SON OF HEAVEN

CHUNG KUO

SON OF HEAVEN

CHUNG KUO

BOOK 1

DAVID WINGROVE

CORVUS

First published in hardback and trade paperback in Great Britain in 2011
by Corvus, an imprint of Atlantic Books.

This paperback edition published in 2011 by Corvus.

5 7 9 10 8 6 4

A CIP catalogue record for this book is available from the British Library.

ISBN: 978 1 84887 526 5

Printed and bound by CPI Group (UK) Ltd, Croydon, CR0 4YY

Corvus
An imprint of Atlantic Books Ltd
Ormond House
26–27 Boswell Street
London
WC1N 3JZ

www.corvus-books.co.uk

CONTENTS

For Susan. Always for Susan.

PART ONE

The Last Year of the Old World

AUTUMN 2065

> Oh, for a great mansion of ten thousand rooms
> Where all the poor on earth could find welcome shelter
> Steady through every storm, secure as a mountain!
> Ah, were such a building to spring up before me,
> I would freeze to death in my wrecked hut well content.
>
> —Tu Fu, 'My Thatched Hut is Wrecked by
> the Autumn Wind', 8th Century AD

CHUNG KUO

Chapter 1

LUCKY MAN

A thin layer of mist wreathed the meadows all the way down to the reeds that traced the meandering path of the river. In the early morning light, the few trees that jutted from that paleness seemed iron black, leafless now that the season had changed. This had all been heath until a few years back, from Corfe to the South Deep. Now the sea had encroached upon those ancient fields, covering stretches of the lowlands to a depth of several feet.

Jake stood there on a ridge of higher ground, surveying the scene, his shotgun tucked beneath his arm. He was dressed for the season in a thick sheepskin coat and warm britches, a hunter's cap and black waders. Close by stood his son, Peter, fourteen and the image of his father, down to the gun beneath his arm. Beside him was Boy, their eight-year-old border collie, his coat sleek and black, his sharp eyes and ears taking in every movement.

A cuckoo called; possibly the last of the year. For a moment after there was silence, then a slushing noise and the sound of beating wings, a heavy sound in the early morning air. As they watched, the bird flew up. Jake's eyes followed its path, then settled on the ruins of the old cottage.

Until six years back this had been a busy, bustling place. Jed

Cooper and his family had lived here. A cheerful man, Jed had shared the cottage with his equally cheerful wife, Judy, and their twin boys, Charlie and John, who had been Peter's age. Only then the sickness had come and they'd been swept away, along with scores of others in the surrounding villages. Last year the roof had fallen in and now the walls were crumbling, nature reclaiming the building, its damp brickwork sinking back into the earth.

Jake looked down and sighed. At his back, a mile to the west, the land climbed steeply to a ridge. There, its ruined keep outlined against the sky, was the castle. Almost a thousand years it had stood. When the Normans came, they'd built it to subdue the locals and place their mark upon the land. Later, in the years of the Civil War, it had been partially demolished, yet still it dominated the skyline, its ruined towers like slabs of living history.

Boy tensed. Peter looked down at him and smiled.

'Seek 'em, Boy! Go chase 'em out!'

The dog was off at once, a streak of darkness cutting through the mist. Jake raised his gun. Beside him, Peter did the same, the two of them waiting patiently as Boy turned the game towards them.

Two gunshots echoed across the meadows, barely a pause between them. Boy slowed then barked, settling beside one of the fallen rabbits.

'Good lad,' Jake said, looking to his son and smiling.

They walked across, Peter going straight to Boy; kneeling down to ruffle his neck and hug him close, telling him again and again what a good boy he'd been.

Jake stooped, once, then a second time, to lift the dead rabbits and slip them into the big leather satchel at his side. He straightened up. The gunshots would have frightened off any other game, but they had plenty of time. The fields beyond the river were pocked with rabbit holes.

'Dad?'

'Yes, lad?'

'D'you think it'll ever come back?'

Jake thought about it a moment. 'I dunno... It's just... if it were coming back, then I guess it would have by now. Only...'

'Only?'

Jake looked down at the dog. Boy enjoyed being petted. His eyes looked back at Peter adoringly, his tail wagging eagerly.

Only nothing. But he didn't say that. It was gone, that old world. Never to return. And good riddance. Only Peter, who had never known it, was fascinated.

'Well?' Peter insisted, getting back to his feet.

Jake laughed. 'You'd have hated it.'

'Why? I mean... all that great stuff you had.'

They had this conversation often, and as so often happened it led nowhere. The Past – the great computer age – was dead, and most of the 'great stuff' with it. All that was left were the husks.

'Come,' Jake said, walking on, not letting his mood be affected by such talk. 'What's gone is gone, lad. It's no good grieving over it.'

'But, Dad...'

A look, a raised eyebrow, and Peter fell silent.

'Come, Boy,' he said, standing, shouldering his gun.

They paused at the ruins, baring their heads, paying their respects, then walked on. Cooper and his family were buried in the churchyard. Long buried now, along with the rest of those who had died that winter. Six years it had been. Only it didn't seem that long. To Jake it seemed like yesterday.

And there too was another truth. That back in the old days they would have survived. Most of them, anyway, if not all. A jab of something and a week in bed and they'd have been right as rain.

Only these weren't the old days.

Jake pushed the thought away, then looked to his son once more.

'Come, lad. Let's go bag some more before breakfast.'

★

Two hours had passed and they had just decided to turn back, when Jake spotted the strangers, some distance off to the north-west, out on the Wareham Road.

His satchel was bulging with dead game. That, and the sight of strangers on the road made up Jake's mind to leave. Now, before they were spotted.

There was an old barn, partway up the slope. There they hid, Jake perched in the gaping stone window, the Zeiss-style glasses – a pair of Bresser Hunters his father had bought more than fifty years before – to his eyes as he checked out the newcomers.

It was as he'd thought. They were refugees. Just a small party, eight strong. Five adults and three children, all of their worldly possessions either on their backs or on the sled one of them dragged along.

He moved from face to face, seeing the tiredness there, the fear. They were a peculiarly shabby lot, with an emaciated, almost haunted look. As far as Jake could make out, a small, fussy little man was leading them; stocky and balding, he never seemed to stop talking. Alongside him was a much taller woman. She was a pale, consumptive-looking creature with lank hair and a pair of broken spectacles that gave her a slight academic air. There were two other men – nondescript fellows with shaven heads and the kind of faces you instantly forgot, they were so generic. Working men, Jake thought, seeing those faces. At least, they would have been, once upon a time. But these two were barely into their thirties. They'd have been ten at most when things fell apart.

The last of the adults – another woman – was perhaps the most interesting, and he took his time, studying her. She didn't seem part of this party. She had a distracted air to her and an uncertainty – a lack of ease – that suggested she had joined them somewhere along the way. For protection, maybe. The look of her – the quality of her clothes – did not go with the others. And there was one other thing. She was pretty.

Jake switched his attention to the children. The eldest was a tall, spindly boy of adolescent age. The clothes he was wearing looked thin and ragged. He seemed to hug himself against the morning's chill. Most noticeable, however, were his eyes – pale eyes that were dark-rimmed and fearful, like he suffered from bad dreams.

His siblings, if that was what they were – a boy and a girl, one perhaps five and the other eight or nine – shared the same, dispirited look.

It made him wonder just how long they had been on the road. Three days? Four? Had they eaten in all that time? Were they hungry?

They certainly looked hungry. Hungry and afraid. As always, something in him responded to their plight and wanted to help; only he couldn't. He had learned that lesson long ago – not to trust anyone in these untrustworthy times. Not strangers, anyway.

Even so...

Jake focused again on the little man, the fussy one, trying to get some clue to it all. A lot of people made the journey west. He'd been told that life was a lot better out here. Only this party didn't seem to be driven by the desire for a better life. No. They looked as if they had been chased out.

Jake lowered the glasses. 'They're no threat,' he whispered. 'But let's get back anyway and warn the others, just in case.'

Peter nodded, then turned to Boy. Boy had been lying there, silent, patient; now he jumped up, eager again.

Peter leaned in close, speaking in a whisper to the dog. 'Hush now, Boy. We're going home, right?'

Normally Boy would have given off a bark – an eager response – but Peter had trained him well. When he used that hushed voice, Boy was to keep quiet.

Jake, looking on, smiled. He was a lovely dog. One of the best. He hadn't known how good it was to have a dog until they'd had him. He put out his hand and Boy came across at once, nuzzling him, licking his fingers and giving off the faintest whine.

'Come...'

They moved quickly, purposefully, up the steep grassy slope and along the Ridgeway, the castle – a massive thing of fallen tawny stone, huge chunks of which were embedded in the grassy hillside – directly ahead. Beyond it, beyond the broad green slope of the castle's enclosed lower field, nestling in the curve of the valley, was Corfe itself. A V-shaped spill of grey-brown two-storey cottages that hugged both arms of the forking road, the parish church with its square tower thrusting up from amidst that great sprawl. It was a sight Jake never tired of, and as always he paused, to take it in, sensing a connection that was beyond his own lifetime. For some reason this was his place and he had come here out of instinct when it had all gone wrong. Here and nowhere else. Because here was where he belonged.

Some of the locals were at the Bankes Arms Hotel already, despite the early hour, unloading carts and carrying bits and pieces through to the garden at the back of the big coaching inn. They were preparing for the evening ahead, it being their custom, once a month, to hold a gathering of all the surrounding villages. It was a celebration – of life and friendship, and of the Past, of the quite astonishing fact that any of them had survived these past twenty or so years.

Jake's best friend, Tom Hubbard, was there, with his youngest daughter Meg, who was Peter's age. While Peter ran across to talk to her, Boy at his heels, Jake sidled over to his old friend.

Tom met his eyes. 'Somethin' up?'

Tom spoke with the same Dorset dialect as Jake's son, Peter, and even as he answered him, Jake was conscious at some level of the lack of that same richness in his own voice. He had been here for more than twenty years, but he was still, in some important way, an outsider. This place, home as it was to him now, was still foreign parts.

'Strangers... on the old Wareham Road. No threat, I'd judge –

they're a bit of a ragtag assortment – but we ought to send a warning round.'

Tom nodded, then turned and whistled through his teeth. 'Alec! Young Billy!'

Two young heads appeared from behind the cart. *'Yeah?'*

'Leave that for now. There's strangers on the Wareham Road. Best put out a warnin' to Stowborough and Furzebrook... oh, and East Holme while you're at it.'

He turned to Jake again. 'How many was it, Jake?'

'Just the eight. Three men, two women and three kids. It's just that they looked hungry, and hunger makes thieves of us all.'

Tom turned and gestured to the two youngsters, who ran off at once. He turned back, then nodded towards the bulging satchel.

'It's a wonder there's any rabbits left, what with you and the lad.'

Jake grinned. 'Thought I'd bag a dozen or so for the do tonight.'

'An' the rest?'

But it didn't need to be said. Tom knew who Jake had bagged them for. Old Ma Brogan, down on the East Orchard. If Jake hadn't brought her a brace of rabbits every now and then she'd never have tasted meat at all, now that her son had run off.

'How's Mary?'

Tom looked up again. 'She's fine. Lookin' forward to tonight. Like a bloody teenage girl, she gets. Can't get no sense out of her or our eldest pair. You'd think it were Christmas.'

The two men laughed, then fell silent. There were shadows over everything they said these days.

They were living on borrowed time and they both knew it. But life had to be lived, not feared. You had to get on with things, no matter what was headed your way. And sometimes that was enough. Only it made it hard to plan anything, hard to look beyond the immediacy of things, and that, so the more astute of them realized, robbed the experience of something precious. When you didn't have a future, what *did* you have?

Jake turned, taking it all in – the castle, the village, all of it unchanged for centuries – and felt a shiver pass through him. It was like living in a vacuum some days. There was Peter, of course, and his friends, but what was it all for? What was the point if it could all be swept aside in an instant?

He patted the bulging satchel, conscious of the smell of the dead creatures which hung upon him.

'Anyway... I'd best deliver these.'

Tom smiled. 'You know what? I'm glad it happened... cos if it hadn't...'

He reached out, holding Jake's arm.

It wasn't like Tom to comment on the past. Neither was it like him to be quite so tactile.

'You all ready for tomorrow?'

'Packed up and ready to go.'

'Good.'

Jake walked away. He ducked through the narrow entrance, stooping beneath the low-silled door and out into the garden. Stepping back into the sunlight, he called out to the little group of wives who were gathered around the big trestle table halfway up the grass.

'Bessie... Mell... who wants the job of skinning these little fellas?'

There was laughter and for a moment the shadow passed. But walking home afterwards with Peter at his side and Boy trailing them, he saw Tom's face again, saw something there behind the eyes, and wondered what it was.

Old Ma Brogan was working in her vegetable garden when Jake came calling.

Straightening her thin, age-worn frame, she raised a hand to shield her eyes, straining to see who it was. Stray wisps of long grey hair lay across her deeply lined face. There was mud on her boots and on the hem of her long, green velvet skirt. *Elegance gone to seed,*

Jake thought, studying her a moment before he unlatched the gate and stepped through.

'It's all right, Mother. It's only me.'

'Ah, Jake, my love. Come give me a kiss. Been a while.'

He went across and gave her a hug and a kiss, then stepped back, admiring her handiwork. For a woman in her eighties she was something else. Frail she might have been, but there was no sign of that frailty in her vegetable garden. Nothing but straight, healthy rows of carrots and beans. The last of the season.

'I've brought you some conies, Ma. Skinned 'em and prepared 'em, I have. Where d'you want me to put 'em?'

A smile beamed out from that ancient face. It made him realize how beautiful she must have been as a young woman.

'Ah, you're a good boy to me, Jake Reed. A better son than that good-for-nothing boy of mine.'

'Now, Ma... he had his reasons.'

'*Reasons!*' She spat the word out contemptuously. 'You're too kind to him by half. Let his cock rule him, more's the truth!'

Jake smiled. He was used to Ma Brogan's foul mouth. Besides, it was true. Her son, Billy, had been infatuated with a girl, and she only half his age. 'Cock-struck' was how Ma Brogan had termed it at the time, and so he was. When she left, he went after her, leaving his aged mother to fend for herself. It was cruel, but it was also life.

'So... where d'you want these?'

'Through here,' she said, turning and leading the way along the brickwork path towards the back door. 'You goin' along tonight, lad?'

'I am.' And he smiled again as he said it. He liked being called 'lad', as if he were Peter's age again. And he liked being mothered. More than that, he liked Ma Brogan's irreverent approach to life. Some didn't, but he did.

In the kitchen doorway she half turned, looking to him. 'You want a brew, boy?'

'I'd love one, Ma. If *you're* having one.'

'I am. Now put those conies down on the side, then take a seat and rest your legs while you tell me all the latest gossip.'

Which is precisely what he did for the next hour, sat there in that low-ceilinged, heavily shadowed kitchen, among the overflowing shelves and the clutter.

Back in the old days he might have scorned it as a waste of time, but now he knew. This was what life was for. Not for accumulating wealth, or making an impression. It was for this. The old lady – *Margaret*, she insisted, flirting with him – made him laugh. Not only that, but she made him think, and if she'd been thirty years younger he might even have slept with her.

He knew a great deal about her life, about her work as a painter and as a potter, and the children she had raised, never to see again. But aspects of her history were still a mystery to him, even after coming here these past twelve months.

'Margaret?'

'Yes, my love?'

'Can I ask you something deeply personal?'

She turned to face him. 'You may.'

'How many lovers did you have?'

Her smile broadened, stretching the thin parchment of her skin. 'You cheeky boy. That is personal. But as it's you...'

She hesitated, searching her memory, the smile fading then returning as she remembered something, or someone. 'My god, it's years since I thought about it...' She gave a little shrug, then. 'Twenty? Thirty, maybe.'

Jake feigned shocked surprise, which made her laugh.

'You wanted an honest answer, you got one.'

'For which I thank you. But now I want to know something else. Who was the love of your life?'

She stared back at him and for an instant her eyes were still young in that otherwise ancient face. It made him think of the old saying – that the eyes were the windows of the soul.

'What's got into you today, my boy?'

'I don't know... It's just that I've been missing her these past few days.'

'Ah...'

A faint, wistful smile had come to her lips. She met his eyes again.

'His name was Matthew. Mattie, I called him. My beautiful Mattie. Ah, he could stoke the fires, that one.'

'Was he your husband?'

'Good Lord, no! My husband, hah! I had three husbands and a fat lot of good any of them were, especially the last! First he ran off, and then his son!' She gave a snort of exasperation, then, after a long breath and more calmly she said, 'No, my love... Mattie was my secret. We'd meet as often as we could, in his room, sometimes, but more often in hotels. Sixteen years younger than me, he was, and I knew it couldn't last, only...'

Jake frowned, seeing how deep the pain still was, and felt a moment's regret at having raised the subject. 'Look, I'm sorry, I...'

'No... don't be. It wasn't like that, you see. He didn't leave me. Or rather, he did, but not through choice. He said he'd love me forever. But then he died. In a car crash. It was awful. I didn't know what to do with myself. His family didn't know, you see, and if they had they wouldn't have approved. But the funeral... Oh, it was terrible, Jake. I couldn't stop crying. And no one there knew me. No one even bothered to ask who it was sitting there at the back of the church sobbing her heart out. No one.'

For a moment he felt like holding her, comforting her for what was clearly still an unhealed wound, even after all these years.

'How old was he?'

She wiped at her eyes. 'Twenty-six.'

Jake caught his breath. It was the same age he had been when it had all come crashing down.

'I'm sorry. I shouldn't have asked.'

She reached out and touched his arm. 'No. No, you should. I like talking about the past, even if it hurts. Even if…'

She shook her head.

'What?' he asked gently.

'Oh, it's nothing, Jake. Just that some days it feels like some dreadful illusion. That none of it really happened and I imagined it all. *Dreamed* it.'

He nodded, understanding. It was exactly how he felt some days. How most of them probably felt, those who had survived the world coming apart at the seams. Simply to be here now seemed something of a miracle.

Jake got to his feet.

'You got to go?'

He nodded. 'I've got a lot to do before tonight. You goin' along?'

She laughed. 'Not me, boy. My old bones aren't up to it any more. The walk there would do for me.'

'You sure I couldn't come get you? You could sit on the cart…'

'It's very kind, my love, but no. You need to enjoy yourself, and how could you do that if you had to keep an eye on me, eh?'

'But, Ma…'

'*Margaret*.' Her voice had an insistent tone to it. 'And *no*. I'll be fine.'

Jake kissed her, held her to him a moment, then quickly hurried away, before he saw the tears welling in her eyes. But halfway up the long slope that led to Church Knowle he turned and looked back, noting how the cottage seemed embedded in the landscape, the thatched roof the same brown as the surrounding fields.

He turned away. What he'd said to her was true. He had been thinking about Anne a lot these past few days, and he felt he needed to do something about it. As it was he felt haunted, and as a rational man he felt uncomfortable with that.

I should go see her. Talk to her. Yes. But first he'd pack, ready for tomorrow.

The farmhouse was a long, low building, set back off the main street, the grey of its slate roof peppered with small patches of green and orange. It was a sturdy house, an unfussy house, functional in a way so many of the local houses weren't. They were more picturesque, more pretty, but Jake had chosen well. It was warm in the winter and the roof never leaked. And besides, it had cost him nothing.

The front door was unlocked. It was never locked. Not these days. If you couldn't trust your neighbours, then who could you trust? Jake stepped inside, into deep shadow. The kitchen was at the back, overlooking the yard, the living room to the left. Both bedrooms were upstairs.

He went through. There were long shelves both sides of the hallway, crowded floor to ceiling with books. Like the house, he had 'inherited' them, and again, like the house, he had come to appreciate with every passing year just how carefully they had been chosen.

The kitchen was neat and clean. The skinned and washed rabbits that the women had prepared had been hung up in the larder. Fresh wood had been cut and stacked. The oak table had been wiped, the breakfast things washed up and put away.

Jake smiled. Peter was a good boy. A dependable boy. He worked hard and never complained.

He crossed the room, standing there a moment at the sink, looking out through the long window, wondering where Peter was. Only he knew where he was. He turned and saw at once that the bucket was missing from the hook.

Jake washed his hands and dried them, then stepped out, into the yard. From there he had a view down the lane towards the well. He could hear the pigs snuffling in the shed at his back, the chickens restlessly clucking. Bessie, their Jersey, was in the barn nearby, sleeping no doubt.

Jake shielded his eyes to look.

Peter was sitting on the broad ledge of the well, Meg beside him. They were holding hands, staring at each other in that lovesick fashion Jake had noticed of late. Boy lay nearby, one eye open, looking out for his master.

Again Jake smiled. In that too they were lucky. To have met such people as the Hubbards, here at the end of things.

Normally he would have left them on their own for a bit, but there was much to do. And besides, there would be plenty of time later on for them to gaze adoringly at each other.

He walked down the sloping lane towards them, his booted feet crunching on the gravel. Hearing it, their hands fell apart. Snatching up her bucket, Meg hurried away, giving Jake a smile as she went.

Embarrassed, Peter jumped down. He lifted his own bucket and began to walk towards his father, Boy jumping up to follow.

Jake smiled. 'It's okay, you know... holding hands. You *can* hold hands. It is allowed.'

Peter didn't look at him. He was blushing now. But Jake, studying his son, saw how tall he'd grown, how close he was to being a man.

How his mother would have loved to have seen that.

They were at the gate now. Jake watched as Peter expertly nudged the old latch and pushed through, the heavy bucket swaying in his hand.

'You know what, lad?'

'What?'

'I thought we'd go see your mum, later. Once everything's done.'

The young boy turned, meeting his eyes. 'You all right, Dad?'

Jake looked away. It was his turn to be embarrassed. 'I'm fine...'

'Yeah...?'

'Yeah...' Only he didn't have to say. Peter was watching him now, a perfect understanding in his eyes.

'I'll cut some flowers for her.'

'That'd be nice.'

Only what he felt at that moment couldn't be contained in words. To have been so lucky and unlucky. To have found her at all and then to have lost her. No. Sometimes words – even whole hallways full of words – were not enough.

St. Peter's Church stood on a mound at the turn of the road, as it had since the early fourteenth century, a neat, solid-looking building of grey stone. Old as it was, it was merely a replacement for the old Saxon church after which the village – Church Knowle – had first been named. Priests had read the ancient services in Latin long before the great castle had been built a mile or so to the west, and there had been a rector resident since 1327. It was here that the locals gathered every week, not to sing hymns or say prayers like their ancestors, but simply to talk – to air grievances, seek help, to raise any problems they might have, and generally to keep things 'ticking over', as they liked to call it. Few among them were religious in any special way, yet they shared a feeling of connection to the land that was almost pagan in its intensity – a sense of *belonging*.

It was over there, on the far side of that lushly grassed space, near the back wall, that they had buried those who had died six years back. And it was there, now, that Jake and his son came, to put flowers down on the neatly kept mound that was Anne's grave.

Jake had carved the headstone himself from a solid slab of oak, fashioning it in the shape of a tree. It had taken him all of three months, but it was a fine piece of work, one of which he was immensely proud. Back in the old days he would have struggled to have finished such a task – things were so easy, so 'throwaway' back then – but this was something different. This was something *meant*, his own small monument against Time, and he had poured all of his feelings for her into the simple design. As for the words...

Jake gave the smallest shake of his head, thinking about it. He had never found anything quite so hard as choosing what to carve into that smoothly varnished surface. After all, what did you say? 'Passed in her sleep'? No, because she hadn't. She had been in torment until the last. It had been agony – sheer hell – to see her suffer all of that. So what then? How to express the utter totality of his loss, his grief? And there were Peter's feelings to consider, too, for it was *his* mother who had been snatched from him so brutally. Jake had felt honour bound to make sure his son had his say. Because this mattered. How you honoured the dead, how you remembered them after they were gone, *that* mattered. He understood that now.

And so, between them, they had honed it down to the simplest of words. Words which might somehow prove a vessel into which all of their grief, all of their painful memories, might pour themselves:

'Our darling girl. Missed beyond words.'

Jake knelt there a moment, his fingers tracing the hand-carved words. Then, taking the special scissors from his jacket pocket, he began to trim the grass.

He was just finishing, wiping the surface of the slab with a damp cloth, when he grew conscious of another presence close by. He turned, looking up into the sunlight. 'Mary...?'

She stood there, staring past him at the headstone, a faint wistfulness in her expression. She was Anne's sister, three years her elder, and as Jake looked at her he could see reminders of what he had lost in Mary's face: her eyes; her long, dark, curling hair; in the very way she stood there, her weight on her left foot, her head slightly tilted. It was precisely how Anne had always stood.

She was holding a small spray of flowers. Lilacs. Anne's favourites.

'It never seems to get easier, does it?'

'No... No, I...'

He left it unfinished. Then, realizing that he'd done all he'd come to do, he clambered up, brushing the grass clippings from his knees.

Mary spoke again, quieter this time. 'You know... I always thought it would be me. I always expected her to tend my grave.'

'Really?' Yet even as he said it he saw the truth in it. Anne had always been the healthy one, the more vigorous of the two. Even if Mary had not already been Tom's wife, he would have chosen Anne, had it come to it, purely for her vitality. She had possessed so much life. Yet it was Anne who had succumbed to the fever, not Mary.

'Have they decided?' he asked, changing the subject.

A smile lit her face. She knew without asking what he was referring to.

'*Far From The Madding Crowd.* You know, the old version, with Alan Bates, Terence Stamp and Julie Christie.'

Once a month, as tonight, they would haul out the old generator, fill it with oil, and show a film. Something from the Past. 'Who chose that?'

'The women. We wanted something *romantic* for a change.'

He nodded to her and made to leave, calling Peter and Boy to him. But at the gate he looked back and saw her, kneeling by the grave now, talking to her sister as he so often did, holding the lilacs out to 'show' Anne, a strangely fragile love there in the muscles of her face.

So fragile, and yet so strong. Jake turned back, looking to his son, noting, as he so often did, how he too carried the familial genes.

'I am the family face...'

'Dad?'

Jake smiled. 'Old words, boy. Just old words.'

Darkness had fallen. In the long, high-walled garden of the Bankes Arms Hotel, a massive bonfire cast its warm, flickering light over the crowded scene, bathing everything in an ever-changing cloak of gold and black.

Above the chug-chug-chug of the ancient, oil-powered generator, music played, struggling to make itself heard against the babble of a hundred voices.

Every one of the big bench tables was filled to overflowing. People had come from miles around, bringing their families. Relaxed now, their faces shining, they ate and drank and talked, while all about them their children ran and played, carefree and happy.

Jake and Peter were seated at the table closest to the generator, sharing it with Tom, Mary and their daughters, Cathy, Beth and Meg. Boy, as ever, lay hidden in the shadows beneath, his jet black eyes reflecting back the firelight. From time to time he would lick his chops, a faint whine escaping him as he sniffed the air, taking in the mouth-watering scent of roasting meat that, mixed with the strong burned-chemical odour of the generator, filled every breath.

The music was much louder where they sat, close by the speakers, but Jake didn't mind that. Music – especially music from the old days – was his passion, one that he shared with Old Josh Palmer, the landlord's father. Josh was in his eighties now, but he was still fit, still sprightly. He lived in the attic of the hotel, in two large rooms with sloping eaves that, apart from his bed and a small sink in one corner, were crammed floor to ceiling with his 'collection'. It was offerings from that collection that they were listening to now, a collection that anyone would have been proud of, even back in the old days. In these latter days, after the Collapse, his boxes of ancient plastic-sleeved CDs and even older vinyl seemed an absolute treasure trove, most of it irreplaceable; things you'd never see, or ever dream to see, at market. Things that were old before Old Josh was born. Now they seemed even more precious, for these were the last remaining vestiges of an easier age. An age that had passed for good. That, but for this, Jake would never have guessed existed.

Right now they were playing one of his absolute favourites, 'Erin Go Bragh', its rapid, almost staccato acoustic guitar underpinning the delicious, broad Scots accent of its singer, Dick Gaughan. Jake leaned back, half-filled beer mug in hand, and closed his eyes briefly to listen to the flute that seemed to float out of the speakers, so sweet and high, mouthing the words to himself as he did.

As the song ended and he opened his eyes again, he saw, looking about him, how they were all watching him, suppressed laughter in every face. Seeing his surprised expression, there was an eruption of delighted laughter.

'What?'

He looked to Tom for an explanation.

'It's just you, Jake. That look you have sometimes. Lost you are. Totally bloody lost.'

'Yeah?' He smiled and shrugged. 'Well...'

But he wasn't going to let it ruin his enjoyment. If the truth were told, he lived for these evenings, when the hot, scented air was filled with music. Annie had loved it too. Sitting there, he could imagine, sometimes, that she was beside him still.

In spirit, anyway, he thought, pushing the memory away. Yet as he did, so another song began, making him catch his breath.

'Oh, well done, Josh...'

He looked across at Josh, seated by the controls of the old mixing desk and clapped exaggeratedly, making the old man grin toothlessly.

'River Man'. Oh, how he loved this song. Loved the sweet, gently English voice of its singer, Nick Drake. Loved its understated lyric.

Above all, what got to him was the bittersweet poignancy of it. The idea of lilac time. Of a time free of all cares.

'Dad?'

He turned, meeting his son's eyes. 'What, boy?'

'These songs...'

'What about them?'

'It's just...'

Peter shrugged. Jake knew his son didn't have the same love of this music. Peter liked his music harder, heavier than this. More modern, too. Even so, Jake felt he ought to reward his son somehow. He'd been a real help lately. Fishing in his pocket, he brought out a handful of local coins, stamped with the simple standing stone motif of Wessex. Taking one, he handed it to Peter.

'Go on... Go and ask Old Josh for a request. But nothing too outrageous, eh?'

Peter's face lit up. Scrambling up, he ran across to where the old man sat, leaning in to shout into his ear.

Jake watched the boy a moment, warmed to the pit of his stomach by the sight. Sometimes what he felt for the boy surprised him.

Turning back, he found himself meeting Mary's eyes. She had been watching him. He saw that instantly. But why?

The question must have been in his eyes, for she leaned towards him, laying her hand on his, and smiled.

'I was just thinking... remembering when you first came here. You've changed, you know.'

'Yeah?'

'Beyond recognition.'

Jake looked away. Tom was watching him now too. Like he and Mary shared a secret. He sipped at his beer, then, seeing Peter returning, turned and called out to him. 'What did you ask him for?'

Peter grinned. 'You'll see...'

'Oh, god...'

Peter slipped back into his seat, reaching down to pet Boy before meeting his father's eyes again.

'No, Dad... you'll like it. Really.'

Jake was about to protest when the unmistakable opening bars began.

Hendrix! It was fucking Hendrix!

From all around, people were getting to their feet, taking up hunched, head down air guitar poses as 'Voodoo Chile' pounded from the speakers.

Jake looked to his son again and grinned. 'Boy, I raised you extremely bloody well.' And ignoring Peter's disgusted look, he too got to his feet and started playing along. As the music faded, Jake opened his eyes again, to find Tom and Mary watching him again, their eyes delighted.

'You enjoyed that, didn't you?' Tom said, getting up and gesturing to Jake to hand over his now empty glass.

'I bloody well did.'

'It's good to see.'

'Yeah?'

'Yeah.'

Jake looked down. He knew what Tom was saying, beneath the words. He must have been hard to be with after Annie had died. His mood had been so dark, so... unremittingly morose. He had forgotten how to have fun. If it hadn't been for Peter. Well... who knew what he'd have done? As it was, the pain lingered, but he could deal with it now.

As Tom went off to get the beers, he looked to Mary again. 'Am I that fascinating?'

She smiled.

'Well?' he asked, when she didn't answer. 'Just that you seem to be watching me tonight.'

'Do I?' The smile broadened. 'Just that it's good to see you smiling again. I never thought...'

She stopped, her expression changing. A new song had begun. Another old folk song, its mood wistful this time. Jake didn't recognize it, but it had a distinctly gaelic feel.

'D'you want to dance?'

Her question surprised him. 'I... don't.'

'You used to. With Annie.'

That too was different. Before now they had come to a kind of unspoken agreement not to talk about Annie and how things used to be. But that had changed, apparently.

'Have you and Tom been talking?'

'Talking? That's what married couples do, surely?'

'I mean about me.'

She shrugged, but there was a smile on her lips now. 'You're our best friend. Of course we talk about you.'

'Yeah? So what have you been saying?'

He was conscious, suddenly, of the children listening in. From seeming bored, they were now attentive. Mary, too, seemed to suddenly become aware of it. Looking about her she shooed them all away.

'Go on, go... This is adult talk.'

When they were gone, Boy trailing in their wake, Mary turned to him again.

'So?' he asked. 'Why am I suddenly so interesting?'

'You've always been interesting.'

He shook his head. 'The truth.'

Mary looked down. It seemed to him that beyond her playful teasing she was steeling herself to say something. Only right then Tom returned, and Jake sensed that the moment had passed. He wasn't sure why, or what it was about, maybe nothing, only it wasn't how she usually was with him. She or Tom.

'Got it all ready for the morning, have you?' Tom asked, handing Jake his beer.

Jake nodded, but he was staring thoughtfully at Mary.

'Your wife...' he began.

'Is a very, very, very fine wife.'

Tom put his arm about her, hugging her to him.

'Maybe... Only I sense she means to meddle in my life.'

'Oh?' Tom sounded surprised. 'And how would she be a doin' that?'

It had come to him, just a moment before. What she was doing.

'I think she means to find Peter a new mother.'

Tom looked to Mary then back to Jake. He was smiling now. 'Would that be so very bad, Jake? I mean... you need a woman in your bed.'

There. As blunt as that. 'Do I?'

'You know you do,' Mary said; but she looked down as she said it and seemed to blush.

'If I needed a good fuck...'

'It's not the same,' she said, meeting his eyes defiantly.

No, he thought, thinking of Annie. *It never was*. But there was something odd going on here. He only had to look at Tom to see it. Tom had a secret, and he wasn't a man to feel comfortable with secrets. Only Jake guessed Mary would have made him swear not to tell. Whatever it was.

Jake looked up, recognizing the song that was playing. It was Sandy Denny, 'Who Knows Where The Time Goes?'.

He smiled, feeling a sweet sadness. Annie had always loved this song.

'You're a sweet woman, Mary Hubbard,' he said, looking back at her. 'But you must leave me be. I am as I am. If I loved your sister too much, then there's no blame in that. I'm not ready yet, okay?'

'Okay. I'll leave you be.'

But she said it softly, and to his ears it sounded much like Annie would have said it, had Annie been there.

A faint breeze ruffled the huge, makeshift screen, making the image ripple, as if the dreamlike aura of the ancient movie were suddenly revealed for what it was. A chimera. A fiction about a life that now seemed equally a fiction.

Even so, nothing, at that moment, seemed more real, more true, than what was unfolding on that screen.

Sitting there among those who loved him best, his face all but hidden in the half dark, Jake wiped away the tears that had been rolling down his cheeks unchecked. It was absurd, he knew, but this scene – where Sergeant Troy stooped over the coffin of his dead love, Fanny Robin, and kissed her cold, dead lips – always got to him. Nothing had the power to move him more. Watching it, he knew Troy's despair; knew just how he could utter those awful, soul-destroying words to the living woman he had so cruelly and mistakenly married.

To prefer the dead ideal to the living reality. It was absurd... but true.

Beside him, Peter was quietly shaking with emotion. It was, as so often, all too close to be comfortable. Jake wanted to reach out and take his hand, but there was that awful restraint between them – that inability to talk of the matter. And so each suffered it alone.

As the final frame finished and the credits ran, Jake quickly made his way across to the back of the inn, squeezing through the packed back bar – where the men were crowded round the tables, talking and smoking their pipes – and into the gents.

He was standing there, relieving himself, when Tom Hubbard came and stood beside him.

'"And married the woman that had the gold..."'

Jake smiled. It was a line from an old song, and, as so often, it said perfectly what he had been thinking. He himself was no Troy – no adventurer. Oh, he had been in the past, but not these days. No. Nowadays he was more of a Gabriel Oak figure, sturdy and reliable. But when it came to love...

He glanced at his old friend. 'It all comes full circle, don't you think?'

Tom shrugged. 'I dunno. Watching that... well, the whole damn twentieth century might as well not have happened. I sat there thinking... this is about *us*, *now*. Only, if none of that had happened – all that stuff that came between times – then we'd not have had the film. Ironic, eh?'

'We live in ironic times.'

'Maybe. Yet we're comfortable enough, don't you think?'

Jake buttoned himself up. 'Another beer?'

Tom shook his head. 'Not me, boy. I'm headin' back. Need some rest before our trip tomorrow. But the girls are stayin' on.' He glanced at Jake and smiled. 'We're not abandoning you.'

Again, there was something behind the words, only Jake was too muddled to work out what. He'd have another beer himself then go. Tom was right, after all. You needed your wits about you on the road.

They made their way back out into the long back bar. There, at the crowded central table, Geoff Horsfield, a tall man in his sixties – a historian by profession, who had run the school in Corfe for the past twenty years and more – was holding sway.

'I was just saying,' he said, looking up at Jake and reaching out to hold his arm. 'Some'at's got to change. How we are... how we live... it can't go on. We're driven as a species to evolve, socially as well as biologically. This here... this little pocket of warmth in which we exist... it's not viable. Not long term, anyway... It's no more than a sideshow. I'd say the main event's to come, wouldn't you, Jake?'

Only Jake didn't *want* to say. He'd had this feeling in his gut the past week or so – a feeling that the presence of the strangers on the Wareham Road that morning had fed, like tinder to the flame. A giddying sense of uncertainty. It was like they were all on the edge of a cliff. One single push was all that was needed and they'd be over the edge again and falling.

'I dunno...' he began, but Tom took that moment to interrupt.

'How we live, here in Purbeck... I'd say it was all pretty civilized, wouldn't you? Tonight, for instance. Who here would have it different? Or do you forget how it *was* before the Collapse?'

'No one forgets that,' Will Cooper said, speaking from where he sat just across the table, ruddy-faced and dark-eyed, his sparse grey hair stretched thin across his sun-burnished pate. 'None of us wants that back. But Geoff's right. We can't stand still. We 'ave to move on. This is all well and good, but it feels to me like we're all just sitting on our arses waiting to die.'

There was a strong murmur at that. Some were in favour of what Will had said, but most were against. Such talk was old ground, of course. Time and again they had sat here late into the night, in the light of the old log fire, drinking the landlord's best ale and chewing this one over. But tonight there seemed a sudden urgency to their talk.

'Things're changing,' Dick Grove grumbled, shaking his head in a foreboding manner. 'Word comin' up the road is that's some-thing's 'appening out east.'

'Rumours,' Tom said. 'Nothing solid.'

'Maybe,' Geoff answered him, 'but *some'at's* 'appenin', make no mistake. And perhaps it's time it did. We've got too cosy. Too complacent.'

'You think so?' Tom asked. 'You think we've got soft?'

'Not soft so much as *accepting*.'

'Accepting?'

'Oh, I'm not advocating a return to how things were. God help us, no! It was like bleedin' Sodom and Gomorrah, remember? The Age of Waste. A whole society living beyond its means. Yes, and we're better off without it. But Mankind has to move on. It's in our natures. It's how we're wired genetically. To sit on our arses, as our good friend Will so eloquently put it, that just isn't an option!'

'You *would* say that,' John Lovegrove chipped in, pointing a long, bony finger at his friend, 'but that's cos you're a 'istorian. I'm just a farmer and I rather like things as they are. Things weren't good afore the Fall. Sod'em and Gomorrah, like you said, and all on live TV!'

There was laughter at that, yet as it faded Jake found his atten-tion caught by the music drifting in from outside. It was Coldplay. 'Everything's Not Lost'. He smiled at the irony, then looked back, his eyes moving from face to face, tracing the circle of his friends. As Geoff talked, they looked on, their ruddy faces intent, their eyes aglow in the fire's warm, flickering light. They were good men, every last man jack of them, but right now they were afraid. He could sense it. Something had changed. None of them knew what, but there was the feel of it in the air.

Change. It was coming. Only none of them knew from which direction.

Tom leaned close, speaking to his ear. 'I've got to go. See you in the morning, eh?'

Jake nodded, looking on as Tom said his farewells, then went outside, back into the crisp late evening air.

The bonfire had burned down. In the cleared space near where Old Josh sat behind his speakers, couples were slow dancing now, lost in the music, while overhead the moon sat full and large in the cloudless sky, a pearled circle against the dark.

Jake smiled. The world could fall apart and still people would be dancing.

'Jake...?'

He went across. Their table was in deep shadow. Only one figure sat there now, hunched in to herself, as if against the cold.

'Mary? Where are the others?'

'Gone off.' She smiled at him, then patted the bench beside her. 'Come and sit with me.'

He sat, feeling her shuffle up to him, her warmth against his side.

'Been putting the world to rights, have you?'

He smiled. 'Tom's gone home.'

'I know.' She took his arm, put it round her shoulders.

'Mary?'

'I'm cold, is all.'

He closed his eyes, feeling her snuggle in against him. It felt nice. Warm and friendly.

'Jake?'

'What?'

'What we said earlier. About you needing a woman...'

He looked at her again; saw how intently she was watching him.

'What's goin' on? You and Tom. You've been odd tonight, the pair of you.'

'Odd?' She feigned offence, then smiled. 'It's nothing... You want to dance?'

'I don't do dancing.'

'No?' She sighed. 'Oh, go on... Please, Jake. For me. Just one dance? I'd dance with Tom, only Tom's not here...'

Jake shrugged. 'All right. But just the one. Cos Tom's not here.'

She held his hand as they walked across. The song ended. As the next began he took her in his arms. It was The Verve. 'Lucky Man'.

'Oh, Jake... I love this song...'

He held her close, closing his eyes, letting himself succumb to the warmth of her. Enjoying the way she pressed against him, swaying gently, the way she softly sang along to the words of the old song.

'You know what?'

'What?' She spoke into his neck, a lazy drawl, her breath warm against his flesh.

'I feel like I've been set up.'

She laughed, then drew her face back slightly, looking up into his face. She was about to say something more, then changed her mind. She looked down, away from him.

He slowed, then stopped. 'What?' he asked gently. 'What is it?'

'Nothing...' She met his eyes again and smiled, as if to reassure him, but there was a shadow now behind the smile.

'*What?* Tell me.'

'It's nothing. *Really.* Just hold me, Jake. Just dance with me.'

★

Peter drew his face back, away from Meg's, then gave a little shiver. Her mouth was so soft, so sweetly moist, so deliciously yielding to his own. And her eyes...

He squeezed her hands, which lay in his, and smiled.

They were leaning against the castle wall, at the top of the great slope, the ruins of the King's Tower silhouetted against the sky at their backs. Below them and to the left, they could see the inn, its long, walled garden seeming to glow like a broad gash of gold against the darkness of the surrounding countryside. From where they were they could see people coming and going, hear the music drifting up from below.

'Do you think we're always gonna live here?'

'I dunno,' she said. 'I s'pose so. Unless we get our own place...'

'Is that what you want?'

'Don't you?'

'Yeah... I s'pose so. Only...'

He looked away, across the dark countryside towards the sea.

'Go on,' she said. 'Only what?'

'Only I'd like to see things. You know...'

She smiled then shook her head. 'No, I don't, silly. Tell me. What kind of things?'

'Oh... things. Places, I guess. I mean, it's daft. I've never even been to Dorchester!'

'You will. When you're older.'

'Yeah, but that's not what I meant. I want to see lots of different places. London, for instance...'

'Lunnun?' She gave him a look of horror. 'What d'you wanna go see that for? It's a horrible place. A place of living corpses.'

'So they say. But what if they're wrong?'

'They ain't wrong. They've spoken to people who've been there. There's cannibals there... yeah, and worse things!'

He looked away, impatient with her suddenly, then relented. It wasn't her fault. It was this place. It was like his dad said, the locals devoured rumours, and the more garish the rumour the more gullible they seemed. But he wasn't going to argue with Meg over it.

He stood, putting his fingers to his teeth to whistle. 'Here, Boy!'

Almost at once, Boy came bounding out of the darkness, prostrating himself at Peter's feet to be stroked and fussed over.

He looked to her again. She was watching him, contrite now. 'Sorry...'

'No, it's me.' He straightened up, then, moving closer, gently placed his hands upon her shoulders. Once more they kissed, a long, slow kiss.

Drawing back from her, he smiled. 'I'd best get you home. It's late.'

Her smile mirrored his own. 'Race you down the hill...'

He laughed, then nodded. 'No cheating, mind...'

And off they ran, whooping as they did, down into the dark bowl of the inner courtyard and on, through the ancient gate, running full tilt, Boy barking excitedly as he ran, the sound of their childish laughter echoing up into the dark.

One dance had become a dozen. Slowly the villagers had gone home, until now it was just he and she, unwatched, unnoticed on the dance floor.

Now, as Old Josh announced the last song of the night, Jake sighed deeply then kissed her on the tip of her nose.

'Tha's nice,' she said, nuzzling in to him. 'You sha...'

'You're drunk, Mary Hubbard.'

She giggled. 'I know. I...'

He put a finger to her lips. 'One more dance and I'll take you home. Tom'll be wondering where you've got to.'

'Tom knows where I've got to. I'm wi' you.'

It was said slurringly. But she wasn't falling down drunk yet. Neither did he intend to let her be.

'What's up?' he asked her gently, as the first bars of the song rang out. 'What's the matter, my pretty girl?'

She laughed huskily, then pressed closer. 'I like it when you say that. And this song...'

Old Josh had done them proud, classic after classic, but this was the best of the lot. 'Nights In White Satin'.

Jake closed his eyes. Normally he didn't dance. Even when Annie had been alive he'd been a reluctant partner. But with Mary...

Perhaps it was because he'd been so long without a woman, but this last hour had been magical. Her closeness had robbed him of his senses. The scent of her, the warmth of her all too female body against his own, had been intoxicating.

He squeezed her gently, feeling a real tenderness for her at that moment. 'Thank you, Mary. You don't know how pleasant it's been.'

She met his eyes again. 'You're welcome, my love. Any time.'

He laughed. 'You really are drunk, aren't you?'

She nodded exaggeratedly. 'Really, *really* drunk.'

'But thank you, anyway. You and Tom. For being such good friends. For...'

She put a finger to his lips. 'Nuff...' She smiled at him again. 'You're a good dancer, you know. You have the feel for it.'

'Do I?'

'You do. And I bet you're a good kisser, too.'

'Yeah?'

'Yeah.'

Only when she smiled this time he had to look away, because he really wanted to kiss her. She was Tom's, yes, and he would never hurt his friend, only he so wanted to kiss her. Wanted it more than anything. Only, if he kissed her, what then?

'Jake? Are you okay?'

She drew his face back with her fingers. Made him look at her again.

He studied her face, seeing both how like and unlike Annie she was. In some ways more beautiful, in others...

'I miss her, Mary. Every fucking day.'

Her face creased in sympathy. 'I know. I miss her too.'

'Yeah... but that's not what I meant. In my bed. You were right.'

'Ah...' She looked down, suddenly less drunk.

'Tonight...' He took a long, shivering breath. 'Tonight's been magical. I'm glad you were here with me. I...'

She pushed her face up into his and kissed him, full on the lips, a soft, warm, welcoming kiss that, after dancing with her so long, he had no power to resist. In an instant he was kissing her back, passionately, the two of them locked in an embrace, her body pressed against his own.

He broke from it, gasping. He wanted to take her, right there and then. And he knew for a fact that she would let him – that she wanted him. He had only to take her. Only it wasn't right. She was Tom's. She had always been Tom's. And he owed Tom everything.

'Mary... I...'

Mary stood there a moment, staring at him wildly, then took a step back. She looked away, up into the sky, then back at him. 'You'd better go...'

He took a step towards her. 'I'm sorry. I really am. I...'

'Jake! For fuck's sake go!'

It had a sobering effect. He stared at her, seeing how troubled she was, how agitated, then turned and fled. Away from her, as fast as he could run. Yet as he ran, out along the curving, chalk-lined path and left onto the Knowle road, he could still see her in his mind, could feel her lips, moist yet burning against his own, her breasts pressed softly against his chest, and knew he would not sleep.

'Oh, god... Oh, Jesus Christ, Tom... forgive me...'

Worst of all he kept seeing her eyes – eyes that were like his own sweet Annie's eyes.

'Oh, Christ... oh, Jesus, no.'

Too late, he thought. Too fucking late.

CHUNG KUO

Chapter 2

THE NATURE OF THE CATASTROPHE

J ake slept badly. He woke before first light and, unable to lie there, went down and lit a fire in the kitchen grate. Then he sat and cleaned his gun, his mind returning again and again to the events of the previous night.

Until now he'd been all right, or, if not, then he'd at least been able to cope. Much of that was down to Tom and Mary. When he'd been at his most desperate, in those awful first few months after Annie's death, it was they who had helped get him through.

One kiss and it had all changed.

The thing that nagged at him was this: that he didn't know why. It clearly wasn't because Mary was unhappy. He had only to think of her last night, hanging on Tom's arm, laughing at his awful, corny jokes, to know that she was still in love with him. That much was self-evident. Why, then, tilt her cap at him? Or was that Tom's doing? Was Tom's friendship that unselfish that he'd offer up his wife? If so, then why now? What had changed to make him suddenly so generous?

Only that was it. Jake just couldn't imagine how, were he in Tom's place, he could even think of sharing the woman he loved. It went against nature.

What then? What had made Mary come on to him? Why, when she had never asked before, had she asked him to dance with her last night? Was it the drink?

He knew it wasn't. He'd seen her much more drunk than that. Falling over drunk. But she had never made a pass at him; never given the slightest hint that she harboured any hidden feelings. Until last night.

Jake sighed, then set the gun down.

So what now? Did he pretend it had never happened? Greet Tom with a cheery welcome? Slap Tom's back and ignore the feelings Mary had woken in him?

It was that which disturbed him most. That he had liked it. That he had wanted it. And much more than just a kiss. In the secrecy of his thoughts he could admit it now. Feeling her against him, kissing her, had affected him profoundly. In the darkness he had dreamed of her. Dreamed of lying naked with her. Of kissing her neck and breasts. Of fucking her.

He closed his eyes. In the corner, sprawled out in his basket, Boy shifted, gave a low growl and then a bark.

Peter stood in the doorway.

'You didn't have to get up yet, lad.'

Peter knuckled his eyes and yawned. 'It's still dark out. You all right?'

Jake smiled. 'Just a bit hung over. Did *you* have a good evening?'

Peter grinned. 'Yeah. We hung about a bit, up on the battlements.'

'All of you?' But Jake knew the answer even before he asked. In any case, Peter, accustomed to his father's teasing, dodged the issue expertly.

'Shall I make breakfast?'

'You don't have to, lad. We'll stop off at Wareham and have something there.'

'Tea, then?'

'Coffee, if you're doing it.'

Peter looked at him, surprised. Coffee was a luxury item. It was rare for them to have it. He nodded, then, filling the kettle, set it on the grid above the fire, whistling to himself all the while.

'You like that tune, son?'

Peter turned his head. 'What tune's that?'

'The one you're whistling. Josh played it last night.'

'Oh... right. Did he?'

Again it was a game they played. Peter pretended that he didn't like any of the old stuff. But he did. He was humming or whistling it all the time.

'You packed, lad?'

Peter nodded, then reached up to get the coffee tin down from the shelf above the sink. Whenever Jake went on one of his trips to market, Peter – and Boy – went to stay with the Hubbard women. So it had been these past six years.

Jake looked down. 'Anything special you'd like me to bring back? We've got a bit spare. Or should have, once I've traded in a few things. Something you need, maybe?'

Peter had been spooning the coffee granules into the cups. Hearing what his father said, he stopped. 'I...'

He was hunched suddenly, awkward. There was something he wanted.

'Go on, boy. If we can afford it.'

Peter steeled himself, then turned, facing his father. 'I... I wanted to get Meg something... A ring.'

'A ring.' But Jake knew better than to mock his son over this. He could see in his face just what it meant, asking for this. 'Is that all?'

For a moment Peter seemed surprised. Then, quickly, he shook his head. 'No... just that...'

Jake smiled. ''S'all right, lad. I'll make sure it's a nice one.'

There was the briefest flash of gratitude in the boy's eyes, then he turned back, busying himself, hoping that his father hadn't noticed he was blushing now. But Jake had noticed.

He stood, then went over to the window. The sky was brightening. The blackness of the yard had been solid a minute or two ago, but now you could discern familiar shapes.

Jake turned, looking across at the old, walnut-cased clock that stood on the mantelpiece. He didn't have to be in Corfe for another hour yet, but maybe he'd go a bit earlier this time. Get there before Tom and make sure everything was okay between them.

'You all right, Dad?'

Jake turned, surprised to find Peter there beside him, holding out the cup for him to take. Had he let something show in his face? He took the cup from the boy.

'Yeah, I'm fine, lad. And thanks. I thought I might try and get us some cocoa this time. As a bit of a treat, eh?'

Peter grinned. 'Cocoa... wow!'

Jake nodded. They couldn't afford it, really. None of it. Tea was cheapest, but even that was a luxury these days, as supplies dwindled. But without such treats life wasn't worth the candle.

'Dad?'

'Yes?'

'Those people we saw on the road yesterday. D'you think something's happened. You know, in London?'

Jake shrugged. 'I dunno, lad. I really don't. But we're sure to hear something when we get to market. That place is awash with rumour. Aye, and some real news too, occasionally. If anyone'll know, they will.'

Only Jake wasn't sure he wanted to know what was happening in London. Or anywhere else outside Purbeck, come to that. He'd been at the centre of things once, and look where that had got him! No, this was his life now, this 'island', geologically shorn off from the rest of England. This place and these people.

Which was why he had to go and speak to Tom. To set things

straight, or at least to make sure everything was fine between them. Because if it wasn't...

He sipped the sweetly sugared coffee, then closed his eyes, smiling with the rare pleasure of it.

'That's good, lad. That's a damn fine cup of coffee.'

For once he shunned the road, taking the back way through the meadows, a full pack on his back, his gun slung over his right shoulder. At this time of year the way was often waterlogged by heavy rains, which was why, with the wagons, they took the main road north to Wareham. But today it was fine, the ground beneath his boots firm rather than muddy.

This was the scenic route and, in summer, he often took it for its sheer beauty and peacefulness, but today he chose it for a different reason – so as not to meet up with Tom. Not yet, anyway. He hadn't rehearsed yet in his head just how he was going to play it.

His natural instinct was to tell Tom everything – to lay it all before him and beg his forgiveness – but how did you tell your best friend that you'd spent the night dreaming about fucking his wife? That wasn't an option. Best say nothing, maybe. Pretend it hadn't happened. Only he felt awkward about it. He didn't like the idea that he was somehow betraying his best friend, even if it were only in his head.

Thought crime, he realized, recalling the classic novel. There were those, of course, who'd not think twice about it. But he wasn't one of them. The very idea of hurting Tom filled him with horror. It would have been the same as hurting Peter, or Annie, come to that, when she'd been alive.

As he walked he looked about him, taking in the sheer beauty of the place. Some days he felt almost like he had died and come to heaven. At least it would have seemed so, had Annie been at his side. Coming out from the trees beside the Ridgeway he found himself waist deep in a meadow full of wild flowers, their bright, natural colours stretching all the way to the low grey walls of the old graveyard that lay in the shadow of the castle.

Jake slowed, taking it all in, his mood brightening at the sight.

He had done Tom no wrong. He had kissed Tom's wife, yes, but he had gone no further, and what was one small kiss between old friends? And maybe Tom knew that already. Maybe she had gone straight home and told him, and he had laughed and said something like 'Poor old Jake. He needs a woman in his bed.' Which was true, only...

Jake stopped, reaching out to pluck a strand of wild lavender, studying it a while, conscious suddenly of how fragile it all was; of how easily all of this was brought to ruin. Transient, it was. And thus meaningless, some might say. Only it was that very brevity that made it beautiful, that gave it meaning. It was like Annie. Even though he had lost her, he would not have chosen never to have met her, not for all the suffering. Never to have had – never to have risked having – that was worse. Far worse.

He came in from the back way, walking up the long, curving slope of West Street. There beneath the Martyrs Cross, two small, horse-drawn wagons were waiting, packed tight with trading goods, their drivers seated on the steps of the old stone cross, drawing on their pipes. Seeing Jake, the smaller of the two stood and hailed him.

'Jake! 'Ow's 'e?'

Jake grinned. Ted Gifford was a small, wiry man in his fifties. He had been born in Corfe and had remained here, and his accent was as local as it got. His companion was his son, Dick, who was much taller than his father with a shock of red hair. It was said by some that Dick was a clever man, though as he rarely spoke it was hard to tell, but one thing Jake did know: Dick was the best shot in all of Purbeck, and he had never see him flinch or run in a fight, even when things looked bad, so he was glad to see him there that morning.

'How are you two? I didn't see you last night?'

'We got some shut-eye,' Ted answered. ''S long journey. An' the road this year...'

He didn't finish, but it was clear he thought they were in for trouble. Not that Jake disagreed. It was why he'd brought an extra magazine.

Just then the wind changed direction. With it came the sound of the dogs.

'Thar' they be,' said Ted, pointing with his pipe towards the Bankes Hotel, and as he said it, so the three dog sleds came into view. At the same time two other figures came striding round the corner to the left: Tom Hubbard and Jack Adams, a beefy, bearded man in his mid-thirties who lived on the far side of their village.

Driving the sleds were Eddie Buckland, a local man from Corfe; Dougie Wilson, a slender, taciturn fellow from Kimmeridge; and Frank Goodman, from Langton Matravers, down Swanage way.

As the two parties merged, there were shouts of greeting, while in nearby houses, doors and windows were flung open, as people got up to watch the men get ready to depart.

As Tom came closer, he glanced across at Jake and nodded, the faintest smile on his lips.

'You're looking rough, old friend.'

'I'm getting old. I can't drink the way I used to.'

Tom's smile broadened. 'Ne'er you mind. You'll soon walk it off.'

And that was it. If Jake had thought there'd be any more to it then he'd been wrong. As Tom turned away, his movements as natural as ever, Jake breathed a sigh of relief. Tom was no actor, and if he'd noticed nothing strange about Mary's behaviour, then there was probably nothing to notice.

Maybe he'd left her in bed, sleeping it off.

Only if it were he setting off for a four-day trip, he'd have made sure he'd woken her. As he always did with Annie.

41

People were emerging from their houses now, bringing a last few items to take to market and trade. Afterthoughts. Things they had no need for. Old Josh was one of them, and, spying Jake, he came across.

'Jake, boy... you know what I'm looking for. If there's anything, get it for me, and bugger the cost. But use your judgement, eh? It's gotta be playable.'

He placed a leather pouch of coins in Jake's hand.

'Christ, Josh... must be half your savings here!'

Josh leaned closer, lowering his voice. 'That's it, boy. Every last crown of it. But I reckons thar'll be some'at this time, what with all the strangers on the road. But you know what I'm lookin' for. No crap, mind. You come back with a Kylie album and I'll be sorely pissed off wi' you.'

Jake laughed. 'You can trust me, Josh. If there's anything, I'll make sure it's yours, all right?'

'Thar's a good boy, Jake Reed. Good as a son to me.'

'It was fine music last night, Joshua. Some of the very best.'

The old man nodded and grinned. 'Thar's naught like the old songs, eh, lad?'

Jake slipped the coin pouch into his inner pocket, then, the last few pieces stashed, climbed up beside Ted Gifford on the first wagon. There was quite a crowd by now – fifty or more, gathered about them – and as Tom led the party down the slope towards the barrier, so the villagers followed, their chatter filling the morning air.

Ahead of them, the two watchmen – Dick Sims and John Gurney – heaved at the gate, straining to move the massive barrier, once a part of a level crossing, back against the wall. Then they stood aside, joining the others in waving and cheering the party through.

As they went round the curve of the castle mound and out of sight, Jake reached behind him and took his rifle from where he'd stowed it temporarily, then loaded a fresh clip into the magazine.

They were moving slowly, at walking pace, the two ponies straining, heads nodding, as they pulled the fully laden weight of the wagon.

Jake always liked this part of the journey, down Challow Hill, following the old railway line – the tracks long since removed – and across Middlebere Heath towards the ancient Saxon town of Wareham. There was something eternal about the place, something untouched, that stirred his soul. There were one or two farmhouses here and there, scattered to either side of the track, but you barely noticed them, they were so much a part of the landscape.

Jake leaned out, turning to look back at the rest of the party. Directly behind them, its two ponies keeping pace for pace with theirs, was the second wagon, with Dick Gifford at the reins. Beside him on the long bench seat was Eddie Buckland. Seeing Jake, Eddie touched his cap and grinned.

'Fine day, eh, Jake?'

'Looks like it!' Jake answered him, touching his own cap, acknowledging him.

Beyond the second wagon were the three sleds, the dogs straining eagerly, keen at this stage of the journey to press on, while at the very back of the party, keeping up a brisk walking pace, were Tom and Frank Goodman.

Jake didn't know Goodman that well. It was only recently that the villagers down there had decided to throw in their lot with Corfe, and on the one occasion Frank Goodman had come along, Jake had stayed at home. But Tom spoke well of him and he was a big, tough-looking man.

Seeing Jake looking, Tom waved, then called out to him.

'Keep an eye out, Jake! And no nodding off now! You can have a kip when we get there!'

Once more the gentle, teasing tone of Tom's voice reassured him.

Jake looked beyond them. From where they were all you could

see was the great green rampart of earth that formed a natural barrier against invaders. Only as you got further away could you see the castle again, tall and elegant even in its ruination, dominating the landscape for miles around.

He turned back, glancing at Ted Gifford as he did. But Ted was miles away, lost in his own thoughts, snatches of old songs – for the most part unrecognizable – escaping him from time to time.

Beside Ted on the bench seat, Jake noted, was his handgun. A Smith & Wesson M327 with a .357 Magnum calibre. An 8-shot. One of the finest handguns ever made.

'You think they'll come at us, even as we are?'

Ted looked at him. 'Not 'ere. Not out in the open. But there's places… We need to be cautious, old friend. Things is 'appening.'

There it was again. That sense they all had. Something had changed, but no one knew quite what. Only that it made them all a little edgy.

'You lookin' for anything special this time round?' Jake asked, changing the subject.

Ted shrugged. 'Thought I might buy a nice mirror if they got one. You know, with bevelled edges. Betty'd love one. The old 'un smashed, see. Apart from that…'

He shrugged, then turned back.

They were pulling out round the Ridgeway now, heading directly west. In a while the great mound of earth would fall away behind them and to their left, leaving them in the midst of a low, slightly marshy heath that stretched away into the distance. Wareham itself was only three miles away and if your eyes were good you could make it out, far off to the north-west.

This had never been a hospitable land. It was too rough, too raw and untended to be admired in a traditional sense, yet its wild beauty was undeniable. Men had lived here for thousands, maybe tens of thousands, of years, and yet they had never conquered it.

Up ahead, the broad path dipped down and to the left, the old railway track they'd been following ducking beneath what had once been the main route into Corfe, the old A351. Slowing the ponies, Ted manoeuvred them down past a row of old cottages that had been long abandoned, and up a small steep slope onto the road. It was a bit of a struggle, what with the full weight of the wagon, and Jake had to jump down and add his strength to that of the ponies to get them up over the lip.

There they paused for breath. Ahead of them the old road stretched off in a straight line across the ancient heath, its surface badly cracked, covered in a thick layer of weed, wild flowers and bracken. Yet the line of it was still discernible, running like a long, thin scar across the landscape.

They came out here from time to time and tried to clear it, making it a day out for the surrounding villages – a picnic of sorts – but their efforts never lasted long. In a week or two it would return, no matter how thorough they'd been. Yet at least it was passable. Like much else about their lives, they made do with things as they were, and this was one of them.

As their party formed up on the road, so Jake and Tom, Eddie and Frank went ahead, using long-handled scythes to cut a way through where the path was overgrown.

Slowly they made their way, while just as slowly the sun climbed the sky, coming up over Studland Bay, to their right as they laboured.

''S gettin' warm,' Eddie murmured, pausing from his task to wipe his neck. 'I thought it would be a lot colder than this.'

Tom laughed. 'Just think of the pint that's awaiting you...'

'And a good fry up,' Frank added, grinning and looking about him. 'Now set to, lads, else we'll be here all bloody day!'

They set to work once more, hacking away at whatever lay in their path, and slowly they progressed, the wagons and dog sleds edging their way closer and closer to their first stop. Just over an hour later, covered in sweat from their exertions, they stepped out onto the cleared section, just across the river from the old town.

'There's got to be an easier way,' Frank Goodman said, wiping his brow with his handkerchief.

'If there is I don't know it,' Tom answered. 'But I do know this. It's spared us a lot of grief over the years. Just as it's hard for us to get out, so it's just as hard for roaming bands to get in.'

Jake looked away. Maybe that was true, but it was far from perfect. They'd lost many a good man to raiders over the years. Yes, and women and children too. But things were far worse elsewhere.

'Come on,' he said, looking to the others. 'Let's go and freshen up. I don't know about you, but I've a thirst on me could kill a man.'

Wareham lay on the far side of the river, the back walls of its southernmost houses right up against the water's edge. In ancient days it had been a walled town, built by Saxon kings, and its street plan remained unaltered from those times. Like the Isle of Purbeck of which it was a part, it was a place of great history. Owing to its geographical position, however, it had long been a town in decline. Now it was a total backwater, a place one passed through on the way east. Even so, it had its compensations, among them the finest inn in the locality.

The Quay Inn was on the right as you entered the town, just past the bridge, its long terrace overlooking the river. As they pulled up in the courtyard, two of the tavern keeper's sons came out, greeting them by name and asking them what their fancy was.

While the others ordered breakfast, Tom and Jake went inside to see the landlord.

Jack Hamilton was a big, cheery man, in his sixties now, but brimming with good health. He had been landlord of the Quay Inn for almost thirty years. When the Collapse had happened, he had helped man Wareham's defences against the bands of murderers and thieves that had plagued the land back then. Now that things were more peaceful, however, he indulged in what he called his 'other favourite sport' – that of talking.

But there was a purpose to their talk that morning. Jack wanted something from market, and he was prepared to pay handsomely for it.

'I dunno...' Tom said, feeling ill at ease with the request. 'Goods are one thing, Jack. But this...'

'Tom... you of all men must surely know... and you, Jake... A man needs a wife. And where in this godforsaken town am I likely to get one? No. I needs to get one where one's available, and where's that if not Dorchester?'

'But, Jack... what if I chose the wrong girl for you? What if—?'

Jack cut in. 'I won't hear it. I know you've the eye for it. Your Mary now... and you, Jake... your Annie, bless 'er soul... You men knows a good woman when you sees her.'

'Maybe,' Jake said, sharing Tom's unease, 'but why not go your-self? Or come along with us. I mean, if that's what you want...'

'Oh, no,' Jack said, frowning now, troubled by the suggestion. 'Me? Why I'd just choose the first one they showed me, and probably pay twice the price she were worth. No... I need someone who knows how to haggle. Who can get me a good, fresh girl... an *unspoiled* girl, if you knows what I mean. Someone as'd be good at cleaning out rooms and serving the odd pint now and then.'

Tom looked to Jake and shrugged.

'All right,' Jake said, relenting. 'But if we don't see anyone we think is suitable, then we're not to blame, right? And we're not bringing back anyone as doesn't want to come, you understand? You're not buying a servant, Jack Hamilton, nor a slave. You're buying a wife, okay? Someone you'll respect.'

The big man grinned. 'Now there's friends for you! I'll bring you the cash straight away. But you relax now and have a good meal and a refreshing pint. It's on me, my lads. It's my pleasure.' And he turned away and was gone.

Tom looked to Jake. 'Are you sure? I mean, what if she runs?'

'Then we choose one who won't. Who wants to settle. Who'll

see this as a chance for a good life.'

'And how are we gonna know that? What if she lies to us?'

'We'll know.'

Tom stared at him a moment longer.

'*What?*'

'I was just thinking. I mean, while we're sorting old Jack out...'

Jake sighed. 'I told you last night. I'm not interested.'

'No?'

But Jake could see Tom was teasing him again. He grinned. 'Come on. I'm hungry.'

'You're a man in need.'

Yes, he thought, but he had to look away, lest his best friend saw through him and caught the vaguest shadow of his thoughts.

They were sitting at the long table by the window when Eddie, who'd been put on guard duty, put his head round the door.

'Tom... Jake... we've a couple of strangers snooping about...'

They were up at once, every last one of them, grabbing guns and piling out the door. The wagons were where they'd left them, beside the sleds in the middle of the yard, the horses tied at the trough nearby. The dogs were sprawled out beneath the wagons, fed now and resting.

'Where?' Tom asked, looking about him.

'They must'a gone,' Eddie answered. 'They must'a seen me go in.'

Tom climbed the steps up to the roadway and looked about him. Jake joined him there, just in time to see two men slip down a side street, clearly in a hurry. Tom looked to him.

'Fancy a look?'

Jake nodded.

Tom turned, looking to the others. 'Finish off then get the animals in harness again. We're going to set out in twenty minutes. Meantime, Jake and I'll go check those two out.'

'You sure?' Ted Gifford asked, looking concerned. 'What if they're bad 'uns?'

'We're going to have a look, that's all,' Jake said. 'Check them out. Make sure they're not a threat.'

'They're not local,' Eddie said, gravely. 'Least, I didn't recognize them.'

'But they were sizing us up, eh?'

'They seemed real curious.'

Tom looked to Jake. 'Ready?'

'Sure. Lead on.'

Jake took the safety off his rifle then followed Tom.

They went quickly, looking this way and that, careful not to let anything escape them. Locals scattered as they came near, ducking into shops or down side roads. As they came to the street the two had disappeared down, they stopped.

'Cover me,' Tom said. 'I'm going to cross over. See if I can see anything.'

Jake raised his gun, and as Tom ran across, he leaned round the corner, aiming at whatever he could see.

The street was empty.

Jake looked to Tom, who stood there in the open, out in the middle of the street.

'Well?' he mouthed.

Tom gestured for him to step out alongside him. Jake quickly went across.

'The Antelope?'

Tom nodded. At the bottom of the street was another inn. The Antelope. They knew the landlord. He was a bit of a braggart and a bully. Not only that, but his beer was sour.

'What if they come out to face us?'

'Then we run like fuck.'

Jake grinned. 'You sure you wanna do this?'

'I don't want the bastards pursuing us all the way to Dorchester.

I wanna know who they are and what their intentions are.'

Only right then they heard noises from the road behind the inn; the sound of booted feet running away. Briefly they saw movement at the end of the street as a dozen or more men took off. Jake made to follow them, but Tom reached out and took his arm, holding him back.

'Well... now we know. They're not friends.' He looked to Jake, concerned. 'We'd better get going straight away. Try and keep ahead of those fuckers.'

'Right,' Jake said. 'But one thing first. We go speak to the landlord. Find out what he knows. How many of them there were, and what they looked like.'

'You think he'll tell us?'

'I'll make him tell us.'

Tom considered that a moment, then nodded. 'Okay, let's go speak to him. But, Jake...'

'Yes?'

'Don't get angry with the man. I don't want to fight him unless I have to.'

Eddie and Ted were waiting for them at the top of the steps when they came back. They looked anxious.

'Well?' Ted asked. 'What do we know?'

'There's a dozen of them, maybe more,' Tom answered, looking beyond the two on the steps to the others. 'Landlord of the Antelope says they're just traders, but how many traders do you know who travel that light? No. They're raiders. And they're headed the same way as us. So we need to stay vigilant. And we need to stay armed at all times. You see one of the fuckers you don't ask him any questions, you just blow his fucking head off, got me?'

'I'll be glad to,' Frank Goodman said. 'Be a *real* pleasure.' Which made the rest of them laugh.

'Good,' Tom said. 'Then let's move on.'

★

Peter stood at the top of the tower, the highest point of the ruins, leaning out over the edge, looking out across country to the north-west. Much as he liked being closer to Meg and her sisters, he hated it when his dad was away. Hated how it made him feel, like everything was suddenly much more fragile. He didn't like that stomach-wrenching sense of uncertainty it gave him, that anxiety he carried with him every waking moment; the fear that he would never see his dad again. It was awful, and nothing Meg could say or do would make it go away. But then Meg didn't understand. She hadn't lost someone the way he'd lost someone. She didn't realize just how brittle it all was.

He wished Jake had let him go with him. At least then he'd have known what was happening.

'Peeee-ter... Peeeeeee-ter...'

He turned, looking down the bisected slope of the ruined castle. It was Beth, calling him in for lunch.

'Coming!'

He took one last, fearful look to the north, then ran quickly down the cracked and uneven steps, leaping the gaps.

For a moment he wondered what it must have been like, back in the old days, before things fell apart. His dad had told him once about how some of the people back then had had tiny communicators, specially-designed 'chips' which were like tiny slivers of silvered metal, sewn into their heads so they could speak to other people as and when they liked. He had had one himself, in fact, only he'd had it removed years back, long before Peter was born. He still had the scar, a neat little purple line on his neck beneath his right ear, but that was all.

If they'd had them now he could have spoken to Jake and found out what he was doing and how he'd been feeling. Only that was just wishful thinking. When it all collapsed, all of that had gone with it. All of the clever stuff.

51

Beth was waiting by the gate to the castle's lower field.

'You all right?'

'Yeah.'

'Just that you have this look sometimes...'

Beth was the Hubbards' second daughter. Seventeen now, she looked every bit a woman. In some ways she was much prettier than Meg, but she was more of a big sister to him than anything else.

'Do I?'

'Yeah. Like you're sad. *Are* you sad?'

None of your business, he wanted to say, only that would have been rude. Besides, she was only being concerned.

'Where's Meg?'

'Helping Mum.'

Beth began walking down the slope. He followed, two or three paces behind, trailing her.

She turned, looking to him again. 'You're a moody little bugger, you know that?'

'Am I?'

'See,' she said, turning to him and laughing. 'You need to relax a bit. Loosen up.'

He could hear her mother, Mary, in the way she said it. Only wasn't that the way of it? Didn't he catch himself, sometimes, sounding like his dad?

'Sorry,' he said, looking down, ashamed suddenly of being so stupid. So moody. Of course his dad would come back. Didn't he always?

Beth looked to him again and smiled. 'I thought we might play a game tonight. Scrabble, maybe. Or Monopoly. Or... well... you can choose.'

He looked to her and grinned. 'Beth?'

'Yeah?'

'You'd make a good sister-in-law.'

'Yeah?' And then she saw what he meant and her eyes widened a little. 'Yeah?'

'Yeah... Don't tell Meg, but I've asked my dad to get a ring... you know, from the market.'

'Oh, Pete-ie...' She came over and, holding his face, gave him a kiss. 'You darling boy. Do Mum and Dad know?'

Peter looked down, blushing. 'Not yet. I was going to ask them... when the men got back.'

They had come to the lower gate by now. He slowed, then looked to her again.

'We're not too young, d'you think?'

But Beth was smiling broadly now. 'Not if you're sure. Not if you're absolutely sure.'

He thought about that a moment, then smiled. 'I'm sure.'

Out on the road again, heading west, they made good time. The route had been pretty much empty, with no sign of the strangers, but now, some three or four hundred yards ahead, the trees to either side pressed in close to the old cracked surface. From here on, for a mile or so, they would be inside the wood.

Tom stood there a long while, staring at the gap between the trees and stroking his chin. They had to go through. There was no alternative. Only it was certain that this, if anywhere, was where they'd make their move.

'Well?' Frank Goodman said, coming over. 'You got a plan?'

'Me? I'm just savouring the air, Frank. Enjoying being alive, while I still am.'

'So what do we do? Turn round and go home? Wait another month? Or do we blast our way in and blast our way out again?'

Tom smiled. 'Sounds about as good as anything I could come up with.' He turned, looking to Jake. 'What d'you think, Jake?'

'We've done it before, and there's not a man here who's afraid of doing it. And as Frank says, the only alternative is to let those fuckers chase us off.'

Jake turned, looking to the others. 'All those in favour of going home...'

There was not a movement. Not a flicker of an eye.

'Okay... all those in favour of the blast-us-in-blast-us-out plan...'

Six hands went up, then a seventh. Finally all eight were raised.

'Good,' Jake said. 'Then that's decided.' He looked to Tom. 'You think they're watching us?'

'They're pretty stupid if they're not.'

'Then they're not far in. They're probably thinking to unnerve us. To hit us immediately we're inside.'

'Or just outside,' Dick Gifford said, surprising them all by even speaking. 'So why don't we just leave all the stuff here and crawl towards them, army style, and take them on, man for man? We can come back for the stuff after we've dealt with 'em.'

Jake looked to Tom, who, like him, was grinning now. Tom nodded, then looked to Dick Gifford.

'Fucking brilliant plan, Dick. And one they won't expect. We go in there, yeah? And hunt 'em down, one by one.'

Jake's heart was racing now. But he wasn't afraid. He'd done this far too often to be afraid. As Tom fixed the details of the attack, Jake looked from face to face, seeing how each of them met his gaze unflinchingly. In the early years after the Collapse, they'd had to do this three, four times a year – mainly in the summer – seeing off raiding parties, fighting for their lives against desperate bands of men who would have taken everything – their food, their women and their children. It had schooled them to be hard as well as fair, to be unsparing when it was called for. There wasn't a single one of them who hadn't risked his life a dozen times and more.

Last of all his eyes locked with those of the new man, Frank Goodman. 'You good for this, Frank?'

Goodman nodded. There was steel in his gaze.

'Okay,' Jake said, 'then let's do as Dick says. You see any kind of movement, you target it. Only I've got one change of plan. We don't go in. We stay *outside*, keeping low, until we're sure we've got most of them. All right? We don't go inside unless we have to, because once we're inside we won't know who's a friend and who's not. Are you all good with that?'

There were nods all around.

'Good, then let's load up and get at them.'

They marched towards the trees in a straight line, the eight of them spread out like gunfighters, guns raised. Tom gave the order at a hundred yards and they went down, onto their stomachs and crawled forward, army fashion, rifles held up in front of them. The way they'd trained to do it years back.

Fifty yards out and the first few shots came from the woods. They whizzed past their ears like angry hornets, or threw up tiny chunks of dirt.

Dick Gifford was the first to return their fire, his single well-aimed shot bringing a howl of pain from among the trees. Next to him, some four or five paces to Jake's right, Frank Goodman laughed, then opened up.

One thing was clear immediately: the raiders weren't that well armed. It was likely that only half their number had guns, and not good ones at that.

Too easy, Jake thought, letting off three quick shots at a movement to his left. There was a cry, followed instants later by a terrible screaming that went on and on.

An answering shot whizzed past his ear.

Dick opened up again, a rapid burst, and the screaming stopped.

For a moment there was sporadic fire, single shots, carefully aimed, and then they all opened up at once, the eight of them getting off shot after shot. For a moment the raiders returned a desultory fire. Then, seeing that the game was up, they began to turn and flee.

Or tried to.

Far to Jake's right, Tom was kneeling now, taking aim at the running men. Dick Gifford was also on his knees, as were Eddie and Frank. In a moment they were all kneeling, picking off anything that moved.

In the silence that followed a thin haze of smoke settled. The smell of cordite was strong in the air, while the barrel of Jake's gun felt warm against his hand. There was a pulse throbbing in his brow.

He stood up very slowly, still cautious, his gun still levelled at the trees. There wasn't a sign of life in there. Not a moan or a whisper.

Jake swallowed. They were going to have to go in and make sure. He looked across at Tom and smiled, but it was a strained expression. He'd never liked this part.

He walked towards the trees, his rifle moving slowly, left to right and back again, ready to blast anything that moved, but he could see already how devastating their fire had been.

He could hear a faint moaning now. One or two were still alive, if barely, just away to his right.

Three of them had fallen in a heap about ten yards in. They were clearly dead. Just beyond them another lay sprawled out on his face like he was sleeping. Only there was no movement, just a lot of blood.

Jake turned full circle, trying to make out how many bodies there were. A dozen at least.

Tom stepped up alongside him. 'You all right?'

Jake nodded. Dick Gifford and Frank Goodman came and stood with them, guns lowered.

'Serves the fuckers right,' Goodman said, looking about him contemptuously. 'Thought they could pick us bare.'

Jake took a long breath. He could smell the dead men. Could smell their blood and faeces. At the end they'd been afraid. As well they ought. They'd not had a clue who they'd taken on.

He knew he ought to be unsentimental about all this, but when it came to it he couldn't stop himself. He always felt sorry for them. No matter how much he tried to convince himself that it was 'us or them', as Tom so often argued, it simply didn't matter. They were still living, breathing human beings. Or had been, until a few moments ago. That was why he couldn't share Goodman's contempt, his cynicism.

The moaning came again. Goodman turned, looking towards the noise, then went across. There was a gunshot, then, four or five seconds later, a second.

Again it made sense. There was no use taking chances, and they couldn't afford to take on a badly injured enemy. Even Jake knew that that made no sense. Yet it seemed a touch too ruthless somehow.

Goodman returned, his face hard. He passed by them silently.

'He lost a brother to raiders,' Tom said, speaking quietly, for Jake's ears only. 'Ten years back. His brother bandaged the guy up. Saved his life. First opportunity the bastard had he shot him... in the back. So now Frank doesn't take chances.'

Tom straightened up, looking about him, then raised his voice. 'Guess we'd better see what they've got.'

Again, Jake loathed this part. Stripping dead bodies – it seemed indecent somehow. He himself would have left them, but it made sense. Life these days was about surviving, and anything that helped tip the balance had to be embraced. They had no one but themselves to rely on.

He walked across to the one who lay face down, then, steeling himself, turned the body over.

'Christ...'

It was a girl. A teenage girl. Her face was scabbed and pale and her hair was cut shoulder length, but there was no mistaking it.

Tom came across, then winced. 'Jesus...'

Jake looked into his face; saw what he was thinking.

It could so easily have been one of his girls.

'Leave her be,' Tom said quietly. Then, looking about him again, he gave another order. 'We've not time enough to bury them. But we can't leave 'em here. Who knows what diseases they'll spread. We'll pile 'em up and burn 'em, okay?'

There were nods at that.

'Look at this!' Frank Goodman said, straightening up above the corpse he had been searching, his face lit up with a beam of a smile. 'It's a watch. It's a fucking gold watch!'

Tom took a step towards him.

Crack!

Jake was still staring at the girl. For a moment he didn't understand. It sounded a bit like a gunshot, only they'd stopped firing minutes ago and all the raiders were dead.

Crack!

Wood splinters flew from a nearby tree.

Tom grunted, then dropped to his knees.

'Tom...?'

Behind him, Frank Goodman was crashing through the trees, heading further in. After a moment two shots rang out and then a third.

There was a yelp, then further crashing.

Jake knelt beside his friend. 'Tom... where are you hit?'

Tom gasped for breath, then let out a tiny moan. 'My shoulder... my right... shoulder...'

Jake looked to the Giffords, who were staring out through the trees, watching the pursuit.

'Ted... Dick... give me a hand. We need to carry Tom over to the wagons, and we need to do it now. He needs this cleaned up and bandaged.'

From deep among the trees, Frank Goodman's voice floated back to them. 'What was the fucking matter with you, you stupid cunt! You'd got away! You'd fucking got away! Now look what you've done!'

They heard the click as he cocked the gun again, then a soft, almost muted explosion.

Jake closed his eyes. It was best not to imagine.

'You'll be okay,' he said, helping Dick and Ted get Tom to his feet. 'We'll put some iodine on it and some nice clean bandages. Then we'll get you home...'

Tom shook his head. 'No, Jake. We've got to go on. We haven't got time to go back. I'll be okay. It's just a flesh wound. A few painkillers and I'll be fine.'

Just then Frank Goodman returned. He had a sour look on his face. 'There were three of them, further back among the trees. I got one of them, but the other two escaped.' He looked at Tom. 'What's the damage?'

Tom grimaced. 'It stings like fuck, but I'll be okay. At least he missed my head.'

Goodman nodded. 'Well, I didn't fucking miss his. You should have seen his eyes when I put the gun in his mouth...'

'They're just boys,' Eddie said, coming across. 'There's not one of 'em over twenty.'

'City boys by the look of it,' Jake said. 'Shanty-dwellers, I'd say. But what are they doing this far west?'

And the girl...

They had come to the edge of the trees, but every tiny movement was making Tom wince with pain.

'Sit him down,' Jake said, taking charge. 'Let's bring the wagon over.'

They did as Jake said. Ten minutes later it was done. The wound was cleaned and bandaged, while a heavy dose of morphine had numbed Tom's pain.

Jake crouched beside him, watching as the others made a pile of the bodies in the clearing beside the road.

Frank Goodman took the petrol can and poured it over them, then looked across at Jake. 'You want to do the honours, Jake?'

They were all here. All fourteen of the dead. And Eddie had been right. There wasn't one of them over twenty, and most of them were younger than that. A lot younger. And then there was the girl...

Unsentimental, he told himself. You've got to be unsentimental.

He struck the match and let it fall, standing back as the flames roared up.

They would have killed us. They would have left our bodies to be pecked clean by the birds.

But it didn't matter what he told himself. They were just kids. Just fucking kids.

Peter sat with the Hubbards, at the head of their old kitchen table, in the 'man's chair' as they always called Tom's seat. He liked being there; liked the way they always made him welcome, as if he was their brother, not just a cousin.

He always ate well at the Hubbards'. Much better than at home. Not that he complained. His dad did his best. But he wasn't half the cook Mary Hubbard was.

The girls were messing about right now, giggling and whispering to each other. They were up to mischief, but for once Peter couldn't be bothered to find out what was going on.

Mary had cooked a casserole. She brought it in, wearing thick oven gloves to carry the steaming pot. It smelled delicious. Prime beef with all the trimmings. But Mary herself seemed distracted for once. She went through the motions of being there, but her mind clearly wasn't. Peter could tell she was thinking about something. When she looked at you, she would smile, as always, but the smile would fade after a moment, as if it hadn't the power to sustain itself.

He ate, trying to enjoy the meal, slipping the odd piece of meat beneath the table for Boy. Only he was too distracted now. The more he observed Meg's mother, the more certain he was that something was wrong. It wasn't just the air of distraction that surrounded her, it was something deeper. She seemed sad. Only that made no sense. He'd been with the Hubbards dozens of times when Tom and Jake had gone to market, and she'd always treated the occasions as a kind of holiday, to be celebrated. They'd always had a lot of fun. Today, however, she seemed positively miserable, and there seemed no reason why.

There was no way, of course, that he could ask, but it preyed on his mind. When they went out into the garden after lunch, he didn't join in the girls' game, but stood there by the end wall, looking north, Boy settled by his feet.

They'd be a fair way along by now, he reckoned. At East Stoke, maybe, halfway to Wool. That was, if they hadn't made it to Wool already.

'Peter?'

He turned as Meg ran up. 'Yeah?'

'We're going in to Corfe. You wanna come?'

'Nah... later, maybe.'

Meg looked disappointed, but she didn't argue. As she ran off, Peter looked down at Boy, then knelt to pet him and rough up his coat.

'You're a good dog... You liked Aunt Mary's stew, didn't you? You could've eaten a whole bowl on your own...'

He stopped, straightening up. He thought he'd heard something.

'Boy,' he whispered. 'Stay. I'll be back in a minute.'

While Boy did as he was told, Peter crossed the garden. He moved slowly, quietly. At the back door, which was partly open, he paused.

Mary was at the sink, her back to him. She was hunched forward, her head lowered. At first he thought he'd been mistaken, but then he saw how she was shaking and heard the noise again.

She was crying. She was standing there with her hands in the soapy water, sobbing her heart out.

Peter turned away. Something had to be wrong.

As he walked back, Boy came over, sensing his mood, nuzzling him, as if to somehow comfort him.

'There's my beauty,' he said softly, bending down to pet him again. 'There's...'

The first few shots could have been anything. It could have been a hunter, out in the meadows. What followed, however, was anything but normal. It sounded more like a fireworks display. Not only that, but he could hear the distinctive sound of a semi-automatic, and he knew Dick Gifford had a semi-automatic. A .338 Browning.

Oh, Christ...

They'd been ambushed. He was certain of it.

He ran across. 'Aunt Mary! Quick! Something's happening!'

She came out, wiping her eyes with her apron, then stood there looking north, listening intently. But it had died down now. Then, another brief flurry, before it all went silent again.

'It's them,' he said. 'It's got to be.'

'It hasn't *got* to be...'

But he could see she thought otherwise.

'Aunt Mary...?'

'What?'

'Just now... in the kitchen...'

The way she looked at him, he could see that she wasn't going to answer.

'Peter. You'd better run in to Corfe. Let them know that the men might have got into trouble on the road. Maybe they can get someone out there. Find out what's been happening... And, Peter... don't say anything to the girls.'

He nodded, then ran off, Boy in hot pursuit.

Be okay, he thought, picturing his father clearly in his head. *Just be okay.*

*

It was difficult knowing what to do with Tom. If they'd been coming back from market it would have been okay. They could have laid him down in the back of one of the wagons and let him get some rest. As it was, he had to sit up on the bench seat, between Eddie Buckland and Jake, who had an arm about his old friend, making sure he didn't topple off.

They had decided to stop at Wool. It wasn't far, only a couple of miles on from where they'd been attacked, and it marked the halfway point of their journey. Usually they'd press on, all the way to Dorchester in the one day. It meant they'd have to set off early the next morning if they were to get to the market when it opened.

As they trundled along, Jake kept Tom talking. The morphine, aside from numbing the pain, was making him sleepy, but Jake didn't want him to fall asleep before they arrived in Wool and got him in a proper bed. And so they talked about old times.

'Back then they'd have seen to you properly,' Jake said cheerily. 'Given you an implant and grown new tissue within a week. And not even a scar. Like new.'

'You think they've still got all that stuff, Jake? I mean, in America or somewhere like that?'

'It's possible, I suppose. And I guess once you've discovered all that stuff you can't un-discover it. But I reckon it'll be years before any of it comes back. When things fell apart, they *really* fell apart. I saw it, remember? When things come crashing down like that, it isn't easy to reconstruct. It isn't easy at all. I read somewhere... oh, a long time ago... that the United Kingdom could only feed ten million people from its own resources. All the rest had to be imported. Well... when things stopped... when we stopped shipping in food and other stuff... people died. Died in their millions. In their *tens* of millions.' He sighed. 'Sometimes I think it's a wonder *any* of us survived.'

Tom smiled; a sickly, pained smile. 'You know what, Jake?'

'What?'

'I find myself wondering sometimes just what's going on else-where. You know... in America and Africa and Europe. Someone must be trying to put it all back together again, don't you think? I mean... they can't just let it stay as it is.'

Jake shrugged. 'I guess not. But they're taking their damned time about it, don't you think? You'd think someone would have set up a radio station, you know, to get the news out to everyone. It's been over twenty years, after all!'

'Yeah, but what's the point?' Eddie chipped in. 'Thar's no 'lectric to run the sets.'

'That's true. But there's those sets you can wind up. We've seen 'em at market from time to time.'

Tom gave a little moan. Jake looked to him at once.

'You all right, Tom?'

Tom swallowed painfully. 'It aches. And I think it's weepin'.'

Jake had a cursory look. Tom was right. The bandage was wet with blood. He looked about him at the countryside. Wool was no more than a mile away.

'Think you can hang on, Tom? It'll be fifteen minutes at most.'

Tom closed his eyes and nodded. He looked drawn suddenly, his face grey.

'Dick!' Jake called, hailing the wagon in front of him. 'Think you can up the pace a little?'

'Right-oh!' Dick called back, putting out an arm in acknowl-edgement. At once his ponies quickened their pace.

Jake looked to his friend. 'We'll get you there, don't worry. Get you laid out in a nice comfy bed.'

Tom smiled weakly. 'Thanks...'

Jake was silent a moment. 'You know what I think, Tom? I think it's going to take a hell of a lot to get it all back together again. As it is, well... it's just too easy to stay as we are... lots of little king-doms warring with each other. It'll take a big man to get it all up and runnin' again.'

'Another Genghis Khan?'

'Or a Hitler.'

'You think?' Tom shifted a little, trying to get comfortable.

'I think. I mean, whoever's going to do it, they aren't going to be nice, are they? Where's nice going to get them? No. People are harder now, more suspicious. They're not going to sign on for anything they aren't *forced* to sign on for. And there'll be a lot of tin-pot kings and so-called "emperors" who'll not be willing to hand over the reins of their little kingdoms, so I imagine there'll be a lot of blood shed setting up our brave new world.'

'And our kids'll bear the brunt of it, is that what you're thinking?'

Jake nodded. He hated to think of it, but it was true. Bad times were coming, and their darlings, their loved ones, would have to face them. All he and Tom could do was prepare them for it. 'Take our own so-called King of Wessex, Josiah Branagh. You can't imagine *him* giving up all his perks without a fight. Unless, of course, he's allowed to keep it all, *nominally*. But that'd be no better. No... if someone wants to create something new, then they're going to have to clear away all of the clutter and build it up from scratch, and who knows how long *that* will take!'

Tom nodded. His eyes were closed now, but he did seem to be listening.

'You know what?' Eddie said, giving the reins a tug. 'I think it was a good thing it all came apart. I mean... look at the way things were headin'. Those were bad times, Jake, as you well know. An' if we lost some'at, then we gained an awful lot too.'

Jake couldn't disagree. Take his own life. He'd been doing well by the system. Very well indeed. The rewards for his job had been phenomenal. By any standard he had been obscenely rich. Only it was a world and a way of living that *deserved* to be destroyed. He looked back at it now and saw how greedy his kind had been, how wasteful and selfish. Even so, he couldn't shake off the memory of how awful those first few years had been, immediately after the Collapse; the savagery and plain evil he had been witness to. He didn't want to see that come again. Didn't want his son – no, or any of his friends' children – to suffer all that again. Only maybe he didn't have a choice. Maybe it was coming, whether he willed it or not.

They were climbing a slight gradient now. Wool was just up ahead.

'Tom?'

But Tom was asleep finally, snoring, a look of peace on his face.

Eddie laughed. 'He's gonna be okay. He just needs some rest, is all. Just a little bit of rest.'

The landlord of the Wessex Arms was an old friend, Billy Haines. They'd helped him out many a time, and now he repaid the favour, preparing a room for Tom. As chance would have it, one of his customers had been a doctor back before the Collapse, a man named Padgett. He'd been retired a long while now, but he was sent for.

So it was that an hour after they'd arrived, Tom was being looked at with an expert eye, sitting up in bed while the doctor slowly removed the bandage.

The shoulder looked swollen, badly bruised, but the wound itself looked clean. The bullet, it seemed, had gone straight through, missing the bone.

'You were lucky,' Padgett said, sitting back. 'If the bone had been splintered it might have been different, but as it is I'd say you have a perfect chance of it healing by itself. I'll clean it and re-bandage it, then you can get some rest. I'm sure Billy here will be happy to look after you while your friends are gone.'

'No chance!' Tom said. 'I'm goin' with them. I can get a bed when I'm there. They can dose me up if they like, but I'm not missin' it. There's things I need.'

'I could get them,' Jake said, but Tom gave him a warning look.

Jake shrugged and turned away.

'Well, my advice would be to stay here,' Padgett said, clicking his medical bag shut. 'After a shock like yours has had, the body needs to rest. And it would be good if I were here to check on it every few hours. Make sure there's no infection.'

'There's doctors in Dorchester,' Tom said, insistent now. 'It's kind of you, Doc, and you, Billy, but I need to go. If I'd wanted to stay at home, I'd have stayed. I won't exert myself, I promise. But I have to go.'

'Then I won't stop you. But be careful. It looks fine to my eyes, but get it checked out again when you get to Dorchester. And get it looked at once more before you start back. You don't want to get blood poisoning. You do, and there's nothing we can do for you, understand? It's not the old days. Even in Dorchester...'

Tom raised a hand wearily. 'I know. And I'll be careful. Only I've got to go. No argument.'

Afterwards, alone with Tom, Jake asked him what was going on.

'What's this about you having to go? Since when was it imperative? I could get you what you need. Just give me a list.'

Tom looked away, avoiding his eyes. 'There's people I've got to see. Urgent business. I can't explain, Jake. Just trust me, eh?'

'Trust you? Trust you about what? Since when did we two have secrets between us?'

'I can't say... I... I promised Mary.'

That made Jake frown. What the fuck was going on? But Tom wasn't going to say. Jake could see that.

'It'd better be good.'

'*What?*' It was said tetchily, but Jake could see how tired Tom was and relented.

'Never mind... I'll go along. I always do.'

Tom smiled. 'Thanks. But now I need you to fuck off. I need to sleep.'

'Here... let me help you.'

Tom let Jake lay him down again, wincing as Jake put the slightest pressure on his shoulder. Doc Padgett had given him some tablets – painkillers and sedatives – but their effect was limited. Tom was still hurting.

'I'll leave you now, okay? But I'll check in again in about an hour. Make sure you're fine.'

'Thanks... Oh, and, Jake?'

'Yes?'

'This... it's okay. We got off light. We always have, eh?'

CHUNG KUO

Chapter 3

DISTANT SHADOWS

I n the clear, bright light of early morning the party made its way
along the road. On their left, the green swell of the Downs
obscured their view of the sea to the south as they made their
way past the sleeping village of Owermoigne.

It was just after six, and, providing there were no delays, they
would be at market in plenty of time, half an hour before it opened.

They had rented a cart from the landlord at Wool, hooking it on
to the rear of the first wagon. As they trundled along, Jake walked
alongside, keeping an eye on Tom, who lay there on a straw palliasse,
wrapped in blankets to keep him snug against the crisp morning air.

This stretch of the A352, which ran in a great loop from Wool to
Dorchester, was kept clear most of the year by Branagh's patrols,
its broken tarmac surface swept free of vegetation. This close to
the county capital, those same patrols made it their business to
stop and search anyone they didn't recognize, or who couldn't produce proper identification. While that could mean trouble, usually
they knew better than to pick on genuine traders. If word got back
to Branagh it meant trouble for them, so generally they did their
job, keeping an eye out for bandits and thieves and leaving genuine
citizens alone.

It could have been worse. Corrupt as many of Branagh's officials were, there was a limit to their greed. They knew precisely what they could get away with, and with whom.

For the last mile or so Tom had dozed off again, and Jake had been left to his thoughts. He had been musing about what Tom had said the previous day. About how they had 'got off light'. It wasn't true. Frank Goodman wasn't the only one who had lost a brother. There was barely a family who had not lost sons or brothers, or who had had wives or daughters raped or beaten. Added to which there had been deaths from disease and accident and all manner of misfortunes. All in all, it had been a hard life these past twenty-odd years. Harder than he could ever have imagined. And yet rewarding, too, compared to the life he'd had.

Jake sighed. As ever, he shied away from thinking about all that. It was better to think about the present. Better to live life in the now.

They had stayed up late last night, talking to the locals. Wool itself had been attacked twice in recent months, the last time only a week or so ago. From the sound of it, it was the same bunch of rogues they had encountered in the woods, but that news was far from good. The party they'd dealt with was, it seemed, part of a much larger, marauding band, some forty or fifty in number. It was only because Wool's defences were so good that they'd not been overrun. That and the fact that, like their friends from Corfe, they had the better weapons.

He wasn't expecting the raiders to try again just yet. The two who'd got away would have told the others just what they might expect, and he'd have been surprised if they'd come back for more. Not only that, but this part of the county was well patrolled.

If they *were* going to try again it would be on the way home, tomorrow.

Unless...

Unless they've gone to try their luck against Corfe itself.

The thought had formed in his mind last night and, concerned that he might just be right, he had paid the landlord a crown to send one of his boys back to Corfe that very evening, to warn them to take care, and to give them the news about Tom.

He had written a note to Mary, for the boy to deliver, telling her not to worry; that Tom's injury was a scratch and that they were taking good care of him, signing it simply, 'From your good friend, Jake', nothing more.

Tom himself had had a reasonably good night. Thanks to the tablets and the earlier dose of morphine he had slept like a log and woken refreshed, with a far better colour. The doctor had come just before they'd left to check the wound and bind it again for the journey, expressing his satisfaction with the way it was healing. But Jake was still worried. He couldn't help it. He had seen it too many times: how a simple wound could kill a man in days from gangrene or blood poisoning. It was one of the big disadvantages of living in a post-technological age. That said, there was a hospital in Dorchester, and a good one at that, and Jake was determined to get Tom looked at just as soon as he could. Doc Padgett was a good man, but he was no expert.

Another mile had fallen behind them. The tiny hamlet of Warmwell was to their right now. Ahead, about a mile and a half further on, was Broadmayne, where the first of the watchtowers that encircled Dorchester stood. A couple of miles beyond that was the town itself.

It was as they passed the village of Conygar, where the ancient pylons lay, fallen and rusting in the fields to either side, that they met their first patrol. Six men on horseback, led by their 'boss', a big, muscular man by the name of Hewitt, who had been their guest at Church Knowle many a time.

Ted Gifford slowed the ponies and brought them to a stop. Seeing who it was, Hewitt gave the signal to his men to wait, then climbed down and came across.

'Hey up there, me lads... how's things?'

They gathered about Hewitt, letting Jake do their talking.

Noticing Tom, Hewitt asked Jake what had happened.

'We ran into a raiding party. Sixteen strong. We killed fourteen of them. Built a pyre of their bodies back on the roadside near West Holme. Tom got hit late. We thought we'd got them all, but three of them was hiding further back.'

'I saw to one of those buggers,' Frank Goodman said, and laughed.

Hewitt was grinning. 'Fuckin' good news, lads. Fourteen dead, eh?'

Jake nodded. 'Yeah. Only they were part of a much larger group that attacked Wool a week or so back. The villagers fought them off – gave them what for, by all accounts – but there's still thirty or more unaccounted for.'

Hewitt's smile had gone. 'Thirty, eh? And well armed?'

Jake shook his head. 'They're just kids. Teenagers. Shanty-dwellers, by the look of it. Though what they're doing this far west this late in the year I don't know.'

'No...' Hewitt stroked his beard thoughtfully. This was un-welcome news.

'I saw another lot,' Jake said. 'Up on the Wareham road, two days back. A ragged bunch of miscreants. Five adults and three kids. They looked hungry.'

Hewitt nodded, chewing over this new information. Then, as if confiding to them, he leaned closer, lowering his voice.

'A word of warning, gentlemen. You're going to market, I can see. Well, bear in mind that things 'ave changed since you were here last. It'll cost more. A lot more.'

There were murmurs of discontent among the men at that.

'What do you mean?' Jake asked. 'How much more?'

'Prices 'ave gone up, that's all I'm sayin'. You'll see for yerself and, I hope, ask more for your own produce. No one's gonna do you no favours, I warn you. Bad times are comin', me boys. Bad times.'

Bad times, eh? Jake thought, once the patrol had gone and they were on the move again. *But why?*

Hewitt's warning concerned him. He had been counting on having enough to pay for Tom's hospital treatment. It would have been a bit of a scrape even as it was, but if prices had gone up it might prove difficult.

As a one-time futures broker, he knew instinctively what such things meant.

Trouble. We're heading full speed into trouble. And the first thing that happens is that things get more expensive. It's the first sign.

Yes. But what kind of trouble?

The answer, most likely, was up ahead, in the taverns of Dorchester. Someone there would know. Someone would have word of what was going on.

The old county capital was directly ahead of them now on the road, some three miles distant to the north-west, its wooden, pallisaded walls coming slowly into view across the meadows. The ancient Bronze Age mound of Maiden Castle was visible, too, a mile away to the south-west, the stone walls of Branagh's 'palace' sitting atop its lush green slopes.

This had been the centre of government for three, maybe four thousand years; a fortress town, bounded by the River Frome to the north. When the Romans came in AD 43, they had conquered the surrounding lands and built a wooden fort here – turning the area into what was basically a frontier town. Durnovaria, they had called it, back then. In the next two centuries they'd expanded their little hilltop fort into a proper town with buildings made of stone – a forum, a marketplace, public baths, and the great houses of the rich. They had built an amphitheatre, too, and a great aqueduct to the west of the town. By the fourth century the wooden pallisade had been replaced by walls of stone. But the Romans had come and gone, their towns, including Durnovaria, burned down and plundered by the invading Saxons. In time Arthur had built his Wessex here. Arthur, King of the Britons. It had a ring to it that 'Branagh, King of Wessex' had never quite acquired, perhaps because Branagh – in his sixties now – had been a salesman before the Collapse.

The thought of it made Jake smile.

'Penny for 'em,' Tom said, leaning up a little on his pallet.

Jake looked to him. 'It's nothing. I was just thinking about the history of this place. How're you feeling?'

'Not bad. It aches, but...' He made to touch his shoulder, but Jake reached across and tapped his hand, like he would a child.

'Leave it be.'

'Where are we?'

'An hour short. Broadmayne's coming up.'

He said nothing about meeting the patrol. Nothing about what they'd learned last night in Wool, or of what Hewitt had said. He didn't want Tom to worry. Didn't want anything to get in the way of him getting better. As for what it'd cost to get him seen to at the hospital, he'd have to do what he could.

'You know what I was thinking, Jake?'

'Go on...'

'I was thinking I might get something... for Mary and the girls. Some little trinkets. There was a stall last time...'

Jake smiled. 'I was going to look there myself. The woman with the funny eye. Becky, I think her name is...'

'With the funny eye...' Tom laughed; the first time he'd laughed in days, only laughing hurt him.

'Oh, damn... Now it's weepin' again...'

'We'll soon be there, don't worry.'

Jake smiled reassuringly as he said it. Only he *did* worry. He couldn't help it. If Tom got ill – badly ill – how would he explain it to Mary?

'You're going to be fine. I'm going to make sure of it, okay?'

Tom looked back at him with gratitude. 'Okay,' he said softly, then closed his eyes. 'Just wake me when we're there.'

They had dropped off their goods at McKenzie's storage warehouse, parked the wagons and stabled the ponies. Now, while Frank Goodman saw to the dogs, Ted and Eddie went off to see what they could get for their produce.

Hewitt had been right. Everything was much more expensive. The gate fee – levied on each wagon, cart and sled – had doubled. Similarly their stabling fee had risen, if not by quite so much. And from what they had glimpsed of prices in the market itself, they were going to have to skimp on one or two items.

But not on Tom, Jake decided, as he helped his friend down the long side alley that led to the hospital. He was going to make sure Tom got the best treatment he could while they were there, even if it meant skimping on luxuries like tea and coffee.

'You mustn't fuss so much,' Tom protested. 'I'm fine. It'll heal of itself.'

'Maybe,' Jake answered. 'But I'm not taking any chances. Besides, it would be a false economy. What would Mary say if you were ill for a long time? How would she cope? No, Tom. They need you.'

Tom looked down at that. His silence seemed significant, but Jake didn't know why.

'Look... we'll get you checked out. Make sure you're okay, right? Then we'll go to that stall we were talking about. Buy your girls something nice.'

Tom looked up again and smiled. 'You think we can afford it?'

'Who knows? Maybe we'll use some of that money Jack Hamilton gave us to get him a bride.'

Tom looked askance at him. 'But, Jake...'

Jake grinned. 'I'm only joking. I wouldn't think of it. But if there's some over… Well, we could repay him later. Jack wouldn't mind.'

Tom considered that, then shrugged. 'I guess…'

They emerged out into a busy square. Just across from them was the front entrance of the old building where the hospital was housed. The real hospital had been burned down in an earlier campaign, and they had utilized this old factory instead. It was far from perfect, but it was better than nothing.

Being a market day, they had to wait some while, but then they were ushered through into a cubicle. A moment later a young doctor appeared, dressed in a long white coat and holding a clipboard.

'Right, gentlemen, I…' Only, seeing Tom, he fell quiet. 'Ah… I thought…'

'I've been wounded,' Tom said, speaking over the young doctor, as if to prevent the man from saying anything more. 'The bullet went clean through my shoulder. Missed the bone. It's been cleaned and bandaged, but we need to make sure it's not infected.'

Jake looked from one to the other. It wasn't even as if the man had introduced himself. But he knew, for a certainty, that Tom knew the young doctor and the doctor knew Tom. Only how?

He watched as the doctor removed the bandage and studied the wound. It looked less bruised now, less swollen, and after cleaning and bandaging it again, the young man looked to Tom and smiled.

'It looks fine, Mister Hubbard. Whoever cleaned it up did a good job.'

'That's Doc Padgett of Wool,' Jake said, his curiosity burning now. He wanted to ask what was going on, but Tom seemed keen to get away, now that he'd done what Jake had asked.

'Do you need any painkillers?'

'No,' Jake answered. 'I think we're fine.'

'Okay…' It was as if the doctor had a query on his lips, only he wasn't going to ask it. Not while Jake was there, anyway.

Tom stood. 'So what do I owe you?'

The young man drew in a long breath. 'We'll call it five crowns, yes?'

Five crowns! Jake narrowed his eyes. What was going on? He'd expected to pay ten at the very least, maybe as much as twenty.

Tom counted five large coins out into the young doctor's hand, then gave him a nod.

'Thanks.'

Outside, in the street, Jake made Tom round to face him.

'What's going on?'

'What d'you mean?'

'That doctor. He *knew* you. He'd met you before.'

'Yeah, well...'

'Go on... I'm dying to know.'

Tom looked away, unable, it seemed, to meet Jake's eyes. 'Last time we were here. I... I came to see him. I had a problem, see.'

'A problem?' And then it dawned on him what Tom was saying. 'You mean...?'

Tom nodded. 'It must have been the time before that. I saw a girl, here. You know...'

'At Flynn's?'

Again he nodded; only there was a look of shame in his face now. 'I... I got a rash.'

'Christ, Tom... Those places...'

'I know...' Tom glanced at him, then looked away again. 'Worst part was telling Mary.'

'You *told* her?' Somehow that shocked him.

Tom nodded. 'Had to. Wouldn't have been fair not to. Didn't want to give her what I had, did I?'

'And now? Are you all right now?'

'Yeah. He gave me something for it. Some cream and some tablets. I...'

Jake raised a hand. 'Enough... I don't want to know.'

Only he did. He wanted to ask Tom why. He'd thought Tom was happy with Mary. He'd thought...

Fuck. What *had* he thought? That Tom was some kind of saint?

'Christ,' he said softly, imagining it now. 'That must have been hard. Telling Mary...'

Tom's eyes were desolate, recalling it. 'Worst thing I've ever had to do. Broke her heart...'

'But she forgave you?'

Tom's smile was wintry. 'Yeah. But things ain't the same, Jake. They just ain't the same...'

Jake looked away, his thoughts in turmoil. So that was why. He'd thought it odd. But he would never have guessed. Not in a million years.

'Let's find that stall,' he said, gently taking his old friend's arm, seeing how frail he looked after his confession. 'And no word of this when we get back, okay?'

'Okay,' Tom echoed; but there was something in his face now that spoke of a deeper, more grievous wound than the one he'd sustained in the ambush – something that Jake completely failed to see, being so tied up in his own thoughts as he was. Something which ate away at the older man. Something unshared.

A secret.

For the moment, however, things were all right. Back on an even keel.

For the moment.

The undercover market was a big space just off the Maumsbury Road, a sprawling, noisy place of several hundred stalls which, on market days, was one great bustle of activity. One could buy almost anything beneath its awnings. Anything that was still being made or grown, that was. And even some of the old stuff, from before the Collapse, was still available, at a price. There were specialty stalls, like those that sold CDs and records, and others that specialized in books and magazines from the old times. There were stalls that sold leather goods – belts and jackets, harnesses and saddlebags. There were others that sold household chemicals – rat poison and detergent, as well as soap and shampoo. Two or three stalls sold home-made sweets, while a good half dozen were stacked high with vegetables of every description. Fruit and clothes, candles, tyres and spectacles, blankets, wallpaper, clocks and watches, seeds, toys and sewing materials – all were sold beneath the market's brightly striped awnings, along with knives and swords, writing paper and pens. There were even two stalls piled high with broken machinery, for those seeking spare parts. In shops nearby guns and ammunition were available, along with liquor and wine and cider. One could buy a strong pair of boots or some delicate, elegant shoes. Tapes, cassettes and videos could be found too, on a stall which flew a banner reading 'Overtaken Technologies Inc.'. Paint and jewellery, hats and football memorabilia, all were on sale, while at two adjacent stalls at the very centre of it all, a small crowd queued for haircuts and basic dentistry.

Right now, however, Jake and Tom were looking at the wares on the trinket stall, run by a young woman with a lazy eye, Becky. She was busy, helping them choose their purchases.

'Now that's a lovely one,' she said, her rich Dorset accent rounding off every word. 'A real bargain, especially in these times. Look at the engravin' on it! An' it's real silver. Look, there's the mark.'

Tom studied the leaf-shaped brooch a moment, then looked to Jake. 'What d'you think, Jake? D'you think she'd like it?'

'I think she'd love it. Only can you afford it?'

Tom took a long breath. He'd already selected necklaces for his three girls. This last purchase was for Mary, and in light of his recent confession, Jake could see why he took so long to choose. He wanted to get this right.

'No discount for bulk purchases, then, Becky?' Jake asked, winking at her.

Becky was a buxom lass with a fine figure, and but for her 'funny eye' she'd have been snapped up by some local male long ago. As it was, however, she would probably never marry.

'I wish I could,' she said, blushing now. 'But the price of silver has soared, I tell you gennelmen. 'Ard times are comin'.'

'Not by just a couple of crowns, my sweetheart?'

He could see his flattery was slowly winning her over.

'I tell you what,' she said, reaching under the stall and bringing out an old black leather briefcase. 'You were sayin' you was lookin' for a ring... for your boy... Well, I've a few nice 'uns here.' She snapped the case open and laid it out before Jake. 'You give me my price for the brooch and the rest of it, and I'll take a coupla crowns off the price of the ring. And you gennelmen can sort it out between you.'

Jake was about to say something, but at that very moment he saw it.

'That one,' he said, pointing to a simple gold band at the top left of the black velvet-backed display. 'That's the one.'

Becky plucked the ring from the display and handed it across.

Jake studied it a moment, then looked to Tom. 'What d'you think?'

'It's nice. But a bit small for Pete-ie, wouldn't you say?'

Jake looked to his friend and laughed. 'It isn't for Peter. Least ways, it's not him'll be wearing it.'

Tom looked blankly back at him, and then he clicked. 'Oh... you mean for Meg?'

Jake nodded slowly.

Tom's eyes widened, understanding flooding them. 'You think...?'

'I know. Least, with your permission.'

Tom laughed, but he was looking very serious now. He turned, facing Jake fully. 'I think it's a very good ring, Jake, my dearest friend, and I'd like it very much if your son were to be my daughter's partner in life. I think...'

A tear rolled down Tom's cheek. 'Fuck it, Jake. You know what?

I can't think of *anyone* I'd rather she were with.'

'You don't think he's too young, then?'

'Too young?' Tom shook his head, then wiped away another tear. 'No, Jake. Not at all. You *know*, you see. It don't matter how young or old you are. You just know.'

Jake grinned. 'Then let's settle up and go and find the others. Maybe have a wee drink or two to celebrate, eh?'

Jake turned back, looking to Becky, who seemed dewy-eyed at the prospect of one of her rings being the occasion for such happiness.

'Becks, love, you've got your price! It's a deal!'

And, reaching across, he drew her closer and gave her a kiss on the cheek that made her blush furiously.

'It's my pleasure,' she said, looking at Jake wistfully as Tom handed over payment. 'Any time, gennelmen... any time...'

Peter was chopping wood out back, when Meg came running up. Seeing her, Boy jumped up and bounded over to her.

'Hey, Boy,' she said, kneeling down to stroke him vigorously, the way he liked it. She looked to Peter and smiled.

'You'll never guess what...'

Peter stood a log on its end then looked to her. 'What?'

'I overheard some'at Ma was sayin'.'

'Oh, yeah?'

He swung the axe, cleaving the log in two. Boy barked, as if applauding.

'Yeah... seems as Jack Hamilton is lookin' fer a wife.'

'A wife?' He stood up another log, but he was grinning now. 'Go on...'

'Yeah... Seems he gave your dad a purse to go purchase 'im a bride in Dorchester.'

Peter had been about to swing the axe, but he stopped, staring now at Meg.

'Buy a wife?'

'Yeah... one who can cook and clean rooms and serve ale at the bar.'

'A skivvy, you mean?' And he brought the axe down hard, making the two halves of the wood fly up into the air. Boy barked again.

'Well, I think it's romantic. Even if 'e is in 'is sixties and 'e's 'avin' to pay. 'E's been far too long on 'is own.'

Peter glanced at her, trying to see if she was somehow alluding to his father, but her words didn't seem to have any hidden meaning. He set up another log.

'Mind,' she said, coming over and placing a hand on his bare arm, 'it does make you wonder...'

'About what?'

'Well... say you had to buy me... what kind of price would you pay? How deep would you dig in your pocket to have me?'

He stared at her, stunned by the words. She laughed, then squeezed his arm. 'I'm only kiddin'.'

'Yeah?'

'Yeah...' Meg walked over to the wall and stood there, looking out across the fields. 'I mean... money's important, but...' She shrugged, then turned and grinned at him. 'You know what? If I were someone else... you know, a young girl, without no prospects and livin' in some awful town like Dorchester... well... I think I might just jump at the chance, even tho' 'e's old.'

'Would you?' Peter looked crestfallen now.

'No, silly. I don't mean me. I mean... Oh, now you've got a face on. I knew I shouldn't 'ave told you.'

He set the axe down and stood up straight. 'Ask me again.'

'What?'

'Go on. Ask me again how much I'd pay for you.'

Meg frowned, then, with a shrug, asked him again.

This time he didn't hesitate. This time he said it clearly and not just in his head.

'Every penny I had, Meg Hubbard. Every last penny I had.'

Jake could have murdered a pint when they got back, but their drink had to wait. Ted Gifford was waiting for them by the door, and he had bad news.

'It's gone mad, Tom. Totally fuckin' mad!'

'What d'you mean?'

Tom sat on the nearby bench. He looked exhausted.

'I mean the price o' things has gone through the roof. We managed to get a bit more for our own load, but nothin' like enough. We've no option, Tom. We're going to 'ave to borrow some money from somewhere.'

Tom leaned forward. For a moment he closed his eyes, then he looked up at Ted again. 'How much d'you think we need?'

'I dunno. A coupla hundred crowns... three hundred, maybe? Heating oil alone has trebled in price. As for clips and cartridges...'

'You've been to Hardy's gunshop?' Jake asked.

Ted nodded. 'Frank went. Says it's absurd what they're askin'!'

Jake sighed heavily. 'Three hundred? Even if we could get someone to lend us that kind of sum, we'll be bankrupt in a month or two at this rate. Is there no way we can make cutbacks?'

'We've done that. You must have seen how things are.'

Jake hadn't, but he understood what was happening. In times of trouble, essentials, those things that people had to have, went up in value sharply, especially if someone was hoarding them, while luxuries, those things that were desired only when money was plentiful and people could afford them, went down. Most of the stalls he and Tom had visited – Becky's apart, for gold and silver nearly always held its value – were selling luxuries of a kind, and so wouldn't really have been affected much.

Jake sat down. 'What d'you think, Tom? Should we ask old Harry? Or maybe Liam, at the stables.'

'You think either of them can spare that kind of money?'

'I dunno. But it won't harm to ask. They know we'll pay 'em

back. We're old friends, after all, and we've been coming to them the best part of twenty years now.'

'Then ask.'

Only he could sense, behind Tom's words, that Tom didn't like the idea. He didn't like the thought of throwing himself on someone else's mercy, even if it was only short term. He'd rather not buy at all than borrow to buy.

Tom looked to him. 'I could take back the things we bought...'

Jake was uncompromising. 'No. You won't.'

'But we've got to have ammunition, Jake. We've got to be able to defend ourselves.'

'Then we buy some.'

'But...'

'No buts, Tom. I'll go see Harry now. He's probably in the back bar. What I'll do is ask Harry for half of it, and Liam for the rest. That way neither man's too stretched. Besides, I'll make it worth their while. I'll give 'em ten crowns interest apiece. That's not a bad return, I'd say, and I can bring it back myself, three days from now.'

'But, Jake...'

'No arguments. It's done. As for you, Tom Hubbard, you need to stretch out on a nice soft bed.' Jake looked to Gifford. 'Ted... give me a hand, won't you?'

Only Jake didn't plan to go and see Harry, or Liam either, come to that. He'd had an idea. Not one that was guaranteed to work, by any means, but he was going to try it anyhow.

'Give me half an hour,' he said to Ted Gifford, once they'd got Tom settled. 'If I don't have the money by then, then we'll find some other way of raising it. I'll meet you outside Hardy's, okay?'

'Okay...' But Ted hesitated. Jake could sense he wanted to say something.

'What's wrong?'

'What's goin' on here, that's what's wrong. I can't help thinkin'...

well, *feelin'* rather... like this is 'ow it felt first time roun'. You know... when it all fell apart. Only... what's left to fall apart? We're down to basics as is. So why's things gone 'aywire?'

'I don't know, to be honest. Scarcity of goods is driving some of it, but I don't know why that should be. There was plenty last month. Maybe Branagh's hoarding stuff. He's certainly put up all the fees.'

'I never trusted that bastard.'

'Nor I... But look... let's just deal with this right now, eh? Let's get our stuff and get back home, and worry about the rest of it later.'

Jake, too, was worried now. Walking through the crowded space, he kept on seeing that same concern in every face. Normally amiable people were bickering now, arguing over the slightest little thing. In the past this had been a pleasant place to do business. There had been laughter and a lot of good-natured banter, but now there was a tetchiness about people. He could see it in the way they spoke to each other. More than once, as he passed by a stall, he would find buyer and seller locked in a bitter, irritable exchange. There was a lot of gesturing and shouting, too. 'Fuck you!' one of them would say, giving the finger, and they'd be off again, the babble of angry voices seeming to grow as Jake got deeper in. None of it came to blows – Branagh's men, who were out in force, saw to that – yet there was a simmering anger that could easily have spilled over into violence.

What made it worse, as far as Jake was concerned, was that no one seemed conscious of it. It was like they were all too preoccupied to notice. He stood there a moment, looking about him, feeling for that instant like the sole still point amidst a swirling mass of humanity. He saw how people were going about their business, saw the urgency with which they made their way from stall to stall, like tomorrow was the end of the world and they were all stocking up against it. There was an air of desperation mixed with panic, the kind that happens sometimes when no one knows clearly just what's going on, only that disaster is imminent.

Which made it all so much more of a mystery, for as yet he'd not heard a word of rumour that made sense.

Right now, however, he had something to do; something which, if it worked, might kill two birds with a single metaphoric stone.

Becky looked up as he stepped in front of the stall, her vaguely troubled look becoming a beaming smile as she saw who it was.

'Jake! 'Ow lovely to see you again. You come to buy something else?'

'You could say that...' He hesitated, then, 'Look... I know this is asking a lot, but could you close up for half an hour? I need to talk. I... well, I thought we might go to a tavern... somewhere quiet, and have a word or two.'

She looked surprised.

'I dunno... half an hour...'

'I'll pay you. Pay you well.'

Her eyes narrowed. 'I 'ope you don't think...'

He put his hands up defensively. 'It's nothing like that. But I do have a proposal for you. One I think you might find to your advantage...'

'Yeah?' But he could see she was intrigued. 'Okay. 'Alf an hour. But you pay me ten crowns for loss of trade.'

Jake smiled. 'Sure.' And as he said it, he wondered what would catch Jack Hamilton's attention most, that disconcertingly lazy eye of hers, or her voluptuous figure. Either way, both he and she could do much worse, and she would be her own mistress still.

He watched her as she covered things over, then got her neighbouring stallholder to keep watch for her. Then, and only then, did she come round to him, smiling and taking his arm.

'All right, Jake. Let's go and 'ave that talk,' she said, pressing against his side. 'You got me right puzzled, you know that?'

'I know,' he said and grinned, knowing in that second, for a certainty, what her answer would be.

Ted was waiting where he said he'd be, outside Hardy's gun shop at the southern end of the market, Frank Goodman, Eddie, Dick and the rest in tow.

'Did you get the money?'

'I got two-ninety of it.' And he handed over the big leather money pouch Jack Hamilton had given him at Wareham.

'But that's...'

'Ours, till we see Jack again. I got him a bride, like he asked, and for free. She'll be travelling back with us. In the meantime we're going to use our good friend's money to buy what we need. We can pay him back when we next see him.'

They were staring at him now, wide-eyed.

'A bride?' Ted asked. 'For *nothing*?'

But Jake wasn't going to be drawn. 'You'll see. Now let's get what we came for. Frank... take one-eighty of it. That should be enough, don't you think?'

'It'll do,' Goodman said, turning to Ted, who had begun to count the money out.

'What else are we lacking?'

'We need some spectacles for Ginny Harris...'

'And boots for young Sam Webber...'

'We could do with some more seed...'

'And scissors...'

Jake raised a hand. 'Okay. Let's make up a new list. Prioritize. There's things we have to have. Seed, yes. Candles... Petrol for the generator... what else?'

And just like that their anxiety was gone.

'I've never seen them like it,' he told Tom, two hours later, when he was back at the inn, sitting at Tom's bedside. 'That one small thing – that sudden rise in prices – and it was like their whole world had been undermined.'

'Yes, but it's not just that,' Tom said. 'It's a feeling in the air. We've both had it, I know, these past few weeks. Only here... well... it's heightened, I guess.'

Jake nodded. 'You're not joking. It's like some form of mass hysteria. I just hope it blows over. Winter's coming and hopefully that'll put a lid on things for a while. And then maybe, in the spring, we'll feel differently.'

'We've had it easy for too long,' Tom said quietly.

'You think? It's felt like it's been hard to me.'

Tom chuckled. 'Then you've a bloody short memory, Jake Reed.'

'Yeah?'

Jake looked around the room. As ever at market times, the land-lord, Harry Mason, had crammed six beds into the room, to take advantage of demand. Tom's was pressed up against the wall, beneath the casement window. From outside came the noise of the market. It would be closing in two hours.

Jake got to his feet, then, for want of something to do, leaned across Tom and felt his brow. It was hot, but not feverish. And his colour looked better than it had been.

'I'm going to ask that doctor if he'll come.'

'What's the point? We'll be back home tomorrow evening.'

'Yes, and when you are, Mary can fuss over you as much as she likes. Until then, I'm in charge. And I want the doctor to look at you again.'

Tom seemed agitated suddenly.

'No, Jake. It's a waste of money, and money's tight right now. I'm fine, really I am.'

'I don't care. He's going to look at you, and that's that.'

'Jake...'

'I'll send the pot boy to get him. Not now, but later. Last thing. Maybe he can give you something to help you sleep.'

Tom tried to get up, but he was clearly weaker than he thought.

'Jake...'

'What?'

'All right... send for the doctor if you must... but I want to come down for a bit. I want to sit with you all, in the bar. I don't want to be up here all night, on my own.'

Jake would have said no, that Tom had to get his rest, but he could see that this meant something.

'All right. For an hour or so... but that's all.'

Tom smiled. 'Thanks. Now you can go.'

'Well, thank you.'

In the doorway, Jake turned, looking back into the room. Tom had closed his eyes. He looked peaceful now, in the last light of the day, but his injury had clearly exhausted him. He had always been such a strong man, a great oak of a man, but now he seemed drawn, almost frail.

We're too fucking old for this, Jake thought, stepping out into the hallway. Worn out too bloody soon.

They and the world they lived in.

He stepped outside, then went back beneath the awnings, walking among the stalls, knowing that he had one last task to perform. He had promised Josh he'd find him something. One last gem to add to his collection. Only as he made his way through the press of bodies, Jake found himself thinking not about that, but about Tom and what had happened last time they'd been here. Had he *really* had unprotected sex with a girl? It was hard to believe, knowing Tom, because Tom was always so cautious, so... *reliable*. Not only that, but he couldn't think when Tom might have found the time, for they'd been together almost constantly.

And yet he must have.

Rory's Record Shack was where it always was, tucked away in the darkest corner of the market, between a stall that sold buttons and another that sold picture frames and scented candles.

Rory himself was a big, black-bearded man who wore black

leather from another age. He grinned as he saw who it was, then addressed him in his broad South London dialect.

'Jake, me old mucker... it's good to see you.'

They shook hands warmly.

'You got anything for me?'

Rory's smile broadened. 'I was hoping you'd show. You want something for Josh, I take it?'

Years ago Rory had called in to the Bankes Arms when he'd been passing and had sworn he'd never seen a better collection than Josh's. He knew what the old man liked.

'I said I'd try and find him something special.'

'Then you've come to the right place, my friend. Here...' And he reached beneath the counter and handed across an old vinyl record, in its polythene-protected cover. 'I guess he might have it, but...'

'No!' Jake said quietly, looking at the cover of the album with pure delight. 'Jesus, Rory, where the fuck did you get hold of this? It's priceless!'

'I know. Some kid brought it to me. Didn't know its worth. Said he found it, but I reckon he half-inched it, meself.'

But Jake was only half listening. He was looking at the grainy black and white image that filled the twelve by twelve cover. Five young men were coming down a set of stairs, next to an old street telephone box, while to the right of the cover a big sign on the window of a cheap motel read '$6 a night'. He flipped it over. There, on the back, was the band's drummer, Ed Cassidy, his hand raised in peace, his distinctive bald head made yet more anonymous by a pair of dark glasses. Behind him was what appeared to be a wasteland.

Josh had been looking for this for years. And here it was. West Coast rock at its very finest.

He looked to Rory. 'What are you asking?'

'I'm not asking anything. It's a present. For Josh. You two have been good customers over the years. Fuckin' fine gentlemen the pair of you. But now it's time to move on. I'm off to Cornwall once I've packed up here, so if there's anything else you fancy, you can have it half price. Closing-down sale. One day only.'

And he laughed again, a warm, kindly laugh that was so unlike anything Jake had heard all day that he found himself joining in.

'Shit, Rory,' he said, holding the album against him carefully. 'Josh is going to wet himself when he sees this. Are you sure?'

Rory grinned. 'Sure as sure and a bit more sure after that. He can put it in with Quicksilver, the Dead, Airplane and the rest. I'd play it for you now, only I don't want to risk scratching it.'

'No... You got any punk?'

'Late seventies punk or late twenties?'

'The real stuff.'

''Fraid not. Had a Vapors single, but it went. Got ten crowns for it.'

'Then you're lucky.'

'Yeah...' Rory's smile faded. 'Looks like the shit's hit the fan at last.'

'Yeah...' Only that was too morbid. Jake looked at the cover again. Josh had some of the other Spirit albums, *Clear* and *Twelve Dreams*, but this was the band at their best.

'*The Family That Plays Together*... it's a great title, don't you think?'

Rory grinned again. 'Not bad. My favourite is *Bless Its Pointed Little Head*, by the Airplane. Not that I've ever seen a copy...'

'Hey... you want to come and join us for a drink tonight?'

Rory shrugged apologetically. 'I'd love to, only I've got to get packed up and on my way. I'm meeting my daughter down Helston way.'

'You've got a daughter?' All these years and he'd never known that.

'Yeah... Roxanne. Fuckin' awful choice of name, I know, but blame her mother. She's twenty in a month or so. Lovely girl. Wants me to go and live with her... now that her mother's dead.'

'Oh...' Jake stared at the man, surprised. How long had they known each other? Fifteen years? And they'd never had a proper conversation. It had always been about music. Nothing but the music.

Jake came away with two more items: a CD of JakPak's first album, *Suture*, from '27, and an old vinyl single of 'Glad It's All Over' by Captain Sensible, which he'd bought partly as a joke – to give to Josh.

On his way back to the inn he ran into Frank Goodman.

'Jake...'

'Frank... everything okay?'

Goodman nodded. 'The main load's stowed on the wagons and locked into the stall for the night. I just came out to see if I could find any last-minute bargains.'

'What're you looking for?'

'Something for the missus. A bracelet, maybe.'

'Then go see Becky... or rather, let Becky sort you out. I reckon as she'll give you a good deal if you say you're with me.'

'Yeah?' Goodman almost smiled. 'Point me in her direction, Jake, and I'll see what she can do...' He hesitated. 'I've only got seven crowns left... d'you think that'll be enough?'

'It'll be plenty. Now get going. I'll see you back at Harry's...'

After checking on Tom, Jake got washed and changed, then went downstairs. The bar was already packed out, the air thick with cigarette smoke and the heavy buzz of conversation.

Jake hadn't eaten since breakfast and was feeling famished. They had paid Harry up front for bed and board, so if he wanted anything, it was just a question of him ordering from the menu. But they'd not paid for their beer, and with things having soared in price, he knew that finding beer money would be difficult. Taking Harry aside, he asked if they could have a slate this once.

Harry's momentary hesitation spoke volumes. Jake clearly wasn't the first to ask.

'All right,' he said, nodding. 'You're good customers o' mine. But I want payment within a week, right?'

'A week?' Jake considered that, then, 'Done!'

The two men spat on their hands and shook.

Just like in the film, Jake thought, watching as one of Harry's girls, Jessie, poured him a foaming pint of Best.

Ted Gifford and a few of the others had taken one of the big tables on the far side of the bar. Jake made his way over.

'Room for a little 'un?'

Tankards and glasses were raised to welcome him. Someone shifted a little and Jake squeezed in, between Dick and Ted's old pal, Brian Leggat, from Abbotsbury.

Talk was of how expensive things were, and of the latest rumours coming down the road. Everyone was in the same boat when it came to the price of things. There'd been no warning, and a lot of them had been left short.

'God knows 'ow we'll manage next time roun',' Dick Cooke, who came from Cerne Abbas, said. 'As it is I've only 'arf o' what I meant to get. An' if this winter's a bad un'...'

It was a fear they all had. That they'd be without essentials over the winter months.

'The price o' vaccines...'

'Couldn't buy one for love or money...'

'Gonna have to chop a fucking heap o' wood to get us through...'

'The cost of fuckin' salt... *unbelievable!*'

And so it went. But Jake kept his silence. He'd seen what was going on. What he wanted to know was why, and none of his friends, concerned as they were by the situation, could answer him.

'So...' Eddie said, turning to face him. 'Where's old Jack's bride, then? I thought she was comin' back with us.'

'And so she is. But she's got to get packed and ready.'

'A local girl, then?'

'She is.'

Ted Gifford groaned at that. 'Fer fuck's sake, Jake... tell us... I can't stand the suspense no more.'

But Jake ignored him. He finished his pint and set his glass down. 'Who's having another?'

'I meant to say about that...' Eddie began.

Jake leaned in, as if confiding to them all. 'Harry's given us a tab for the night. You can order what you like, boys...'

There was a great cheer at that. Eddie and Dick stood, taking orders, then made their way over to the bar to get them in.

It was just after ten past five.

'It's gonna be a long night,' Leggat said from where he sat to Jake's right. 'Men'll be drinking to forget their sorrows.'

Jake nodded. That was the truth. And they had the time to get oblivious.

'How's your Jean?' he asked, after a moment. 'She okay? And the kids?'

Leggat grinned and pulled out his wallet, searching through it, then presented Jake with a small colour photograph, which showed him, his wife and their two children.

'Christ! Where d'you get this?'

'Tinker... came róun' our village. Was chargin' five crown a picture. No end of takers, I tell you. Ain't seen nothin' like it for years. Bloody thing actually developed in the back of the camera. Guy sez they 'ad cameras like that fifty, sixty year ago.'

Jake stared and stared at the photo, then handed it back.

'Fuck...'

'You a'right, Jake?'

'Just that. It's so nice. To have a picture of you all.'

Leggat laughed, then shook his head. 'Yeah... yeah, it is.'

'Look, I just gotta go sort Tom out. I said he could come down for an hour or so. I'll see you in a bit...'

Outside, on the back stairs, he stopped, holding on to the rail for dear life.

That picture had got to him.

Jake took a long, shivering breath. He had been close to tears back there, just thinking. What a treasure it was. What a priceless fucking treasure. It had got him thinking. *If only I had the like of it. Some image of her.* Because all he had were the pictures in his head.

Tom was awake. As Jake came into the room, he yawned and made to stretch, then winced.

Jake smiled. 'You forgot for a moment, eh? That's a good sign. It means it's healing.'

The light outside was fading now, the room in half darkness. Jake lit the bedside candle, then leaned across and drew the curtains.

'What's the time?'

'A quarter after five.'

'It seems later...'

Jake looked down at his old friend. In the candlelight, Tom seemed to have aged. Perhaps it was just a trick of the light, but he seemed tired. Not tired the way a young man got after an exacting day, but the kind of tiredness that seizes on the old. A drawn kind of tired.

He sat Tom up, then felt his brow again. It was cool.

'How're you feeling?'

'Better.'

'The pain...?'

'Is manageable. It's a dull ache now, most of the time.'

'Good. But I'm still getting the doctor, right?'

Tom made no move to argue.

'Okay,' Jake said. 'Let's get you dressed.'

At the top of the steps, Tom paused and looked to Jake.

'Let me do this on my own.'

'Fine. But hold on to the rail.'

'What am I? Eight?'

Jake chuckled. 'Okay. But they're steep.'

'I can see that.'

'Let me go first...'

'What? So I can fall on you? That'd be useful, having the both of us in hospital.'

'Then stay in bed.'

'Stop fussing, man.'

He stopped fussing. But he couldn't stop worrying until Tom was safely at the bottom. There, Tom let Jake help him again, Jake putting an arm about his waist as they stepped out into the bar.

'There 'e be!' Ted Gifford said, getting up to welcome Tom.

There were smiles all round.

'Get the man a beer!' Frank Goodman called, looking to Eddie, who was up out of his seat and on the case already.

'Pint of Best, Tom?'

'And no flies in it this time!' Tom shouted back, alluding to the time, back in the summer, when a half-drowned bluebottle had spoiled Tom's first mouthful.

Tom nodded, then squeezed into the seat, between Ted Gifford and Dick Cooke, the Cerne Abbas man.

Jake took a seat just across from them.

'How you feelin', boy?' Ted asked, touching Tom's good arm. 'Not still weepin', is it?'

'No. It's good. The doctor's looking at it later.'

'Ah... good...'

Jake watched Tom take the tankard from Eddie and, after a salute to all those gathered there, raise it to his lips, savouring the taste.

Like old times, Jake thought, only it wasn't. They were relaxed now, sure, but not as relaxed as in the past. There was still an underlying atmosphere. A sense of unease.

'So when's this woman comin'?' Frank Goodman asked, looking to Jake.

'Soon,' Jake said, amused by their persistence. 'Just be patient.'

'I don' reckon she exists,' Frank said, his gaze never leaving Jake's face. 'I reckon Jake's 'avin' us on.'

Jake smiled, taking no offence. 'Is that what you think?'

'Well... where'd you find one, just like that?'

'In the market... that's where...'

They all turned, their faces a mixture of shock and surprise. It was Becky, and she was glammed up to the nines. Lazy eye or no, she looked in excellent shape.

'Becky,' Jake said, standing and offering her his seat, 'meet the boys. Boys... I think you know Becky. Becky Hamilton, as'll be.'

'Well, I'll be...' Ted Gifford began.

'No, you bloody won't,' his son chipped in. 'Not if she's Jack Hamilton's missus!'

And they all roared with laughter, Becky included.

'What you 'avin', Becks?' Eddie called. 'It's on the tab...'

Becky squeezed in, waggling this way and that to get comfortable, much to her neighbours' delight. 'A pint o' Best'll do me, Eddie, my love.'

'Quite a change of career,' Brian Leggat said, grinning at her.

Becky turned to face him, her one good eye focusing on him. 'Oh, I'll still be comin' back 'ere to market from time to time, don't you worry. Bein' Jack 'Amilton's missus won't change that!'

'If 'e'll 'ave you,' Leggat said mischievously.

Oh, 'e'll certainly 'ave me!' And she winked outrageously with her good eye, making them all roar with laughter.

Peter stood there in the quiet of the shadowed hallway, listening. Apart from the steady tick of the old grandfather clock, and the sound of Boy gently panting, there was nothing. The house was silent, empty.

He walked through, into the comparative brightness of the kitchen. The room was lit from outside by the moon, a great white circle in the dark, halfway up the sky over Kimmeridge, away to the south-west.

Boy padded after him, then gave a tiny growl.

'Quiet, Boy...'

Even so, he went to the pantry and, reaching up, took down one of the long, leathery chews that hung there and threw the dog his share of their last pig. Boy jumped up and caught it in the air, then settled with it, chewing away contentedly.

Peter went to the window and looked out into the yard. Everything seemed fine. The wood was where he'd stacked it earlier, the lid to the water barrel padlocked. There was a brief, faint noise from the chicken coop and then silence again.

He looked back at Boy. 'Okay, Boy... all's well here. Let's go look around the barn.'

He walked back out into the hallway. His gun was in the case on the wall, where he'd left it earlier. Taking the key, he unlocked the mesh-protected door and took it out.

He breached the gun, checked it was loaded, then clicked it shut again.

'Come, Boy... let's go see if there's any foxes...'

Boy growled at the word, but held on tight to his chew-strap, even as he padded after his master.

There was a faint breeze blowing from the east, coming across Poole Bay and Studland. In the distance he could hear an owl. It was a fine night for hunting.

The barn was further down the slope, backing on to the high wall of the New Inn tavern. Back in the old days, so he'd been told, this had been a really popular spot, and every evening, during the summer, the great car park at the back of the inn had been filled with motor cars. There'd been parties here running late throughout the summer, with the electric lights blazing out and the music drifting across the night-cloaked fields.

Peter sighed. There hadn't been any cars these past twenty years and it didn't seem likely that there were going to be any ever again. Which wasn't a bad thing, according to his dad. Only sometimes he found himself wishing he could ride in one, just once. Just to know what it was like.

He looked up, out across the fields. From here, at the top of the long slope, you could see the sea, like a shimmering sheet of metal in the distance.

Boy had stopped suddenly. Now he began to growl. A moment later he dropped the chew and began to bark. It was the kind of bark he gave when it was someone he didn't know.

Peter raised his gun. He had a whistle on a string about his neck. When this kind of thing happened he was supposed to take it out and blow it hard and people would come running. Only he didn't.

He walked on, slowly, silently, moving out a little, away from the barn.

'Hush, Boy,' he whispered.

At once the dog was silent. But Boy was fully alert now, his ears pricked up, his body crouched low to the ground, like he was hunting game.

Slowly Peter circled, trying to make out who or what was there. At first he couldn't see a thing. Boy had to be mistaken. Either that or it was some small animal. But then he glimpsed something.

He took the safety off, then began to edge closer.

There were three of them, stretched out on the straw pallets at the back of the barn. At least, two of them were stretched out. The third was sitting up, his back against the end wall. From small movements of his head Peter could tell he was awake, even if the others weren't.

Keeping watch...

He crouched, making himself less visible.

They didn't seem to be armed, but he couldn't be sure. He couldn't see any weapons, but maybe they were resting on the floor beside them, or tucked away in their clothing.

There was the faintest groan. One of the 'sleeping' men turned a little, moaning as he did, as if he were wounded. The watchman leaned in, saying something, but Peter couldn't make out what.

He crept closer, Boy shadowing him, moving as he moved, looking to his master with bright, eager eyes.

He could pick them off from here, easy. Could have two of them before they even moved. But he was curious now. Who were they?

Peter glanced round. Behind him, to his right, near where the old pet sanctuary had once stood, was the Hubbards' house. They'd be expecting him back, and soon. He could see candlelight in one of the upstairs windows and wondered which of the girls it was. Beth probably. It was her room.

He looked back, and felt his stomach lurch.

He was gone! The watchman had gone!

Peter turned, looking this way and that. Then, from behind the barn, came the sound of someone pissing.

He let a long breath escape him.

As the man came back, buttoning his flies, Peter got a good look at him in the moonlight. He was a stout man, in his thirties, with a straggly beard. A very ordinary man, except for the look in his eyes.

He was afraid. And he had every right to be. You didn't cross the countryside these days without being in fear of your life. To be a drifter was to be a problem. A problem that was solved more often than not with a bullet to the head.

Boy had been silent until that moment. Now, seeing the stranger so close, so clear in the moonlight, he let out the faintest whine. Immediately the man froze, looking out towards where Peter crouched beside Boy.

'Japhet... Japh...'

The words issued from the man in a low, urgent hiss. Their answer came from the darkness inside the barn, the word slurred and sleepy.

'Wha...?'

Peter's gun was aimed directly at the watchman's chest. With his left hand, he reached inside his shirt and drew the whistle out. He had only to blow it.

Only if he did, they might run off, and then they'd be up half the night chasing them round the countryside. As it was he had them. Provided he played it right.

The question was, what would his dad have done?

He knew without having to ask.

Straightening up, he raised his gun to his shoulder and took two paces towards the man.

'Run and I'll shoot you dead!' he said in a loud clear voice. 'I'm a fuckin' good shot and I won't miss. Now put your hands up where I can see them!'

To his surprise, the man groaned and sank to his knees, his hands raised in surrender. From the barn came a similar groan of anguish and a babble of words.

'Oh, shit... oh, fuckin' shit...'

This was where he'd have to be careful. If either of the two in the barn were armed...

Only he knew they weren't. If they were they'd not be so afraid of him.

'Boy! Guard them! Go on, Boy... make sure they stay!'

Boy leapt up at once and went across, barking at the two men who were there. One of them lay there still, oblivious to all that was happening. The other was sitting up now, his hands raised in surrender.

Good. Putting the whistle to his mouth, he blew. Once. Twice. A third time.

There was a moment's pause. Then there came the sound of slamming doors, the noise of running feet. The kneeling man – the watchman – was whimpering now. He knew the game was up.

Peter stayed where he was, not showing himself fully. The man could see the glint of moonlight on the gun's barrel, however, and would know that Peter wasn't messing.

As the first of the villagers ran up, Peter gestured towards the barn.

'There's two in the barn... and this fellow here. I don't think they're armed.'

He glanced round; saw that it was the butcher, Matthew Hammond. Behind him Jack Randall and his wife, Jenny, were hurrying down the slope, coats thrown on hastily, both of them armed with shotguns.

Hammond nodded to Peter then stepped past him, going right up to the one on his knees. He pointed his rifle at the man's head.

'Okay... who the fuck are you? And what are you doing on our land?'

Others were arriving now, among them Mary and her daughters. They too had pulled on coats. Mary had a gun, while the girls had clubs and knives.

The kneeling man tried to answer, but he was stuttering now. 'W-we're just p-passing through.'

From his accent he sounded like a Midlander.

Hammond looked across, to where Jack Randall stood over the prone figure, while the other man cowered against the back wall, Jenny Randall's gun pointed directly at his face.

'This one's injured, Matty...' Randall said. 'Badly by the look of things. I'd say our friends here have been in a bit of a ruck.'

'That true?' Hammond asked, touching the man's neck with the barrel of his gun.

The man look petrified. As well he might, for half the village was out now. Men and women were hurrying down the slope, coats thrown over their shoulders hurriedly, every last one of them clutching a weapon of some kind.

'It's t-t-true... We... w-we were part of a p-party... out of B-b-b-Bromsgrove.'

'Bromsgrove. In the Midlands?'

He nodded.

'So what were you doing here, in Purbeck? How many of you were there?'

'Th-th-three th-th-thousand... maybe m-m-more.'

There was a murmur of surprise at that.

'Three thousand?' Hammond sounded stunned.

Again the man nodded.

'So what happened to the rest?'

'Th-they g-got t-turned back... on the b-big road north of here. Armed t-troops... they c-came out of n-nowhere. Th-that's how my f-friend got h-hurt.'

'Must be Branagh's men,' Randall said. 'Can't think who else it'd be.'

Charlie Waite, the landlord of the New Inn, arrived right then, with two of his sons. They were carrying torches, and in their flickering light they could see the faces of the men for the first time, see the blood-caked clothes of the one who'd been injured.

'Christ...' Jenny Randall said quietly, appalled by the sight. 'The poor boy's been peppered with bullets!'

But Hammond wasn't concerned with that. He nudged the kneeling man again with his gun.

'Why were you on the road?' he asked. 'Three thousand men... what were you? An army?'

'R-r-refugees,' the man stuttered. His eyes were wide. You could see he expected every moment to be his last.

'Refugees, my arse,' Charlie Waite said, coming up alongside Matthew Hammond, the two big men towering over the kneeling stranger.

Waite reached down and grabbed the man by the neck and shook him. 'Tell me the truth, you fucker!'

Peter looking on, grimaced. He had seen this side of Charlie Waite before. The man had a short fuse and no sympathy. His intercession could only mean trouble.

'N-n-not just men... w-women, t-too. And k-k-kids.'

The wounded man groaned and opened his eyes. Jenny Randall looked to her husband, concerned.

'We've got to do something... the poor boy...'

Charlie Waite looked round, enraged by her sympathy. ''E's like that, Jenny, cos he *deserves* to be like that! I bet a crown to a penny they were mercenaries. Not a woman or child among them.'

'Then why've they no weapons?'

'Because that's what mercenaries do. As soon as things turn against them, they throw away their weapons...' He looked back at the man he still had a grip on and shook his head. 'They would have marched straight through if Branagh hadn'ta intercepted them. And where'd we be then? Facing the same dilemma, only with a thousand times as many of the bastards! Let's have done wi' 'em, I say.'

There was a loud click as he took off the safety on his gun.

Peter acted instinctively. Before Waite could place the gun to the man's head, he stepped in and knocked the gun aside, then stood there, between Waite and the now hysterical man.

Waite looked astonished. 'What the...?'

Peter glared at the innkeeper. 'I didn't blow the whistle so you could come and kill them. I could have done that myself. You want to kill them, you're going to have to kill me first, and then you'll have to deal with my dad. No, we keep them... tie them up and lock them away somewhere safe, till the rest come back. Then we decide. And Jenny's right. We give them the benefit of the doubt, and tend to that one's wounds. Then if he dies, it's not our fault.'

Waite sneered at him. 'You think that matters, *boy*?'

But Peter wasn't having any of it. Waite didn't scare him. 'Oh, it *matters*, Mister Waite. It matters more than anything.'

It was just after eight when, unexpectedly, Rory from the record stall turned up after all, a very pretty young woman on his arm.

'Tom... Jake... this is my daughter, Roxanne.'

'Rory!' Jake said, delighted, jumping up to welcome him. 'I thought you were heading off to Cornwall...'

'I was... then her ladyship turned up, out of the blue, so I thought...'

'Oh, you're very welcome. Both of you! Shove up, everyone... make some room for our good friends here!'

Jake had given up on the idea of getting Tom back to bed an hour past. He only had to look at his friend to see what good this was doing him. Him and them all, if the truth be told, for the anxieties of the day had been washed away in a tide of alcohol.

'Wha'ral'i'be?' Eddie asked, getting to his feet unsteadily. 'A pi' fr you, Ror? An' wha'ral'a-gir'ave?'

Dick Gifford snorted with laughter. 'Lissen to 'im! Pissed as a fuckin' newt!'

'A pint would be ace,' Rory said in his best cockney, for that moment the only truly sober man among them. 'An' the same for Roxie, ta.'

Eddie leaned closer, winking at the girl. 'S'on'a'tab...'

Jake looked to the girl, then back at her father and shook his head. 'Nah... I don't reckon she's yours, Rory. Much too beautiful.'

Rory grinned. He didn't care what people made of him, but clearly any praise of his daughter was very welcome. And she was a good-looking girl, full-figured with long curls of dark brown hair. Looking at her, you could see why Becky had found it so hard to get and keep a man. Roxanne, on the other hand, probably had to fight them off.

'So what do you do, Rox?' Tom asked. He was sat right back now in his chair, a look of autumnal mellowness about him.

'I engrave glass... words... designs... flower patterns...' The men were leaning forward now, attentive to what she had to say; every last one of them smiling as they took in this new breath of fresh air to their table.

'Thar's a stall in the market,' Billy Leggat said, gesturing with his pipe, 'that 'as a few pieces like that. Lovely things, they are. 'Spensive, though...'

Roxanne grinned. 'Those are mine.'

'An' tha makes a livin' from it?' old Ted Gifford asked.

'Truth is, no,' she said. 'Not a great call for it, if I'm honest. But it's what I want to do. And Dad helps me out from time to time, so...'

Rory put his arm about his girl and squeezed her to him.

Just then, Eddie reappeared with their beers. He had spilled a bit, but most of it was there.

'Ror... Rox...'

'Fuckin' Japanese, ain't it?' Frank Goodman said, nudging his neighbour, then putting his fingers up to his eyes to make slits of them. 'Wha' you fink of it so far? Ror-rox!'

One or two of them laughed, but Tom and Jake were clearly a bit embarrassed.

'Don't mind him,' Jake said, quietly, apologetically. 'It's a lovely name. Did your mother take it from the song?'

Roxanne, however, looked blank. Rory leaned forward. 'Her mother didn't like music.'

Tom laughed at that. 'Christ, Rory... you do pick 'em!'

'Don't I?' He looked at his girl again. 'Mind... she does look a lot like her ma did at that age. That was when I first met her. We were on the road, both of us. Refugees. She was tryin' to get home... to Cornwall... while me... I was just trying to get as far away from London as I could. Bloody madhouse it was.'

About the table there were dark looks at that mention. For the first time in an hour or two they'd been reminded. Of how things had been. Yes, and how they might yet be again.

'Well, she's a lovely girl,' Becky said, smiling at her rival. 'Such lovely 'air... I used to 'ave 'air like that...'

'Jack 'Amilton used to 'ave 'air, too,' Ted Gifford said drily, and they all set about laughing again, Becky included.

The talk had got little further when their old friend Hewitt, Branagh's man, made an appearance. He looked like he'd been riding hard, for the sweat still clung to him and his face was black with dust.

'Jake... can I 'ave a word?'

Hewitt took him outside, into the cold air. His patrol were nearby, their horses tethered. Like their captain, they all looked like they'd not washed in days and their eyes had a tired, desolate look to them, like they'd seen too much.

'What is it?'

'Just wanted to warn you. There's been an encounter...'

'An encounter?'

'We had word something was happening a few days back, from other travellers. We didn't let it get out, of course, or people might not have come here for market. Anyway... a force of four hundred men were sent north to intercept. They took up a position at Sherborne, on the bridge over the River Yeo. We hit the bastards hard, before they had a clue what was happening and—'

'Hold on,' Jake said, interrupting him. 'You said to intercept. What were they intercepting?'

'An incoming force. Three, maybe four thousand men. Some of them were armed, but most of them had little but makeshift weapons.'

Four thousand men... Jake felt a flicker of fear at the thought. There'd not been a force like that for years.

'And we beat them?'

'Drove 'em off. Killed a fair number, but most of them fled back north, over the fields, heading for Glastonbury...'

'But not all of them.'

Hewitt nodded. 'A small body of them doubled back. Last thing we saw they were headed south-east, down your way... that's why I thought I'd warn you.'

The thought of it chilled Jake. 'Thanks... but look, who were they? I mean... four thousand men...'

'Midlanders. They'd been driven out, from what we can ascertain.'

'Midlanders?'

'That's what the ones we've questioned say. And those accents... you can't mistake it.'

'Christ... and Branagh knew about this?'

'Knew about it and acted.'

Jake thought about it. His instinct was to set off at once and come back for the wagons later if need be, only it was far too late for that. The men were much too drunk.

He went back inside, sobered by what he'd heard. Should he tell them? Spoil their evening? He decided not to. There would be plenty of time in the cold light of dawn to decide on a strategy.

Pray god I'm not wrong, he thought. Pray god eight hours won't make a difference. Yes, and pray god they're all safe at home when we get back.

Jake tried not to let what he'd heard make any difference, but it did. He couldn't sit there now and laugh with them at this trifle or that; couldn't enjoy the moment. The thought that they were sitting there while armed strangers were heading towards their homes was too uncomfortable to bear. He finished his beer – his last beer, he decided – then turned to Tom. If anyone knew what to do, it was Tom.

He leaned in, speaking quietly to Tom's ear. 'I think I know why things were like they were today.'

Tom was less drunk than he seemed. He turned and met Jake's eyes. 'Something Hewitt said?'

Jake nodded.

'I wondered when you'd tell me. When you came back in... your face... it looked like you'd seen a ghost.'

'More like a bloody army of ghosts...'

Tom's eyes narrowed, taking that in. 'What was it?'

'Branagh sent his army north... to Sherborne... they had a battle there.'

'Christ...'

'Yeah. Four hundred men – well armed and well trained... against a band of marauders.'

'I take it they won.'

'Yeah.'

'Then why aren't we celebrating? Why aren't the bells ringing out?'

Jake took a long breath, then told him. 'The invading force. Hewitt says there were near on four thousand men. Midlanders. They drove them off, but... well, most of them fled north, but some, he doesn't know how many... went south... south-east, to be accurate.'

He saw Tom think about it, then realize what that meant. 'You mean...?'

'Hewitt doesn't know. Only that they seemed desperate. Something drove them out. And what could drive out a force of four thousand men?'

There was the faintest tremor. The glasses on the table began to clink. Conversation faltered and then died as the men looked to one another, trying to make sense of it. The tremor grew, became a shaking. Pint glasses fell from some of the tables, shattering on the floor, while in the background the pounding boom of engines filled the air.

Everyone was on their feet now, a look of panic gripping them. Across the bar, on the far side of the room, someone was screeching anxiously, like they'd totally lost it.

Jake too was on his feet. 'What in Christ's name...'

A sudden, brilliant light hit the square outside, flooding the bar. Men shielded their eyes, stumbling against each other. There was an uproar of voices.

Jake pushed through, forcing his way outside, even as others staggered out into the brilliantly lit space. Out there the pounding pulse of the engines was deafening. It made the very air itself vibrate. Like the scouring, unforgiving light, it was coming from the sky directly overhead. Only that made no sense. It was over twenty years since there'd been any sign of aircraft in the sky.

Besides, whatever it was, it was no plane or helicopter. No. This was something new; something entirely alien.

Jake shielded his eyes, trying to make out the shape of the thing, its size. Only the light was so intense, so blinding, he could make out nothing.

A gun went off, then another.

'You idiots!' he screeched. 'Don't fire at it! But his words were swallowed up by the noise of the craft, the twin pulse of its engines, which was so loud it seemed to be inside him now.

And then, as suddenly as it had struck, the light went out, the blackness in those first few moments so total, so absolute, there was a great moan of fear.

Jake blinked his eyes tight shut, then opened them again, craning his neck to look up at the ship. For a moment he could see nothing. It was as if he had been blinded. All he could see was the burned-in image of the craft's searchlight on his retinas. Then, as that began to fade, he got the vaguest glimpse of its outline, the silvered shape of it in the moonlight as it withdrew; a strange, inhuman-looking craft, much larger than anything he'd ever seen.

The pulse withdrew. Slowly the air grew still.

'D'you see that?' someone yelled. 'D'you see that on its wings? Fuckin' aliens!'

But Jake had seen it too, right at the end, even as it had accelerated out of sight.

Dragons. Those markings... they were dragons.

And as he thought it, so he could feel the touch of the finest silken threads on his face, the faintest trace of sulphur and cinnamon on his tongue. And, pervading all, like a coil of swirling, dark red smoke, the outlines of a face. Oriental. Brutal.

Jake fell to his knees, recognizing the triggered memory; knowing now without a shred of doubt who it was.

'It's the Chinese,' he said, looking to Tom, who stood nearby, his shocked face turned to the sky. 'It's the fucking Chinese...'

PART TWO **The East is Red**

SPRING 2043

Barely fifty, but already my face is old, my hair white.
I travelled this whole coast fleeing from The State.
Rough cloth saved my shivering bones
As I roamed the awful cold.
Thus began the years of my disease.
Everywhere the people were mud and ashes.
Between heaven and earth,
There's nowhere a body is safe.
We may never find the roads back home.
We weep our eyes dry in the river.

— Tu Fu, 'Running From Trouble', 8th Century AD

Chapter 4

FUTURES

The datscape explodes upon my skin. Cascades of dark violet flakes drift through an umber skein of smoke as I step in. Close by, a magma heave of glowing cerise rests at the centre of a landscape of outrageous geometric shape, outrageous colour. If I gently squeeze my eyes within the mask, vision reveals the ghostly layers beneath, another dozen data levels, all of it painted in vital, vivid colours, like a child's spilled toy box, distortedly alive, in constant movement, constant flux.

Everything has meaning here. Our senses are fine-tuned to discriminate. Colour denotes commodity, density value, fluidity the transferability of stock.

It is a market, after all.

The great curve of the dome arches above me, studded with glowing metallic teats – ten thousand and more – spinning fine threads of information into the flow, like coloured silk, building and demolishing the datscape nanosecond by nanosecond, like the universe itself, a constantly unfinished work.

Layers. There are endless layers to this. The datscape has the power to make a metaphor quite literal. It is a massively complex feedback system, the computer world's most powerful metonym, accurately reflecting the world of markets. Subtle changes of colour, of texture, of flow, all of these are significant, for everything here has a mathematical expression. In the instant it exists, everything here has a precise monetary value.

I move on, past massive termite towers of a dense cyan blue, past pulsing, globular moulds of bright magenta. Skeletal trees of silver-black thrust skyward, their branches rippling like the innards of some pulsing, transparent insect. Beyond lie massive hills of coloured geometry and shape – mushroom growths heaped up alongside crystals of a thousand different hues, subtle variants of shade from which furred golden leaves and sinuous chains of bright red stickiness emerge like parasitic growths. And through it all flow streams of fierce, glowing colour, steaming and vaporous, while in the air a spectral, flickering snow storm of fine crystals briefly blurs the sensory feast.

Dali's migraine. Cyber art meets cyber commerce.

A world of avatars and avarice. How does it look? I'm often asked. How does it feel to be inside? But it isn't how it looks that strikes one most, or how it feels. It's how it *smells*.

For just as every stock and share, every commodity and company has its own colour and shape, its own density and viscosity, its warmth or frigidity, so it also has its scent. It can be fresh or stale. Colour and shape, they're indicators, certainly, but smell is what I 'look' for, what I sniff out, as I make my way.

Freshness is all. At least, for what I do.

Trading results, capital growth, investment and R & D, recruitment policy, new patent registration – all these are reflected in the smell of a company's shares. If the company is young, dynamic, get-ahead, it has a green, spring-like freshness to its smell. It will emit... pheremonally, that is. Whereas an ageing company whose sales are falling, whose staff are leaving; a company dependent on financial cushioning, let's say. Well... do you know the smell of dead meat?

I close my eyes sometimes – metaphorically speaking – and smell my way about the datscape, sensing the acid-taste of some giant plastics company on my tongue, the tickle of shipping stocks in the fine hairs of my nasal passages.

There is a primacy to smell. It doesn't lie the way that colours lie. A fresh paint job... you can't do that with a smell. You can try to mask it, to deodorize it, and only a fine nose can discern that.

Which is what I've been trained for. It is all breathed in, you see, through the fine filter of my mask. Information. Endless information. Processed not as a computer might process it, but in a primal, instinctive fashion, using the back brain. For my job is a process of letting go. Of submitting to the Market.

The best of us don't simply look around, we trawl the Market. We suck it all in, let it fill our pores and overload our senses, hunters in some dark, primeval forest. A hundred and fifty thousand years of instinctive decision-making gathered in, life and death stuff, fine-tuned, fine-focused for this brave new world.

But I mislead you. You might think I am alone here. Far from it. The datscape is alive with avatars; not only the servants of the eight big companies that service the virtual Market, but those of the fourteen hundred and ten much smaller brokers that prey like lampfish in its stygian depths.

How many? Fifty thousand, perhaps, at any one time. It depends. Some are conservatively 'dressed', as samurai, perhaps, or famous captains of industry, but there are pirates too and dragons and other mythical creatures, gods and heroes, lobsters and robots, lions and Lilliputians, hill trolls and hobbits, bulls and bears, spiders and grey-bearded sages, Eurydice and...

Whatever the imagination can devise, you'll find it here, walking the Dantean circles of this great Erewhon – this nowhere place – crawling up its walls or flapping their great wing-ed arms across the inner sky.

Only right now I am heading for the future. And before you ask, let me answer you. You can walk there. You need only move your virtual legs and there, on the far side of the cavern, lies a doorway, or rather, a membrane. You just have to step through. There, on the far side, in a cooler, less-crowded, less eye-disturbing place, the future waits, silent and sterile, a great warehouse of what-will-be.

There is marginally less here than in the present, and as one walks on, further into the weeks and months ahead, so the landscape grows less crowded still, until, a year or so ahead, there's empty floor space under foot. Here, one can identify stocks and commodities at a glance.

Yes, and here's where I do much of my business: identifying what's going up and what down, which is a good risk and which poor, using what I've learned from the 'Now' of the datscape, to gamble on the 'Then' of this other place. Buying cheap to sell dear a year from now. Guaranteeing supplies for my masters and oiling the wheels of commerce in the years to come. Making sure it all continues.

Futures. That's what I do. I deal in Futures.

The cameras stopped. Behind the actor, dangling in his harness, the elegant curve of the blue screen reappeared as the projection vanished.

'Okay, Jake... that's great... word perfect... and great visuals too...'

Slowly they lowered him.

'Jeez, it's hot in this...'

He was dressed as a massive go piece; a huge black stone, tiny limbs and an equally tiny head sprouting from the curved, unblemished surface.

'Stop moaning,' Carl, the director, called to him. 'You're being paid twice what you're worth!'

It wasn't true, but it didn't matter. He liked doing this stuff.

As his feet touched the floor, the prop men hurried over, unhinging the costume and letting him step free.

'Have a shower, Jake, then we'll talk.'

Jake nodded. He liked Carl. They had the same acerbic sense of humour. And Carl knew what he was doing. He had understood at once what Jake was getting at.

As he showered, Jake thought about the shoot. When he'd first become a *login* there had been no guidelines, no training 'immersions' to help him find his feet. He'd been thrown in at the deep end to sink or swim. But things had been different back then. The virtual Market had been so much smaller, so much easier to deal with. In the last ten years more and more companies had signed up, until now it was impossible to float a company without being in the datscape.

Now training was all the thing, and he, their star turn, their golden boy, had been asked to make the latest training immersion.

He stood beneath the hot air stream, drying off. Because of the shoot he had been given the evening off. Friends were coming round. They were going to have a meal and watch the latest episode of *Ubik*.

Chris and Hugo were coming, along with Jenny and Alex. And, of course, Kate.

Speaking of which...

Jake pulled on his shorts, then pressed the tiny implant that lay beneath the skin just below his right ear. At once he was connected up.

'Get me Kate. Voice only.'

The implant vibrated gently. As it stopped, Kate's voice filled his head.

'Hi, sweetheart... how did it go?'

'It went wonderfully. We got it in one. You still okay for this evening?'

'Be there at seven.'

'You can come earlier if you want.'

Her laughter made him smile. She knew what he meant.

'Seriously. I've just got to have a quick word with Carl, then I'll be home.'

'Maybe... but I'm not promising. I've got to finish a few things.'

'Okay... I love you.'

'Love you, too.'

He cut the connection.

Turning, he noticed the steward standing against the wall across from him. The man's head was bowed, his eyes averted, but Jake had the feeling that he'd been being watched.

'You...'

'Yes, Master?'

'Book me a hopper. I want it on the roof in twenty minutes, okay?'

'Yes, Master.'

Jake watched him go. Chinese. Of course he was. The Chinese got in everywhere these days; body servants and cleaners, receptionists and doormen. It seemed like there wasn't a single service industry they hadn't infiltrated.

He finished dressing and went back upstairs. Carl was waiting for him, sitting in the bar, the big picture window behind him giving a view of the river and the dense mass of high-rises that was the City.

'What are you drinking?' Carl asked, getting up and coming across.

'Just a Coke.'

'You don't drink?'

'Oh, I drink... but only when I've a day or two to recover. You can't take any chances when you're inside. You need your senses about you.'

Carl grinned. 'Literally so, from what you were saying... A Coke it is, then.'

They went over to the bar.

As Carl ordered the drinks, Jake studied him.

'If you don't mind me coming to the point, what is it you want?'

Carl turned, handed him his drink. 'From you? Well, I certainly can't match what you make with Hinton, but... if you want to do some more of this stuff... and I don't just mean the corporate packages... well... I'd love to work with you.'

'That's very flattering...'

'No. Not at all. You're good. One of the best I've worked with. You've got a real gift for it, Jake. And that text... I loved it...'

'I wish I could claim sole credit, but I had help from my friend, Hugo.'

'Well, introduce him to me. Here's my chip.'

Jake took it, stowed it in his pocket, then raised his glass to the other man. 'Maybe... let me talk it through with my fiancée.'

'You're engaged?'

'She doesn't know it yet, but... yes...'

Carl's eyes flew open wide. 'You mean...?'

'A permit, yeah... it came through yesterday.'

'Christ! Then we *have* got a reason to celebrate!'

Jake smiled 'I'd love to, only... Another time, eh?'

'Sure. Take a copy of the chip for yourself. You're welcome to call any time, day or night. My avatar fields all my contacts.'

'Thanks. I will.'

The hopper was waiting for him on the roof, as he'd asked. There was no sign of the steward. Then again there was no reason for him to be there, only...

You're getting paranoid...

Maybe, but they had been warned only last week. Industrial espionage was on the up. Yes, but the man worked for Bellini's, and Bellini's were a top-class establishment. They'd have double-checked his credentials before hiring him. Jake relaxed.

Even so, you had to be careful what you said and to whom.

He fingered the chip that was in his pocket. Carl, for instance, was extremely open in giving him his chip, especially as it was being handed on to someone he'd never met. It showed trust. Only trust wasn't a strength these days. In some circles it was seen as a distinct weakness.

As the craft lifted and banked out over the river, Jake looked out to his left. He loved this sight, especially at this time of the day, with the sun turning the river into a snaking coil of silver and gold. He was looking back, past the enclaves, towards the poor districts. From this high up you could see the enclave walls, their creamy marble almost Mediterranean in the sunlight.

Like a fortress within that ancient sprawl.

Slowly they climbed. It was only five minutes to his apartment, but he wasn't in a hurry. It was hours before his guests would turn up.

Across from him the new-builds began to climb the sky, endless needles of dark glass that surrounded the central 'hub' built in and around the ancient heart of the City. *Like something from the datscape.* The Hinton building lay in the shadow of two other massive buildings, on old Eastcheap, its H-shaped structure adding a faint tinge of green to the blacks and greys and whites of the nearby buildings.

It wasn't the biggest, not by a long way – that was the great pagoda-shape of the China Construction Bank – but it was getting a reputation as the best. In these harsh and unforgiving times Hinton rarely got it wrong, and Jake and the hand-picked team of *logins* he worked with were almost entirely responsible.

Hence today's 'immersion'. For if they were to maintain their steady climb to the number one spot, then they had to recruit the best and give them the best training possible.

Jake had bought his penthouse apartment in direct line-of-sight to his place of work. Every morning he would wake and go out onto the broad balcony and look across at it before breakfast with a kind of possessive fascination. Mind, it was hardly surprising. Hinton had recruited him at fourteen from among thousands of eager, fresh-faced applicants. They had sent him to their academy in the wilds of Cumberland. There he had begun the intensive training that had led to this, first as a 'runner', then as a 'boardman' and finally as a *login* – a 'web-dancer' as they sometimes called them.

It had been an exhaustive education and he had come out of it with Firsts in History, Economics and Political Science. The world had been his oyster – provided he stayed with Hinton.

Jake took out the tiny black and silver-blue chip Carl had given him and studied it a moment. A tiny hologram of Carl's smiling face looked up at him from an octagonal inset at its centre.

It was flattering of Carl to offer him work – especially work in the media – but he enjoyed what he did far too much. In fact, some days he would simply stop and laugh aloud to think that they paid him so much to do the thing he loved.

Not that his bosses didn't know that, but they pampered him anyway, keeping him 'sweet', giving him whatever he wanted.

Which was why he had his own entry pad to the Market, located in his apartment: a vaulted box room they'd had specially built. It was intended to be used only in emergencies, but he went in there sometimes, when something was troubling him.

Tonight, however, something else dominated his thoughts.

The permit... Should he tell her tonight, when everyone was round, and ask her to marry him? Or should he wait until they were alone?

Of course, if she came early he could do it then.

As the craft set down on the roof of the private apartment block, Jake leaned forward, thanking the pilot.

'Cheers, Sam. Put me down for two flights, will you? I've had a very good day...'

'Thank you, sir. And have a good evening.'

'I will... I most definitely will.'

He stood back as the craft lifted away, then turned and made his way down the single flight of stairs that led to his apartment.

As ever, everything looked spick and span. The panoramic glass windows gleamed, not a speck or a fingerprint on them. Jake liked that. He was a highly meticulous man. He didn't like mess or clutter. It got in the way. The only 'mess' he liked was inside, in the datscape. That was a mess he revelled in.

They were four hundred and fifty feet up here. Fifty floors, give or take. And the view was spectacular. He never tired of it.

'Trish... give me news,' he said, speaking to the air. 'Non-Market specific.'

At once the big screen on the wall behind him lit up. He turned to face it.

'Afternoon, Mister Reed...'

'Hi, Trish... How're David and the boy?'

Trish was Jake's filter avatar, his very own AI, programmed to keep Jake's diary, run his apartment and field all calls.

Part of her job was to trawl the media for items that were specifically to Jake's taste or that he'd find of interest. She didn't really exist, but it made it more pleasant to pretend she did. Jake had given her a husband, a young child, and a two-bed in one of the orbitals. He'd made her his own age, twenty-six, but there any similarities ended. Jake was 'exec' status, Trish wasn't. She was 'service'.

'They're fine, Mister Reed.'

'Good... so what's been happening?'

'First up is the new manned mission to Mars.'

As he spoke, the screen showed the massive *Shenzou 41* rocket thrusting its way up into the clear North China skies on a plume of fire and roiling smoke. The bright red craft had a large gold star facing four smaller ones painted on its flank. Inside, its crew of twelve – six males, six females – smiled broadly and gave a thumbs-up for the watching cameras.

'You think they'll beat the Americans there?'

'The Chinese say it doesn't matter. There's room enough on Mars for everyone.'

'They say that now… Next?'

The image changed, showing the British Prime Minister, the Right Honourable Andrew Isaiah Yates, addressing the House of Commons.

Trish gave commentary.

'As you can see, the PM forced a new package of vagrancy laws through parliament last night in a lengthy late night sitting. At the same time he announced yet another crackdown on the "un-protected".'

Again the image changed, showed the Security forces, 'suited and booted', in full riot gear with truncheons drawn, charging a line of stone-throwing citizens while water cannons fired over their heads. Buildings were burning, and in the air close by a number of massive police hoppers shone their searchlights down on the masses. The air was full of the pop-pop-pop of gunfire.

Just another night in the suburbs.

'Next…'

The image changed, showed what was clearly the avatar of a beautiful woman. Naked and full-breasted, she held a bright red apple up to the camera and smiled. Behind her, perched on the open door of a black iron-barred cage, was a massive jet black crow. There was a small coin in its beak, while its golden eyes stared out from the screen in a challenging, almost threatening fashion.

Music played quietly in the background.

'On the media front, diva Eve Adams is releasing a new album, her first in four years. It's called *Crow-Nickel*, and will be available in all formats from today.'

Jake smiled. He liked Eve Adams. 'It's a dreadful pun… Old stuff or new?'

'New,' Trish answered. 'But as you've noted, the album's a kind of personal chronicle. Adams says the songs reflect what's been happening in her life. It's fairly dark...'

'But then so is her life... Next...'

A new image, this time of a grey-haired African, shaking hands with a smart-suited Han. Behind them was what looked like a massive chemical plant.

'What's this?'

'It's a big new deal...'

'I thought I said non-specific...'

'You did. But I thought this one would interest you. That building in the background... it's a drilling station.'

'I don't understand...'

'It seems they're going to tap deep into the earth's core,' Trish went on. 'Into the magma itself...'

'What are they looking for? New energy sources?'

'That's just it. What they say they're doing is generating oxygen.'

'Oxygen,' Jake laughed. 'Air, you mean?'

'That's right. It seems the atmosphere's been depleted these past twenty years, and they want to do something about it. It's a pilot scheme...'

Jake stepped closer, trying to make out the details. He'd not heard of anything like this before, and for the Chinese to be doing it seemed strange, to say the least.

'Next.'

'A personal one this time...'

The image changed. Seeing who it was, Jake grinned.

'Hey, that's Hugo...! What the hell is he doing?'

'It's a charity show... for the Campaign For Legal Representation. He's written a new piece, for electronics and orchestra. They're going to perform it next week.'

Jake was in two minds about Hugo's charitable activities, but he kept that to himself. If Hugo wanted to be a liberal, let him be one.

'I'm surprised he didn't say...'

'You've been busy,' Trish said, as the image faded, the pixels breaking up like the dissolving pieces of a puzzle.

The screen was now filled with the image of a windswept field of grass of that perfect shade of green Jake found most relaxing. The same green that, in the datscape, represented 'liquid' cash.

He smiled. 'Thanks, Trish... We'll speak later.'

'Sure thing, Mister Reed.'

Jake turned away. He ought to have been speaking to the chef, sorting out the menu for tonight, only he didn't feel like it.

No, what he felt like was seeing Kate. Only Kate had things to finish off.

He walked through, into the bedroom, then stretched out upon the low, Japanese-style mattress.

The room, like the rest of the flat, was minimalist. Jake didn't see the point of surrounding himself with things when you could hire whatever you wanted and have it delivered at a single command. Why keep things when someone else could store them for you?

And by now, on what he was earning, he could afford to have things shipped from anywhere. Almost anything he wanted. Jake closed his eyes. The session today had been exhilarating. He hadn't enjoyed anything quite so much in ages. Anything 'outside' that was.

So maybe he'd do some more, after all. Take up Carl's offer. That is, if Hinton let him.

He closed his eyes. Found himself thinking about China.

There was a Chinese painting on the wall. It had been here when he'd moved in and he hadn't bothered to have it removed. As far as he knew, it was an original, on loan to Hinton Industrials from one of their clients.

He spoke to the air.

'Trish... what is that painting?'

Trish knew without asking which painting he meant.

'It is Emperor Hui Tsong's copy of Lady Kuo Kuo's Spring Outing.

The original was by Chang Hsuan in the eighth century.'

Jake rolled over and looked at it. It was very pretty. The stylized horses, the faint pinks and lime greens of the ladies' skirts, the whole thing, in fact, demonstrated a highly delicate sensitivity.

'Have you told me this before, Trish?'

'Several times.'

'When I was drunk, you mean?'

'I wouldn't wish to comment...'

But there was the faintest hint of amusement in Trish's reply that implied that he had indeed been drunk. As you'd expect, perhaps. Jake had, after all, programmed her himself.

Oxygen generators... now what's that all about?

The latest space launch did interest him, however. Since the space race had begun again in earnest thirty years back, it had been a matter of national pride. As a student at the academy, he had had pictures of astronauts on his wall. Americans, Russians, Chinese, Europeans, including one or two pure-born Englishmen. Those were the new heroes. And when he'd graduated at eighteen, it was an astronaut he'd really wanted to be, not a *login*.

Logins... sounded so prosaic. And so unreal, from what he'd heard. But he knew better now. This world of theirs depended on *logins*. Without them things would grind to a halt. Astronauts, romantic as they were, were a luxury.

Hugo, of course, thought otherwise. He thought them the saviours of the world. Or, at least, the pioneers of new and better worlds.

Jake, however, didn't believe that. He thought it was a lot of sentimental bullshit. He'd seen first hand what really happened. Seen how the moon-based ore companies had trebled and quadrupled their profits these last few years.

Brave New World, my arse, he'd say. It's the new Klondyke.

There were colonies on the moon already. The Chinese had six, the Americans four, the Russians a further two. The EU had built one, but there'd been an accident and they'd all died. And now there would be colonies on Mars.

Jake stretched, relaxing, wondering what it was like up there.

And after Mars?

Jake felt a faint vibration in the tiny insert behind his ear. He sat up.

'Kate?'

There was a moment's silence, then Kate's voice filled his head.

'Hi, sweetheart... I'm incoming... I'll be there in five...'

'Thought you had things to do?'

'I did. But I cancelled them. You sounded needy.'

'Needy?' He laughed. 'I could have sent for one of the company women.'

'Over my dead body.'

He smiled at that. 'See you in a bit.'

'See you.'

They cut contact.

Jack sat there a moment, wondering just how he was going to play this. Should he tease her? No. It was too big a thing for that. Well, then, maybe he'd just hand her the sealed packet the permit had come in.

Yes. That was it.

And afterwards? Did he ask her then? Or did he take her to bed? Show her how much he wanted her, then ask her, in the afterglow.

Jake let out a long breath. This was the start of it. The permit meant they could get married and have children. Without it the whole thing was a non-starter. Any child they'd have had would have been outside the protection of the legal process, would have been 'unprotected', and whether you agreed with that or not – and there were many, Hugo included, who didn't – it was how things were.

Yes, the permit was the key. It opened doors.

★

'Hey...' Hugo said as he stepped from the lift, handing Kate the flowers and Jake the wine, 'something's up, I can sense it.'

Kate looked to Jake.

'Not yet,' he said. 'Wait till the others are here.'

Hugo let Jake take his coat. As he turned back he saw that Jake was smiling.

'What?'

'I saw you earlier, on the news...'

'Oh, the campaign... you don't approve...'

'Someone's got to help the UPs. But I was more interested in the piece. You didn't tell me you'd written something new.'

Hugo shrugged, as if it was nothing. It wasn't that he was modest, he just kept things to himself. It had always been this way, since their schooldays. You always had to drag out of him what he was up to.

'Where's Chris?' Kate asked, as they went back inside the apartment. 'I thought he was coming with you.'

'He'll be along. Something cropped up, last minute. You know how it is...'

Chris was Hugo's partner. He was ten years older than Hugo and ten or twenty million Euros richer, but you wouldn't have known it.

As the door irised shut, Hugo made an exaggerated gesture of sniffing the air.

'God, that smells wonderful! You got a new chef, Jake?'

'I thought I'd try Bellini's... I was there today.'

'At Bellini's?'

'Yes... making a new immersion for the firm.'

Hugo looked impressed.

'Remember that piece you helped me write... you know... about being inside the datscape?'

'Sure.'

'That's what we used. The director, Carl, loved it. So much so, in fact, that he gave me his chip to hand to you. Says he'd like to work with you sometime.'

Jake handed him the chip. He'd not had time to look at it himself.

Hugo stared at it a moment, then slipped it away in his pocket. 'Serendipitous,' he said. 'I was about to look for a director... for the new piece.'

'Well, Carl strikes me as a good man. He's keen, intelligent...'

'Gay?'

Jake laughed. 'No... at least, I wouldn't have said so.'

Kate reappeared at that moment with drinks. She had put on an ice-blue, full-length dress for the evening, and had tied her hair back in a bun, giving her a classical, almost Grecian appearance.

'You look stunning,' Hugo said, accepting his glass with a nod. 'Not only that, but you look like a girl with a secret...'

'All in good time,' Jake said. But Kate was blushing now.

'I won't spoil things,' Hugo said, as if he already knew.

Trish's voice rang out. 'Your other guests are here, Mister Reed. They'll be touching down in approximately one minute.'

Jake looked to Hugo and smiled. 'Trust Jenny to make an entrance...'

They went out on to the roof to watch the hopper set down. It wasn't a 'taxi' or a company hopper, but one of the big military versions, similar to those Jake had seen on the news item, the craft bristling with heavy armour.

As Jenny and her partner, Alex, stepped down from inside, two uniformed guards saluted Alex, then stood back as the door hissed closed and the craft lifted, merging into the darkness.

They came across. Jenny was giggling now.

'Sorry about that,' Alex said. 'Just thought I'd cadge a lift.'

Alex was Security. 'Plain clothes', as he liked to call it. But Jake knew he was special forces. Jenny had told him when they'd first started going out together, three years back.

Back inside, Kate brought more drinks, then looked to Jake.

'Have we *got* to wait for Chris?'

'Oh, no, don't...' Hugo said. 'You know what he's like... it could be *ages* before he gets here. Just tell us...'

'Tell us what?' Jenny asked, intrigued. She was wearing red, but otherwise, she and Kate could have been twins.

Jake looked to Kate. 'You want to tell them, or shall I?'

She blushed and looked down. 'You do it...'

'Okay... but before we do, I think something special's called for... a bottle of the eighty-one, possibly. No... let's go mad... two bottles!'

There was laughter.

Jake went out to the kitchen, returning a moment later with a tray of glasses. He had obviously prepared for this moment.

As they took their new glasses, Jake looked across at Kate and winked.

When he'd told her earlier she had gone very quiet. At first he thought that maybe she had a problem with it. Then he realized what it was. She was crying. Crying with happiness.

They had made love, gently, tenderly, like it was the first time. They couldn't conceive, of course – Kate would have to go to the clinic to have the implant removed – yet it felt different. It wasn't just sex any more, it was creating.

They had 'created' once more before showering and getting ready for their guests, but Jake had never seen Kate so happy, so bright-eyed and rosy-cheeked. Hugo was right. She looked stunning.

As he raised his glass, the others copied him.

'To my future wife...' he began.

'A permit! You've got a permit!' Jenny squealed, almost spilling her drink in her excitement. She put her glass down then rushed to hug Kate.

'Oh, you darlings! You precious darlings! I am so happy for you!'

Hugo was grinning in a kind of 'I told you so' fashion, as if he'd known all along – which was quite possible, knowing Hugo. Alex, meanwhile, had a calm smile on his features. 'Well done,' he said. 'I'm really pleased.'

Kate met Jake's eyes, then raised her glass to him. 'To my future husband...'

'Oh, Jake...' Jenny said, tears in her eyes now. 'Don't stand there like a lemon... kiss her...'

He kissed her. The others cheered and raised their glasses high.

'To Jake and Kate,' Hugo said, looking about him. 'May they have health, wealth and happiness... and many children...'

'Hear, hear!' Alex said, nodding vigorously.

But Jake only had eyes for Kate.

Sometime in the past, Jake had been at a party. It was a firm 'do' – Hinton had thousands working for them at all levels – and they had hired Hampton Court Palace for the evening, flying their employees in along a protected corridor over the ghettos of Wandsworth and Wimbledon.

He'd spent an hour talking to colleagues, making an appearance, 'networking' as they called it, though why he, a rogue creature of the datscape, should need to 'network' was beyond him. To be frank, he had been bored. Bored shitless, as he'd later recalled when telling the tale. He had decided to seek out his line-boss and then leave. Get a good night's sleep and get in early – make the firm some profits before the sun came up.

It was then, as he'd crossed the room, having spotted old George Hinton, to whom he nominally reported, that he ran into her – almost literally.

She had turned and stepped backward, even as he made to move past her in the crowded room. As he later said, he didn't have a chance.

'She literally threw herself at me.'

It was Kate, of course.

'I am *so* sorry,' she said, her face an agony of embarrassment. 'I really, *really* didn't mean to do that.'

Jake had picked himself up and, putting his hands up as if to ward off any further assault, answered her. 'No, that's perfectly fine... you didn't see me... I was moving very fast...'

'Very,' she echoed, but she was smiling now that she could see he wasn't angry with her.

'And you are?'

'Kate...'

It was almost a whisper. People were watching now, amused by this sudden entertainment, and Kate clearly didn't like being the centre of attention.

Jake liked that. He had liked it immediately.

'Well, Kate... I'm Jake, and I am *really* pleased I bumped into you.'

She seemed surprised. 'Are you?'

'Yes, actually, I am.'

He had been a *login* only eight weeks back then. A novice, making up with keenness what he lacked in skill and subtlety. And Kate? Kate was the daughter of the chief exec of one of the City's biggest insurance companies. One he knew by touch and scent. A very ash grey kind of company.

That was how it had begun. Accidentally. And now this.

As Kate cleared the table, he watched her, pleased that he'd done so well. She was grace personified and, as far as his bosses were concerned, the perfect partner for such a high-flier as he. Now, when he got an invite to a Hinton 'bash', it was for 'Kate and Jake', as if she too were an employee.

'Kate...?'

She looked to him from the doorway, pausing, the tray full of dirty plates balanced tremulously. 'Yes, my love?'

'Have we any of that glorious stilton your parents bought us?'

'I'll get it.'

And she was gone.

Jake turned, looking to Alex, who was facing him. Alex was staring down into his brandy glass, slowly swirling the dark liquid about. Sensing that Jake was watching him, he looked up.

'You're a lucky man, Jake. A very lucky man.'

'I know...'

'Looks, brains... she'll be a good mother, too, I bet... but d'you know why you're so lucky?'

Jake shrugged. 'Go on... tell me.'

'Because she's kind.'

It was a very un-Alex kind of thing to say. Alex was always so formal, so... *closed*. But he had drunk a lot tonight – they all had – and he had loosened up considerably as the evening had progressed.

'She is,' Jake said, nodding his agreement.

He looked to Hugo. 'Have you given up on Chris?'

'I don't know... he's probably buggering some poor little office junior...'

'Hugo!' Jenny protested. 'He'd never...'

'Oh, *wouldn't* he.' But they could see he was teasing. In truth he trusted Chris absolutely. Chris was, after all, the love of his life. 'Jake... about what you were saying earlier... about the Chinese...'

'The Han,' Jenny said. 'They call themselves the Han.'

'The Han, then... Do you really think they're still our enemies? I mean... it's been more than fifty years since they joined the global economy. They're fully integrated into our world. I mean, it's *their* world too, only...'

'What the fuck are you trying to say?' Alex asked.

'I don't know...' Hugo shrugged. 'It's just... well, I deal with a lot of them... you have to... more than half our sales are in the Far East... only I've never felt I've got close to any of them. I can't say, even now, that any of them are my friends.'

'We don't mix,' Alex said, leaning forward, his face serious now. 'Half the cases I deal with these days... well, I can't say, of course... but I know who's at the bottom of most of them. The Chinese.' He looked to Jenny. 'The *Han*. Horrid and Nasty, we call them. And you know what? They are. They've got whole armies of hackers, hacking away at our data. Stealing it or corrupting it. Like burglars, breaking in and sniffing our dirty underwear.'

Jenny looked appalled. 'Alex...'

'I know. We do it, too. Only for them it's like a mission. They don't have ideas of their own, they steal ours. Always have done, ever since they came out of the dark ages and started to trade again.'

Hugo sat forward at that. 'Oh, unfair, Alex... You can't say that. They're every bit as creative...'

'As us? See how we talk "us" and "them" when it comes to the Han. We don't talk about the Yanks that way.'

'No, but the Yanks *are* us. Genetically. They're Europeans. The Han...'

'Are Ha-han, o-o-ho...' Alex said, doing his best Elvis Presley impersonation.

There was laughter, but beneath it there was a sudden, darker edge to things.

Kate reappeared, carrying a large platter filled with various cheeses.

'Oh, Kate,' Jenny said, jumping up to help her. 'They look wonderful!'

'You wouldn't catch a Han eating cheese,' Alex grumbled. 'Just bloody noodles...'

Jake looked down. He wished now he hadn't mentioned it. Wished he'd kept it to himself. But there was some truth to what Alex was saying. If they weren't enemies, then they most certainly were rivals. He knew that from the datscape. When it came to the acquisition of raw materials, China was voracious. Was a giant mouth that demanded to be fed. It was the only reason they were out in space...

Trish interrupted his thoughts.

'Mister Reed... two more guests have arrived. They're coming up in the lift right now...'

Hugo jumped up, casting his serviette aside. 'It's Chris... I wonder who he's brought...'

Jake felt a brief flash of irritation. Chris might at least have asked. It was, after all, a private occasion. Now he'd have to make small talk to some stranger.

Only it wasn't a stranger. It was a very old friend.

'Alison... how in god's name...?'

'I found her,' Chris said, stepping past Jake to give Hugo a peck on the cheek. 'Hi, hon... having fun?'

Jake just stared. 'The last time I saw you...'

'...was on the steps of New College five years ago.'

She stepped closer, embracing him. It wasn't a hug, Alison never hugged, it was more the slightest physical touch, an establishing of boundaries. It reminded Jake of why they'd broken up; of how insular, how self-contained she was. There was the faintest scent of perfume about her, but the dominant impression was of her cleanliness. Hair, clothes, manners, all were so neat and precise.

'Jake?'

He turned. Kate stood there, smiling, looking to him to make an introduction.

'Kate... this is Alison. Alison, this is Kate, my fiancée.'

'Ali...' Hugo pushed past Jake to take Alison's hands, leaning in to plant a kiss on her cheek. 'I wondered when you'd make an appearance...'

Jake turned back, looking to the others for an explanation.

Hugo answered. 'We bumped into each other a month or two back, at some gallery or other... I meant to tell you...'

'But it escaped your mind...'

Jake glanced at Kate, could see how she was dying to know who this new woman was.

'Hugo and I were at uni with Alison. She was majoring in art history...'

137

'A big mistake,' Alison said, as if it were amusing, only there was no amusement in her cold blue eyes.

'So what do you do now?' Alex asked. He alone had remained seated.

'I work for GenSyn.'

'GenSyn?' Alex frowned, trying to locate where he'd heard the name. 'What do they do?'

'Genetic Synthetics. We build things. Living things.'

'That's one hell of a change of direction.'

She nodded, acknowledging that. 'They retrained me.'

Kate opened her mouth, as if to ask something, then seemed to change her mind. She smiled, becoming the perfect hostess once again.

'Look... I'm being very rude... what'll you have to drink?'

'I'll have a large brandy,' Chris said, 'and a carbonated soda for the lady.'

Kate looked to Alison, who nodded.

'Come, take a seat,' Jake said. 'Are you hungry?'

Again Chris answered for her. 'Gods, no... we gorged ourselves on canapés, didn't we, Ali?'

'We did,' she conceded, letting herself be led over to the table. Hugo brought another chair in from the back room and placed it between his and Chris's seats.

'Are you married?' Jake asked, knowing even as he asked it how pointed a question it was.

She smiled; a neat, formalized smile that gave nothing away. 'No.'

'Boyfriend?'

'Not right now. I haven't time.'

'No?'

'No. You could say I'm married to the job. It's very demanding. We're a small family firm...'

'I know.'

Jake recalled it now. When she'd first mentioned the company's name, he'd not made the link, but now he had. It was why he was so good at his job. Attention to fine detail.

'The Eberts... right?'

She bowed her head a little. 'Very good... But then I'm told that you're the best at what you do.'

Jake looked to Chris who shrugged. 'Only telling the truth, old boy. You're the bee's fucking bollocks.'

Hugo laughed. 'I think it's dogs, not bees...'

'Mixed metaphor,' Chris said, waving a hand dismissively. 'The best kind...'

'Who'd a thunk it,' Alison said, making Jake look at her again, surprised that she'd remembered.

Old dead comedians...

But then, why would she forget? Had he forgotten?

Kate returned with the drinks.

'So what do you actually do at... GenSyn, is it?'

Alison looked up at Kate, accepting the fluted glass. 'I evaluate.'

'Evaluate?'

'Potential lines of research... projects, I guess you'd call them. Whether they're viable... whether we'd make any money out of them...'

'So they got you in the end, eh?'

Alison turned her head, looking directly at him. 'They got us all, Hugo aside...'

'Oh, no,' Jake said, finding himself, for a moment, back in the conversational mode of earlier years, 'they got Hugo, too. Didn't they, Hugo?'

'Golden hook, line and sinker...'

Trish's voice interrupted them.

'Forgive me, Mister Reed, but you asked me to remind you when your programme was about to start...'

'Thank you, Trish...'

Alison looked about her for an explanation.

'*Ubik*,' Chris said.

'Ah... I've not...'

'Not seen it?' Hugo was appalled. 'You can't not have seen it! It's...'

'Ubiquitous,' Jenny finished. And there was laughter. Only not from Alison.

What are you doing here? Jake thought. And why tonight? Why, when I was finally over you, do you turn up again in my life?

He turned his head, looking to Kate. She was watching Alison, a hardness in her eyes, as if she were trying to work out who this new woman was and what her role in things might be. And she was right to, because Jake had only ever loved two women, and here they both were.

'Trish... full wall...'

They went and settled on the sofas as the opening credits ran.

'It's sci-fi,' Hugo explained. 'From the good old days. One of Dick's best...'

'Dick who?' Alison asked, and there was laughter. She smiled and looked about her. 'What did I say?'

'It's Philip K. Dick,' Jake explained. 'He was the writer.'

'Ah... And he's good, is he?'

'He saw it all,' Chris said. 'Seventy-odd fucking years ago he wrote this, and boy did he know what was coming!'

They fell quiet, watching the wall. This was the last episode of four, the finale, and it had taken the media by storm. Everybody was talking about it.

How did you not know about this? Jake wondered, glancing at her, seeing how she watched the giant screen, trying to understand what was going on. *Is your life really that circumscribed?*

Apparently not, for she went to galleries.

Yes, but what was she doing here? Why had she let Chris talk her into this?

'God, this is weird,' Alison said quietly.

'Isn't it?' Chris said excitedly.

The others made hushing noises.

Kate shifted a little on the sofa next to Jake, pressing up against him and putting her head on his shoulder.

He smiled.

On the screen the 'anti-psi', Joe Chip, was trying to climb the stairs. Trapped in the threatening nightmare of the 'half-life' world, he struggled to climb each step, like Sisyphus, or like a diver coming up from the depths of the ocean bed. None of it made sense. Not yet. But it would, and when it did...

Jake shivered. Back then, when Dick had written this, in sixty-nine, there had been no internet, no world wide web or datscape, no virtual worlds. Yet what was the world of *Ubik*, if not that? A half-life... yes. Sometimes, not always, he felt like that; like he was trapped inside some hallucinogenic, drug-induced dream.

'What's with the spray cans?' Alison asked.

'Later...' Hugo said, reaching out to touch her arm. 'We'll explain it all.'

Yes, if we can make sense of it...

But that was why it was so good. Because it made so little sense to begin with. But now it was all joining up. All the stuff about pre-cogs and telepaths, and the evil little boy, Jory... And Ella Runciter...

As the end credits ran, they sat back, great sighs of satisfaction and amazement escaping them.

'Fuck, that was good!' Chris said, shaking his head.

Jake looked down. 'It's strange, but it's like that at work some days... All those outrageous-looking avatars. There's even some based on Dick characters. Palmer Eldritch for one... Some of them try to get into your head...'

'How do they do that?' Hugo asked. 'I thought it was all about surfaces and using your senses...'

'It is. But there is penetration.'

There was a comic 'ooh' from several of them at that.

Jake shook his head. 'Come on, now. I'm being serious. That's what it feels like. That they're trying to get right inside your head. They hack in, you see. The datscape acts fast, of course, to shut them down. It doesn't like penetration, but in those first few moments, when they're in... well... they can find out a lot. They can do a hell of a lot of damage.'

'But at a cost, eh?' Alex asked.

'Sure. Those who do it find themselves locked out.'

'But they're expendable?'

'I guess.'

'Our friends again, eh?'

Alex was talking about the Han again, the Chinese. And he was right. They *were* the chief culprits.

Alison stood. 'Look, I'd better get going. I've got an early start.'

Kate stood, smiling at her. 'Must you? I was going to do coffee and some little pastries.'

Unexpectedly, Alison smiled back at her. 'That's kind, but I really must. I need my sleep.'

'*Moi aussi*,' Chris said in his best mock pretentious style, standing and stretching, as if he were suddenly tired. 'We could share a hopper, eh, Hugo?'

Hugo was clearly still thinking about *Ubik*. He looked up, meeting Chris's eyes. 'What's that?'

'Alison's got to go... I was offering her a lift.'

'Oh... we're not staying then?'

Jake grinned. 'As it happens, I've got an early start, too.'

Kate looked to him. 'You didn't say...'

No, and Jake hadn't really thought about it, until a moment ago. But now that he'd thought about it, he was determined. He didn't like being away from the datscape for too long – and eighteen hours seemed a very long time.

He stood, looking to Alison. 'Are you *sure* you won't stay for coffee?'

'No. I must go. I only came because—'

She stopped, conscious that they were all listening.

'Go on,' Jake said, surprised by the strange change in her face.

Alison looked down. 'It's just... my father died. Yesterday. I know how much he and you got on...'

'Oh, Alison...' He stepped forward, as if to hold her, then realized that her body language screamed at him not to make a fuss over it. Besides...

'I didn't know,' Chris said, all sympathy. 'You poor dear...'

'I'm so sorry,' Jake said.

Alison met his eyes. Her own were clear. 'I just wanted to tell you, that's all. For old times' sake.' She looked to Hugo, forcing a half-smile. 'He'd been ill some time, but... it's still a bit of a shock... when you hear...'

Fuck, Jake thought. And now she's alone. No wonder she came.

Her mother had died while they were at Oxford. He had attended the funeral with her; stood at her side while they put the coffin in the ground. And now here she was.

And she was right. They had got on. Like father and son. But when he'd stopped seeing Alison, he'd cut all links to her father.

'He was a lovely man,' he said quietly. 'A really lovely man.'

'Thank you...'

Afterwards, when they were all gone, Kate came over to him.

'She was very pretty.'

'You think so?'

'Yes. Were you lovers?'

'That's very direct of you.'

'I'm a very direct kind of girl.'

He hesitated. 'Yes. We were. And we probably still would be. Only she wanted more than me. More than what I was, anyway.'

Kate had looked down. 'How long were you together?'

'Three years.'

'Ah...'

She hadn't known. But, then, he hadn't told her. Hadn't made anything of it.

She brightened. 'Did you know... Alex got his promotion.'

'What?'

'He's full captain now. Jenny told me when we were out in the kitchen.'

'No wonder he was in such a good mood. I did think it odd. He's usually such a surly bugger. But why didn't he say?'

'Didn't want to take the edge off our news, I guess.'

'That was nice of him.'

'Wasn't it.' She paused then. 'I know you two don't see eye to eye on things, but... he's a good friend.'

'Yeah...' And when he thought about it, he realized it was true. But a captain, eh? In Security. What did that mean? That he was in charge of torturing suspects?

Jake didn't want to think of it, but that was how it was these days. The Oil Crash of twenty-two had jolted politics to the right in a major, some felt irreversible way. Social welfare as a political concept had died, stoned to death by angry, rioting mobs.

'Jake?'

'Yes, my love?'

'Do you really have to go in early? I was thinking maybe we could get up late and have breakfast together on the verandah.'

He wanted to please her. To say yes, why not? Only the datscape called him. Not so much an addiction as a basic need, stronger than sex. Even so, he didn't want to spoil her special evening.

'Okay... but I'm going in at ten, all right?'

She grinned. 'Yes. Now come to bed. I want to drive all thoughts of any other woman from your head.'

'You don't have to...'

'Worry? I don't. But I want to show you that I want you. As you are. I don't need more. I have all I need.'

Jake stared at her. He was a lucky man. He knew that. But just how lucky he hadn't realized until that moment. In that sense it was good that Alison had come tonight. In one regard it was perfect timing, for he knew now he had nothing to regret. He had loved her, yes, but that was in another life. He had been a different person back then.

He took her in his arms. 'Kate... I love you. More than words can possibly say. And the thought of having children with you...' His smile broadened. 'I can't wait...'

She sighed. 'Only you'll have to. Apparently it takes four to six weeks for the effects of the implant to wear off. The body has to adjust...'

He kissed her, mainly to shut her up, but the kiss seemed to light something in them both and after a moment they were tearing at each other's clothes, ignoring the fact that the big panoramic window was unshuttered. It didn't matter.

'Fuck me, Jake,' she said, naked beneath him, her mouth warm against his ear, using that word she never used. 'Just *fuck* me!'

Chapter 5

SOLID AIR

As it turned out, they never had that breakfast. At 5.19 a.m., Greenwich Mean Time, Jake was woken.

It wasn't Trish. It was Daas from Hinton.

'Forgive me, Jake, but you're needed instantly.'

Jake sat up, blearily rubbing at his eyes. Beside him, Kate slept on.

'Hi, Daas. You want me to go into the room?'

'No. You need to come in. I've spoken to George. He says he'll meet you there.'

'I see. I'll shower...'

'A company craft will be on your roof in ten.'

'I'll be there.'

Daas was DAAS4, the Datscape Automated Analysis System, Version 4, an enhanced intelligence unit. Its job was to keep alert to sudden Market shifts.

An alarm bell was ringing. Something urgent was happening.

As he showered, Jake wondered what could possibly have got George Hinton out of bed at this unearthly hour. Something big. It had to be. But what?

Everything had been fine when he'd left, with not a single sign of anything resembling a run. There'd been no tension, no pressure either to buy or sell. No, nor none of those uncertainties that sometimes precipitated a scramble. In fact, nothing unpredictable at all. The Market had been solid.

George met him in the Wiring Room fifteen minutes later.

It was called a Wiring Room because, in earlier incarnations of the datscape, the operatives had stayed outside, literally wired-in to the interface, data pulsing through their synapses. Of course, there were still operatives – 'boardmen' – who performed that function, sat there at the great long curve of a desk, plugged in directly to the mainframe. Their job was to back up the *logins* and process the information – the purchases and sales – that the *logins* made on behalf of their clients. But there was a special room for that now, surrounding the central core where the datscape was held, the 'Dealing Room' as it was known. The "Wiring Room" had become a kind of anteroom; a place where you put on the immersion skin and mask. That done, you were fitted into the harness and pushed through the membrane. Inside.

George was one of the younger Hintons, a nephew, not part of the inner circle, but still an important man, and the fact that he wanted to go inside and see for himself intrigued Jake. George Hinton wasn't at all comfortable in there; he didn't have the *feel* of it, so if he wanted to go and look for himself, then it had to be serious.

'What's going on?' he asked as the engineers fussed about them, fitting their 'skins'.

'It happened an hour back. There was an attack.'

'What kind of attack?'

'That's just it. We're not sure. It was all rather hit and miss. A few companies. Various stocks. It was all made to seem quite random.'

'Only it wasn't.'

'Quite.' George Hinton looked entirely different in the skin.

Even without his mask on, he looked transformed from the business-suited 'chap' he normally was. Not only that but he had developed a middle-age paunch, which the skin accentuated.

Like a fish out of water.

'What do we know for certain?'

'We had five *logins* in at the time, three of whom we've had the chance to debrief...'

'And?'

'That's just it. They saw nothing.'

'But there was damage?'

'Quite considerable damage. But limited. Like they were flexing their muscles.'

'They?'

'As I said, it only happened an hour back. We've not had the chance to analyse it properly just yet. Oh, and before you ask, there's nothing in from MAT. They're keeping this all very quiet.'

MAT was Market Activity Tracking, the Market's own version of DAAS4. It was designed to prevent runs on the Market. To anticipate and act. That they'd not issued a warning suggested that they didn't yet know what they were dealing with.

Jake spoke to the air. 'Daas? Anything to add?'

'Just that the attacks seemed to come from four separate sources, but were timed to coincide.'

'And those sources?'

'Melted away as soon as we put tracers on them. They must have been re-routed twelve to fifteen times.'

So. Serious stuff. Major-league hackers by the sound of it.

'What if it's schoolboys?'

Daas was silent a moment, in case George should choose to field the question. When he didn't, it answered.

'I don't think this is schoolboys, Jake. It was a particularly vicious attack.'

'And schoolboys aren't vicious?'

'Not in this fashion. It was too sophisticated. And besides, we've got information on all the known hackers. This didn't have the fingerprint of any one of them. It was... well... *unique*.'

Daas's choice of that word fed Jake's curiosity. Daas had seen it all before, many times over. It was why it was such a good system. And if Daas didn't recognize something, then maybe it was a big thing.

And there was that phrase George had used. *Flexing their muscles*. Now why would anyone do that? Why draw attention and then run away?

He didn't know. But he was going to find out. He was going to go in and look at the evidence. *Forensically*. Because everything you did in the datscape left a trace.

He followed George, their harnesses jolting along the guide rails.

Inside was a massive sphere, within which hung the *logins*. Compared to the virtual space of the datscape it was incredibly small. Less than a thousandth the size. But it didn't need to be big. It only needed to be large enough for the company's *logins* to hang there, in their harnesses, while data flooded their skins and masks. 'The drying room' some of them called it, because that's what it looked like to the engineers who had to go in there sometimes to make repairs.

It was all an illusion. The very best available.

Jake stepped inside.

He'd not mentioned it yesterday when he'd been making the immersion. Explosion wasn't really the word for it. Sensory overload, more like. Every time he 'stepped' through. Like an all-body orgasm. The drugs from the immersion skin helped, of course, sensitizing him, letting his real skin merge with the artificial one. It was one great data feed, only translated into see, feel, smell and touch. SFST, or a walk down Science Fiction Street, as some wag had called it.

If his avatar had had a cock, it would have been hard every second he was in there.

'Christ,' George said quietly. For a moment he had forgotten.

Jake glanced to his side. George's avatar was hardly subtle. He was a British grenadier from the eighteenth century, complete with cocked hat. A major, by the look of his regalia.

Jake stopped, looking about him at the sweeping vistas of that rainbow-coloured landscape, seeing, in the distance, a number of other figures wandering about.

Everything looks fine. Fine and healthy.

That was the other thing about the datscape. The silence. It was all a great dumb show. Not a cry or echo.

Some companies even hired the deaf, thinking they were perhaps better sensitized to such a place, but Jake knew better. One filled that absence with one's thoughts.

Besides, if anything, the removal of one sense enhanced the others.

To his right, great melted slabs of glaucous blue climbed the air like some nightmare giant's causeway. Beyond them was a riot of sienna and slate-grey crystalline shapes, while to his left, beyond George, piles of tiny blocks of shining amethyst fought for space with massive spikes of olive green. Steaming flows of hot pink lava ate narrow gullies into the surrounding rock-like edifices, whilst just above them to their left, a waterfall of forest green and ivory particles fell in a constant tumble from a ledge of startling black crystal. And always, everywhere, were the data threads, like rainbow-coloured smoke trails.

'Daas? Where the fuck are we heading?'

Daas answered at once. 'I'll put up a guide thread.'

Instantly, a pulsing thread of bright, golden light appeared, snaking its way through the geometric chaos into the distance.

He looked to George and pointed, mouthing the words.

'You go first.'

Like Orpheus in the underworld...

Or like Joe Chip in the half-life world.

Only he knew where he was here. And if there was danger you had only to cut the connection and in an instant you'd be back there, in the drying room, hanging limply in the harness.

Jake smiled and walked on, following the portly figure of the grenadier.

The smell of it hit him from twenty paces away. A sickly sweet, charred kind of a smell. Not healthy, like the smell of cooked meat. This was something rotten, something suggestive of corruption.

'Archer and Simmons,' George said, kneeling over it to conduct an examination, ignoring the stench.

Instantly, Daas fed him data. Archer and Simmons had been bond merchants, specializing in Far Eastern bonds, commodities and London financial futures. Now they were little more than a charred space on the floor of a virtual landscape.

In the real world they would be arriving any time now, to find their doors barred, their company wound up and in administration.

Poor bastards. They never knew what hit them.

'Systematic destruction,' George said, straightening up. 'Only why? Is this someone getting their revenge?'

Jake spoke to Daas. 'Can we see a re-con?'

At once a massive, opaque bubble formed about them. An instant later, the datscape shimmered and then jumped. They were back two hours.

The reconstruction began.

Jake watched. Saw how good a company Archer and Simmons had been. The tiny clusters of purple, grape-like growths that represented it were bulbous and had a healthy shine. You could smell how rich and fine they were.

And then, suddenly, and with a savage intensity that took Jake by surprise, the attack began. For a moment there was nothing, just a kind of pulse in the air, and then a swarm of tiny orange crystals, no bigger than dice, seemed to materialize from nowhere and descend on the grape-like clusters.

It was over in seconds. Literally in seconds.

They slowed it, ran it back.

'Jesus... look at that...'

Slowed down you could see how the tiny crystal shapes attacked, like a pack of jackals, prising the skin of the company open and manoeuvring themselves into the tiny fissures that formed in the bruised purple of the clusters. Once they were in they began to digest it piece by tiny piece, devouring it in moments, leaving only the tiniest traces of it to linger, like some vile calling card.

Leaving just the rotted carcass smell.

Jake stared at it, impressed, but also the tiniest bit afraid. He had never seen its like. This wasn't malware or a virus, not even of the most complex kind. This was different. As different as one species from another, for each crystal had been programmed to work with every other crystal, like a tiny army of super-efficient soldiers. This wasn't hacking in its traditional sense. It went way beyond that. To visually conceive this was one thing – to programme it quite another. As he ran the re-con again and again he realized just how astonishingly complex they were, the code written in counterpoint, like tiny symphonies. Yes. But who could have written anything quite so beautiful, quite so devastatingly destructive?

And one other thing. Where had it all gone? The bonds. The company's assets. If this was a metaphor, what did it represent? Because something must have happened to them. They had to be somewhere, didn't they? Archer and Simmons had been worth six billion Euros. So who had that money now?

George looked to him and shook his head. 'Come, Jake. Let's move on. I want to get this done, before the board meets at ten.'

*

While the board met, Jake went home. Kate had gone, but she had left him a note, propped up on the kitchen table.

Gone to see M & D. See you later. K xxx

Jake smiled. So she'd gone to tell her parents.

He showered again, standing there in the fine hot mist of water while he thought about what he'd seen.

They still had no idea who was behind the attacks. Whoever had written the attack programmes had made sure that the datscape tracers that latched on to them were led a merry dance, this way and that, until they fell off cliff-edges or found themselves in virtual cul-de-sacs.

Exasperated, Jake had run several of the complex 'fox and hound' programmes he had developed for this purpose, trying to discern patterns, to work out just how they had slipped in and out again, under the radar. Trying to get under the skin of what happened, to understand it better.

Only it hadn't worked. Whoever had devised these attacks had known someone like Jake would try something like this. They had anticipated it. Had written it in.

Part of the 'beauty' of these rogues was the fact that they were so efficient, and that had happened because someone had spent a long time analysing the datscape's protection system, looking for its fundamental weaknesses.

Given time, data-shields like MAT and DAAS4 were programmed to deal with such intrusions. However, they had first to identify them. Thus there was a delay in responding. Not a long delay – in both cases it was less than four seconds, real time – but a delay nonetheless. A *hiatus* in which an aggressive interloper could break in and cause havoc.

All four of the attacking viruses had played on that. The longest had taken 2.357 seconds start to finish, the shortest a mere 1.670 seconds. All four had been tightly coordinated, such that the intrusion took just 2.623 seconds in its entirety.

Daas hadn't stood a chance. By the time it had realized they were hostiles they were gone, leaving smoke trails and a false scent.

Not only that, but each was quite distinct. One tore its victim-host apart. Another stripped it to shreds. The third vaporized its victim. And the last – Jake smiled as he thought about it – the fourth had simply frozen the assets of the company it had attacked. Left them intact but made them valueless. He wasn't sure how they had done it, but they had.

So. Four coordinated attacks on four quite random, unconnected targets, each of them frighteningly efficient. Each utterly untraceable.

Muscle flexing. That's what George had said. But by whom?

The truth was, he didn't have a clue. Couldn't begin to think who could benefit from this.

Maybe George was right. Maybe it was school kids. Geeks. After all, there was a long history on the internet of smart-arse kids fucking about with so-called 'secure' systems. Why shouldn't this be simply another instance?

It was a possibility, but a very remote one. Because it would take an absolute genius to have devised those programmes. A regular Beethoven of the computer keyboards, a Michelangelo.

Or four teams of slightly lesser talents, each team working on a single programme. For *years*.

The idea, once he'd had it, stuck.

Okay. But who would put the money into that kind of intensive research. And why?

He didn't know. Not yet. But he would.

Jake dried himself, then sat down at his console in the bedroom.

'Trish... give me what you know about GenSyn.'

'Is that wise, Mister Reed?'

He turned, looking to the ceiling, as if she were physically there. 'I'll be the judge, thank you, Trish. I'm not going to see her again, if that's what you're thinking. I'm just interested, that's all.'

There was a second's delay, then Trish responded.

'On-screen, or shall I give you a summation?'

'Just tell me, Trish...salient facts. When the company was formed, how it's doing, what it's developing.'

'And your friend?'

He smiled. 'Make it brief. I'm just intrigued as to why she joined them.'

'Okay. The company was formed twenty years back, in 2023, by Gustav Ebert and his brother Wolfgang.'

'What lovely names...'

'Gustav, it seems, was a genetics specialist. He'd been working at the University of Heidelberg. He'd done his doctorate there and stayed on to do pure research. It was while he was there that he came up with something. A year later he had formed the company with his brother.'

Jake interrupted. 'Came up with something... what do you mean by that?'

'It's not clear. He's never specified in any of the interviews he's done since. But within the first ten years of its existence, GenSyn registered over three hundred and forty patents with the WPO, all of them within the field of modified genetics.'

'I see... and the finance for all this?'

'Wolfgang was the financial genius. He raised sufficient capital up front to build his brother a new block of labs and, three years down the line, a fully mechanized factory just outside of Bremen. They call it "The Farm".'

'Any reason for that?'

'It seems that one of the things they specialized in is modified animals, for the pet market. Super-intelligent mice, that sort of thing.'

'And the others?'

'The *other*... Enhanced human replacements.'

He waited, knowing Trish would explain.

'Their clientele is very rich,' Trish said. 'They don't deal with just anyone. It might interest you to know that your own CEO, Charles Hinton, is among them.'

'And what did he buy from GenSyn?'

'It isn't specified,' Trish said. Only Jake knew she was keeping that information from him. And who could blame her? She *belonged* to the Hinton organization, after all.

'But what kind of thing do they provide?'

'Replacement organs. Replacement limbs. Full-body doubles.'

'Sorry? Body doubles? What do you mean?'

'Precisely that. Genetically precise copies of their clients' bodies. They grow them, it seems, in vats.'

Now why the hell haven't I heard of this before? Or was I simply not attending when that was on the news?

'And these doubles... these *golem*... are they alive?'

'Physically, yes. Mentally... no. They have no intelligence whatsoever.'

Jake shivered at the thought. So that's what the ultra-rich are spending their money on these days. They've done with yachts and private jets. Now they're buying themselves new bodies, to replace the old ones when they wear out.

'Okay... and they're doing well out of this?'

'Very well indeed.'

'Then why haven't I come across them in my work?'

'Because they're still a private company. There are only two shareholders...'

'Gustav and Wolfgang?'

'Yes.'

'And Alison's role in this?'

'Is precisely what she said it was. She looks at new projects and evaluates whether or not they're worth pursuing. The Eberts think very highly of her. If she says yes to something, then they put money behind it. If she says no...'

'It's no.' Jake smiled. Some things never changed. 'Okay. Forget I ever asked.'

'It's forgotten already.'

Jake stood, meaning to go and dress, but Trish hadn't quite finished.

'One other thing,' she said. 'A little bit of gossip. About Ubik...'

He sat down again. 'Go on...'

'It's about Drew Ludd. He's finally signed a deal with Chinese media agents *Huang Chin Shih Tai*...'

'Never! I thought he said he'd rather erase everything he'd ever done...'

'That is what he said. But he's struck a deal. A very good one, too. He's all set to become the biggest grossing actor in Hollywood, dead or alive!'

Drew Ludd was the actor who had played Joe Chip in the media drama of *Ubik*. Until now he had been Hollywood's most vehement opponent to 'morphing' – the use of computer-generated actors' faces, gestures and voices by studios and advertising agencies. Thus far he had insisted on doing things 'the old way', using live performances and working with a cast of real actors. But now, it seems, he had sold out to the highest bidder.

'Do you think it was just a bidding ploy, then, Trish?'

'There's a lot of commentators who are saying that, but there's also a feeling that HCST offered so much that he just couldn't turn it down. There's word that he's giving half his future earnings to charity.'

Jake whistled. That would do him no harm, either. He was already the most popular actor on the planet.

'Have they said anything about what kind of thing we're going to see him in?'

'Well... rumour has it that they plan to re-make the old TV show, *Band of Brothers*, with Drew Ludd playing alongside Spencer Tracy, Marlon Brando, Robert De Niro, James Dean, Daniel Day-Lewis,

Al Pacino, Peter O'Toole, Charlton Heston, Kirk Douglas, Elvis Presley and John Wayne.'

Jake nodded. He liked the sound of that. What he didn't like was when media companies used their licences to bring out crap. The *Shou Wei* company, for instance, had spent a fortune acquiring the late Johnny Depp's image-package, together with those of a whole number of nubile young actresses, only to bring out a stream of hardcore porn movies. It wasn't right, especially as in most cases the actors themselves weren't alive to defend themselves against such exploitation.

'Thanks, Trish. Is that all?'

'That's all.'

Jake dressed, then pottered about for a while in the kitchen, making himself a late breakfast. He would have preferred to have been at work, there inside the datscape, but George had wanted him out, along with all their other *logins*, until they knew for sure what they were dealing with.

In one way that made sense. In another...

He had kept thinking about it. The only way to trace it was to be there when it happened. To have a whole team of them, hundreds strong, inside there, waiting for something to show up and then reacting instantly, not four seconds later when it was too late.

He was standing there, lost in his thoughts, when Hugo rang through.

'Jake? You there?'

He put the wall on visual. 'Hugo? What's up?'

Hugo beamed down at him from the big panel that filled the upper half of the kitchen wall, twice life-size.

'Just wanted to let you know. I met up with Carl this morning. He's real cute, isn't he? Offered me a job, too. Not that I'm going to take it, only... well, it's nice to be flattered.'

'It's not flattery, Hugh... you're good at what you do. Maybe the best.'

'Don't overdo it now. I know how good I am... and how far short I am from being the best. But I like what I heard.'

'What's the offer, then?'

'Soundtracks... he's linked up with some big Chinese media company... *Huang Chin*—'

'*Shih Tai*,' Jake finished for him.

'How'd you know that? Did he say something?'

Jake told him about the Drew Ludd deal. Hugo whistled.

'Christ... you don't think...?'

'I imagine they have hundreds of projects on the go at any one time.'

'Yeah... and I doubt they'd want to use a novice first time out...'

'No, but it'd be nice, eh? You can dream...'

Hugo grinned. 'Yeah... and I kept thinking to myself, what a nice arse this guy's got...'

'Hugo!'

'Oh, I know... but I can look, can't I?'

After Hugo had signed off, Jake sat there, feeling at a loose end. Maybe he should contact Kate and see how she was, find out if she'd told her parents yet and how they'd reacted.

He could picture their delight. Only even as he made to connect, George's voice filled the air.

'Jake... are you there?'

He sounded breathless, agitated.

Jake stood. 'What is it?'

'Something's happening. I think you should get back here.'

'I'll be there at once.'

'Right.' And George cut. No formalities, he just cut, which was the surest indication of how serious things were, because George never forgot the formalities.

'Trish. Get me a hopper.'

'It'll be here in two.'

'Ah... right...'

George must have ordered it.

'Trish... do we know *anything* about what went on in that board room?'

'Nothing. It's all level-A.'

'Right... Then let Kate know I'll probably be late.'

It wasn't really necessary. Trish always knew best what to do. But it gave him the illusion that he was still in charge, and who knew, after what he'd seen earlier, whether they were in charge of things or not. Only time would tell. Time and, he hoped, a little bit of luck.

As he stepped inside he could feel the wind blowing and knew a change was coming to the Market. The wind, like all else, was an indicator. Its strength reflected the flow of stocks and shares, the amount of trade that was taking place.

A warm wind boded well. A cold one...

Jake shivered. There was a distinctly icy edge to this wind. It was an East Wind, blowing over a landscape of extraordinary forms. Things had changed in the hour or so that he'd been gone. There were cracks now in the surface of the datscape, like fault lines, crusts forming and crumbling over the bubble and heave. He looked about him, noting how the surface of everything was sweating now. That always happened when the Market got as volatile as this.

Only why? What had set this off?

Usually it was obvious. Normally, in this place where geometry met geology, one could trace its every stage, its every movement. But today was different. That wind was like a faint but steady pressure. It felt... *fake* somehow, like someone was forcing things, was artificially driving prices down. But how could that be?

George had met him outside, in the Wiring Room.

'What did they say?' Jake asked. 'What's the plan of action?'

'There isn't one. They just want you to go back in there. Try and calm things down. Steady things. The Market's edgy after that attack.'

'They still think it's schoolboys?'

'I told them what you said, Jake. About the complexity of the programming. But I think they could see that for themselves. We got the MAT report while we were in session...'

'And?'

'They haven't a clue, either. But this new development... it has to be linked, don't you think?'

Jake didn't know how, but it made sense. This new *pressure* on the Market came too soon after the other not to be connected.

Maybe what happened earlier was them firing off a few shots, testing them to see if they worked. Finding their range. Maybe the big bombardment was yet to come.

It was a crazy way to think of things, but what other way suggested itself?

He walked on, feeling the crunch of tiny pellets beneath his boots. It was warm in this sector, a faint tang of citrus and rosebuds contrasted with the strong metallic odour of some nearby mineral stacks.

The wind gusted. Things shimmered, trembled, rattled silently. A flurry of azure dust gusted by, leaving a frosting of dark blue crystals on his arm.

Jake slowly turned 360 degrees, taking everything in.

Where's the source of this? Or is this so subtle that it's coming from a thousand different sources?

Follow the wind, he told himself. Check out its source.

Yet even as he thought that, even as he took the first step towards it, so he felt something else. The sensation that something had latched on to him. That his feed was suddenly contaminated.

There was an expression for this. *Being ridden.*

Jake reacted immediately. 'George... flush me through. I think I've got a rider.'

A second later he felt the surge as his sensory feed was dumped then re-established. It made him stagger but he didn't fall. What's more he was alone again. The intruder had been shaken off.

'Put up blocks. And a trace. I want to know who's jumping on my back.'

It happened sometimes. Other traders, not necessarily *logins*, tried to get a free ride – looking through his eyes and using his experience to make money. But this felt different. It was as if they'd wanted him to know he was being watched.

Only why would they do that?

Ahead the land sloped down, an outgrowth like a giant pile of melted orange sugar blocked his path. Jake eased round it, jumping over a narrow stream of aquamarine ooze that flowed sluggishly down its track.

And stopped dead, facing what looked like two identical huge red beetles. The two of them stood upright on their jointed back legs, their forearms and antennae twitching.

Jake had never seen them before; never, in all his travels in the datscape, encountered anything like them. You met all kinds of weird and crazy avatars but he had rarely come across any that were quite so hostile as this pair. It was like they were physically blocking his way.

Only this was the datscape. It wasn't etiquette, but he could walk right through them if he wished.

'Who are they?'

'We're tracing now,' Joel, the senior engineer, answered.

'Hi, Joel... Where's George?'

'He's been called away.'

'Ah...'

Three seconds passed. The two giant beetles held their position.

'They work for the *Chung Kuo Ts'ang K'u*, the China Storehouse. It seems they've had a corporate redesign. The dat's crawling with them.'

'Well, can you ask them to fuck off out of my way?'

Joel sounded amused. 'We'll ask them nicely.'

A further ten seconds passed. The beetles moved aside. But even as Jake made his way past, he sensed them turn and watch him go, as if interested in him for some particular reason. Only, again, why should that be?

I'm getting paranoid, he thought. I've been watching too much *Ubik*, that's what it is.

And walked on, following the wind.

The pressure on the Market was sustained for the best part of six hours, and then it eased. Ten minutes later it was gone. The 'air' inside the datscape was untroubled once more. The wind had ceased to blow.

'What's the damage?' Jake asked as he peeled out of his suit.

'To us? Not much. A couple of hundred million...'

'And the Market in general?'

'Three or four trillion.'

Jake had followed the wind. He had traced it back to source, only whenever he thought he'd got there, the source had vanished. The wind had changed. Was blowing from somewhere else.

Weird, he thought. Really fucking bizarre.

But others had reported the same experience. And MAT, which recorded everything, had no answers either. Again there was a randomness to things that was hard to understand.

Because who in their right mind would want to lose money? Who could possibly benefit by depressing the Market and driving down prices? Who but a madman? And madmen generally didn't have the money to operate at this level. So that ruled that one out.

Jake went home, to find that Kate had been and gone.

'She said she'll be back later,' Trish advised him. 'I believe she's gone shopping. She said she needed a few things.'

Jake felt tired now. He had had barely three hours' sleep last night, and what with the nervous tension of the day...

'Trish... I'm going to put my head down for a bit. Wake me if it's anything important. Otherwise, say that I'm out... that I'm... well, shopping with Kate.'

Only sleep didn't come easy. His mind wouldn't let go of the problem.

In the end he got up again and, making himself some coffee, sat there with an old-fashioned pen and notebook, jotting down anything that came into his head.

So what did he know?

The red beetles for a start. He hadn't liked the red beetles. And not just the first two he'd run into, but the rest of them. A regular infestation, it had been.

That was how some companies liked it, of course. They wanted to emphasize that their employees were team players, not mavericks. But you could take that too far.

What had Joel said? The *Chung Kuo Ts'ang K'u*... the China Storehouse. He'd look into that one for a start.

Not that there was necessarily any connection. In fact, the more he thought about it, the more it didn't fit with the rest of it. It was too upfront. Too easy to check on.

It was probably only coincidence that they'd had a corporate redesign at the same time this had blown up. As for their belligerence...

Jake smiled. They probably weren't very nice people. After all, it took all sorts to make a market.

So what else?

He had barely got going when Kate returned.

'Hey,' he said, getting up and going over to her. 'I'm really sorry about this morning.'

She let herself be kissed and fussed over. Jake sat her down and poured her a glass of wine, then sat across from her.

'Well? Were they pleased?'

Kate lit up. 'They were just so happy. I thought Mum was going to explode with happiness.'

'And your dad?'

'You know how he is. All very laid back. But I could see he was excited. Deep down. He likes you, Jake. They both like you.'

'And I like them... which is why we ought to have them round. For a special celebratory dinner. Would you like that?'

'I'd love it.'

'Then you can organize it. Get what you want. Something special, maybe.'

'Can I?'

'Sure.'

She hesitated, then asked, 'What was it? Why did you have to go in so early?'

'There's been a bit of a run, that's all.'

'But I thought the Market was fine. I thought... well, everything seems so rosy. All the signs...'

'Are good. So don't worry. It'll right itself. We just have to calm the jitters, that's all. Make sure that people don't lose confidence.'

Kate smiled. She was reassured. Just like that. If Jake said it was okay, it was okay. She trusted him.

But Jake himself was worried, not by the severity of things – he'd seen the Market in good times and bad – but by the lack of explanation. The fact that they had no idea where this was coming from.

'Kate?'

'Yes, my love?'

'I might have to go in again... later on. They might need me.'

'Okay.'

She didn't argue. Didn't sulk. And that was why she'd make such a good wife, he realized. He was just so lucky in that regard. He knew other *logins* whose marriages were really under pressure. Others who had split up. But Kate wasn't like that. She understood him.

'Jake?'

'Yes...'

'Let's skip dinner. Let's just go straight to bed again, eh?'

He should have slept. Tired as he was, he ought to have slept. Only he couldn't. Something was happening in the world, something big, and he couldn't shake that from his mind. Even as Kate slept on beside him, her gentle snoring filling the room, Jake found himself thinking back and analysing the situation, reminding himself just how they had got to this point.

The Oil Crash of 2022 had been the turning point, the 'make or break' moment for them all. Jake had been three when it had happened, and had experienced, through infant eyes, the bewilderment of the months that followed. It was globally catastrophic, but the problems had been there a long time, a decade and more before he was born, in those heady days when China had first emerged as an economic superpower.

It was hard to think of now, but only sixty years ago China had been a Third World country, militarily strong but powerless economically; at best a sleeping giant whom no one thought could escape the lethargy of its recent past, or the tight control of its communist regime.

Deng Hsiao Ping had changed that. He had freed China from its shackles, and in the next three decades China had grown... and grown and grown.

And therein lay the seeds of future problems.

At first that growth was beneficial, and not just to China. For as China became the manufacturing hub of the world economy, so prices came down. In that first golden glow of globalization, everything looked rosy. Four hundred million Chinese were raised from poverty. China boomed. But the cracks in the great edifice were there from the outset.

By 2009 the United States' net international debts had reached a staggering three trillion dollars. At the same time, China, by maintaining an artificially low exchange rate, had built its own foreign exchange reserves up past the two trillion dollars mark. In one sense this was a good thing. China's purchase of low-yield US bonds and bills had kept money cheap and international interest rates low. They had fuelled the boom. But it could not go on.

For a time things held together, even as recession slowed China's growth from the steady 10 per cent it had enjoyed. But the cracks were growing larger. As China's trade had grown – as its vast infrastructure had expanded, filling the eastern coastal plains – so its voracious need for raw materials had grown with it. Slowly the negatives had begun to outweigh the positives.

Meanwhile, in America, the protectionist lobby, suspicious to the point of paranoia over China's intentions, grew more and more vociferous. The Republicans, coming to power in the shadow of the deepest recession in memory, wanted to do away with free trade. In a frenzy of nationalistic rhetoric, they sought to replace globalization with protectionist tariffs. They wanted to pull up the economic drawbridge, just as their predecessors had after the Wall Street Crash of the late 1920s. 'Buy American' was their slogan.

It was a mistake. When the inevitable crisis came there was not the will to solve it. The USA reintroduced tariffs in 2016 and in the years after the world came close to war, not once but on three separate occasions.

Africa was the first flashpoint.

China's links to Africa went back to the 1960s and the years of the Cultural Revolution. Back then the USA and Russia, locked into Cold War mentalities, had used Africa as a covert battlefield, their opposed ideologies tending to destroy whatever they came into contact with. China, however, took a different path. It had helped build infrastructure, becoming Africa's friend. Then, in 2000, with a new industrial revolution taking place at home, the Chinese once again looked to Africa, investing billions of dollars and sending hundreds of thousands of workers to kick-start African industry. That was just the start. By 2018 over forty million Chinese had emigrated there and close on two hundred and fifty billion dollars had been invested.

It was hardly altruistic. China *needed* Africa. Needed its untapped resources – its platinum and copper, its iron ore and gold, its coal and wood. And more than anything, its oil.

As push came to shove and the price of oil per barrel soared to four hundred dollars, the USA responded angrily. In a session of the United Nations in March 2019, perhaps frustrated at being shut out of the by-now lucrative African market, it had accused China of 'colonizing' the dark continent. More than that, it had demanded that China's 'special relationship' with thirty-eight African states be examined by the World Trade Organization and those countries 'opened up' to international trade.

China's response had been blunt, and memorable. Their delegate had stood and, in perfect English, told the American delegate: 'Go fuck yourself!'

What had followed was six months of tit-for-tat legislation, each of the two great superpowers vying to outdo the other in sheer pettiness. By Christmas 2019, any pretence of being trading partners was gone. As, effectively, was globalization. The days of free trade were over. Protectionism was now the key. The world economy began its slow slide.

Then, two years later, another flashpoint.

By then the recession was beginning to bite. America's close neighbours (Mexico, Venezuela, Costa Rica, Panama, Nicaragua, Guatemala and El Salvador), facing a massive economic downturn, did what had been unimaginable only ten years earlier and linked themselves politically with the now rampantly right-wing giant that had for so long dictated their policies. Plebiscites were held, and in all seven countries an overwhelming yes vote was delivered. On 29th October 2021 the United States of America became the

'Fifty-Seven States'. Over the next three years it was to add another twelve – including its biggest neighbour, Canada.

Before then, however, one other event threatened to shake the tree, and once more it was to do with oil.

Back in the heady days of expansion – in 2008 – China had struck a deal with its neighbour Burma, to build a nine-hundred-mile-long oil line from Kyaukphyu, on Burma's western coast, through Mandalay to Kunming in China's Yunnan Province.

It was a visionary venture, for until then, 80 per cent of China's oil had had to come through the Strait of Malacca, a channel of water about five hundred miles in length that was 'policed' at one end by the US naval base at Changi in Singapore, and at the other by the US Indian Ocean Fleet, operating out of Diego Garcia.

For China this was equivalent to the US having its fingers on their windpipe, even with the extra oil from Burma. It could not be tolerated, and led to the fast-track construction of a Chinese deep-sea fleet, further raising military tensions.

Even so, all might have been well and the balance kept, except that in November 2021, just four weeks after the formation of the Fifty-Seven, the Attorney General of the United States expelled more than fifty Chinese embassy officials in response to yet another Chinese spy plot.

China followed suit, expelling more than two hundred Americans.

Stubbornness became belligerence. By the end of that first week, and in the shadow of a further twenty-dollar rise in oil prices, the US threatened to blockade the Strait of Malacca unless China backed down.

It was now a matter of face.

For the next four days, as shipping ground to a halt, China was entirely dependent on its Burmese pipeline. War seemed imminent. And then it happened. The oil pipe was attacked and blown up, thirty miles south-west of Mandalay.

The United States denied any involvement. In fact, it protested its innocence. Even so, the world held its breath.

At urgent meetings over the next forty-eight hours, senior officials from both sides desperately cobbled together a peace. A treaty was signed. The world drew back from the edge.

Only the damage had been done.

China, in particular, was suffering now. While the slowdown had not been as catastrophic as some had predicted, it *had* caused problems, especially in the countryside, where the margin between eating and starvation had always been slender.

For years there had been local uprisings against corrupt officials. China's communist elite had accepted this as the price of modernization. Now, however, as the markets slumped and oil prices reached a peak, that fragile margin vanished. The spectre of starvation faced the seven hundred million who lived in rural China and the revolts began.

Anhua, in Hunan Province, was the first. 'Old Mud Legs', as the peasant farmers were known, had had enough. Local officials were strung up. Two thousand peasants marched on the nearby town. They burned down government buildings and looted government storehouses. The authorities tried to suppress news of what had happened, but it had already leaked out on the internet. Local farmers, seeing it, joined the angry protest. Within the hour, Taojiang, Yiyang, Wangchang and a dozen more northern Hunan towns were in flames.

The army was sent in. Two battalions from the regional capital, Chang Sha. Drawn from distant provinces – a measure the government had taken to try to avoid local boys having to subdue their own 'brothers' – the soldiers ought to have stayed loyal to their commanders. Only they didn't. They understood the farmers' plight only too well – weren't they the sons of farmers themselves? – and they refused to fire on them.

The riots spread. To Sichuan and Hubei, to Henan and Shantung and Kuei Cho. Soon every province had its burning towns. There was talk that the 'Mandate of Heaven' had been broken and that the leadership would have to stand down.

It was then, on the fifth day, that they acted.

Word of it flooded the news media just after dawn. Peasants, waking to another day of protest and violence, found themselves instead staring at the big TV screens in their local towns and watching an unbelievable scene.

From above it seemed as if the sea was full, from horizon to horizon, of ships – Chinese navy ships – while overhead hundreds of planes, fighters and transporters, filled the sky.

The invasion of Taiwan had begun.

Since 1949, when the remnants of Chang Kai Shek's *Kuomingtang* army had fled to what was then known as Formosa, the communists had wanted Taiwan back – to unify the Middle Kingdom and make it whole again, ending the long years of humiliation at Western hands. A defence treaty between Taiwan and the United States had meant China had held its hand all these years, but now they played it, meaning to take the country by force, whatever the cost in lives.

It was cynical, of course. An act of desperation in the face of civil war. But it worked. No more buildings were burned – unless they were those owned by Americans. 'Old Mud Legs' stopped his shouting of angry anti-government slogans and stood in curious groups before whatever screen was available, watching the unfolding of events with bated breath.

The United States reacted instantly. The diplomatic agreement between the two powers, which had stood since 1st January 1979, was torn up. The US sent its Seventh Fleet north. Fighters were scrambled from on board the *Abraham Lincoln* and the *Enterprise*.

Jake had seen only recently – on the History Channel – what had happened next. For a full three days the two great fleets had faced each other in the Strait of Taiwan. The Chinese flagship, the *Hung*

Se Huang Ti (or 'Red Emperor'), pride of their deep-sea fleet, sailing north, shadowed by four US destroyers, then south again, like some ancient warrior king riding out on the battlefield in front of his army.

And all the while the rhetoric grew and grew. China must have Taiwan, and how could that possibly be resolved except by violence?

Even so, both sides held back from escalating the conflict. No one wanted to be the first to use nuclear weapons. Both fleets had missiles enough to blow each other to kingdom come, but neither used them yet.

And then, at the eleventh hour, just as the rhetoric reached a crescendo and it seemed war was impossible to avoid, the US withdrew, leaving the battlefield – and Taiwan – to the Chinese.

It was as abrupt as it was shocking. One minute it seemed as if it was the prelude to Armageddon, the next the Chinese were wading ashore unopposed, along the two-hundred-mile-long stretch of coast between Taipei and Kaohsiung.

China, the Middle Kingdom had been reunited.

Only later, as word leaked out of what had really happened, did the withdrawal make any sense. A deal had been made at the highest level. The last of all such deals between the two, as it turned out. The world was to be divided up into two spheres of influence. The East would go to China, the West to America, as when the New World was divided up between Portugal and Spain by the Treaty of Tordesillas in 1494, five centuries before. The USA had abandoned Taiwan. Had traded it for a bigger slice of the global cake.

No one else was consulted. It was done, and Taiwan was the deal clincher. The Battle of the Taiwan Strait – potentially the biggest single battle between two superpowers – gave way to 'The Taiwan Compromise'.

As it turned out, however, events were to overtake them. China might have solved its internal crisis, and America fashioned an empire of sorts, but oil was still the number one problem. Even as the two great superpowers strove to lay their new foundations, so that problem escalated.

The oil was running out, and in the last week of May 2022 the problem became a crisis and, in a matter of days, the crisis became a crash.

Oil production – artificially maintained at a high level – peaked then began to fall away dramatically. And as it fell, so companies fell with it. By the middle of June demand outstripped supply by seven billion barrels a day.

A modern, oil-based economy was no longer viable. Catastrophic recession was about to hit the world hard. Things were going to have to change.

Jake remembered how his own father had come home that day, a look of sorrow and bewilderment on his face, to tell them that he had been laid off. He was no longer an insurance broker. He had joined the long ranks of the unemployed.

As it turned out, his father had found another job, and they had done all right. But the UK, like most of the world, underwent radical changes in the years that followed. There was a massive swing to the right. And, with it, a massive polarization of society. In the convulsion of that year, a new modern world was formed.

It was an uneasy birth and as the divide between rich and poor, have and have-not, widened to a gulf, there was increasing social unrest. Rioting and acts of terrorism characterized those first few years after the Crash. In the UK, as in so many Western countries, the right-wing government, elected on a populist mandate, began a crackdown. Many complained that they were living in a police state, and it was not far from the truth. But the public unrest settled. Slowly life improved. Only things had changed. There were two camps now, two kinds of citizen. And a third kind, who weren't even citizens. The unprotected, or UPs.

Jake sighed. It was the world he knew. The world he'd grown up in.

For a time he slept. The sleep of innocents and fools. And then he woke.

Daas woke him. For a moment he wasn't sure where he was. He had been dreaming. In the dream an army of bright red scarab beetles had appeared one by one from nowhere, unfolding, it seemed, from solid air, like baby universes.

He sat up, knuckling his eyes, then glanced at the sleeper-clock.

4.17 a.m.

Christ, he thought. *What now?*

He got ready, then went up onto the roof to wait.

Ten minutes later, sitting there in the shadows at the back of the hopper, waiting for clearance, the great dark sprawl of London spread out below, the City a bright-lit fortress embedded in its midst, Jake found himself thinking of the past.

The years had shaped the landscape down below. From pagan settlement to Roman town and on through the centuries to now, men had come and gone and left their mark on the land, expanding and extending, though rarely with anything like the fervour of the last twenty years. Yes, while the greater world had suffered, some, like himself, had thrived. So it was. So it had always been. Nothing stayed the same for long. Nothing ever did.

Jake snapped out of his reverie as the hopper lifted off.

'Are you all right, Mister Reed?'

'I'm fine, Sam.'

'Sorry about the delay. They're ultra-cautious tonight for some reason.'

'That's okay.'

'And the Market...?'

Jake looked across at the pilot. 'Why, what have you heard?'

Sam hesitated. 'It's just... signs... you being here at this hour, for instance. But yeah... there's a vibe. Rumours... a feeling that things aren't quite right.'

'You pilots discuss this kind of stuff?'

'Not usually, but... well, today's felt different. I don't know why...'

Joel was waiting for him in the entrance hall. He was still wearing his wiring suit, his long-lens data glasses slung about his neck.

'How's the Market?' Jake asked, going over to him.

'Quiet...'

'Then what...?'

Joel took his arm and led him aside, away from the reception desk so they wouldn't be overheard. He seemed excited.

'We've heard from MAT.'

'And?'

Joel smiled. 'We've been accepting that what we saw in the datscape was what went on. It wasn't.'

'What do you mean?'

'I mean they've been using what MAT call perception distorters. Imagine a programme that takes what's there in the datscape and feeds it back to us as something else. A programme that distorts not merely how we see it, but how it feels and smells. How we *perceive* it as a totality.'

'Perception distorters... So it was there all the time?'

'Staring us right in the face. The rogues didn't appear from nowhere, they were in the data threads.'

'And how did MAT find that out?'

'They've got four dead spinners.'

'Ah...'

Jake almost laughed. It was obvious when you thought about it. After all, the only way to get a programme into the datscape was through the data nodes, and the only way to do that was to go through the guys who fed in the data: the 'spinners' as they were known. The rogues would have ridden in on the data threads, their presence masked by the fact that yet another programme – a perception distorter – was sending back a signal that simply didn't register to the observing sensory equipment.

'It's an amazing programme,' Joel said. 'We're calling it IM.'

'IM?'

Joel smiled. 'Invisible Man...'

'And the four dead spinners?'

'No links whatsoever, as far as they can establish.'

'Yet the attacks were coordinated to within a fraction of a second. Do we know *how* they were killed?'

'They're checking that out right now.'

'Oh, but they must know by now...'

Joel had gone quiet. 'Word is they were suicides.'

'Suicides?'

That made no sense. No sense at all. Why would four men who didn't know each other kill themselves? What possible motivation might they have had? Was this some new form of terrorism?

The glass door across from them swished open. It was George.

'Joel... Jake... You've heard the news?'

They followed him through, into the interior.

As George and Jake skinned up, Joel went to his desk to check on the situation inside the datscape.

'So what's the plan?' Jake asked.

George met his eyes. 'I want to have another look. Now that we know how, I want to see if there's anything we might have missed first time round.'

Jake couldn't see how, but George was his line-boss and if George wanted another look...

'How is it?' George asked, looking past Jake to Joel, who had just returned.

'Much as it was. Trade has slowed since the attacks. Word's got out and people are a little jittery, but it'll pick up. Now that we know what to look for...'

Jake stopped what he was doing. Was that it? Was all of this just a feint? To make them look in one direction when the attack was coming from another?

Maybe. But it all kept coming back to one question. Who in god's name would want to do this? Suicides. No, it made no sense at all.

They went in, the sensory rush washing over them.

Standing close by and to his left, the portly grenadier lifted his arm and pointed. 'That way, I think...'

It was quiet. *Unnaturally* quiet. In a metaphorical sense.

The datscape was a twenty-four-hour-a-day phenomenon, open everywhere and all the time. It never ceased. But this felt like it must have felt back in the old days, in the gap between when one market closed and another, on the far side of the world, opened.

Jittery wasn't the word for it. Afraid, more like.

Yes, people were afraid.

Are we really that fragile? Jake asked himself, as he clambered down a slope of cornsilk rocks.

Even the data threads seemed listless. They lacked the pulse and vibrancy they normally possessed.

George's voice sounded in his head. 'Is it me, Jake, or has this whole place gone to sleep?'

Jake nodded. 'It's not you, George. It's...'

He stopped. The wind... it had begun to blow again. Faintly, like a silent rustling in the branches or the slightest rippling of a stream. He could feel it on his chest and arms and on his face. A gentle breeze that made the hairs stand up.

He shivered. Across from him George was looking about him.

'Where's it coming from?'

Jake licked his finger and held it up.

'There,' he said, pointing east. 'Right there.'

'What's happening?' George asked Joel, keeping his channel to Jake open so Jake could hear.

'I don't know,' Joel said uncertainly. 'We're trying to get a trace. Daas is on to it... Oh!'

That 'Oh!' made Jake stop in his tracks.

'*What?* What is it?'

'There was a jump... I don't know... like a power surge. Didn't you feel it?'

Jake shook his head. 'No... George...?'

'It doesn't feel right, does it?'

Jake closed his eyes. Did it feel right? It didn't feel *wrong*...

'Let's press on,' he said. 'Do what we came to do and get out.'

The wind blew a little stronger. Beneath Jake's feet, a tiny rivulet of dark magenta grew agitated.

'Someone's dumping stock.'

'What kind of stock?' George asked, pre-empting Jake's explanation.

'Animal foodstuffs. Media. Industrials. Consumer goods...'

'Random stuff, then?'

'Looks that way...'

'So who's dealing?'

'Small traders mostly... maybe they've heard something...'

'Heard what? It doesn't work that way.'

'It isn't *supposed* to. But what if they've been talking outside the loop? Anyway, nothing's happening. There's no reason anyone should be selling.'

'Right,' George said. 'Only they are. And you know what it's like... unless we put a damper on this and quick...'

'How are we going to do that, George?'

'Government intervention.'

'The UK couldn't afford it...'

'I don't just mean us. I mean internationally. Like in 2008. Get the central banks to calm things down.'

'Is that what you discussed the other day?'

'One of the things.'

'So you anticipated this?'

George turned to face him, conscious that they could be overheard, if someone really wanted to overhear them.

'We discussed a lot of options. But we were agreed on one thing. The attacks were a prelude. To what we don't know. But something's happening, and we've got to be ready to respond to it.'

Flexibility, Jake thought. That's the key. That's what will see us through.

Only what if their rival's game plan included that?

Jake sat in George Hinton's office, a big bulb glass of brandy in one hand, listening in as George reported back to his uncle, Harry, who was Head of Strategic Planning.

The wind had blown all morning, strong and cold, like a hand pushing against their backs, though never hard enough to warrant action. No. Because for all George's talk of intervention, action at this point would merely have fed the fires. Would have paradoxically confirmed that there was a problem.

No. They had to keep their nerve and only act when things got bad. That was the way with the Market. It had always been the way.

Confidence. That was the secret. Confidence.

'... true, true...' George was saying, 'only I don't see how. The brokers we've spoken with confirm what MAT discovered. It's customer-led. They've had specific instructions to sell. And when you're told to sell by your clients, you sell. It's a free market...'

Yes, Jake thought. But is it? Or does someone stand to make a lot of money?

And that was where he ran up against a wall, every time. Because what other motive could there be? Speculation. It was the blood and sinew of the system. And there *had* to be a profit to be made, even if he couldn't see how.

And if *he* could make a profit?

Jake considered it a moment. Would it be so wrong to capitalize on this? To make money out of this misery? Wasn't that what his instincts cried out to do? In normal circumstances he wouldn't have hesitated. He'd have been in there, sniffing out the bargains. Only this wasn't a normal situation. Instinct told him there was no profit to be made from this. After all, 5 per cent of nothing was still nothing.

No. For once he had to fight this, not embrace it.

George ended his call. He turned and looked to Jake.

'You want to go home, Jake, or do you want to stay on?'

'I have an option?'

'Just that if this carries on the way it's been, we may need you in there for quite some time. I'm thinking twelve-hour shifts...'

'You think it's going to get worse.'

George nodded. 'Whoever's driving this... whoever's feeding false information to the Market, or whatever it is they're doing, they're doing it for a reason, and that reason will come clear after a time. I'd like you to be in there when that happens, Jake. I want you to evaluate just who and what it is and tell us how you think we ought to act.'

Jake let out a breath. 'You discussed this at the board meeting, too, I take it?'

'We did.' George paused. 'You're our best, Jake. Maybe the best. If anyone can work out what's going on, then you can. Only...'

'You don't think the crisis point has come just yet.'

'No. Which is why I'd recommend getting some rest. Maybe take a shot. The next session might be rough.'

Jake considered, then gave a nod. 'Okay. I'll do what you suggest. But, George?'

'Yes?'

'I think you should ask a few of those clients just why they've given their instructions. I think you need to confirm that this is rumour-led.'

George's face had been deadly serious throughout. Now he gave the faintest smile. 'We're doing it already.'

'Good.' Jake stood and put the untouched brandy on the table next to him. 'Then call me when you need me.'

'Oh, I will, Jake... I most certainly will.'

He'd hoped to find Kate there when he got back, but she was out having lunch with Jenny. He left a message, then, knowing he'd not sleep without it, took a shot of KalmEaze and went to bed, giving Trish instructions to wake him in six hours.

If George was right, and this was some speculatory gambit – some rich man's ploy to get even richer at the Market's expense – then that would surely become clear before much longer. To give the Market time to defend itself made no strategic sense. If it were he, he'd strike fast and hard. That was, once the tipping point was reached. Once confidence had been sufficiently eroded and the circumstances were ripe.

Because that was his guess right now. That this was a process of slow erosion. A softening-up before the onslaught.

There had been a similar incident in the early days of the datscape. Back then – and he was talking twelve, fifteen years ago – the datscape had been in its infancy. It had been incomplete. *Flawed.* And someone had taken advantage of its flaws to propagate a massive fraud. Things had tightened up since then. The datscape was a perfect model now, matched one-to-one to the outside. Not only that, but its defences had grown sophisticated. But so too, it seemed, had those who sought to penetrate those defences.

He kept thinking of the strange perfection of those four attack programmes. If he'd been a 'scrip' – a writer of programmes for the datscape – he'd have been immensely proud. There was a real art to seeming so effortless.

Jake yawned. The KalmEaze was taking effect. He would be out of it in five.

'Trish,' he said lazily, almost slurred. 'Doh wake me less you muss...'

*

181

He woke to find Kate beside him. No alarms, no urgent voices, just Kate, lying there, reading a book. Seeing he was awake, she set it aside, then rolled into him, letting him cuddle her.

'Hi, sleepy head... You snore, you know that?'

'Do I?' He breathed in the scent of her. On the datscape she would be a high-value bond with a smell like that. A solid investment.

'I was surprised you were home. What with all the stuff that's been going on...'

'Yeah? Like what?'

'It was on the news...'

Jake looked past her at the screen on the wall. 'Trish...?'

'Not yet,' Kate said, placing her hand on his chin and turning his face so that he was looking at her again. 'I thought we might... you know?'

'Mister Reed?' Trish asked.

'Nothing, Trish... just dim the lights.'

Only now he was wondering what it was that had been on the news and how it was connected to the Market.

After a minute or two, Kate sat up. 'Your mind's not on this, is it?'

'I'm sorry... creature of habit and all that. Just let me see what it is, then you'll have my full attention.'

Kate huffed, then, 'Trish. Show him.'

The screen lit. There were fires and gunshots and...

'Where is that?' he asked, only vaguely recognizing it through the swirling smoke and the gun flashes.

Trish answered instantly. 'It's P'ei Ching. Tiananmen Square. It seems that a number of members of the State Council have been killed... assassinated. Hence the unrest. There's talk of a coup of some kind, but everything's vague right now...'

'And the Market?'

'There's renewed pressure...'

He looked to Kate. 'I ought to go in. I'm surprised they didn't...'

She pushed him down onto his back, even as Trish cut the feed and the room fell silent.

'If they need you, you can go. Until then you're mine.'

The hopper set down on the roof of Hinton Industries. As its engines growled to a halt, Jake looked towards the pilot, meeting his eyes in the mirror.

'Sam?'

'Yes, Mister Reed?'

'What do you think about what's happening in China?'

'I think it's worrying.'

'Worrying? You think it will affect us, then?'

'Everything affects us. It's that kind of world these days.'

That was true. Jake nodded. 'Thanks...'

'That's okay. They called you back, then?'

'Yes... looks like we're in for a bumpy ride.'

Sam smiled stoically. 'Looks like it.'

Joel met him in reception. He was only in his thirties, yet he seemed to have aged ten years since Jake had last seen him.

'I know,' Joel said. 'I need some sleep. But come through. I have to show you something.'

Looking past him, Jake noticed that they had doubled the usual number of guards. Tonight, eight of the hugely muscled 'firewalls' were making sure that no one got in from the outside. It made him wonder why.

He followed Joel through reception. Only this once they didn't turn right towards the Wiring Room, but to the left, following the corridor along to the Dealing Room.

The noise hit him as he stepped through. Every seat at the great curving board was filled. Sixty or more 'boardmen' were plugged in and dealing, the delicate looped cables like a cat's cradle between men and machine.

He looked to Joel. 'Looks like a full complement.'

Joel nodded. 'We've got every spare boardman in and working, and we still can't cope. The volume is abnormal. I've never known anything like it.'

'When did this start?'

'It's been like it the past two hours... since events broke in China.'

Jake nodded. It was the kind of thing that could affect a jittery market. But was that part of it, too? Those killings were deliberate, sure, but were they linked to this?

'Anything strange going on in there?'

'We've a full team inside, Jake. I've left one suit free, naturally...'

'Then fill me in as I'm getting ready.'

Jake made to turn away, expecting Joel to follow him through to the Wiring Room, but Joel reached out, pulling him back.

'It's like I said, Jake... I have to show you something.'

'But I thought...'

Jake had thought he'd meant the Dealing Room. The abnormal volume of work.

He looked at Joel properly this time, saw that he was keeping something back.

'Come,' Joel said. 'You've got to see this.'

He followed, through the long curve of the Dealing Room to the door at the far end, beyond which was the Overseer's Office.

Jake normally had little to do with Walter Ascher, the Overseer. The only time they ever came into contact was at strategy meetings, and then they barely ever spoke. Ascher was a number-cruncher. His job was to make sure Hinton Industrial was solvent; that its profits exceeded its losses, and that it was taking its due cut from clients. He was old-fashioned in that regard. He would have preferred if their business had been wholly client-driven, as some were. He didn't trust 'web-dancers' like Jake. He thought it all too cavalier.

Or had. For it didn't matter now what Walter Ascher thought, because Ascher was dead.

Jake went across. Ascher was slumped in his chair. His face was ashen and his hair was standing on end, like it had been weirdly styled with gel. Someone – Joel? – had removed his plug-ins, disconnecting him from the board, but you could see from the scorch marks around the tiny input holes at his temples and at his neck, that he had suffered a fatal overload. A *surge*.

Jake turned and looked to Joel. 'What happened?'

'I'm not sure. I found him like this twenty minutes back. Security are on their way.'

Jake studied Ascher a moment longer. '*Was* there a surge?'

Joel shrugged. 'If there was, it was highly specific. No one else was affected. Inside... well, it's not good, but there've been no power surges.'

Then it was likely Ascher had been targeted. But how? And why him?

'I don't want to pre-empt things, Joel, but I think we should contact some of our competitors. Find out whether they've had similar problems.'

'That's George's call, surely?'

'Where is George, by the way?'

'Inside...'

Which was where *he* ought to be. Security could deal with this. Maybe it *was* faulty wiring. Maybe something *had* gone wrong with the machine. Only these systems were supposed to be safe. One hundred per cent safe. They only went wrong when someone deliberately tampered with them.

'Joel... get me inside. I think it's time we took back the initiative.'

Two hours in and Jake had to rest.

Thus far they had done well, fighting fires and damping down activity like they were old hands. For the last hour they had focused on locating and isolating those places where the wind blew strongest and capping them, like you'd cap a gush of oil. Neither was it just Hinton. All of the 'big eight' now had bodies out there in the datscape, firefighting.

Outside, too, they were finally taking action. The eight had met and decided there was only one solution, to *freeze* the Market. Only not just yet. First they would try to calm things down, to persuade the smaller brokers and their clients not to sell, even to lean on them if necessary.

For Jake it had been an eye-opener. The unhealthy smell had hit him instantly. It was like sour sweat and rotting cabbage. An awful smell for one who loved the Market. And the wind...

The wind was gusting now, little tornadoes scurrying across the floor of the datscape. It was a phenomenon he had never seen before, and he wondered what it meant. Normally he was able to read every twist and turn of this virtual environment, but not tonight.

Tonight it was different.

As a landscape it seemed suddenly to have aged; to have shrivelled and lost its bloom. Here and there the great geometric shapes had been eaten away as if by acid, while elsewhere there were signs of atrophy, and of a strange blight that left sickly grey-green patches on whatever it affected.

Neither was this process natural. That was, as far as 'nature' could be applied to the datscape. None of these changes mirrored anything that was happening in the real world. Not as far as Jake could ascertain. They were programmes, they had to be, and if that was so then they had to be coming in on the threads. There had to be more spinners out there, feeding this stuff in, working for their enemy, whoever it was.

It was while he was sitting there, his boots immersed in a faint grey slush, that Joel came through to him again.

'Jake? Good news. The cavalry's arrived.'

'Yeah?'

'Yeah. We've got intervention.'

Jake grinned. It was the best news he'd heard all day.

'About fucking time, eh? Mind, we could have done with it an hour back. It would have made it so much easier. What are they putting in?'

'Sixty trillion to start with. And a further forty if necessary.'

It was a lot of money to throw at the problem, and to be effective they would have to buy-in at above the odds. But the alternative – to do nothing – would very likely cost them more, much more.

'When's it happening?'

'Midnight, GMT. They're going to spread the purchases throughout the eight. Let each identify where it can act best.'

It sounded good. Sounded the kind of aggressive measure that might just stop this dead in its tracks. For the first time in days, Jake felt that maybe things were turning in their favour.

'And Ascher? We got any word yet on what happened?'

Joel's answer was subdued: 'Same as happened to all the other Overseers. They must have targeted the lot.'

The news stunned Jake. 'Not possible. How... I mean... just the codes...'

'I know. It's unimaginable. Yet that's what they did.'

'You say *they*, Joel. Have we any inkling yet of who's doing all this?'

'Not a single fucking clue.'

'No. I didn't think so.' Jake swallowed. 'Hey... let me know any news. And take good care of yourself, yeah?'

'Yeah...'

And Joel was gone.

Jake looked about him. It was eleven minutes to midnight. Eleven minutes to keep things ticking over, and then they'd kick this bastard's arse. Whoever he was.

*

'Chao?'

'Yes, Master?'

'What are they doing now?'

'It is called intervention, Master.'

'Intervention...' The small man considered that a moment, pulling at his beard as he did. Then, 'And how far do they intend to intervene?'

'At first, sixty trillion. And then another forty... if they must.'

'Oh, they must. They really must.' And he laughed, a low, pleasant laugh.

'Master?'

'Yes, Chao?'

'Should we let them think they're winning?'

'I thought this was your show, brave Chao. I thought...' He paused, an idea coming to him. 'Tell me, Chao, how hard would it be to project my face into that place?'

'Your face, Master?' The other considered that, then shrugged. 'I guess I could. Why... would you like that, Master?'

'At the end of things, yes... if it is possible.'

They were silent for a moment, then the one called Chao, who had been watching his own computer screen, looked up again.

'Their tactic's working, Master. The wind is dying. Should I...?'

'Not yet, brave Chao. Give them hope. Remember what Sun Tzu teaches us. We must show them a small avenue of escape. The faintest possibility of hope. And then...'

Chao looked down, smiling. 'As my Master wishes.'

They waited, watching as the signs grew hopeful, as the wind died and the colours slowly changed to brighter hues.

'There,' the small man said, pointing towards the figures on the screen. 'Have your man focus on that one. The one in green, on the right there. I want to see his face as it all changes back. I want...'

The image changed. The man's face – his mask – became larger, clearer.

'Good. Good... now let's end it. Let's kick the fucking legs from under it, eh, Chao?'

Chao chuckled. 'As my Master wishes... but what would you have me sell?'

The small man was smiling now. A broad, triumphant smile. 'Sell glass, Chao. Sell every last share we have in glass!'

'Glass?' Jake stood there, stunned by what Joel was saying. 'They're selling glass?'

'Yes,' Joel answered. 'Like there's no tomorrow...'

Unfortunate words, Jake thought, because now he knew. The Chinese. The fucking Chinese were selling every share they had in glass. And why would they do that? Why in god's name disinvest in something they needed so much of?

'Oh, fuck... Oh, Jesus fucking Christ!'

Joel, it seems, was still listening in. 'Jake? What's up?'

The Chinese are selling glass, that's what up. And if they're selling glass now, then all the rest...

'It's the Chinese, Joel. It's the fucking Chinese!'

Joel laughed. He actually laughed. 'It can't be.'

'Why not?'

'Because they're suffering more than anyone.'

'So?'

The wind had died. There was a sudden freshness to the air. For a moment or two it had almost seemed that it was over. And then the Chinese had begun to sell glass.

Jake turned, aware suddenly that someone was behind him.

'God...'

It was Jory. Jory from *Ubik*. At least, an avatar that looked like Jory, complete with shovel teeth.

'Who are you? Who the fuck...'

His avatar seized, became catatonic for a moment, locked. All but his eyes, which were somehow permitted movement.

It's him, Jake thought. The one who made all of these things happen.

It made no move to come and get him. To try to eat him, as it tried to eat Joe Chip. No, it just stood there as all about it the datscape slowly died.

He wanted to understand. He wanted to ask it why it had done this. But he couldn't use his mouth. Only his eyes. As if some highly specific programme were controlling him now.

He was expecting it to speak. To tell him why he had been chosen at the last. But it said nothing, merely looked at him, disdainful in its triumph.

The backdrop flickered, speeded up, then slowed. A voice sounded in a long-drawn-out drawl. It was Joel, speaking in his head.

'Who-oo-oo's sqeeeee-ziiing iiit?'

The bandwidth. Joel meant the bandwidth. Someone was 'squeezing' it.

Things grew pale, faint, instabilities began to appear in the surface of things – tiny black holes forming where things were missing suddenly, like gaps in reality. Only none of this was real. None of it.

He tried to cut out of there, but, paralysed as he was, he couldn't.

Trapped. I'm fucking trapped.

'Not trapped,' a voice answered him, as if it read his mind. 'Beaten, yes, but not trapped.'

Was that him? Was that Jory? Only his mouth hadn't moved. He hadn't spoken. But someone had. Someone had finally got inside him.

And as he thought it, he could feel the touch of the finest silken threads on his face, the faintest trace of sulphur and cinnamon on his tongue. And, pervading all, like a coil of swirling, dark red smoke, the outlines of a face. Oriental. Brutal.

★

Jake woke, covered in sweat. Joel was leaning over him.

He looked about him, panicked. 'What happened? What the fuck...?'

'They froze it. Closed the datscape down.'

'Closed it...?' He nodded. Of course. That's what they had decided. 'So things are... all right?'

'They're hardly that. But they've declared a three-day holiday. To try and sort things out.'

'And China?'

In answer, Joel pointed to a screen above Jake's bed. 'Look for yourself. China's burning. They're no threat to anyone.'

On the screen, the Forbidden Palace was in flames. The great square in front of it was filled with angry people, shouting and fighting. As the image jumped from city to city it was more of the same. People fought and buildings burned.

'I don't understand...'

'It's madness now, but things'll calm down. People were afraid, that's all.'

Jake stared at him a moment, then let his head fall back onto the pillow, closing his eyes.

Something had happened. Something bad. Only they were all in denial about it. They thought they could close it all down for a couple of days and everything would be fine. Only it wasn't. Neither would it be. Not if China had its way.

He kept seeing that face, forming in the smoke, and knew now where he'd seen it before. It was on a TV bulletin, about a year ago. He couldn't remember the man's name, but he would. In time.

He turned his head, opening his eyes to look at Joel again.

'So what's the plan?'

Joel smiled. 'You go home. Sit tight for a day or two. Then come back here and start it all up again.'

'And meanwhile?'

'We're going to analyse what happened. Run it all back and see what we can see. We've got a good idea, thanks to you, Jake. We know what we're looking for. And we'll find it, I guarantee.'

'Yeah?' Only he wasn't sure they would, for once. The one he'd faced – the one behind the Jory avatar – must have known they'd close things down as soon as they got bad. He'd anticipated all the rest, why not anticipate that?

No. Whoever he was, he was good. Possibly the best. Those programmes he'd written. It was like he understood things in a different way.

But why bring it all down? Why that?

Joel ordered him a hopper. It was after five and, standing there in the dark, he wondered what their next move was. Because this hadn't finished yet. What the Chinese had begun, they'd finish, because that was their way.

As the hopper touched down on the pad, he ran across, bent low. 'Mister Reed...'

He clambered inside, grateful for once to be heading home. 'Hi, Sam. How are things in the real world?'

'Not good, Mister Reed. Been a bad night...'

'Yeah?'

Jake was surprised. Sam was normally so cheerful, so positive. Yet as they climbed above the tops of the high buildings, he could see back down the river. P'ei Ching wasn't the only place that was burning. All down the river, on both sides, there were patches of golden flames among the blackness.

'God... what's been happening?'

'News gets out,' Sam said. 'Word is the Market had to close.'

Jake nodded. 'That's so.'

'Then things must be bad, yeah?'

'I guess.'

There was a brief silence between them, then Sam spoke again. 'Mister Reed?'

'Hey... call me Jake.'

He saw in the mirror how Sam smiled at that.

'I'd love to, Mister Reed. You're a nice man. But it'd get me the sack. No... what I wanted to say was this. Hard times are coming. Maybe the hardest we've seen for years.'

He wanted to say no. To reassure him the way he knew he was going to have to reassure Kate. Only he couldn't. Sam deserved better than that.

'Yes,' he said finally. 'I think that's so. I think...'

He saw it coming up at them. Sensed its brightness long before he felt it strike the craft.

'Jesus Christ!'

The world exploded in the air about him. Bits flew past the seat where he was cocooned in the back.

The hopper shifted to the right, then began to fall.

'Hold on!' Sam yelled above the sudden noise of wind.

The engine juddered, died.

'Oh, fuck...'

Jake closed his eyes. It was like one of those funfair rides. All of his weight was suddenly transferred. Everything was suddenly so much heavier. Only this was no ride. He wasn't in the datscape now. This was real. And there was nothing between him and the earth. Nothing but the river.

He fell, faster and faster, strapped into his seat, the craft beginning to swing round and round in the air, pirouetting madly.

And then it hit.

Chapter 6

FRAGMENTS

Jake came to, lulled by the gentle rocking motion of the craft. It was dark and damp and his ribs ached. There was the faintest gurgling sound, a soft electronic crackle and the steady hiss of spraying water.

From the blackness in front came a groan.

'Sam...?'

There was no answer.

Jake fumbled for the catch to release him from the restraining harness. As he did he noticed the wetness surrounding him.

'Fuck...'

The seal for the inner compartment had been breached. Maybe some piece of shrapnel from the explosion had got between the two surfaces, preventing them from closing properly. He didn't know.

The water wasn't deep. Four or five inches at most. But if they couldn't get out then they were in serious trouble.

'Sam? You okay?'

Another groan.

Maybe someone was coming. Maybe someone had seen the missile hit and had sent for help. Or maybe Sam had sent out an

194

emergency signal. Only he couldn't count on that. What if no one knew they were down?

He had to open the seal and take his chances. Swim for shore and hope it wasn't far. That or wait for the water to fill the capsule.

He sat forward, then winced with the pain. The strap must have cut into him. It felt like someone had taken a blunt knife and run it down the length of his chest from left shoulder to right hip.

Forcing himself to ignore it, he hauled himself up out of the seat and through the gap. There was a lot more light here in the front. He could make out Sam's figure, slumped over the controls. Leaning across, Jake put his hand on the side of his neck. It was warm. And there *was* a pulse.

'Sam... we've got to get out of here... the capsule's filling up...'

Sam groaned.

The control board in front of Sam was faintly lit. There were thirty, maybe forty switches, none of them clearly marked. Which of them activated the seal?

Did he just keep flicking them until he got lucky?

'Sam... we've got to get out of here...'

Sam stirred, his head lifted. 'Wha' the...?'

Jake reached up, touching Sam's face, tracing his nose and forehead with his fingers. They were sticky with blood.

'The seal, Sam... which switch opens the seal?'

Sam groaned again.

That was another thing. If he breached the seal, he was going to have to grab hold of Sam and somehow get him ashore, too, because Sam wasn't going to make it on his own.

At least I know how, he thought, his eyes moving from one switch to another, hoping he might recognize something.

He smiled wryly. So all of those old swimming safety lessons were about to pay off. Who'd a thunk it?

It made him think of Alison, and in turn of Kate. He had to get out. For her sake as much as for his own.

'Sam... I'm going to press a few of these switches until I find the right one, then I'm going to get you out of here and back onto dry land. You got that?'

Sam's groan seemed almost articulate this time. He gave the vaguest nod.

'Okay. Good. But you couldn't help me here, could you, buddy? Just press the right switch for me, eh?'

Sam moved his head, almost as if he were focusing, then his hand went out, his fingers covering a switch.

Nothing happened, but now Jake knew which switch he had to throw.

'Okay,' he said, talking to himself now. 'Count to three and we're out of here. One, two...'

The solid thunk as the seal came open and the sudden inrush of cold, stale-smelling water took Jake by surprise. For a moment he lost direction. In the sudden swirl he couldn't make out which was up and which down. And Sam... he had no idea where Sam was.

As the capsule opened like a massive flower blooming, it began to sink. As it sank it dragged him under.

Jake kicked hard, struggling to make his way back to the surface. The pain in his chest and ribs was ferocious, but it didn't matter. All that mattered was to survive. He pumped his legs and arms, striving to break free of the water's grip, then broke surface, gasping.

It hurt. He could hardly breathe it hurt so much.

For a moment he closed his eyes, treading water. He felt like he was going to black out, only he knew he mustn't. If he lost consciousness now he was dead. Dead and no way back.

He counted ten then opened them again, looking about him.

Moonlight silvered the swollen surface of the river. There was no sign of the craft, no sign of Sam.

Jake slowly turned himself in the water, trying to work out where he was.

The hopper's capsule must have drifted upstream quite some way. The City was way off in the distance, its bright-lit towers unmistakable.

Just then something bobbed up onto the surface, some twenty yards away.

'Sam! Wait, buddy... I'm coming...'

Jake kicked out hard, swimming towards him, praying he hadn't already drowned.

Jake left Sam on the tiny stretch of beach and went for help. He had tried to make contact but the implant beneath his ear had been damaged. When he touched it it was moist and painful and the best he got from it was a faint hiss.

He didn't know where he was – Fulham, maybe – or how he was going to make contact, but there had to be a way. Hinton would come for them. They had to. They wouldn't let him down. He was worth too much to them.

There was a set of worn stone steps leading up on to the embankment. It wasn't a cold night; even so he was soaked through and as he stood there, trying to make things out, he found he was shivering.

Cold or shock? He didn't know. Maybe it didn't matter. All he knew was that he had to survive long enough for them to get a fix on him.

It was dark where he'd come out, like it was a park of some kind. An unlit, uninhabited space. Further back, however, beyond the immediate blackness, he could see the fires blazing, sending their lambent glow up into the night; could hear the Security sirens wailing, the baying of looters and rioters.

Jake turned, looking back across the river.

It was just as bad over there. He could make out more than a dozen different fires, could hear the sirens, the distant roar of the mob.

Jake shivered. It was a bad night to be lost.

The trouble was, he didn't know how things worked out here, outside the enclaves. Was there a communications network? Was there some way he could get Hinton on the line to come and rescue them? Or was he going to have to drag Sam with him to a gate and get them to let him in?

That last seemed likely. This didn't look like a place that had a sophisticated, hi-tech communications web. This had the look of somewhere that had been left to rot.

For a full two minutes he stood there, unable to decide. The truth was, he didn't know what to do. For the first time in his life he had no answers. All he knew was that he couldn't leave Sam, even if it made things difficult.

Okay... Think... How can you make this easier?

Some kind of cart, that would be a start. Or a litter. Something he could put Sam in, so that he didn't have to carry him. Only where the fuck was he going to find something like that?

He didn't know. All he knew was that he felt like a castaway on an island full of savages. And with that thought came another, darker, bleaker than the first.

He was going to die here. Ignominiously. Unheroically. Victim of some savage little know-nothing.

It made him feel sick. Made him feel like his whole life had been wasted.

'Jake... Jake...'

Jake went to the rail and looked down. It was Sam, calling him. He couldn't make him out very well, but he knew it was him.

'Wait there,' he shouted back as he ran down. 'I'm coming.'

Sam was sitting up, holding his shoulder. Jake knelt.

'You okay?'

Sam nodded. 'Thanks... you know...'

Jake waved it aside. 'D'you think you can walk? I mean, you can lean on me...'

He helped him up. Sam swayed a moment, as if he were going to fall down again, then steadied himself.

'I'm fine, I...'

'We'll find a gate,' Jake said. 'We'll work our way east and...'

The thought struck him. Sam would have an implant. Even if his was damaged, Sam's would still work.

'Sam... your implant... can you...?'

Sam shook his head. 'Nothing but a hiss. Like everything's dead.'

That made Jake think. What if the communications system was down? What if the Chinese had hit that too? Because he knew now it was the Chinese. They were behind all of this. It was probably one of their agents who had shot him out of the sky.

Which meant he had been specifically targeted. They had somehow known when he'd come out of there – known what craft he was on and had a man there waiting to pull the trigger and send the missile flying up out of the darkness at him.

It was a souring thought. It made him think of the steward at Bellini's. The guy he'd thought had been watching him. Well, maybe they had been watching him all along; knowing he was Hinton's star turn; knowing that if they got to him they weakened Hinton and, through Hinton, the West.

Because if what had happened was what he thought had happened, China had just declared war on the rest of the world. Not overtly, but covertly, by dismantling its systems, by destroying its electronic infrastructure.

Or was that going too far?

Getting Sam up the steps took a long, exhausting time. Sam was hurt. Badly hurt. At the top they had to rest, to let him get his strength back. It didn't augur well. The fastest Sam could do was a kind of geriatric limp.

Jake wasn't sure they were going to make it. If this was Fulham, then they had a good long walk – a mile, a mile and a half through hostile streets – before they'd get to the enclave. And even then, there was no guarantee the gate would be open. Not on a night like this.

He wondered where Kate was. Whether she was at home now, worrying. Whether Hinton would have told her that his craft had gone missing.

That disturbed him, more than anything, because it felt like Hinton had given up on him. That, having lost him, they hadn't bothered to send anyone out to see if he'd survived the crash. It felt wrong, somehow. It felt—

'Jake...'

Jake looked to Sam. He was hunched forward, his head down.

'What?'

'You'd better leave me here. Go get help.'

'But, Sam...'

Every word seemed to cost Sam dear, but he was insistent now. 'No, Jake. I'm just being practical. You try and walk me through those streets you die. And I'll die too. Whereas you leave me here we both have a chance. Just put me somewhere where no bastard can see me. Then you go and get help. Bring someone back, yeah?'

'Yeah...' Jake smiled and gently touched Sam's arm. 'Okay. Let's find a place to hide you...'

It took Jake the best part of an hour to get to the outer wall of the West Kensington Enclave. He'd had to stop and double back a dozen times, to avoid the mob. Once he'd been chased, but they had quickly given up, looking for easier targets.

Keeping to the shadows, moving cautiously from hiding place to hiding place, he had made his way through roads littered with the rusting, burned-out hulks of ancient cars, the debris from fallen houses, slate and broken bricks, soiled rags and human excreta, flattened beer cans and endless other rubbish. It would have been bad at the best of times but tonight it was like a vision of hell. Not a street was untouched, not a single house intact. He had passed endless burning buildings, countless blackened shells from previous nights.

All of which was bad. Yet the worst was by the enclave wall itself, for there the houses had been bulldozed flat to make a space before the wall a hundred metres wide. There, on that flattened pile of brickwork, they had built fires. There, as the guards on the walls looked on, shaven-headed men and women, half-naked with their faces painted savagely, kept up an unearthly heathen chant, thrusting their home-made weapons in the air to the rhythm of a dozen makeshift drums.

Defiant and powerful they looked in that hell's glow, Britain's new outlaw class.

The unprotected...

Jake had never seen the like. On the news they never showed this side of things. It was always the mob fleeing Security. Never this.

The men were bad enough, yet it was the women to whom his eyes were drawn, for in them the transformation was most marked. Whatever signs of femininity they might once have possessed had long since disappeared, devolved into a hard and brutish form.

Those whose heads were not shaved, in the fashion of their menfolk, wore long, matted hair. Streaks of dirt marked their faces, while what clothes they wore were rags and tatters, the cloth frayed and stained. Many of them wore even less, their painted breasts exposed, held up, thrust out towards the soldiers who manned the enclave's gates, as if in defiance of the Eden from which they had been cast.

Looking at them all, Jake felt a certain pity. As fierce as they were, they had a worn and shabby look to them. A *beaten* look. They were like dogs. And mongrel dogs at that. Years of ill-use had given them a furtive appearance, as if at any moment they would fall upon each other, tearing at one another's flesh with tooth and claw. They only *seemed* like a tribe. What they were was a pack.

Respectability had fallen from them, leaving them exposed. Where they lived now was a darker, nastier reality – a world in which each day was a struggle to exist, and god help the one who showed any weakness.

As the wind changed, he could smell them, a sickening, fetid smell that made him want to retch.

Seeing them like this made him wonder how they lived. What they did when they were not taunting the enclave guards or making trouble. What they ate and how they organized their lives. But he would never know. The media would never let him know. All they ever showed was this. This savage barbarism.

It was not their fault. But if not theirs, then whose? His?

Jake pushed the thought away. He was crouched now in the shadows at the end of one of the streets that opened out on to that great swathe of rubble, hidden behind an outcrop of brickwork. Looking on and wondering how in god's name he might get past such a mob, for there seemed to be hundreds of them dancing in the firelight, their ragged voices taunting the men on the wall.

From where he was he could see the gate, over to his left. It was a massive thing, like an ancient barbican, its upper levels heavily armoured.

If he could get there he was safe. If he could get there.

He looked to his right, wondering suddenly if there might not be another, smaller entrance somewhere. Down by the river, maybe, like they'd had on old castles. He couldn't see anything, but maybe he should try it.

Only what if he did that and was seen? What if they caught him?

Jake looked back. The mob was slowly working itself into a frenzy. To even think of trying to make his way through its ranks was absurd.

He would try the river. See if he couldn't get the attention of one of the guards. There had to be a river gate. Had to.

For the next twenty minutes he crept from one pile of bricks to another, across that uneven wasteland, certain that at any moment he'd be seen. Only the attention of the locals was elsewhere. They seemed to know what was happening in the Market, that all was not well 'inside', among the protected.

Finally he made the river. There was an old stone wall, which was crumbling in places, and a metal ladder down, but no sign in the enclave wall of any gate. The pale marble was tall and smooth. Unbroken.

'Shit...'

There were no guards on this part of the wall, but overhead an automated gun followed Jake's every move, its infrared tracker seeing him as clearly as in the daylight.

For a moment his disappointment stopped him thinking.

Where there was an automated gun, there would be a man at a board, supervising it, looking at a screen. If he could speak to him...

Jake raised himself on his toes, waving his arms in the air and shouting, praying that no one was close by, that they wouldn't see him, and that the noise of the mob would cover his own yells. There was only one person he wanted to know he was there – the guard at the board.

'I'm stranded!' he yelled. 'I'm a citizen... You've got to help me!'

He looked round. If they saw him now...

'He-elp!' he yelled again, waving his arms frantically. 'For god's sake help!'

The gun jerked. Jerked again, as if focusing on him, then lifted a fraction.

The sudden chatter made him jump. He could hear the bullets whistle overhead, missing him. Heard a howl, the clatter of disturbed brickwork as someone fled.

Jake closed his eyes. For a moment he had thought he was dead.

And then, suddenly, there was another noise in the air. The pulse of engines.

Jake whirled about. Over to his left four big Security hoppers had swung in over the gate and, spreading out in a half-circle, had begun to fire on the mob below. As he saw the mob begin to scatter, one of the craft rose up over the others, heading directly towards him.

Jake stood there, picked out by the searchlight on the side of the craft, as it slowly drifted in. He still wasn't sure. Still thought that any moment might be his last. But now someone was hailing him, telling him to get his arse across and fast.

Safe, he thought, as the guard's hand gripped his arm and pulled him onboard. *Safe*. Only his problems were just beginning.

Jake stared back at the Security captain, then shook his head in disbelief.

'What do you mean I don't exist? Of course I fucking exist.'

'Oh, you exist... as far as you're sitting in that chair facing me. Only Jake Reed doesn't. Never has, and probably never will.'

Jake shook his head. 'I'm a *login*. I work for Hinton. The pilot... the guy we pulled out of there just now. Sam... He'll tell you.'

The captain sat back. His grey eyes looked sceptical. 'Unfortunately he's unconscious. Took rather a heavy blow to the head.' He paused, then, 'Listen, you may have been dressed like a citizen and cut your hair like a citizen, but there's not a single mention of you in our records, so...'

Jake looked up, met the captain's eyes again. 'There's got to be some mistake. Check again. Or phone George Hinton, he's my line-boss. He'll...'

'George Hinton is dead.'

The news stopped Jake in his tracks.

'Fuck...'

'Yes, as in fucking-outta-luck, eh? Now tell me who you really are and who sent you.'

'No one sent me. My hopper got shot down...'

'Yeah? So why is there no report of that?'

'I don't know, I... Look... contact Hinton... get them to send someone who knows me. Joel Haslinger, maybe. He's known me years. He's chief tech there.'

The captain looked tired. He was clearly fed up with this charade. But he was going to do his job.

'Okay. Last chance, though. This Joel guy doesn't ID you, then I'm throwing you in a cell until you tell me who you are.'

Jake looked straight back at him. 'I'm Jake Reed and I'm a *login* for Hinton... a web-dancer... and I'm engaged to Kate...'

'Enough...' The captain stood. For a moment he stared at Jake silently, as if trying to fathom him, then he turned and left the room.

Sitting there, his hands and feet restrained, Jake could tell what had happened. It was the Chinese. It had to be. Who else would take such care to erase him from the records. And others, too. Just in case they survived the attack.

Thinking about it, Jake was almost in awe of the mind behind this. He could almost imagine that an AI – some new super-intelligent breed of AI – had done this. Only no. This was too good. Too human. There was a man behind all this. One single mind. A subtle, clever mind bordering on genius. And that mind had a face. He existed... somewhere.

It came back to him. The name he'd been trying to remember. The Han he'd seen on the TV. Tsao Ch'un. That was his name. Tsao Ch'un.

Jake smiled. Realizing just how simple it actually was, he said the words quietly to himself.

'Just find Tsao Ch'un and you find him. Whoever he is.'

'What's that?'

The captain had returned. Jake looked down.

'Bad news,' the captain said. 'Everyone you know seems to be dead.'

Jake looked up at him, shocked. 'You're kidding me...'

'Would I joke about this? No. It seems they killed your friend Joel outside his apartment, an hour back.'

'Fuck...'

'However...' The captain paused. 'I did check on the hopper. Seems that one has gone missing, only they had no record that it was going to pick you up. Only that its pilot was your friend Sam in there.'

'So what does that prove?'

The captain smiled. 'I'm fucked if I know. Only...'

Jake stared at him. 'What?'

'The guy at the hopper place... when I mentioned your name, he said he knew you. Said...'

'Go on...'

'It's just that I checked his records and there's no mention of you as a client. So either you *weren't* a client, or...'

'Someone's erased me. All traces of me.'

The captain nodded. 'Do you want to try someone else? Someone who might still be alive, that is.'

Jake had been thinking about that. 'Harry Lampton... that is, Sir Henry Lampton. He's Head of Security for Hinton.'

'And he'll know you?'

'He'll know *of* me.'

The captain stood. 'I'll give it a try...'

Jake watched the man leave, then sat back.

So what do I know?

He knew this much. That he'd been targeted, both inside the datscape and out here in the real world. They had tracked him down and tried to kill him, like they'd killed George and Joel. Yes, and others. Not only that, but they had anticipated possible failure; had taken the secondary measure of erasing him from the records, and that was no mean task when you considered how much personal information a person accumulated in the modern world.

Or *was* that what they'd done?

He sat up, alert suddenly.

It looked like an erasure, sure... but what if all of that information had not been erased but *moved*, 'shifted' sideways somehow. Shunted off into the sidings, so to speak.

It made a lot more sense. To trace all of that information and erase it would have been a gargantuan task even for a highly discriminating super-computer, whereas to modify where it was all stored...

Jake was beginning to understand. Their security had been breached at not one but numerous levels. Their encryptions – which they had thought were absolutely failsafe – had been as much use to them as a piece of string to secure a gate.

Jake shivered, thinking about it.

The man anticipates. He leaves nothing to chance. Not a single detail escapes him. An imagination that wide, that precise and yet that flexible.

It was impressive. No. More than impressive. Awesome.

He smiled, trying to picture in his mind what kind of man this other was. His antagonist.

You play wei chi, don't you? You're a master of Go. These moves. You see the small patterns and the large. You're watching the board all the time, placing a white stone here, another there, waiting for us to make a mistake.

The captain returned, this time with the duty sergeant. He bowed, then looked on as the sergeant removed Jake's restraints.

'I take it Lampton's vouched for me.'

The captain lowered his head, respectful now. 'He's sending his private craft.'

'I don't blame you,' Jake said. 'I'd have done the same. The man we're up against...'

The captain met his eyes, surprised. 'You think this is a single man?'

'Pulling the strings? Yes. It's all of a piece. He's outwitted us. Made us chase shadows.'

'But why?'

Jake hesitated. Did he really want to say? After a moment he shook his head, then lied.

'I don't know why.'

Only he did. Sitting in the back of Lampton's private hopper, swinging back over the river, he saw it all clearly for the first time; pictured the man sat at his computer, moving the pieces while his 'Master', Tsao Ch'un, looked on.

Young or old?

Old, surely, for such wisdom; such insight didn't come to the young. And yet young, equally surely, for such invention; such originality was not a trademark of the elderly.

Whichever, their foe had not beaten them. Not yet. They had been savaged, certainly, but a war was not won with a single battle. A genius he might be, but he was still a single man, capable of being killed.

And maybe that was what he should suggest to Lampton. To track Tsao Ch'un down and deal with him. Because wherever Tsao Ch'un was, this one would be with him.

Yes, send an army. Two armies. Maybe ten. But get him. Make sure the bastard's dead. Then reconstruct. And build it better next time. Stronger.

The hopper flew on, as daylight leaked into the world again.

Yes, we have to kill the fucker. Before he kills us all.

Lampton was waiting on the pad for him as the craft came down.

It was a beautiful house, more country estate than London home, its broad lawn sloping down to the river. But what impressed Jake most were the massive walls that surrounded it, the guard towers and the endless armed security. This wasn't just Lampton's home, it was his fortress.

As Lampton looked on, Jake was searched and scanned. Only then was he allowed to move down, through the cordon of guards, to shake Lampton's hand.

Lampton was a big man in his fifties. An ex-mercenary and SAS man. But Hinton had hired him for his brains not his brawn.

'Jake... sorry about the fuck up... seems the thieving bastards have been plundering our database. You're not the only one who "went missing" from the records.'

They were making their way down the steps into the main court-yard. Guards were everywhere. It felt like they were under siege.

'It's the Chinese,' Jake said.

Lampton glanced at him. 'How'd you make that out?'

'Who else could it be? There's been a coup, right? Tsao Ch'un is in charge?'

'We don't know who's in charge. But Tsao Ch'un would be a good candidate.'

'And towards the end, as we were about to get out of there... I saw a face... a Chinese face. I think it was Tsao Ch'un's.'

Lampton laughed. 'A bit egotistical, wouldn't you say? Besides, it doesn't mean it is them. What if someone wanted us to think it was China?'

'Why would they do that?'

'I don't know. But why would the Chinese – why would this Tsao Ch'un – kick away the supports?'

'So that he doesn't have to fight a nuclear war against the USA.'

That stopped Lampton dead in his tracks. He stared at Jake for a full ten seconds, as if slotting that in to his mental picture of events, then he nodded.

'You know what, Jake? That makes a kind of sense.'

Inside the main building, in what was a huge conference room, the others were waiting for him. Some he recognized, others were total strangers. One thing he did notice, however, was the absence of any Chinese faces.

There were roughly sixty or so of them, mainly men, but with a handful of women, their Savile Row suits marking them out as 'execs'.

'Ladies... gentlemen,' Lampton said, introducing him from a platform at the front of the room. 'This is Jake Reed, Hinton's principal login. Jake's just had the pleasure of being a guest of our Security services. It seems he doesn't exist. He's been erased.' Lampton smiled. 'Fortunately for us, that's not true. Jake... tell them what happened.'

For the next half-hour Jake told his tale. As he ended, Lampton took the stage beside him again.

'Friends... I'm sure you've got plenty of questions you'd like to ask, but time is pressing and you all know precisely why we're here... So let's get on with it, eh?'

Outside, in the corridor, Jake turned to Lampton. 'My fiancée...'

'Kate?' Lampton smiled. 'I've let her know you're okay.'

Jake smiled. 'Thanks. So what now? Are we going back in?'

Lampton nodded. 'We weren't sure we could, but now you're here... Well... we've got everything we need – board room, Wiring Room, drying room, skins, the lot. Hinton had it built here as a backup against possible terrorist activity. You'll be on your own in there, I'm afraid, but we'll be ready to haul you out of there the moment you yell!'

'I understand, but... look, I took some damage. My communicator...'

Lampton had a look at the damaged implant. 'Hmm... Was it hissing at you?'

Jake nodded.

'Yeah, we've all had that. The communications web is patchy to say the least. There're disruptive bugs in the system. They keep having to shut it down and reboot, but it shouldn't affect the datscape. We're running on an entirely different circuit, isolated from the rest.'

'Are we still spinning data?'

'Barely. We're running a skeleton crew under strict MAT super-vision, filtering everything that goes in for bugs and viruses. MAT have sent us six of their best men to help.'

'By skeleton, you mean...?'

'Twenty men... barely enough to maintain the semblance of the Market. But we can't risk anything more than that just yet. And as far as the rest of the world's concerned, we're not even running that.'

'So what are we looking for?'

'Some indicator as to how and when we can get functioning again. Three days will cost us, but any more than that and we're in trouble. We've got to get up and running again, Jake. If we don't...'

But he didn't have to be told. He knew. They had to make this work, or watch it all fall down. *Like Babylon the Great...*

As he was being skinned up, Jake kept up a conversation with Lampton.

'So just how many *have* they killed?'

Lampton shrugged. 'The truth is, Jake, it isn't clear. What with the glitches and the erasures and all of that shit... but we at Hinton have lost at least nine. And the others... well, say a dozen apiece.'

'Just datscape people? Is anyone else getting hit this way?'

'Not that we can work out. It's all very specific. They mean to take us out. I guess they think that if the Market falls, the rest falls with it.'

'Which is the truth.'

Lampton sighed heavily. 'Yeah. So find a way, eh, Jake?'

It had changed. Had become a place of ashes and dust. In the distance great sheets of grey-green lichenous matter streaked with foul browns and blacks dominated the view. It was a wasteland, a corrupted environment, in which were scattered, here and there, like forlorn pieces of sculpture, the hollowed-out, blackened shells of abandoned avatars.

The datscape was sick. Was a place now of sudden, unexpected weirdness. Blind, metallic spiders picked their way back and forth, while on the flanks of dying stocks – their vibrant colours bleached, as if sucked dry – thin, whispering mouths sighed their foul breath into the atmosphere, adding to the acid taint that underlay every scent.

And then there were the eyes, thousands of them, cold, unblinking eyes staring out of every surface, like some pustulent all-seeing rash.

From time to time some small remaining facet of the Market would collapse, tumbling into the putrid flow of waste that slowly sank towards the mid ground of the landscape, all of it turning slowly, like a whirlpool, about the central abyss.

Jake had seen a reconstruction before he'd gone in. Had seen how the Market had been destroyed in a tidal wave of data as, right at the end, China had dumped everything. It had struck him then and it was much clearer now. Tsao Ch'un wasn't playing some financial game. He wasn't looking to make a profit. This was war. A new kind of war. And this wasteland was the result.

Before they'd closed it down, they had sent in their own attack worms, rapid propagation programmes intended to countermand those that the rogues had spread, but they had barely had an effect. The rogues were too strong, too elegant to succumb.

Jake stood there now, looking about him. For all his imaginings, he had not thought it would be so bad. Nothing new was coming in. They had slammed that door firmly shut. Only that didn't matter. The rogues had colonized the datscape. They had dug in, rooting themselves deep into the sub-levels, tapping into the lower level programmes that sustained the datscape, and cannibalized them.

This was their world now, and they were busy eradicating every last trace of the previous occupants.

'Harry? Are you listening?'

'I'm listening.'

'Then hear me. It's no good. It's too far gone. We're going to have to start again. Maybe erase the past two days and begin again from that point... you know... from the moment the first intruders went in.'

'Impossible.'

'Why? We've got the data, haven't we?'

'Yes, but... well... two days of trading... people won't accept that. Some people have made money out of this.'

'Then get them to give it back. Reconstruct. Get the international community to lean on them if you have to. Only we can't do anything with this as it is.'

He heard Lampton sigh. Heard voices talking distantly, no doubt discussing his suggestion. It was radical, true, but right now it seemed the only way. If they could persuade all parties to ignore this *malaise*... to pretend that the last two days simply hadn't happened... then maybe they could begin again, fresh and confident. Put up safeguards against another such attack. After all, it was only figures in a machine. But that was the heresy of his plan. Because they weren't only figures, they were people's lives, their fortunes. What Jake was suggesting was much too arbitrary.

'Jake?'

'Yes, Harry...'

'We need to find one of their avatars. Capture one if we can. See if we can't get some answers.'

Jake closed his eyes. He felt weary now. Even if he found one of their avatars – one of the Jory ones, say – how was he going to capture it? How would he question it? Lampton didn't understand. They weren't in charge here any more.

And besides, he hadn't seen a living avatar the whole time he'd been in there.

'It's no good,' he said again. 'Can't you see that? Just blitz it. Flush it all away. It's worth nothing now, anyway.'

He heard the intake of breath as dozens of wired-in onlookers registered his words.

It's worth nothing now...

It wasn't what they wanted to hear. They wanted him to say it was saveable, that all they had to do was clean it up and things would revert to normal. That if they improved security – upgrading their firewalls and encryption codes – everything would be all right. Only nothing could be further from the truth.

'It's fucked,' he said. 'Can't you see that? Fucked!'

And us with it, he thought. Unless we take radical action.

'Okay...' It was Lampton's voice again, but quieter now, more subdued. 'Let's get you out of there. I think we've seen enough.'

Jake stood outside in the corridor, waiting while they argued it out, the representatives of some of the richest men on earth, trying to decide what they should do.

He'd had his say. Contributed his part to the debate. Now it was up to them.

Has he anticipated this too? Jake wondered. If we do erase it all and start again, from the point where it all began to go wrong, has he a strategy to deal with that?

Jake's best guess was that he *had*. That no matter what they did he would have an answer, a new twist, or some devious way of trumping whatever they did. Because *they* weren't in control any more. *He* was.

So what was he doing standing there? What was he waiting for? Some blinding revelation? No. They were fucked. They were well and truly fucked.

He hesitated, then, without a glance back, made his way out of there, back up onto the roof.

'Get me a craft,' he said to the officer on duty.

'I'm afraid I can't do that, sir. Not without Sir Henry's approval.'

'But I need to get home.'

The soldier raised his hand, then spoke into his lip-mike. For a moment he listened, then he lowered his hand and looked to Jake again and smiled.

'It's okay, sir. Mister Lampton says you're authorized. Oh... and he says good luck.'

Jake swallowed. 'Tell him thanks. And... tell him that I hope we all ride this one out.'

Jake stood there on the roof, watching the craft drop away into the darkness, then turned, looking down the steps.

He had tried to contact Kate on the way back, only the system still wasn't working properly. If she wasn't here then he wasn't sure what he'd do.

For once he didn't have a plan.

Inside the apartment it was dark and silent. He walked through into the bedroom, hoping she'd be there.

She wasn't.

'Trish?'

There was a moment's delay – not much, but more than normal – and then Trish's voice filled the air.

'Mister Reed... what is it?'

'I just wondered if you'd heard... from Kate. Whether she'd been here.'

Again there was too long a gap between his request and her response. It made him think that this too had somehow been corrupted.

'She... left a message.'

'Can I see it?'

He counted this time. Three seconds. In computer terms that was a small eternity. And then the wall screen lit up, showing Kate.

'Hi, Jake... Just wanted to let you know I'm okay. I'm staying with Mum and Dad for a couple of days. You can get me there. Love you. Bye.'

Jake frowned. He didn't know why, but it felt wrong. A lot had happened, but he had the distinct feeling that they were going to have her parents over here. Kate had said nothing about staying with them.

'Trish?'

'Yes, Mister Reed?'

Quicker that time. Almost back to normal.

'Can you get me Hugo?'

'I'm afraid...' There was a long pause. 'There's no signal, Mister Reed. The system's down.'

'Oh...'

He walked across and stood by the window, looking out across the river towards the City. It was a great spangle of lights. Looking at it, one could almost imagine that nothing was wrong; that everything was as it had been.

'Give me the news, Trish. Not the usual trivia. Let me see what's happening in the world. The big items.'

There was no answer, but a moment later the wall screen lit up again. The view was of a baseball stadium – Comiskey Park, it read.

'What's this?'

The camera focused in on a man's face. The instantly recognizable face of James B. Griffin, the sixtieth President of the United States of America. He was smiling, laughing, talking to his neighbour. Then, shockingly, his head jerked back as the top of his skull blew away, fragments of bone and bloodied brain scattered over the rows behind.

'Shit!'

Jake's stomach fell away. The last two days had been bad. But this...

He had to get out. To get away, as far and as quickly as he could. Because this was the end. The rest had been prelude. This was the killing blow that would send it all over the edge.

'Trish... get me a hopper.'

Silence.

'Trish...?'

Nothing. Not even the hiss of static.

He went through to his room, packed a bag, then went out into the hallway. Were the lifts working? Was anything working?

Jake pressed the button, then waited.

When did that happen? An hour ago?

No. It had to be more recent than that. The news must have broken even as he was in the air, coming back. Lampton wouldn't have let him go if something that serious had happened.

So what now? How long did they have before it became a shooting war? Because Jake had no doubt who was behind it.

Tsao Ch'un. He's pushed and pushed and now...

It was astonishing. Audacious, one might say. And very, very risky. But, then, everything Tsao Ch'un had done so far was risky. Which was not the same as saying that this was all a gamble. No. It was all part of a much greater strategy, clearly thought out and confidently carried through. And President Griffin's death was another key part of that, designed to panic America. A symbolic cutting off of the executive head.

The lift arrived. Pinged. As the doors hissed open, Jake hesitated. Maybe he should have left a written message. A note for Kate, just in case she returned. Only what would he have said? He wasn't even sure himself where he was going to go. Just that he had to get out of London fast, before the missiles flew.

Jake stepped inside the lift.

As he descended, he wondered if he'd ever return. Whether anything would ever be the same.

He'd go to Hugo's. If anyone knew what to do, it would be Hugo.

Besides, Hugo had a car. An air-driven Porsche. There was no one in reception. He rang the service bell, but no one came. And when he spoke to the air, summoning the block's AI, he got only silence.

He'd meant to get a cab to take him, but he could walk. It was only ten minutes away. But the big, sliding panel doors wouldn't open.

Jake went over to the reception desk. There was a control panel there. The outer doors were clearly marked. There was also a gun, in the drawer to the left of the board.

Jake stared at it a moment, surprised to find it there, then took it out and checked the chamber.

It was loaded.

He'd done an arms course years back, when he'd first become a *login*. He was licensed to carry a gun. Only there had never been a need for it.

He unlocked the doors and went outside, the gun wedged into the waistband of his trousers, the safety on.

Outside it was cold, the streets dark and empty. Overhead he could glimpse a hopper, one of the big Security craft, heading west at speed, away from the City.

Maybe they were evacuating. Maybe the big people were getting out.

If they'd worked it out, like he had.

He half walked, half ran. By the time he got to Hugo's building he was almost out of breath.

He knocked on the outer glass doors. The guard on the desk looked up, then quickly came across. He was elderly, ex-police, and whilst Jake didn't know his name, they were nodding acquaintances.

'Mister Reed...' he said, letting Jake in, then locking the door securely behind him. 'Have you come to see Master Hugo?'

'Is he home?'

'I'll check for you...'

The guard walked back over to his desk and pressed a connecting switch. He glanced back at Jake. 'Awful business this, don't you think?'

Jake looked across and saw how the silent screen behind him

was filled with images from the assassination. Distraught faces told their eyewitness accounts into camera.

'It's horrible,' Jake said. 'How long ago did it happen?'

'Not twenty minutes back... Ah... Master Hugo... it's James here, down on the desk... yes... your friend Mister Reed is here... Okay... I'll put him in the lift...'

The guard pointed to the lift, which pinged open.

'There you are, Mister Reed. You know the way...'

Hugo was waiting for him upstairs outside the lift. He hugged him, then ushered him inside.

'Where's Chris?'

'Somewhere...'

'You've got to find him. Get him to go with you.'

'Go? Go where?'

Jake swallowed, then launched in. 'Haven't you seen? The American President's dead! Someone blew his head off!'

'I know. I saw it on the news.'

'Then why aren't you packing?'

Hugo looked at his old friend askance. 'It's not good, I know, but... why in hell's name should I be packing? You booked us a surprise holiday?'

'It isn't time for jokes, Hu. We've got to get out of London. It's war...'

'Oh, come on...'

Hugo stared at him, saw how serious he was, then shook his head. 'Okay. What don't I know?'

Chris arrived twenty minutes later. He seemed breathless.

'It's a madhouse out there,' he said, throwing off his coat, then striding through into the bedroom. 'I don't know what's going on, but there are big queues at all the gates, and you can't hire a hopper for love nor money.'

Hugo looked to Jake. 'It's like you said,' he said quietly.

Jake got up and walked through to where Chris was busy opening drawers and taking out clothes to pack.

'You're getting out, then?'

Chris glanced at him. 'Till things get better, yeah. You want to come with us, Jake? We've plenty of room at the cottage.'

'I don't know, Chris...' Hugo said, from where he stood in the doorway. 'I think I might stay. I mean, I can't see how anywhere is going to be any safer than this. If the bombs start falling, I don't think any of us'll have much of a chance.'

Chris turned, surprised. 'Come on, Hu... We can't stay here. If it all kicks off... well... this place'll be ashes.'

'Maybe... but I'd rather die like that, suddenly, in a blaze of light and heat, than have my flesh rot over the months that follow. Nowhere's going to be safe, Chris. Nowhere.'

Jake wasn't so sure. 'I dunno... if I'm right...'

Hugo shook his head. 'Do you really think the US will hold back, Jake, after what you've told me the Chinese have been doing? No. This is what some of those Pentagon boys have been wet-dreaming of these past fifty years!'

Jake turned back, looking to the older man. 'Chris... you've not heard anything from Kate, have you?'

Chris looked across at him and smiled. 'As a matter of fact, I have. She was asking if I'd seen you or spoken to you. Said she couldn't get any kind of response from your apartment.'

'No... it's gone. The AI – Trish – has packed up. I don't know why, but...'

'They targeted Jake,' Hugo said, stepping past him. 'They shot down his hopper and erased all his files.'

Chris turned, aghast. 'They did *what*?'

Jake shrugged. 'It's been a tough day. But look... do you mind if I try to reach her from here?'

'No... go on,' Hugo said. But his attention was taken by Chris, who was still busy packing his bag.

Jake went through into the living room again, then spoke to the air, addressing Hugo's AI. 'Hal... it's Jake... get me Kate...'

There was a ten-second delay and then Kate appeared on the wall screen, twice life size.

'Jake... thank god... I was so worried.'

'Hi, sweetheart, I'm at Hugo's. Chris gave me your message.'

'Where've you been? I've been frantic. I contacted Hinton, but no one there seemed to know what was going on.'

'No, I don't suppose they did. But look... can you get over here? We're going to go with Chris... and Hugo, I guess... down to their cottage. Until things blow over.'

Kate looked round at that. 'I don't know... I'm at my parents'. They're really anxious about things. My sister's coming here... maybe you could...?'

'You want me to come to you? Sure. I don't know how, but... maybe Chris and Hugo can drop me on the way. I don't know how it is on the roads.'

'Can't you get a hopper?'

'Uh-uh... no chance of that. The big people are commandeering all of those.'

Kate swallowed and looked down. She seemed close to tears. 'What happened, Jake? What in god's name happened?'

His mouth was dry. He didn't want to say. Didn't want to scare her even more than she was scared already.

'It's going to be okay, my love. I'll get to you, don't worry. It'll all blow over, believe me... You just hang in there until I see you again, okay?'

'Okay...' But her voice was small and frightened, and as he cut the connection, Jake found himself wondering if he would ever see her again.

The approach roads to the western gate were jammed. No one was being allowed in or out. Which was why, an hour on, they were still there, in Hugo's apartment, trying to work out what was best to do.

They had been following it all on the news. Had seen the panicked crowds, both inside the enclaves and out. And now there was new footage of Griffin's assassination, showing the killer, a big, shaven-headed American in his mid-forties.

They had argued over that – whether he was a Chinese hireling or just a deadbeat with a grudge, but as yet no one was making any threats of war.

For the moment, then, things were all right. Not good, but better than they'd looked like being an hour back.

'Let's leave it a bit,' Chris said, getting up from the sofa. 'Let things cool down, then make our way.'

'Maybe I should try Hinton again,' Jake said. 'See if they can't get us a hopper.'

'Good idea,' Hugo said, bringing a fresh bottle of wine in from the kitchen. 'I reckon they owe you one, don't you?'

He did. But whether they thought that way was something else.

Jake hadn't heard from Hinton since he'd left Lampton's, two and a half hours back. He'd let them know where he was, but no one had contacted him.

'Hal,' he said, 'get me Hinton... no, get me Sir Henry Lampton... specifically him. Tell him who I am...'

'Will do, Mister Reed.'

They waited, sipping wine, the wall screen showing silent images of chaos. Then Hal spoke again.

'He says sorry, that he can't speak right now. But he did ask if you needed transportation...'

'Good man!' Chris said, raising his glass. 'Well done, Sir Harry!'

Jake stood, addressing the air. 'Tell him thanks, and that, yes please... if we could have a hopper at this address... say in fifteen minutes?'

'Will do, Mister Reed.'

'Well?' Chris asked, setting his glass aside and looking to Hugo.

'Are you staying or coming?'

Hugo smiled. The fact that nothing had happened yet had re-assured him. If there was going to be war it would have happened by now, surely?

'I'll come...'

Chris beamed. 'Good... there's my darling boy... now go pack a bag... quickly now...'

Alone with Jake, Chris looked to him. 'You want dropping off at Kate's parents, yeah?'

'Yeah...'

'You think we'll get through this?'

Jake shrugged. 'I don't know. I... What I saw in there scared me, Chris. Tsao Ch'un's a man who's not afraid to take great chances. As for the guy who's working for him... the one who's providing all his programmes...'

They'd not really talked about this.

'Go on...' Chris said. 'What about him?'

'It's just... I've never encountered anything like him.'

'Him? You're sure it's a him?'

Jake nodded. 'Yeah... there's something coldly masculine about what he does. Some unforgiving logic. My guess is that he's infil-trated a lot more than we've yet realized. If what he did to the datscape's a taster, then I reckon he'd have no trouble disabling the whole of America's defence system.'

Chris laughed at that, but his face, his eyes particularly, were serious. 'What, like, shut things down? Stop them using their tech-nology?'

'Precisely that. He has the capability. And my guess is that he wouldn't start what he can't finish. It wouldn't surprise me if, when push comes to shove, the Americans find most of their switches and buttons are connected to diddly-squat!'

'So you don't think there'll be a war?'

'That's not what I said. There might not be a shooting war... but then there doesn't need to be, not if what the Chinese plan is simply to destroy our infrastructure. They can do that without firing a single weapon.'

Chris stared at him a moment longer, not sure whether this was truth or paranoia. Not that Jake knew himself. But his feeling for it was strong. And it was just that kind of feeling that Hinton had paid him for all these years. To outguess the Market.

'So what's going to happen?' Chris asked finally.

'I don't know,' he answered truthfully. 'But let's hope I'm wrong, eh? Let's hope to god I'm wrong.'

The hopper Lampton sent them was one of the big military cruisers, complete with heavy-duty armour, guns and guards.

The three of them sat in the back, in the luxury of the spacious hold, looking at each other and grinning.

'Good old Jake,' Hugo said, relaxing for the first time in hours. 'We knew your connections would come in useful one of these days.'

Jake smiled and nodded. But it made him think. 'What about Jenny?'

'She'll be fine,' Chris said, wriggling back into the plush black leather seat, getting himself comfy. 'Alex'll look after her. He's a captain now, after all.'

'Makes me glad I'm not straight,' Hugo said.

Jake looked to him. 'And why particularly do you say that now?'

'No children. I don't know what I'd have done if I'd had kids, what with all of this happening. It's bad enough looking after yourself. If you had kids...'

Jake nodded, falling silent. It was an awful thought. To think you might not be able to protect them. He swallowed, his mouth gone dry again.

'Jake?' Chris asked.

'Yeah?'

'What you were saying... I can't see it. One man, manipulating it all. Writing programmes... it seems...'

'Impossible?'

'No. Just unlikely. And the Americans... they'll have their own geek geniuses, no?'

'Almost certainly, only...' Jake shrugged, not knowing quite how to persuade them. 'He's just so good. It's like... well, just the way he backs up everything he does with something else. Fail-safes. Ingenious countermeasures. The man uses a whole palette of effects. You can't predict him. Everything you think of he's thought it through beforehand and has an answer.'

'And yet he failed. He tried to kill you and he failed. He tried to erase you from the records...'

Jake looked to Chris and nodded slowly. 'Yes, but that was pure accident. It was *chance*, pure and simple. And you could argue that he didn't need to kill me... just take me out of the game for a time. Which is what he did. So...'

'They should kill him. Send a squad in... special services... and kill the bastard.'

'Yes,' Jake said, 'they should.'

He hugged them, Chris first, then Hugo, then jumped down onto the lawn, turning to wave goodbye as they lifted into the late afternoon sky.

In a moment they were gone.

Jake turned. Kate was waiting for him by the back door, her parents just beyond her, inside the old mock Tudor house.

He'd been afraid he'd never see her again, never touch her, but there she was.

Jake picked his bag up and began to walk towards her, and as he did, so she began to come to him, walking at first, then running, throwing herself into his arms.

'Oh, Jake...'

He lifted her up, whirling her about, kissing her as he did. She smelled so good.

'Thank god,' she said, smiling up at him. 'I thought I'd never see you again.'

It was on his lips to tell her everything that had happened to him. But why trouble her? She'd only be more anxious.

'Well, it's okay now,' he said, gently kissing her brow. 'I'm here.'

They went across. Charles and Margaret were smiling, welcoming him.

'Jake,' Charles said. 'Rum old business with the Market, eh?'

'We'll talk,' Jake said. 'Later on. I'll tell you what's been happening.'

Charles picked up quickly on what he meant. 'Ah... right... Margaret's done dinner... you fancy some?'

Jake hadn't eaten in god knows how long. 'I'd love some. If there's enough...'

'Oh, there's plenty,' Margaret said, stepping closer so he could kiss her cheek. 'And well done, you. The permit... It's wonderful news!'

He'd quite forgotten. The permit... Of course. Not that it meant that much any more. No. Everything had changed. Who knew what the future would bring?

Dinner was pleasant but polite. Barely a word was said about what was happening outside in the real world. And for once that suited Jake. He felt tired. Mentally exhausted. What he really wanted was to sleep for eighteen hours straight. But that wasn't going to happen.

As Margaret cleared away the plates, Jake looked to his future father-in-law.

'Sir?'

'Yes, boy?'

'I wondered if I might ask you a favour... whether I might log on to your computer?'

'Of course... help yourself. You know where it is. Maybe I'll join you, if that's okay. Have a word about things.'

'Sure.'

The two men got up and, after giving Kate a kiss, left the room.

Charles's study was on the first floor of the house, at the back, next to the box room. Jake had often stayed in here when he and Kate had started seeing each other and they'd gone through the charade of pretending not to sleep with one another.

As Jake sat at the console, keying in his details, Charles sat in the chair nearby and lit up a cigarette.

'So what do you make of all this, Jake? Can't understand it myself. The Market was as right as rain. Strong and healthy. But now...'

'Oh, Christ...' Jake said, as it rejected his password. 'I forgot... I don't exist...'

'What's that, boy? Don't exist?'

He turned to face the older man. 'It's a long story, but if you'd log me in on your account...?'

Charles came across and typed in his code. 'There... that should do it.'

'Thanks...'

Jake turned back. Brought down the Hi-Five search engine and typed in 'TSAO CH'UN', then 'WEI CHI'.

'It's all very complex,' he said, as the machine showed up the best matches. 'All I can say is that they're going to have to reconstruct it all from scratch.'

'Reconstruct it all? What do you mean?'

There was a picture on-screen now of a youngish-looking Han – Tsao Ch'un, he realized – looking on as an older middle-aged man sat at a wei chi board, leaning across to place a stone. The caption read, 'Central Committee Member Tsao Ch'un looks on as reigning All-China wei chi Master, Chao Ni Tsu, plays the winning stone.'

Jake typed in 'CHAO NI TSU, WEI CHI MASTER', then 'COMPUTER TRAINING'.

'I mean,' Jake said, turning to face Charles again, 'exactly that. It's been destroyed. Attack programmes have turned the datscape into a wasteland.'

Jake saw the shock in the other man's face. Up until eighteen months ago, Charles had been part of that world. Until he'd taken early retirement for his health's sake. And now, it seemed, it was gone.

'What are we going to do? I mean... all of us... if it's gone...'

Charles had grasped it at once. If there was no Market, there was no wealth. Everything everyone had was suddenly illusory. Nothing was worth anything. Aside, that was, for basics. And how would they get hold of those?

'Oh, god... does Kate know?'

Jake shook his head. 'Like everyone, she knows there's been a bit of trouble... but not the extent of it.'

He turned back. On the screen now was a picture of a man in his early twenties, taken some thirty-odd years ago. He was a Han... or maybe he was Japanese. It was hard to distinguish in this case. But from the caption this was Chao Ni Tsu, and the piece that followed related how he had qualified from Cambridge with a double first in Computing Science, then gone on to write his doctoral thesis at eighteen. Aged twenty-three in the picture, he had now formed his own company.

Jake smiled, then magnified the face, so that it filled the screen.

So there you are...

Any doubts he'd had were gone. This was his man. This was the enemy they had to fight.

Cambridge graduated, eh?

Jake cleared the screen, then turned to face Charles again. The older man was watching him now.

'You fancy a brandy, boy? A large one?'

Jake nodded.

'Good... because I most certainly do. And while we drink it, I want you to tell me everything. From start to finish, leaving noth-ing out.'

'Yes, sir.'

'And it's Charles, boy. If I'm going to be your father-in-law then I'm having none of this "sir" shit, all right?'

Jake smiled. 'Yes, Charles…'

'Jake?'

'Yes, my love?'

'Come to bed.'

He turned and looked across the room at her. She had pulled back the sheets and was sitting up, her small, perfectly formed breasts revealed by the moonlight.

Jake sighed. He didn't know what the coming days would bring, but at least he was lucky enough to have this.

He went across and, slipping from his robe, got in beside her, taking her in his arms and kissing her.

They made love, quietly, as of old, conscious of her parents, there on the other side of the wall in the bedroom next to them. And afterwards they lay there, Kate's head on his chest, her hand laid gently on his shoulder, while his arm lay about her back. As if nothing were wrong. As if the world hadn't changed between the last time they had lain here and now.

After a while he could hear her gently snoring. She was asleep. But Jake couldn't sleep. There was too much going on in his head.

Careful not to wake her, he slipped out of bed and, putting on his robe again, went out onto the balcony, looking out across the enclave towards the City.

You couldn't see it properly from this far out, only a vague kind of glow on the horizon, but the noise of rioting went on, muted but still there, on the edge of hearing.

After Kate and her mother had gone up, Charles and he had had another drink and watched some news.

If you could believe what was on the media, things had calmed. The PM had announced that the Market would open in a week, and that measures had been taken to stabilize the situation. And maybe that was so. Only Jake didn't believe it.

Charles, after what he'd told him, had been subdued. He had tried to put a brave face on it, but what Jake had told him had clearly sapped his spirit. He had looked ashen.

They had agreed not to tell the women just how bad things were; to play it by ear and see what the next few days brought.

'We've a country place we could go to,' Charles had said, 'down in Dorset. We could load up the car and go down there.'

Only Jake wasn't sure that'd be any better than here. At least here they had a well-stocked freezer and a larder full of food. And the enclave itself had sturdy walls. There were far worse places one could be in times like this, and there wasn't the added risk of travelling halfway across the country.

No. If he could, he would persuade them to sit tight and ride things out. And who knew, maybe the world *would* organize against this threat.

One thing nagged at him, however, and that was how easy he had found it to locate Tsao Ch'un's man – his Go-playing computer expert, Chao Ni Tsu.

Wouldn't the man have hidden himself? Or at least made it much harder to find out who he was and what he looked like?

Knowing how devious the man was, how adept at anticipating, Jake would have expected no less. The man liked to leave smoke trails wherever he went, so why not this?

What if it *were* misinformation? Stuff he'd put online to satisfy his enemies' curiosity without revealing anything real.

A faint breeze blew across the garden, rustling the branches of the trees. Within it was the sound of voices, shouting, closer than before.

Jake frowned, looking over to his left, past the scattered rooftops towards the nearest gate, less than a mile distant. It sounded like it was coming from over there.

Here, in Marlow, they were at the north-western edge of one of the larger suburban enclaves. Within its walls, everything was fine. To the south, however, lay Maidenhead, an unprotected zone.

Not now, surely? he thought. But why should the mob keep civilized hours?

He stood there a moment longer, craning his neck, trying to hear. And once again, as the wind gusted, so he heard it: closer now, louder.

There was no mistaking it. A mob of people were heading their way.

He went inside and, dressing quickly, took the gun from his bag. Outside Margaret and Charles's room he hesitated, wondering whether he should wake Charles, then hurried on.

There was a key to the back door, hanging on a hook in the kitchen. He took it, slipped it into his pocket, then went out, running silently across the garden and out through the lattice gate that led onto the lane, heading for the gate.

Others joined him as he ran, having pulled their clothes on hastily. Some had guns, others makeshift weapons, but all of them had a look of grim determination.

At the gate more than a hundred of the local residents had gathered, along with a handful of security guards. The older men, Jake noticed. No doubt the younger ones had fled already.

One of the residents – a big, middle-aged man – had climbed up on to the back of a truck and was busy organizing things, shouting and pointing, clearly in his element.

Jake looked about him. The fencing was solid steel, twenty feet tall, topped with razor-wire. There were men up on the walls, their guns pointed down the approach road. As for the mob, you could hear them clearly now, a great roar of sound coming closer by the moment.

He went across, nodding to people as he went. Some looked excited, others scared, but no one was going anywhere. They were going to turn the mob back here, at the gate. No one was going to get past.

'You!' the man on the truck yelled, pointing to Jake. 'You got a weapon?'

Jake showed him the handgun.

'Good. Then go to the gate. We want as much firepower as we can there. You need more ammunition?'

Jake nodded.

'Okay... then see Will... over there...' And he pointed just beyond the truck.

Jake went across. To his surprise, Will seemed to have half a gun shop in the back of his vehicle.

'What d'you need?' the slightly balding man asked him. 'Here, give it to me... I'll find you something suitable...'

Moments later Jake came away with a whole pocketful of flat, thin cardboard packs of bullets.

Enough to start a war...

Looking through the wrought-iron bars of the gate, you could see the mob now, surging towards them, their torches flickering in the dark; a great mass of bodies impelled by hatred.

The sight terrified him.

This was the world they'd made. This awful world of have and have-not.

Nearby, one of the men was doubled over, heaving his guts up. Looking along the line of men, Jake could see that all of them were frightened now. They may have imagined doing this, may even have talked about it these past few days, but this was for real now. It was kill or be killed, and for many, it was the first time in their lives that they'd had to make such a choice. They had always been the lucky ones. But tonight their luck had run out.

With the mob still some way off, the first few shots rang out.

'Hold your fire!' the guy on the truck yelled. 'Wait till you can see their faces clearly!'

'Fuck off, Napoleon!' one of the men to Jake's right murmured, and there was laughter. Relieving, strengthening laughter. All of them tensed now, waiting for the order.

'Okay… let 'em have it!'

A great volley of shots rang out, and as they did, the whole of the front row of rioters fell.

Just like in the movies…

The mob surged on, breaking into a run now, meaning to take the gate by storm, but the gunfire was creating havoc and they were still a good fifty yards off.

It was then that the hopper flew over them, sweeping in from their left.

Jake turned, following its flight, watching where it went and wondering if it was for him. It was certainly setting down somewhere near the house.

For a moment he hesitated. It would look bad to leave the line, but he had to know. If it was Hinton, he'd have to go.

He backed away a pace or two, then turned and began to move quickly through the press of men.

'Hey… what the…?'

The man on the truck began to yell at him, then crumpled, clutching his gut.

So the rioters had guns too…

But Jake was running now, back through the streets, heading for the house.

He was coming round the corner, into the lane, when he heard footsteps crunching on the gravel up ahead.

Maybe it was Charles, coming for him. But instinct made him stop, made him step to the side and hide behind the hedge.

And not a moment too soon, for down the path came two heavily armoured men, both of them carrying semi-automatics.

Han... they were Chinese.

Jake swallowed. He watched them out of sight, then hurried on, along the path and through the back gate.

And stopped dead, gasping, staring with disbelief at the back of the house.

The house was on fire. The whole of the kitchen was blazing away. Even as he took a step towards it, the windows blew out, scattering glass across the patio.

Jake looked about him. Where was the craft? Had it set down? Or had it just dropped the men and gone?

He ran across the lawn. The key was no use now, but there was a flight of wooden steps going up the side of the house. He went up them quickly and, at the top, used the gun to smash the glass pane, then pushed through into the box room.

The smoke was getting thicker. He could taste it now in his mouth.

Only hours ago he had sat here at the computer console...

Jake ran through, not daring to call out in case one of them was still there, waiting for him to return. Pushing the door to her parents' room open, he saw at once just what he'd feared. They lay there, side by side, sightlessly staring at the ceiling.

Jake took a step closer.

Christ... they had been garrotted.

He felt sick just looking at them. His legs felt weak.

Jake staggered through, knowing now. She was dead. His darling girl was dead. And all because he'd been curious. Had needed to know if his hunch was correct.

There was no other explanation. No other way they could have found him so quickly.

Kate had put up a fight. She had been woken by them – no doubt to ask her where he was – and she had fought them. Even so, the sight of her, doubled up on the floor, the thin flex round her throat, pulled so tight that it had drawn blood, made him whimper.

'Oh, Christ...'

He would kill them. He would find the cunts and kill them.

Downstairs the fire was spreading. Smoke was pouring up the stairs now. He ought to be getting out of there, before the ceiling downstairs gave way. But he couldn't go. Not yet. Kneeling beside her, he gently touched her cheek, then bent forward and kissed her farewell.

'Goodbye, my darling girl...'

For a moment he couldn't move. Couldn't leave her. Then, tearing himself away, he stood and, drawing his gun, stepped out into the hallway.

And almost walked straight into him.

The man was wearing a mask. Even so, Jake could see his eyes. See what he was.

He shot him. Once in the chest and once in the head.

Jake stepped over him, where he lay, and reached down to pull off the mask. The Han was still alive, gasping for breath but still living.

Jake put the barrel in the man's mouth and pulled the trigger.

He straightened up, wiping his mouth with the back of his hand. It didn't matter now whether he lived or died. Nothing mattered now.

As he went slowly down the steps, the kitchen ceiling came crashing down.

The heat was fierce now. As Jake crossed the garden he could feel it at his back.

The first of them came running through the gate at speed. Jake shot him, watched him fall.

The noise from the fire must have masked the sound of the shot, for the other came through the gate a moment later, unaware that he was there.

Jake fired at him and missed.

The assassin swung his gun up.

Jake's second shot hit his shoulder and span him round, sending his gun flying away from him.

Jake walked towards him. Raised his gun again and pulled the trigger.

There was nothing. Just the click of an empty chamber.

He saw the Han's face. Saw that the man thought he had a chance now.

Jake threw himself at him, using the handgun as a club now, hitting out blindly, forcing him down onto his knees, then hitting him again and again and again until his face was a pulp and Jake's hand was sticky with blood.

As the Han gurgled away his last breath, Jake straightened up. He was straddling the man, sitting on his chest.

Jake stood, then looked across at the other one. He lay there, kicking, holding his throat. A moment later he grew still.

Jake walked across and picked up the assassin's gun.

Was that all of them? Or were there more?

Right then he felt like killing dozens of the bastards. Hundreds. Just bring them on. He'd kill them all. He'd fill the world with dead Chinese for what they'd done.

Jake turned, looking back at the house. It was totally ablaze now. Great sheets of flame leaping up twenty, thirty feet into the air. The heat from it was almost too much to bear. Slowly he stepped back, away from it.

As he did the roof fell in, sending up tall showers of sparks.

Everything gone, he thought, the first tear rolling down his cheek.

Chapter 7

WEST

There'd been no time for tears. He'd had to get out of there as quickly as he could, before they came for him again.

That was, if they could find him.

He'd plundered the two he'd killed in the garden, taking one of their guns and all of their ammunition, along with the body armour and helmet of the bigger one.

He had been tempted to make his way to Heathrow, to get a plane out of there and ride things out on the Greek isles, but three things were wrong with that.

First, it would entail travelling back towards London, through the wild lands of Maidenhead and Slough, back towards the chaos of the city.

Second, he had no money. Not that money – either as notes or as a credit balance on an account – was worth anything now. The Chinese had effectively done away with money when they'd destroyed the datscape.

And third, he wasn't sure that he still existed. Officially, that was. Lampton had talked of glitches in the system, but what if those hadn't been dealt with? What if they'd left him off the record?

There was only one answer, to head west and try to get to Hugo and Chris's cottage down in Coombe Bissett, just outside Salisbury. He wasn't sure how far it was – eighty miles, maybe a hundred – but it was better than heading back in. It would mean travelling across lawless countryside, but there would be plenty of places to hide, plenty of places to bed down for the night. Besides, he was armed now.

What he didn't have, and what he needed badly, was a map. An Ordnance Survey would have been nice, but any map would do.

There would be filling stations on the way – places where they sold the compressed air cylinders that most cars ran on these days. They'd have maps there, surely?

That gave him an idea. He'd never owned a car. Never needed to. But they couldn't be that hard to operate. What if he took one and used one of the toll roads?

First, however, he would get to Henley, maybe use the gate at Sonning Common.

He set out, walking through the dark, half-lit streets, expecting at any moment to be stopped and challenged. But, apart from a twitching curtain here, a face at a window there, there was no sign of anyone.

Until he came to the gate.

There, in the streets surrounding it, they had built barricades, using whatever they could find – motor mowers, garden tables and chairs, shed doors and bicycles, bags of compost and old bits of wood. Nearby they had lit bonfires. In their light, Jake could make out sixty men or more, most of them armed.

Jake stopped, trying to make out if there was any other way round. But he had already been seen. Three men came towards him, guns raised.

'Hey… Who are you?'

Jake knew he must have looked quite threatening, what with the body armour and the helmet and the gun hanging from his shoulder, but he tried not to panic them. He raised his hands.

'It's okay... I'm coming from Marlow... my girlfriend's parents live there... Charles and Margaret Williams...'

They spread out, encircling him, their eyes narrowed, watching for any move of his, itching, it seemed, to use their weapons.

'So what's with all this?' their spokesman said, gesturing towards the uniform, the weapons. He had a nasty, hostile expression on his face, like he wasn't going to believe a thing Jake said.

He had to be careful.

'There were assassins... Chinese...'

'What the...?' The man seemed to lose his patience. 'Show me your ID!' he barked. 'And don't think of trying to use one of those!'

Jake shrugged. 'Okay... calm down... I'll move slowly, okay? It's in my jacket pocket, so...

He had almost forgotten. He still had the handgun. It was there, next to his ID card. Not that he'd have a chance to use it. No. He'd be dead before he could get a single shot off.

Jake took out the card and threw it across. The man stooped down and picked it up, glancing at it casually before looking back at Jake.

'This genuine?'

What a fucking stupid question to ask. But Jake didn't say that. He simply nodded. 'I'm Jake Reed. Twenty-six years old. My birthday's the eighteenth of August, and I'm a *login.*'

'A *what?*'

'He's what they call a web-dancer,' one of the others said. 'Ain't that right?'

Jake nodded. 'I work for Hinton Industrial. Or did. I used to buy and sell stocks and shares on the datscape.'

He saw how the man pondered that, turning the card over and over in his hand. Then he seemed to make a decision. He lowered his gun, then stepped across, handing Jake back his card.

'I'm sorry... it's just... we can't take any chances...'

Jake nodded, pocketing the card. 'No need to apologize. But

look... I need to get outside... I'm trying to join up with some friends, down in Salisbury.'

'Salisbury? You won't make it, friend. There's wild mobs out there. Real fucking savages. You'd be better off staying here till things calm down.'

Maybe, Jake thought. Only he needed to be with friends, not strangers. If the world was coming to an end, then he wanted to be with those he loved, not those who'd shoot him if he got his story wrong.

'Thanks for the offer but... my fiancée's there. She's expecting me.'

It hurt him even to say it. Only it made his anxiousness to be away from there believable.

'There's a lot of that shit,' one of them said. 'There's gonna be a lot of people cut off from each other. I'm just glad all mine are home. Fuck knows how worried I'd be if they were the other side of the country. Like Mike says...'

'Look, Mike,' he said, latching on to the name. 'I need a map. A good one, if possible. I'm kind of vague on the route, and...'

'I've got one indoors you can have,' Mike answered, amenable now that he knew Jake wasn't a threat. 'Just wait there. I'll go get it.'

While he was gone, Jake talked to the other two. They were nervous about how things were, sure, but things would right themselves. Just give it a day or two and it would all be up and running again, just see if it wasn't.

If only that were true, Jake thought. If only our leaders had the sense and the courage to sort things out.

Only they didn't. Jake knew only too well who *really* controlled the Market. It was the international speculators. The big fish. And it was their greed, their inability to think of anything but their own fat wallets, that had allowed Tsao Ch'un to get away with this.

Not that it mattered now.

Mike returned, smiling now as he handed Jake the book of maps. It was a big, expensive-looking thing, leather-bound, 1 to 50,000 scale, or just over an inch to a mile.

'I can't...' Jake said, old habits of politeness kicking in. 'This is just...'

'No, take it... it's fine. You're going to need it out there. And... my wife did this for you...'

Jake took the bag from him and looked inside. There were bottles and a number of small packages wrapped in foil – a regular little picnic.

Jake looked back at him, touched by this unexpected gesture.

'Thanks... Look, I... I really hope it all goes well for you. I hope...'

That you all survive, he wanted to say. Only he couldn't. It was too depressing. But it was the truth. The darkest days lay ahead, when people realized exactly what had happened. That nothing had any value any more.

He embraced them. Then, as a number of them kept him covered, they opened the gate and let him pass, out into the wilds. Out into the unprotected dark, gun in hand, hoping he'd made the right decision.

He went south and west, following the old minor roads, through Kidmore End, then across country, arriving at the sleeping village of Whitchurch as the clock struck three.

There was an old toll booth there on the south road. It had fallen into disuse years ago, but the road was still there, boarded off to cars. Jake climbed over the barrier and set off towards the motorway.

There were barriers – fifty feet tall – along the whole length of the motorway, with razor-wire on top to keep out the UPs, but just ahead of him the toll road dipped beneath the highway, emerging on the far side. The town of Theale was a mile or two further on.

As Jake went into the tunnel, he could hear cars on the motorway. There wasn't much traffic, just the whine of an engine now and then as one went past, all of it heading west.

He moved slowly, trying to see into the shadows, his gun out and ready, the safety off. If he was going to be attacked anywhere, it was here. It was a perfect spot for an ambush. Only who the fuck would be walking out this late? Who would be so crazy as to use this route?

Only a desperate man.

The road dipped, then began to climb again.

He could hear the slow crunch, crunch, crunch of his own footsteps. Hear his own shallow breathing.

Something scuttled away, up a bit and to his right. He knew it was only a rat, or some woodland animal, but it made his nerves twitch.

He stopped, straining to hear.

Nothing.

And went on, climbing the slope, the darkness becoming less intense with every step, his heartbeat slowing as the tension eased.

He had been lucky so far. Or perhaps all the rioters had worn themselves out and had gone back home – were now safely tucked up in their beds, like good little savages.

Jake sighed. He'd have to stop soon. Had to get some rest. Travelling at night made sense, only he was exhausted. He had seen too much. Done too much...

At the top of the slope he halted. He could see the faint outlines of houses up ahead. Maybe one of them was deserted. Perhaps he could kip there for the remainder of the night, then set off early.

The implant beneath his right ear had been weeping again. It felt sore and swollen, possibly even infected. He'd have to see to that sometime. Maybe at Newbury when he got there.

If he got there.

As he came up alongside the first of the houses, he stopped, looking across.

How did you tell which houses were occupied and which not? Did you just break in and take a chance?

A barn, then, maybe. Somewhere that wouldn't be checked before the morning.

Only he needed a bed. Needed to lie down and sleep, and he wasn't sure a barn would be any good for that.

Jake let his head fall. Until that moment he had been all right. Until he'd thought of it, and seen himself in memory, there beside her in her bed in her parents' house, her beautiful green eyes looking up at him.

'Oh, fuck...'

He had been walking like a dead man. Numb. Emotionally drained. Pretending it hadn't happened. Only now it came flooding back and he saw in his mind how she lay there on the floor beside the bed, her flesh sickly pale, a line of crusted blood about the plastic cord those cunts had used on her.

He groaned and fell to his knees.

Make it not so...

Only nothing could call it back.

Jake shivered, then remembered. The permit. He still had the permit in his pocket. He took it out, staring at it a moment, trying to make sense of it, then tore it into shreds and scattered it.

His life. His future. Gone. The whole fucking lot of it, gone!

Then why not end it now? Why not put the gun in his mouth and pull the trigger?

Jake got to his feet. Wiped his face with the back of his sleeve. He had to get to Hugo and Chris, that's why. Had to tell them what had happened.

He walked on, his legs heavy now.

This one? No. The curtains are drawn. There's someone in that one. Then this one, maybe? Yes... why not.

At worst he'd wake someone. At worst...

Only he had to sleep. If he didn't he'd fall over.

He walked across and looked inside. The curtains were open, the front room dark. He went round the side of the building and tried the back door. It opened. Inside, in the dark silence of the kitchen, he stopped, straining to listen.

Nothing. The place was empty.

Even so, he checked it out. Checked every room. Then settled in the back bedroom, hauling a small chest of drawers in front of the door before he drew the curtains.

He didn't risk putting on the light, but there was a television – an old wall-mounted plasma screen. He plugged it in, not expecting it to work, only it did.

The electricity's still on!

That surprised him.

The screen lit. Images of burning buildings and riot troops in action. London, he guessed, or one of the other big cities. He turned the sound up slightly.

Two planes exploded in the air, one after another. Bits of one came raining down on an airport lounge as screaming passengers fled the burning building.

The picture cut out, then came back. The sound wavered momentarily.

An elderly man – the US Vice-President, Jake realized – was being sworn in, his generals standing close by, looking on, their faces anxious.

Three men – Chinese by the look of them, bound hand and foot – were led into a courtyard by masked special services men. They were forced down onto their knees then executed, one by one, with a single shot to the back of the head.

The screen went black, then slowly brightened.

There was something about Martial Law being declared, over pictures of streets packed solid with fleeing people. It cut to the announcer again.

The screen went black. This time it stayed black.

Wearily, Jake went across; turned it off then turned it on again. It wasn't the power. It was the signal.

He stretched then yawned; the kind of yawn that almost disconnects your jaw. What he'd seen on the screen, that was just part of it. All over the world fucked-up things were happening. Good people were dying. People who deserved a lot better.

It made him feel sick just thinking about it.

They should have killed Tsao Ch'un. Strangled the little bastard at birth. Like Hitler and all the other sociopathic egomaniacs. Drowned them in a vat of acid, just to make sure.

But he was tired now. Bone tired. He could barely feel his hatred through the thick layers of tiredness.

He lay down, knowing he shouldn't sleep, that he didn't deserve to sleep, not when his darling Kate was dead. But sleep came nonetheless, like a vast wave washing over him, dragging him deep into its sunless depths. Down, down into the dreamless abyss of exhaustion.

Like the dead. Like the living dead.

He woke early, startled back into consciousness, grabbing at his gun in a panic, the feeling that there was someone in the room with him strong. Only there was no one. He was alone.

Jake sat there for a time on the edge of the bed, hunched forward, his head in his hands. He had been too tired yesterday, too concerned with making his escape, for it to have struck home. But now it did, just like last night. Kate was dead. So too the life he'd known, his future.

Maybe, only he was still alive.

In the half-light he could see now what kind of room it was. It had the look of a spare room, with cheap, make-do furniture and a threadbare carpet that smelled old and musty. He had barely noticed it when he let himself in, but now he did. This was the kind of room he'd have to put up with from now on.

Jake pulled the chest of drawers away from the door, then gathered up his things. Downstairs he searched through drawers and cupboards, looking for anything that might prove useful, putting it all into an old green knapsack he had found hanging on a hook next to the back door.

Knives, a torch, two packets of working batteries, a first aid kit, a pair of size nine hiking boots, and other things.

And then, because – who knew? – things might yet turn out right, he left a note, addressed to the householder, itemizing what he'd taken, and giving his old address back in the city.

He went out, pausing in that scruffy, untended yard to listen.

Nothing. Only the call of birds in the copse beyond the houses.

He had a long walk before him, and it would be best if he got a fair distance behind him before people began to get up.

It was a bright, clear morning. Fresh, with not a trace of cloud.

He had no plan except to walk, and keep out of trouble. If he could.

Theale was silent. It seemed deserted. There was not a trace of anyone about. Maybe it was too early. But Jake had the sense of being watched.

No one was taking any chances. Maybe they were all staying indoors and minding their own business until things blew over. It was what he would have done if he were them. Only he wasn't, and his only chance was to get to Hugo and Chris's. Apart from them, he didn't have a friend in the world.

He saw his first sign of the troubles as he came into what the road sign said was Sulhamstead. There, by the crossroads, an inn had been burned out. It must have been done recently, for it was still smouldering. In the car park nearby a number of cars had also been set alight.

Jake took the gun from his shoulder, then walked on.

At Woolhampton a number of windows had been smashed and several of the shops had been boarded up. Someone had spray-canned slogans on the boards and on the walls, together with the age-old anarchist symbol, the A in a circle, which always reminded Jake of an eye.

He walked on. Ahead was Thatcham, and beyond it Newbury. At this rate he would be there within the hour.

As he came to the outskirts of Thatcham, Jake slowed. Up ahead he could see a group of people, a dozen or so of them, gathered on the right-hand side of the road.

After seeing no one at all so far that morning, this little gathering seemed ominous. Should he get off the road and try and make his way round them, or should he press on, directly?

If he was to get to Andover by this evening, which was his plan, then he couldn't afford too many delays. Only he didn't want trouble.

But then, why should they be trouble? What if they were just normal citizens? Maybe they'd simply gathered to discuss things. Wouldn't he have done the same? Only he had in mind what had happened at the gate last night; that hostility bred of fear and uncertainty. These were not normal times. You couldn't expect people to behave as they would normally.

But to try and make his way around them made little sense. At least on the road he could see them clearly. Knew where they were. Off it, they had the advantage. After all, they knew this locality, he didn't.

He walked on, taking the safety off. He didn't mean to use the gun, but if he had to he would. He would keep to the other side of the road. Would greet them politely if they called out to him. Otherwise...

He swallowed.

This is how it's going to be from here on in. A slow march through hostile territory, and not a single friend between here and Salisbury.

As the distance narrowed, he saw how they turned to face him, then stepped out onto the road, spreading out, blocking his way.

Twenty yards from them he stopped.

'I'm going to Newbury,' he called. 'I just want to pass. I won't do any harm.'

'Where d'you come from?' one of them asked in a broad Swindon accent.

Jake looked to him, read him at once. A troublemaker. A fucking troublemaker. Just his luck...

The man had the look of a pub drunk. Belligerent. Aggressive. The rest were taking their lead from him. He could see that at once.

'I've come from London,' Jake said, letting nothing show in his face. 'I'm heading west.'

That was as specific as he was going to get.

'I think you're wrong,' the man answered him, smiling unpleasantly. 'I think you're going east. Back where you came from.'

Jake had been looking along the line. Trying to assess where the danger was. Two of them had guns, which was probably why the man felt confident in threatening him. Only the two gunmen looked anything but confident. They could see he had better weaponry than them, and from the look of him, the body armour and all, he probably knew how to use it.

Jake sighed. 'Look... just let me pass. I don't want trouble. I don't want to harm anyone, got me?'

He looked to one of the gunmen, then the other, then back at the mouthy bastard who was their leader.

'If I have to, I'll blow your fucking head off, understand? But I'd prefer not to. I've had a hard two days...'

'Mike...' one of them began, but the man cut him off with a savage hand gesture.

'Listen, Mister... this is our village and we say who can come through, okay? So just turn around and...'

Jake fired the gun into the air. Saw how they all jumped at that, surprised, most of them taking a step or two back, away from him. The two gunmen were shaking now.

No doubt it's easier under cover of darkness.

'Leave 'im, Mike,' one of them said. ''E ain't worth it.'

'That's right, Mike,' Jake said, smiling now, a cold steel at the heart of him now that he'd been pushed. 'I ain't worth it.'

They were moving to the side now. Clearing a path for him. All except Mike.

'Listen,' Jake said, meeting the man's eyes coldly. 'I'll say it once and once only. Get out of my fucking way!'

Mike hesitated, then, his head dropping, he stepped back.

Good, Jake thought, only he moved slowly, carefully, keeping an eye on them all. Particularly the two with guns, just in case they found a bit of courage at the last. Then he was walking slowly backwards, away from them.

'Arseholes...' he said quietly, beneath his breath. But it had taught him an important lesson. He could not relax. Not for a second. For what had happened had exposed a rawness, a savagery in people, a compound of pettiness and bitterness and spite, that needed to be vented. And who better to vent it on than outsiders? Passing strangers like himself.

No. There would be no kindnesses from this point on. Only hostility. And next time he might not be so lucky. Next time they might shoot first and talk later.

Jake stopped just south of Newbury at a place called Enborne Row, where the A34 crossed the A343.

There, in the cover of the trees, his back to an old stone wall, he ate the last of the picnic he'd been given back at the Henley gate.

For that much, anyway, he was grateful. For the woman's ham and chicken rolls and the bottles of spring water she'd provided. Jake wolfed them down, then, knowing he had a long march ahead of him, took ten minutes' rest.

And woke an hour or more later, hearing voices on the road.

Refugees. He could see them through the trees. Two, maybe

three dozen in total, carrying their possessions, one lot of them wheeling their stuff along on a handcart.

Maybe he should get in with them. Travel south with them to Andover. That was, if they were heading for Andover, and not taking the main road down to Winchester instead.

Jake gathered up his things, then quickly ran after them.

'Hey!'

They turned, looking towards him.

He slowed, seeing their mistrust, their fear.

'It's okay, I...'

One of them grabbed a gun, aimed it at him. 'Don't come any closer!'

Jake knew how he must look. The guns. The helmet. Yes, and a two-day beard didn't help, either.

'Look, I won't harm you. I just wanted...'

The one with the gun – mid-forties, he'd guess – didn't waver. His gun was aimed directly at Jake's chest, and he looked quite capable of using it. 'I don't care what you want,' he said. 'On your way. And now.'

Jake raised his hands. 'Look, I...'

'On your way.'

He took a long breath. They were afraid. Maybe afraid that if they took him in he'd prove a viper in their midst. And who could blame them?

'Okay,' he said, taking a step back. 'I'm sorry... Hey, and good luck...'

Jake stood there for a long time afterwards, watching them go, feeling a longing for company that surprised him in its intensity. That was what he found hardest, he realized. Being alone. Having no one he could call on.

He walked on. Despite the hour he'd lost, it was still early. If he made up time he could be in Andover by late afternoon. And maybe someone would take him in, give him a room for the night.

Maybe...

Only he couldn't be sure. Couldn't be sure where next he'd find a single act of kindness.

For a long stretch of the road south, he saw nothing. Now and then – every ten minutes or so – a car would pass, always travelling south. Hearing them, he'd pull in, concealing himself as best he could, just in case.

Then, just outside a place called Hurstbourne Tarrant, he heard a very different sound – the sound of a small convoy.

Hiding among the bushes at the edge of the road, he watched it pass. There were two armoured cars and five army trucks, the vehicles packed with helmeted soldiers.

He knew this area had, for a century and more, been a training ground for the army, and they had quite a presence here. Especially further south, round Salisbury Plain. But this was the first time he'd seen them. The first time he'd seen *any* sign that there was still a government in place.

There was barely any indication of the disturbances on the way south – no broken windows, no burned-out cars or marauding bands of thugs. But as he came to the outskirts of Andover, first town of any size for some miles, things changed.

The first thing he saw was the wreck of a car, over on the far side of the road. He went across, seeing where the windscreen was smashed. Someone had fired a shot through it. That, doubtless, had made it swerve off the road and hit the tree. Of the driver, however, there was no sign.

Jake felt the bonnet of the car. It was cold.

He was about to walk on, when he noticed something, over to his right. Cautiously, he made his way across, between the trees, then found the driver. He had crawled away from the crash, looking for safety. But he hadn't found it. He had bled out, there by the wall of some godforsaken outhouse in the middle of nowhere.

Poor bastard. He didn't look older than eighteen or nineteen.

There were further signs only a few hundred yards on. An isolated farmhouse had been targeted, the doors kicked in, the windows smashed. Inside, a brief glance revealed that someone had trashed the place.

Then, not a stone's throw further on, a row of houses had been attacked and two of them burned out. Jake walked round them and found the corpse of a young man, lying on his front on the back lawn.

Jake checked the windows, making sure he wasn't being watched, then stooped down and lifted the young man's head.

He had been beaten badly. Mercilessly, by the look of it.

Evil fuckers...

Jake walked on, tensed now, his gun drawn and ready, expecting the worst.

At the first roundabout they'd built a barricade across the road, forcing any cars to either drive up onto the grass verge, or drive the wrong way about the roundabout.

There was no one there, but just across the way Jake saw how they'd built a second barrier, to try and trap those motorists who'd thought to evade the first. It had been cleared away, shunted over to one side. By the army, probably. But the wrecks of four separate cars could be glimpsed just a bit further on, and when he came to one of them, Jake was shocked to see that all four of the occupants had been killed, charred to death inside the burning vehicle.

The sight sickened him. It was hard to tell who they'd been – male, female, young or old, but he imagined them a family: mum and dad and their son and daughter. Imagined how terrified they must have been at the end.

He walked on.

The central part of Andover, according to his map, had been made into an enclave. There was a wall about it and three gates. Or, at least, there had been, for they too had been burned down, the wall breached in several places.

As for the town itself, it showed every sign of having been brutalized. Not a house or shop was undamaged, barely a single window was unbroken. A dozen buildings – maybe more, he didn't venture down some of the side roads – had been burned to the ground. More sickening yet was the sight of bodies, lying untended in the littered streets. He counted more than twenty before he gave up. All of them had been attacked savagely and beaten to death – like the young man he'd seen earlier.

Out in the middle of the main street, Jake turned 360 degrees, his gun searching every window, every shadowed place. It was an hour or more from sunset and he had the feeling that this was not the place to be when darkness fell. But he had walked a long way and he was tired. And not only tired, but hungry.

He let out a long breath.

There was no one about. Andover was a ghost town.

He ran across, then ducked down a side road, checking each doorway, each window as he passed. There at the far end of the narrow street he stopped, facing a small cottage-like building. It was painted a cheerful yellow.

He hesitated, then tried the door. It swung open.

Jake stepped inside.

He'd thought the house was empty. Thought he'd got the knack of telling which ones were, but he was wrong this time.

Or almost wrong.

The sight of the old man sprawled on the sofa, covered in blood, his head smashed in, was a shock. Likewise the woman on the stairs. He thought at first that maybe she was just sitting there, quiet in her sadness, only she too was dead, her sightless eyes staring straight ahead, into infinity.

He didn't know how she'd died, didn't really want to look too close, but it was more than clear how her husband had been murdered. He lay on his back on the big double bed in the back room upstairs, an axe in his chest, a look of surprise frozen on his face.

'Fucking hell…'

It was as he was standing there, staring at the corpse, that she came at him.

If he'd not been wearing the protective armoured jacket, he'd have been dead right there and then. As it was he had a bruise the size of a melon come up later on.

The blow threw him forward, onto the bed. As he scrambled up, wondering what had hit him, she came at him again.

He couldn't get his gun up fast enough, couldn't unlock the safety. Her second blow glanced off his shoulder, taking a slice off his ear.

Jake grunted and tried to back off, tried to warn her. 'For god's sake…'

Only she wasn't listening. Her face was like a fury's. As she threw herself at him again with the big kitchen knife, he opened fire.

Twenty rounds from close range. Enough to take out a platoon.

Jake let out a groan. The force of the blast had literally blown her off her feet.

He stood there, staring down at her in disbelief, his hands shaking violently.

What was left of her chest wasn't worth keeping. It was just a raw and bloodied mess.

She still gripped the knife, tightly, almost convulsively, but she was dead. And her face… Jake staggered to the side and threw up. She was just a girl. Just a wee girl. Why, she couldn't have been older than twelve or thirteen.

He glanced round, then shook his head, in pain at the sight.

'You stupid girl! You stupid, stupid girl!'

Who knew what she had seen? Maybe she'd thought he was her parents' murderer, come back to finish the job. Maybe she'd even been a witness to it all, hidden away somewhere, in a wardrobe or something. He'd never know.

All he knew was that he felt sick to the stomach at what he'd done.

He stepped over her, making for the door. There he'd stopped, holding his wounded ear, taking a moment to look back. There was blood everywhere. And the two corpses...

He staggered away, crying now, ashamed of what he'd done.

After that, he had tried not to break into any more houses. Tried to make do with what he had. To catch an hour or two of sleep here and there, hidden away out of sight. Only that wasn't always possible, and as more people appeared on the road so the potential for trouble increased. These were desperate times, and he saw from the eyes of those few whose path he crossed that desperation bred a kind of pragmatic evil. People were willing to do things they'd never have dreamed of doing. Just like he had.

He spent that night in an old abandoned brewery just outside Andover, in an attic room that could be reached only by a ladder. He pulled the ladder up, like a drawbridge, but in the middle of the night he was woken by the sound of lorries pulling up outside, in the brewery's cobbled yard.

Curious, he crept to the tiny attic window and looked down.

It was the army. Or some of them, at least. Two lorries full of khaki soldiers and an armoured car. Maybe the same as he'd seen earlier, on the A343.

The sight of them cheered him. He had begun to think that everything had broken down, but if the army was still functioning, still keeping some semblance of order, then maybe they still had a chance.

He was about to leave his place at the window and go down to speak to them – to maybe get a lift into Salisbury with them – when he heard the sound of another two lorries rattling down the narrow lane.

These had armed guards riding shotgun at the back of them.

Inside were what could only have been prisoners, for the men who staggered from the back of the lorries were handcuffed, their hands tied so they were right up under their chins.

And one other salient feature. They were all black.

Jake knew at once that this wasn't right. They might have been troublemakers, serious rioters even, only this was Andover and there was not a single white face among the captives.

He quickly packed his bag, checked that his gun was loaded, then returned to the window.

Things were happening fast down there in the yard. They had stripped the prisoners and had formed a circle about them, guns raised.

Jake's mouth was dry. He thought he knew what was coming. Only what happened next surprised him. Surprised and horrified. One of the prisoners was taken from the circle and dragged into a smaller group close by, made up of six big, bare-chested soldiers. Sergeants by the look of them, altogether older and tougher than the squaddies who formed the other circle. These began by taunting their captive, pushing him about and flicking at him, lightly at first, like it was in play, but then more viciously, until they were raining vicious punches and kicks at the man as he lay on the ground.

Jake could see the dull glint of a knuckleduster, heard the crunch as steel-capped boots smashed teeth and bone.

He tore himself away, sickened, unable to watch. But the sound of it went on as the ritual was repeated for another and yet another of the prisoners.

It was now that some of the captives, knowing what fate had in store for them, tried to make a break.

They had no chance, of course. The soldiers had awaited this moment. In an instant some of them drew their knives, while others used the butts of their guns as clubs, wading in, joining in the fun, stabbing and smashing in a real blood frenzy.

It was over in minutes.

While the older men smoked and talked among themselves, the squaddies set to, loading the bodies back onto the trucks, slinging the dead men up onto the platform like they were haunches of beef, laughing and joking as they did.

From where he was, Jake could have taken out at least three or four of them, maybe more, before they'd even worked out where he was firing from. Only what was the point? He'd be dead. They would make sure of it. Whereas if he kept his head down...

As the lorries drove away, Jake sat there with his back to the attic wall, shivering, not from the cold but from an overwhelming sense of hopelessness. The world was going mad and there was nothing he could do. He had given it his best shot, back in the datscape, and he had failed. All he could do now was hide away. Until things got better.

Which was why he was here now, sitting at the roadside near Salisbury, waiting for the crowds to pass, for darkness to fall.

Further up the road they had set up a barrier. Soldiers were manning it, stopping people and checking their IDs, while others observed the crowd from the back of an army truck, looking out over people's heads, making sure there was no trouble.

Were they the same soldiers? He couldn't tell. It had been dark, and he'd not really noticed which regiment they were from. But he didn't trust any of them now.

That way, he realized, was barred to him. Even if his identity was back on record, even if he did officially exist once more, he wasn't sure that he wanted anyone to know where he was. What if an ID enquiry tipped them off? They had found him last time, and double quick. Why shouldn't they be able to find him again?

No. He'd wait for dark then make his way round to the south and then west again. Coombe Bissett was only a short way beyond the town, a couple of miles at most. It made no sense to be impatient, not now that he was so close.

He sat there for another hour, biding his time, then got up and walked away, crossing over the main road and taking a side street, away from the tide of refugees.

He was halfway down when he heard the unmistakable click of a gun being cocked in the deep shadow to his right. He stopped, raising his hands, slowly turning towards the sound, making sure he did nothing to make them panic and shoot him.

The man was roughly his own height, but whether he was young or old Jake couldn't tell. His face was completely in shadow.

'What's ee want?' the stranger asked, in a broad Wiltshire accent.

Fifties, Jake guessed. He cleared his throat. 'Just passing through, Mister. Don't want no trouble. There's soldiers stopping people up there, and I don't feel like being stopped, if you know what I mean?'

The man stepped forward a little, coming out of shadow. His shotgun was levelled at Jake's chest.

'And why be that?'

More like sixties, he re-evaluated. The man's eyes were surrounded by wrinkles, his beard completely grey.

'Maybe because I've seen too much these past few days. Seen what they're capable of. I don't fancy being any man's prisoner.'

The old man nodded vaguely at that. 'Where you be 'eaded?'

'Coombe Bissett. Got friends there. They're expecting me.'

'Coombe Bissett, eh?' His eyes blinked, blinked again. 'Then you best get movin', eh, boy? There's a track goes round that way... keep walking down this road, two, three hundred yards, then right. You'll recognize it. There's a long gate with a broken bar. Climb over that and follow the path... it'll bring you out south of the town...'

Jake touched his finger to his brow. 'Thanks. I'm much obliged to you... And good luck.'

The old man nodded. 'Looks like we'll all be needing it, eh, boy?'

*

The encounter with the old man raised his spirits. Like the picnic, it was sign that there was still some kindness, some decency in the world. That things might yet be okay.

Only every time he thought that, he kept seeing her again. His darling Kate. There on the floor beside her bed.

It was late afternoon by the time he got there, for though it wasn't far, there had been army patrols everywhere and he'd had to hide several times, backtracking each time and trying another way. But finally here he was.

Coombe Bissett was much as he remembered it. Beyond the razor-topped wall, there was a pond and, across from it, an inn – the only one in the village. Just beyond that was a long, sloping lawn with a row of black brick houses to the left, and, at the top, Hugo's cottage, with its thatched roof and whitewashed walls.

Jake tapped in the security code at the enclave gate and waited as it hissed open. Walking past the inn, he was conscious of the silence of the place. There was no sign of anyone.

How many times had he come here in the past? At least six or seven. But he had never been so glad to see it as now.

As he climbed the slope he noticed, to the right of the house, in the yard next to the adjacent barn, a bright red Audi, parked right up against the wall.

Jake smiled at the sight of it. *Jenny's here!*

Only then he remembered his news.

He stopped and turned, composing himself, looking about him. It was all so quiet, so peaceful, after all he'd seen.

Jake took a long breath. He was close to tears. He had been so alone on the road. So fucking terribly alone.

He turned back, imagining their faces. Their surprise at seeing him.

He had never felt so glad to be somewhere. Never in all his life.

Wiping his face, he took the last few strides across the lawn, letting himself in by the side door.

He could hear the radio, playing in the background. Could hear Hugo's voice, speaking over it, then Chris's sudden laughter.

Jake closed his eyes, a tear rolling down his face.

Thank fuck...

He peeled off the jacket and set the helmet down beside the butler sink. Then, careful to make no sound, he laid his guns and knapsack down in the corner by the freezer unit.

He could hear Jenny's voice now, making some joke. Chris was laughing again; that lovely, deep, hearty laughter of his.

Jake froze. The next voice stunned him.

Kate. It was Kate.

He walked through. Saw at once that the room was empty.

To his right the big wall screen was lit up. On it, as large as life, the six of them sat about, half-filled wine glasses and a half a dozen bottles spread out on the low central table, as they laughed and joked, in this very room.

Two years ago, it had been. Jake could remember it like yesterday.

He went across and, crouching down, looked at the projection box. It was on a loop. He pressed pause. At once the image froze.

Jake stood, looking about him.

Maybe they were out. Maybe they'd gone to town, to get food and supplies. But if so, then why all of them? Why hadn't someone stayed to mind the fort? And why had they left the screen on a loop?

He went upstairs. The place had been ransacked. Totally trashed, like someone had been through everything with a fine-toothed comb.

Looking for me. Or for some clue as to where I'd go.

Only where were they? Had they been taken somewhere?

Jake hoped not. But what other explanation was there?

What surprised him most, after all he'd seen these past few days, was that there were no signs of violence. No blood. No bodies.

He grabbed the gun then went outside, checking the barn, the summer house, the garden shed.

Nothing. No sign of them at all.

Jake stood there, back in the lounge, wondering what to do. He'd had no other plan except to come here.

If they'd been here once, then surely they'd come back. And if he were here...

He had to leave. He couldn't risk staying.

Jake found the keys to Jenny's car where he knew she always left them, in the drawer to the right of the sink, then loaded his things.

He should have gone, there and then, before they came. Every minute he was there he was in danger. Only he couldn't leave. Not before seeing her once more. Not without hearing her voice.

Jake went back through and, for the next hour, stood before the screen, watching it all. His life with Kate. One evening of their charmed and wonderful life.

Only then, at the end of it, did he tear himself away and, tears running down his face, reversed out on to the slope, heading away from there, knowing he'd never see any one of them again.

The car got him as far as the village of Pimperne, just outside Blandford Forum. There the compressed air cylinder gave out. Taking his knapsack and his gun, he abandoned the car and set off on foot, heading south, round the town, meaning to get back onto the main road and follow it down to Dorchester. Only it was getting dark and when he got to the roundabout he could see, along the road a bit, that two houses had been set ablaze, and knew that trouble lay that way.

Which was why he took the Poole road.

Two hours later, having made good time on an almost empty road, he found himself on the outskirts of that great sprawl of suburban architecture that was the Poole and Bournemouth enclave.

It lay like a great swathe of brightness between him and the darkness of Poole Bay, that very brightness an encouraging sign. Elsewhere almost everything had been cast into darkness, but here it was different. Here they'd kept things going.

It was only streetlights, he realized, only he had never seen anything quite so welcoming, anything quite so expressive of what they stood to lose.

Even so, it was no use going that way. It might have *looked* welcoming, but there was nothing for him there. Not while *they* were after him.

It was standing there, taking in that stirring sight, that he finally made his choice.

Corfe. He'd go to Corfe.

It wasn't far, after all. An hour's forced march to Wareham, maybe, and then a further hour after that.

And then he'd rest. Jake closed his eyes. The simple thought of it made him realize just how tired he was. More tired than ever. In truth he could have found himself somewhere right there and then and lain himself down, only why prevaricate? Now that he knew where he was going there was no point. Not until he got there. Not until he reached the end point of his journey.

He would walk all night if he had to.

Jake sighed, then, taking the Wareham turn, set off. Away from the light. Out into the ancient Purbeck night.

Jake had no idea at all what time it was when he arrived. The place was in total darkness, not a light to be seen for miles, and the castle was a mere suggestion of a shadow atop the looming blackness of the mound.

There was a barrier, however, blocking the road into the village, and manning it were two, maybe three men. Again he could barely discern the details, it was so dark.

For a moment he thought about throwing himself at their mercy. Of going over to them and begging them for a place to sleep. Only it was late, far too late. After all, he had not come all this way to be shot by some nervous villager merely because it was dark.

Silently he turned away, taking the road that went about the castle's base, recalling it from his childhood. Before his parents had been killed in that awful accident. Back in those heady days of innocence.

There had been a campsite about a mile down the road. They'd even stayed there once or twice. A little way on from that, he knew, was Church Knowle. He would try there. See if he couldn't find somewhere to bed down for the night.

As luck would have it, there was a place, its windows boarded up, a padlock on the door, an estate agent's sign set up against the garden gate. As quietly as he could, he forced the back door and made his way upstairs, finding himself a bed. There, almost as soon as his head touched the pillow, he fell into a deep sleep; a sleep in which, for the first time in several nights, he dreamed of data streams and virtual landscapes.

It was there, in his dreams, that they came for him. And it was there, in that small back bedroom, in the light of a wavering candle, that they woke him, two of them holding him down by the arms, while the third held a shotgun to his throat and smiled darkly.

'Who's been sleeping in *my* bed?'

Jake was dragged down the stairs and out into the dark, his hands roped tightly together, the shotgun jammed into his back.

There, just outside the house, a small group of villagers had gathered in the flickering light of their hand-held torches.

'Where's Tom?' one of them was saying anxiously. 'Go and get 'im! Tell him we 'as an intruder!'

The accent was purest Dorset. The man himself, in that faint light, was of typical local stock, broad-shouldered and dark-haired. He looked to Jake and glared.

'A fuckin' Lunnun-er, I tell 'e!'

Jake lowered his eyes, determined to keep silent. To speak only when he was spoken to. Maybe, that way, he would survive this night.

There were a good dozen there already and more kept arriving by the moment. Then, through the growing crowd, the one named Tom appeared. He was a big man, much bigger than most of his fellows, and he moved gracefully, but what surprised Jake most was his age. He'd been expecting a middle-aged man, or someone even older – some village elder from whom they took instruction – but this one was barely Jake's own age.

'What have we here?' he asked, coming directly up to Jake and looking at him, as if he were some kind of specimen. 'What's your name and where're you heading?'

There was Dorset in that, too, only less than in the others' voices, and it made Jake think that maybe he'd spent some time away from there – at college maybe, or up in town.

He spoke up confidently. 'My name's Jake Reed and as for where I'm heading... well, here, I guess. I used to come here for my holidays when I was young. I...'

Jake stopped, seeing that the other was getting a touch impatient.

'They tell me you had a gun,' Tom said. 'A big thing. A semi-automatic. That's a bit odd, wouldn't you say?'

Jake looked down. 'I took it from a dead man. They... killed my girlfriend. We were staying at her parents', in Marlow. I...'

The man waited. Then, 'Go on.'

Jake shrugged. 'There's nothing more to say. I've walked from there to here. Three days, it's taken me. I was going to stay with some friends, up near Salisbury, only...'

He fell silent. It didn't matter what he said. They would either kill him or not. Or send him on his way, which was just as bad. Because in the end someone would lose patience with him. Or try to rob him, or...

Tom reached out. Undid the rope that bound his hands together.

'Jimmy... you got a spare room till we can find out what to do with this one?'

'I 'ave... you know I 'ave, only...'

'I'll vouch for him,' Tom said. 'I'll even sit up and guard him, if you like.' He looked to Jake and lowered his voice. 'You won't mind that, will you? Me taking precautions?'

Jake almost smiled at that. 'I'd think you mad if you didn't.'

'Then it's agreed,' he said, addressing them all again. 'We meet in the morning, at the church, a'right? Ten o'clock, and not a moment later. And we'll work out then what we're going to do with this here Jake fellow.'

There was a murmur of agreement and then they began to file back to their houses, the excitement over.

'Thanks,' Jake said. 'Thanks a lot.'

But now that the others were gone, Tom's face seemed harder when it looked at him. 'Don't thank me yet,' he said. 'And let me warn you, friend Jake. Don't try anything. Understand me?'

Jake nodded. 'I understand.'

'Good. Then let's get you back to bed.'

That was the morning it began. The same morning he met Annie for the first time. The first day of his new life.

There, in St. Peter's, before a packed hall of more than two hundred locals, he answered all their questions, leaving nothing out. Being straight with them because, as he reasoned later when they talked of it, they either had to take him as he was or end it then. There could be no half-measures.

And so he told it all. Even the mad stuff, the stuff about the Chinese coming after him.

And at the end, when they came to decide, he stood there, naked in his soul before them as, one after another, they stood up to cast their vote.

'Aye,' one would say.

Then 'Aye' again from another.

And Tom would write each one down in the book.

'Aye.'

'Aye.'

Not a single nay.

Jake stood there at the end, humbled and astonished, deeply moved by the strange power of the ritual. Becoming, there and then, one of them. Bound to them by this. For just as they had accepted him among them, so he felt he must prove himself to them. As Tom came up to him and put his hand on his shoulder, Jake smiled, touched, maybe even changed by their kindness.

'Well, my friends,' Tom said, grinning broadly, speaking to the gathering. 'We have a new member of our host. A new friend. A good friend, let's hope. Jake Reed.'

There was applause, then a shout from the back.

'What are we waiting for?'

It was answered immediately. 'Don't know about you, Daniel, but I'm waitin' for the bloody pub to open!'

There was laughter.

'Well?' Tom asked. 'Will you come and have a drink with us?'

Jake looked down. He couldn't meet the other's eyes. Couldn't bear such kindness after all that had happened.

'Hey... it's okay. You're safe now. Among friends. You're home now, boy. Home.'

Jake looked up, gratitude in his eyes.

Home.

He sniffed, then wiped the tears away. 'I guess I am.'

PART THREE   **When China Comes**

AUTUMN 2065

Birds and beasts cry out, calling to the flock.
When flowers crowd amidst dead haulms, no
        fragrance comes from them.
Fish, by their thatch of scales are told apart;
But the dragon hides in the dark his patterned
        brightness.
Bitter and sweet herbs do not share the same field;
Orchid and sweet flag bloom unseen in solitary
        sweetness.
Only the good man's lasting beauty
Preserves its aspect unchanged through succeeding ages.

—Jiu Chang, 'Grieving At The Eddying Wind',
    2nd Century AD

Chapter 8

THINGS BEHIND THE SUN

T om had aged. The journey back, the jolting of the cart, had aged him. Anxious to return, they had not gone to Wareham as they'd planned, but taken the quickest route back, following the old road and then the railway line directly into Corfe. They arrived just after five, in the last few shreds of daylight.

A small crowd was awaiting them there, torches lit against the encroaching dark. Peter, Mary and the girls were among them, but it was Charlie Waite, who owned the New Inn, who pushed in front.

'Jake! We need to talk!'

Jake looked about him, wondering what had been going on, and saw at once that something was up. Peter wouldn't look at him, wouldn't meet his eyes, and Mary – Mary looked troubled.

Jake jumped down, confronting Waite.

'What is it, Charlie?'

Waite took him aside, out of hearing of the others.

'Your boy... he showed me up.'

'Showed you up? How?'

'We've taken three prisoners.'

'Prisoners?'

'Midlanders.'

'So? What's this got to do with Peter?'

'They're scum. Vagrants. I was going to deal with them.'

'*Execute them*, you mean.'

But Waite wasn't in the mood for word games. He was a pugnacious little man at the best of times, and right now he was incandescent.

'Call it what you fuckin' like, Jake, but it's 'ow we deal with it. It's why we've survived. You've killed enough yourself...'

'When it was necessary. But why did my boy intercede?'

'I don't know. Felt sorry for the miserable bastard, I guess. But you need to 'ave a word, Jake. Put the boy in his place. Let him know he should respect his elders.'

Jake's own anger flared a little at that, but he knew he'd have to resolve this. Waite was an old friend – a good man when it came down to it, reliable in a fight, even if his views on life were sometimes questionable. Besides, it was right what he'd said. They hadn't survived from being soft.

Jake changed tack.

'Have you questioned them?'

'They're in my outhouse, under guard. One of 'em's in a bad way. Don't reckon we'll have to bother with him, but the others... Well... we stripped them down and searched them.'

'And?'

Waite almost smiled. 'Come and see for yourself.'

'I will. But first I need to get Tom home and settled. He's had a long day. He needs some proper rest.'

'Okay. But come when you've finished there. We need to settle this. And, Jake... I mean it... have a word with your boy. He means well, I'm sure, but he can't go interfering in our business like he did.'

It was inviting Jake to argue, but Jake wasn't going to rise to it. He'd listen to what his son had to say before making any judgement. But as he walked back to the wagons, he found himself wondering what could have made Peter stand between Waite and a man he didn't know – someone who, he imagined, would as soon stab him in the back as grant him the same consideration.

Back at the wagons, Jake called Peter across.

'Peter... come and give me and your Aunt Mary a hand. We're going to take Uncle Tom back in the cart and get him settled, then you can bring the cart back here.'

Peter met his eyes briefly. He nodded then came across, Boy yapping at his ankles.

'We'll have a word later, eh?'

Mary and the girls walked alongside as they pulled the cart along, Mary holding her husband's hand tightly.

Glancing back, Jake saw just how concerned she was. Such concern that it made him think again about what Tom had told him. Whatever else was in that look, it wasn't the look of a betrayed woman. There was too much love in it, too little sign of damage. No. The sight of Tom in pain was too much for her.

So what then? Had Tom been lying about the girl? Maybe. Only it made no sense. Why would he tell such a story against himself?

It was almost dark. There, just past the castle mound, the great stone ruin high above them to their left, the lane narrowed and went between the trees. As they hauled the cart along, so the darkness intensified, until it seemed they were moving inside a long tunnel, the quiet broken only by the rattle of the cart, the rumble of its wheels, the sound of Boy padding along, panting quietly at Peter's side.

Jake looked back, over his shoulder. It was so dark now he couldn't even see the others, close as they were.

'Mary...?'

Her voice came back to him out of the darkness. 'What?'

'Did Tom tell you about the craft?'

'Yes... yes, he did.'

'And the markings on it?'

'Yes...' She hesitated, then, 'Look, Jake... do we have to talk about this now?'

'No, I just...' He let it drop. Only he had to speak. There was too much going on in his head to keep silent. 'So what happened? With Charlie Waite? You were all there, I take it?'

He had meant to leave this until later. Only he needed to know. Needed to deal with this as soon as possible.

It was Peter who answered.

'He was going to kill him.'

'And that was wrong?'

'It felt wrong.'

They were both conscious of Mary and the girls listening.

'So what did you say?'

Peter's silence was a shrug. Jake didn't have to see him to know.

'Oh, come on... you must have said something. Charlie was very upset.'

'The man's an animal,' Mary said, surprising Jake, because she rarely made comment on their neighbours.

Jake took a long breath, then asked again. 'So what did you say?'

'It wasn't just what he said,' Mary answered. 'It was what he did.'

'Which was?'

'I knocked the gun out of his hand.'

'You...'

Jake almost laughed, he was so shocked by the notion, only it wasn't a laughing matter. Waite's pride must have been severely dented.

Peter spoke again, trying to explain.

'The man... the prisoner, I mean... he had a bit of a stutter. I guess that's what did it. He was afraid, you see, and... well... I could understand that. He didn't *want* to be here. He...'

Peter fell silent.

They were rounding the bend now, the darkness suddenly less intense. Up ahead the trees thinned out and they could glimpse the church, ahead and to their right, the moonlight shining on the tower and on its steeply sloping roof.

'Mary? What do you think?'

'D'you know what?' she said. 'I think Peter showed real courage, defyin' Waite. It was Peter who found them, see. They were 'is prisoners and 'e was right to insist that we wait till you got back. I mean, they weren't armed, nor dangerous, come to that. They were just frightened.'

Jake looked to his son. 'Then you did the right thing.'

Only it made things difficult. Very difficult indeed, because hard times were coming, and it didn't do to be at odds with one's neighbours at such times.

He glanced back again. 'You okay, Tom? We've not shaken you about too much?'

'I'm fine,' Tom answered weakly.

'Good. Because it's not far now. Not far at all...'

Pulling the cart back through the darkness, Boy at his heels, Peter had time to reflect on what had been said.

He had known, even before Jake had uttered a single word, just what his father would say. He also knew that he would have to apologize to Waite at some point, to keep the peace, if nothing else. But he had not been wrong. Not in the least. Because to go along with what Waite had wanted to do would have been evil; would have been tantamount to negating his own existence.

Jake had told him the story countless times, but its impact on him had never been so strong as last night.

When Jake had first come here, he too had been a stranger, he too might simply have been shot and disposed of, had the likes of Waite had their way. Only they hadn't. That choice had been left to Tom Hubbard, and Tom had given his father a chance. A chance to prove himself, to become his friend.

Without which I would not be here...

The thought made him smile. But the smile was tinged with sadness, for Tom, who'd saved his father, was looking bad. The wound itself looked good, looked clean and uninfected, but Tom himself looked wasted.

'Peter?'

He slowed, then stopped. It was Meg. She came out of the darkness like a shadow; a warm, all too real shadow that was suddenly in his arms and kissing him.

Boy barked excitedly.

Peter moved back a little. He couldn't see her, but then he didn't need to. He could picture her perfectly.

'What was that for?'

'For being you. And for doin' the right thing. I didn't say last night but... I'm just so proud of you. I'd 'ave never 'ad the balls...'

He shrugged. 'Waite's okay. He's not really a cruel man. Just pragmatic. He sees the world in simple terms, that's all.'

'But so do you.'

'You think?'

'Yeah... but that's okay.' She squeezed him again, gave him another small, soft kiss.

He chuckled. 'Stop it... I've got to get this cart back...'

'Then get going. I'll 'elp you.'

He turned and began to push the cart again, feeling at once her presence there to his right, helping him.

'Meg?'

'Yes, my love?'

'D'you think your dad's all right?'

She was silent a moment. 'I don't know. I was lookin' at Mum, earlier on, before Dad got back. It's just... I dunno... somethin' in her face. She's seemed so sad these last few weeks.'

Peter took a long breath. 'If I tell you something... will you promise not to say anything?'

They had slowed almost to a standstill.

'Maybe. Depends what it is.'

'No, seriously. You've got to promise me.'

'Okay. I promise.'

'The other day, when you three went into Corfe and I stayed behind... I was in the garden and I heard something, and when I went over, I could see your mum standing at the sink...'

'Yeah?'

'And she was crying.'

They had stopped, there in the darkness.

'Cryin'?'

'Sobbing her heart out.'

He heard her sigh, sensed rather than saw her turn away.

'Meg? What is it?'

'I think somethin's wrong. A few weeks back – remember? – when Dad was away for a couple of days...'

'Seeing his cousin, over in Lulworth...'

'Yeah...' Only she didn't *mean* yeah.

'You mean, he *wasn't*?'

'I don't know.' Meg took his hands. She was trembling now. 'It's just... 'e's not been well. Not for a long while. He keeps up a front, but... well, I've seen it. Seen 'ow tired he gets.'

'So you think he might have gone to see someone?'

'I don't know. Only looking at him just now...'

'He's just tired, that's all. The journey... the stress of it... it can't have been easy.'

'No... no, I guess not.'

'And if there was something wrong, well... he'd have told us, wouldn't he? Dad would certainly have known. You know what those two are like. They're like brothers. They don't keep *anything* from each other.'

Jake was waiting for them near the church, his torch held high, as Peter and Megan emerged from the blackness of the lane.

'Are you ready?'

Peter looked to Meg, then looked back at his father and nodded.

'Good. Then let's go and sort this out.'

The New Inn was just across the way. They went down the little alleyway at the side and out onto the patio. There, on the far side of the long, descending lawn, partway down the slope, was the outhouse. Normally Waite kept various bits and pieces there, fold-up chairs and empty barrels, crates of glasses and the like. For the moment, however, it was being used as a cell.

'Jake...' Waite said, coming across, his two sons shadowing him. 'Peter...'

All three, like Jake, were armed.

Peter bowed his head. Jake was about to say something, but Peter got in first.

'I'm sorry, Mister Waite. Last night... I didn't mean to be disrespectful...'

Waite blinked, then slowly began to smile. 'S'okay, boy. But we gotta sort this. Can't afford to let it drag.'

'No, sir.'

Jake looked to his son, proud of him at that moment. 'Well?' he said, turning his attention to Waite. 'What've you found?'

They went across, following the stout little man, who produced a key to the padlock and handed it to his son, then stood back a bit, gun raised, as he unlocked it.

As the door swung open they were struck by the stench of urine and faeces.

Jake grimaced. 'Christ!'

In the light of the torch he could see two of them huddled in the far corner, off to his left. They had been stripped to their underwear, their ankles and wrists bound with electrician's tape. They looked bruised and beaten, and fearful. But they were much better off than their fellow. He lay unmoving on the straw to Jake's right. From the look of him he was dead.

'I thought—'

Jake stopped, choking off his words, not wanting to get off on the wrong foot. He didn't want to be arguing with Waite right from the start. For once he ignored the fact that Waite had done nothing to help the man – that he'd just left him there to die. Maybe he'd have died anyway. Only it spoke volumes of Waite's attitude. He just wanted to kill the men and have done with it.

He turned and looked at Waite, noting, as he did, the way Waite looked past him at the prisoners; the set look of hatred on his face.

'Will!' At Waite's shout, his younger son stepped forward and handed Jake what looked like a lady's make-up bag.

'What's this?'

Waite gestured with his head towards one of the cowering figures. 'It was on that one... S-s-stammerin' S-s-stan. 'Is little goody bag. Things he stole...'

Handing the torch to Waite's boy, Jake unzipped the small velvet bag and looked inside. There were jewels and coins and...

Jake looked up sharply, looked to the one Waite had indicated, then back at Waite. His whole countenance had changed.

'Give me half an hour.'

'Jake?'

He thrust the bag into Waite's hands, then turned to Peter.

'Peter... get your gun... and spare ammunition. Then meet me by the well.'

As Peter and Boy ran off, Jake checked his gun, then looked to Waite again.

'What is it?' Waite asked. 'He taken some'at of yours there, Jake?'

'Not mine,' Jake answered, but he said no more, just set off, down the slope and through the gate in the fence, heading for the well.

Jake ran across the empty space before the cottage, keeping low. At the back door he paused, then, lifting his head, took a quick glance inside.

He looked back, to where Peter waited in the shadows with Boy, and gave him the signal. At once both boy and dog raced across, scuttling round the side of the building.

Jake heard the faint click as Peter took off the safety.

East Orchard was silent. Not a light shone anywhere. The cottage itself was enveloped in darkness, the moonlight on its ancient tiled roof revealing the only part of it to jut out above the surrounding vegetation.

Jake took a long breath, steeling himself, then pulled the door open and went through, into the darkness of the kitchen. There he stopped, alert to the least noise, letting his pulse slow.

He remembered sitting here, only a few days before, as Old Ma Brogan made him tea and chatted with him. Then this had seemed a fine place to spend an hour or two, but now the darkness seemed ominous.

He walked across. It was dark and he had to feel his way; even so, there was no sign that anything was wrong. Nothing was broken, nothing spilled. Everything was as it had been.

In the hallway, nothing. Only silence and the stale, musty smell of things.

The living room was empty. So too the back room.

Upstairs he paused, sniffing the air.

If there'd been strangers here, they were here no more. The very silence of the house confirmed it. But they had been here. He was certain of it.

He found her in her bedroom, lying beneath the sheets. At first he thought she was asleep. He couldn't hear her sleeping, but then he'd heard that old people slept very lightly.

Scrabbling in the bedside table he found a box of matches and lit the candle. In its burgeoning light he turned and saw at once.

'Oh... Margaret...'

They had slit her throat from ear to ear. Blood caked the pillow under her head.

He leaned across and closed her sightless eyes, then bent close to gently kiss her brow.

Outside Boy barked.

Jake went to the window and called down. 'Peter! I'll be right down.'

He would come back in the morning and see to her. Until then...

Jake stood, weary suddenly, all of the belief he'd had in the goodness of men drained from him. They didn't have to do this. They could have taken what they wanted and let her be. Only no.

He stood. He would leave the candle. Let it burn down.

Let it all burn down.

Maybe it was a good thing. Maybe she'd be spared what was to come. Who knew? Only he did know. He knew that this was evil. This nothing of an act.

Outside Peter was waiting. 'Well?'

Jake shook his head.

Boy barked again, as if he sensed something was wrong. Peter quietened him, but he too seemed agitated now.

'What are you going to do?'

But Jake was done with words. He set off, half running now, seeing in his mind what had to be done. Peter ran after him, for once struggling to catch up.

As Jake came out onto the lawn of the New Inn once again, Waite took a step towards him. He was smiling, but, seeing the look on Jake's face, the smile became a frown.

'What's up?'

Jake pushed past him, pushed his son aside. For a moment he stood there in the doorway, looking in, then, throwing his gun down, he drew his hunting knife from his boot and, crossing the room in an instant, bent down and dragged the younger man – the stammerer – to his feet.

'Who did it?' he demanded. 'Which of you two sick fuckers did it?'

'I d-d... I d-d...'

Jake's voice was unforgiving. 'You d-d what?'

'Dad?'

Peter was standing in the doorway now, tears streaming down his face.

Jake turned, his face like stone. 'Don't *dad* me. You didn't see what this bastard did!'

'I d-d...'

Jake turned and, bringing up his arm, drew the knife quickly, crisply, across the man's throat, then let him fall. Seeing that, the other began to jabber fearfully. But Jake seemed inured to it. Kneeling close, he took the bloodied knife and wiped it on the man's shirt.

'Thieving we might have let you get away with, but murder...'

Jake stood. For a moment he studied his handiwork. Saw how the one he'd cut struggled for each breath now, his bound hands scrabbling at his throat, trying vainly to stem the ebbing tide of blood. A strangled, gurgling noise coming from him.

'Charlie...'

Waite was standing in the doorway next to Peter. 'Yeah?'

'He's all yours.'

Jake was standing there, out on the lawn, holding Peter to him, when the shot rang out. A moment later Waite emerged. He came across.

'What was it?' he asked.

Jake turned to him. 'That bag... it was hers. I didn't realize that at first. I must have seen it, sitting on the side, a hundred times. But what I did recognize was her earrings. Lovely silver earrings shaped like leaves. She always wore them.'

Waite looked to Peter. 'Well? Was I right or was I right? Scum they were! Nasty little cut-throats!'

Peter looked suitably chastened. 'You were right, Mister Waite.'

'Good…' He reached out and ruffled Peter's hair. 'We'll make a proper citizen of you yet, my lad!'

But Jake wasn't so sure. Even so, he looked to Waite and nodded. 'I'll tell Tom it's dealt with. You'll see to the burials, yeah?'

Waite nodded. His whole tone was softer now that things were settled. 'Yeah… leave it with me.'

'Good. Then we'll see you later.'

'Later?'

'Yeah. There's stuff we need to talk about.'

But Waite clearly had heard nothing about what had happened back in Dorchester. He'd been too busy dealing with the prisoners.

'Stuff?'

'We need to call a council of war,' Jake said. 'Decide what we're going to do.'

'Things are that bad, huh?'

'That bad.' And, with a final nod, he took Peter's arm and walked away, the thought of what he'd just done burning in his head, like the after-image of some awful, searing light.

'Peter? Are you okay?'

Peter looked up. It was Beth, Meg's elder sister. She had left the others and come across to where he sat alone at one of the big trestle tables at the back of the New Inn.

He liked Beth. Or, rather, admired her. She was the rebel in the family, the one who never did what you thought she would. At seventeen she ought to have been married by now, maybe even had kids, but she wasn't having any of that. She wanted a different life. She didn't want to be an unpaid drudge, tied to some dishwater-dull farmer. Only what were the options?

'I'm fine.'

She sat, facing him, leaning in towards him and making a face. 'Well, you could have fooled me, cuz. You've been sittin' there with a face like a wet weekend.'

'Have I?' He almost laughed. Only he kept seeing it in his memory, and every time he did it cast the same dark shadow over things.

That his own dad should have been capable of such an act.

At the other table the other kids were chatting and laughing, sipping at glasses of the home-made lemonade that was Ma Waite's specialty. Meg was among them, and from time to time she would glance at him, but she wouldn't come across. Not after what he'd said.

'You two havin' a tiff?' Beth asked, seeing where his eyes had gone.

He looked back at her. 'Yeah.'

'I didn't think you two ever argued.'

'We don't. Only today's different.'

'Yeah?'

'Yeah.'

'All that stuff that's been happening, you mean?'

He nodded. He had heard it from his dad only an hour back. Had seen how worried it made him, like this was it.

'Is that what they're talkin' about now in there?'

Peter nodded. 'Yeah, but it won't be any use, though.'

'How d'you mean?'

'I mean... if it is the Chinese...'

She laughed. 'You really think...?' But she could see he was serious.

'Dad *saw* them. He *saw* the dragons on the craft. And then there's the photograph...'

'What photograph?'

There was this friend of Dad's, at market... he showed Dad a photograph. A polaroid. Only there haven't been polaroids about since before the Collapse... they're self-developing, see, and the chemicals that allow it to develop... Well, Dad thought about it and he couldn't see how it could have survived, how it would have *worked* after all these years. So he had another look at it, and there, in the top corner on the back of the print, were four tiny Chinese characters... *chops*, you call them.'

'And?'

'Don't you see? The guy who had the camera must have got it off them... off the Chinese, that is. Bought it, maybe, or stole it...'

'And what were the Chinese doin' with it?'

Peter shrugged. 'That's not the point. The point is that if he did, then they must be here.'

'The Chinese?'

'Yeah.'

Beth considered that a moment, then looked at him again. 'What if it was made by the Chinese, but someone else brought it into this country? Some trader... that's possible, isn't it?'

'Only...'

'...you like your dad's version better... yeah?'

Peter smiled. In some ways Beth was much better suited to him than Meg. Meg would just have accepted what he'd said.

'I'm not saying categorically that they *are* here, just that if they are...'

'Then we're all fucked...'

'Beth!' But he was grinning now. 'What would your mother say?'

'She'd say I was a big girl now...'

Peter looked up, past Beth's shoulder. Meg was coming across. 'What're you two talking about?'

Beth turned to face her little sister, exaggerating her country accent as she did. 'We wuz tarkin' Aparcollips. 'Bout 'em Chinese fellas comin' 'ere ta Purbeck...'

Peter giggled. The way she said it did make it seem rather funny. But Meg didn't find it funny. She hated being teased.

'You gonna come join us?'

He looked down. Truth was, he didn't want to. Not right then. He'd been enjoying Beth's company. But he could see how much it had cost Meg to come across; how she'd had to swallow her pride.

'Thanks,' he said, looking to Beth as he stood.

'You're welcum, vine zur...' Beth answered him, getting up and curtseying, like she was a milkmaid.

He went round, took Meg's arm. 'I'm sorry...'

She looked up into his face. 'Are you?'

'Yeah... let's have a nice evening, eh? Let's worry about tomorrow when it comes.'

Geoff Horsfield sat back, pointing the stem of his pipe at Harry Miller, who sat just across from him.

'That's all very well, 'Arry, only there's far too few of us and we've no bloody time in which to do it!'

The bar of the New Inn was packed, every table filled to over-flowing. Everyone had turned up, it seemed, brought there by the news of the strange craft the men had seen at market.

'Besides,' Geoff went on, taking a match from his pocket and beginning to dig at the bowl, 'if we want to set up *proper* defences then why don't we use what we've got? I mean... we've a perfectly good castle out there...'

'It's a bloody ruin,' John Lovegrove chipped in.

'Bits of it. We could fill the gaps...'

But Jake had heard enough. They had been talking around the subject for the best part of an hour now, and he was beginning to lose patience. He stood, raising his arms, calling the meeting to order.

'Ladies... gentlemen... please... let's address the real problem. What if they *are* here? Shouldn't we be asking ourselves a few questions? Like... what do they want? And how is it going to affect us, here in Purbeck?'

'Why don't you go and ask 'em?' Ted Gifford said, making everyone laugh.

Jake shook his head. 'I think you're all missing the point. That craft, if it is Chinese, speaks of a highly advanced civilization.

Christ... we didn't have anything like that *before* the Collapse!'

'Not that we knew of...' Will Cooper said. 'But you know 'ow governments are...'

'What if those dragons were Irish dragons,' Jenny Randall threw in.

'For Pete's sake,' Geoff Horsfield answered. 'Is that really likely?'

'Well, they are a creative race...'

'*Chinese*,' Jake said emphatically, feeling like he'd blow a fuse if he couldn't get them to focus on this. 'It was a *Chinese* dragon. I saw it, remember? But I ask again... what do they *want* from us?'

'Why should they bloody well want anything?' Old Josh said, from where he sat on a stool by the bar. 'Maybe they'll leave us alone. Let Branagh rule us.'

'Maybe,' Jake said, conceding the point, some part of him wishing it were so. 'Only I don't believe that.'

'You know why I *don't* think it's them?' John Lovegrove said, sitting forward. 'Because if it *was* them, then it could mean only one thing.'

'An' what's that, John?' someone asked from one of the tables at the back.

'That they want to rule it all...'

'Bollocks!' Charlie Waite said from where he stood behind the counter, drying glasses. 'Why would the Chinese want Purbeck? What fuckin' use are we to them?'

It was a good question. The Chinese had traditionally stayed within their borders. Why should they change that now?

'Not so much Purbeck,' John said, 'but... well... England... you know, the old United Kingdom... I mean, if they were the first to recover... the first to get back on their feet, so to speak well... maybe...'

'Maybe what?' Jake asked. 'A world state...? Is that what you mean? With the Chinese pulling all the strings?'

Jake looked around, seeing the effect his words had had on them all. The idea of it had got through to them, had touched their imaginations for once.

A world run by the Chinese...

'Nah...' Eddie Buckland said, puncturing the mood, signalling to Charlie to get some more drinks in. 'I can't see it, meself. Can't see why they'd bother...'

'But it's a *fact*,' Jake said, exasperated by their complacency. 'They're here. We saw one of their craft. We didn't *dream* that. We *saw* it. It's already *here*.'

'Well, it zertainly wuz massive,' Ted Gifford said, nodding as if to emphasize what Jake had said. 'Biggest fuckin' thing I've ever seen, truth be told. Like in the ol' films... you know, when the aliens invade...'

'Thanks, Ted,' Geoff said, shaking his head. 'Be sure to tell the kids that one afore they go to bed tonight.'

'Yeah, but Ted's right in a way,' Jake said. 'What if it is an invasion? It'd explain all those people on the move...'

'There are always people on the move.'

'Sure, John, but recently... Well, we've all seen it...'

'That's true,' John answered, sitting forward. 'Only why's there been no word of it before now? You know how it is, normally... we hear about such things long before they reach us. What's gone wrong this time? Why has the rumour mill dried up?'

Jake didn't know. Maybe it hasn't, he thought. Maybe they're just much more efficient at keeping word from spreading.

Only how would they do that? People got away. Word got out. Word always got out.

It all ended inconclusively, two hours later. Nothing had been decided. Ted Gifford had suggested that they send a party east, to see if they could find out more, only no one was keen on going and the idea of an expedition fizzled out.

One thing *had* come out of the meeting, however, and that was a general disbelief that anyone – aside from the odd band of thieves and murderers – was actually interested in Purbeck.

Will Cooper perhaps expressed it best.

'It ain't exactly fuckin' Tibet now, is it?'

The general consensus was that it would all blow over; that they'd need to be extra vigilant these next few weeks, but after that...

Jake stood outside, on the patio at the back, looking out across the fields towards the south. It had been an eventful day. He had killed a man and found a good friend dead. Tomorrow he would go and bury Margaret, then deliver Jack Hamilton his bride.

Which reminded him. He had to go and tell Becky that they'd be delayed setting off for Wareham in the morning. If he was to see to Ma Brogan, it would be best if he did it at first light. Yes, and alone. Peter had seen enough.

Peter was with the other village kids, standing idly around, down by the outhouse where it had all happened. Jake went over to him.

'You okay?'

Peter nodded.

Jake looked around. 'Where's Boy?'

'Meg's taken him home. He was hungry...'

'Look... I've just got to nip in to Corfe. I've got to let Becky know we're setting out a bit later tomorrow. I told her eight, but if I'm to... you know...'

'I know. Shall I light a fire?'

Jake grinned. 'A fire would be nice.'

'Then I'll see you later on.'

He left Peter and went back inside. Josh was just about to leave. He was heading back on the wagon with Geoff Horsfield and John Lovegrove, but on hearing that Jake was heading his way, he latched on, holding on to Jake's arm for support, then sitting beside Jake in the back of the wagon as they made their way back.

'Ted was sayin' that Rory 'as a daughter,' Josh said as they entered the darkness of the tree-lined lane.

'He has, and a lovely girl she is. Roxanne...'

Josh sang two lines of the old song, then laughed. 'Bet she gets that a lot.'

'Not from the young 'uns...'

Josh fell silent for a moment, then: 'Did you get me anything, Jake? You know... at market?'

Jake hadn't yet given Josh his surprise. He had meant to tomorrow, after he'd sorted everything else.

'I got you *something*.'

Josh chuckled; a chuckle that became a cough.

'You all right, Josh?' Geoff said, speaking from the darkness just ahead of them. 'Chest not playin' you up?'

'Chest's fine... it's my bloody legs.'

'Didn't sound like your legs,' John Lovegrove said, laughing.

'Been a strange ol' day, ain't it?' Josh said, ignoring him. 'Can't say I'm not glad it's over.'

'Strange you should say that...' Jake said.

'Why's that, boy?'

'You'll see.'

Josh touched his arm sympathetically. 'Been a hard day for you, I know... Poor ol' Maggie...'

'Maggie? Oh... you mean...'

'Ma Brogan... as was...'

'No one blames you, Jake,' Geoff said. 'I'd have done the same.'

'Me, too,' John quickly added. 'I'd 'ave cut 'is fuckin' balls off, if it were me!'

'And fed 'em to him! Bastard!'

Jake looked down. It was strange hearing such vehemence, such anger, from his old friends. They were such kind men. Kind but unforgiving.

'Killing him... that was nothing... he was worth no more... only...'

There were grunts of agreement. They all knew what Jake was talking about. They knew him too well not to.

'The boy'll understand, Jake,' Geoff said more quietly. 'He knows you. Knows that you wouldn't'a done it without good reason.'

'Yeah, but...'

'Geoff's right,' John said emphatically. 'The boy'll be fine. 'E just needs to understand how things are. Needs to know what's wrong and what's right. An eye for an eye.'

Maybe. Only Jake had never liked 'an eye for an eye'. It was distinctly Old Testament, and in his mind he associated it with a kind of right-wing severity that he'd always mistrusted. Not only that, but it seemed to place him there alongside men like Charlie Waite and Frank Goodman, and he wasn't sure that that was where he wanted to be.

Necessity, he thought. That's what it comes down to, necessity.

Only he knew that what he'd done had damaged him in his son's eyes.

He changed the subject.

'You were quiet tonight, Geoff...'

'Was I?'

'Yeah... I'd have thought you'd have had a lot to say on the subject, being a historian and all.'

'Well, maybe I have. And maybe sometimes it's best not to say a word.'

'Yeah?'

Geoff was silent a moment, then, 'You free tomorrow afternoon, Jake?'

'I guess so.'

'Then come and see me.'

'Sounds ominous,' John Lovegrove said.

'Well, maybe it is,' Geoff answered him. 'And maybe I'm wrong. It's the thought that I *could* be wrong that made me hold my tongue earlier. After all, I don't want to go scaring souls for no reason.'

'You think what you've got to say would scare people, then?' Jake asked.

Geoff chuckled darkly. 'I dunno. But it fuckin' scares me, I can tell you!'

Back in Corfe, Jake helped Josh back indoors.

'D'you know where Becky's putting up for the night?'

'Right here, boy,' Josh said. 'She'll be in the bar, I warrant. Likes her drink, that girl...'

Jake said goodnight, then went through to the bar. Only Becky wasn't there.

'She went up a while back,' Dougie, who was cleaning up behind the bar, told him. 'She's on the first floor at the front. Room Three.'

He went upstairs and knocked.

'Who's that?' she called from inside.

'It's me... Jake... I wanted to give you a message.'

'Hang on...'

Becky came to the door. In the candlelight, he could see she had been getting ready for bed. She had washed her hair and thrown on a nightgown.

She smiled. 'Jake... 'ow lovely to see you... come in a minute...'

'No... look, I can't stop...'

But she was having none of it. '*Come in,*' she insisted. 'I've been waiting all day to have a word.'

As she closed the door then turned to him, she laughed.

'What?'

'Just that you almost caught me.'

'Caught you?'

'With my patch on... I wear it sometimes... when I'm on my own. I hate seein' it, see... in the mirror.'

'Ah...'

He looked about him. The room was small and rather shabby,

with a threadbare carpet and cheap-looking teak furniture from the nineteen fifties. There was a wet towel on the bed, and on the bed-side table, beside the candle, was a bottle of whisky and a tumbler.

She saw where he was looking. 'You fancy a nightcap, Jake? It's a single malt. A Laphroaig. From before the Collapse.'

He'd meant just to tell her and leave, but the sight of the whisky swayed him.

'Okay... just a little one...'

She grinned, then went across. 'So what's the message?'

'Just that I'll be a bit later than I said. There's something I've got to do first thing. I thought... well, that you might like a bit of a lie in.'

'Before the big day, eh?'

She poured out a large measure, then turned, offering it to him.

Jake went across. 'Cheers!' he said, taking the glass and raising it to her. 'You all right about tomorrow? I mean... you're not having second thoughts about marrying Jack Hamilton?'

She looked down. 'It's just... well, it's going to be strange... tied to one man...'

'Yeah?'

She met his eyes. 'Yeah... and a much older man, too... I just wonder...'

'What?'

She hesitated. 'Can I tell you a secret, Jake?'

'Go on.'

'I like sex. I like it a lot. And the eye... well, I was born with it, and things 'appenin' as they did, I never got a chance to correct it. But that's not all bad, see... because it's given me an excuse... you know... not to get too involved.'

'Yeah?' Jake said uncomfortably. It was a bit too close to the nub. He took a sip of the malt. 'Christ, that's good!'

'Ain't it?' Becky took it from him a moment and had a sip herself. 'Hmm... only one thing better I can think of.'

'Sex, you mean?'

She handed the glass back.

'And is that it? Is *that* what's worrying you? That you'll have to be faithful to Jack?'

'Partly...' She laughed and looked down. 'That's if I can... I've got some bad 'abits, Jake. Some very bad 'abits... An' I'm not sure as marriage'll cure 'em.'

'So what are you going to do?'

Again she met his eyes. It was disconcerting, certainly, but a man could get used to it. 'Right now I'm going to bed.'

'Oh... right...' Jake took a large swig of the malt. It was a truly magnificent whisky. He loved the way it burned in your throat afterwards, the delicious after-flavour of it. He looked to her. 'I'd better go, then...'

She took the glass from him, sipped from it, then handed it back.

'That's just it... I was 'oping you wouldn't. I was 'oping... well... that you'd stay a bit and let me show you just how grateful I was.'

'Becky...'

'No, Jake. Hear me out. You see, travelling back in the wagon I kept thinking to myself, what can I do for Jake? Seein' as 'e's been so good to me. And I thought to myself, I could fuck his brains out... that'd be a good way of saying thank you, wouldn't it now?'

Jake swallowed awkwardly. 'And?'

Unfastening the belt, she let the gown fall from her.

'I'm a very grateful girl, you see, Jake Reed. I know who my friends are and I treat 'em well...'

Jake stood there, mouth open, taking her in. There was no doubting it, looking at her. She had a lovely figure, and it was years since he had seen a naked woman. Only this was wrong. He would never be able to look at Jack Hamilton again.

No, or himself.

She stepped closer. Taking his hands she placed them on her breasts.

So warm they were, so perfectly formed.

'Becky... I can't...'

'Why not? You ain't doin' Jack no 'arm. 'E don't even know I'm on my way to 'im. An' seein' 'ow it's the last time before I become an honest woman...'

Jake closed his eyes, feeling her hands at his neck, her lips on his cheek. What harm would it do? What harm?

'Becky... I'm flattered... really I am... you're a beautiful woman...'

That much was true. In the candle's light she looked the very picture of desire, like a Botticelli Venus. Even so, he knew he couldn't stay. To even think of starting something with her was madness. And besides, there were ghosts. Only it was hard to tear himself away. The warmth of her flesh against his palms, the soft delight of her mouth against his neck.

'Becky, *please*...'

'You can have me, Jake. Tonight... you can stay all night if you want...'

'I can't... my son...'

'An hour, then... Please, Jake... I'll do whatever you want...'

He groaned as her hand moved down to gently cup his sex.

'Becky, I can't... I *can't*...'

But the stiffness there betrayed him.

'Hush, my darlin' boy... course you can... that's what Becky's 'ere for... to make you feel alive again...'

'Becky...'

But he was lost. Lost and no way back. Her hands, her lips, the fullness of her breasts... He had forgotten the magic of it all.

She smiled at him lovingly as her fingers nimbly, expertly unfastened him. 'You've been dead too long, Jake, my love... Come, my darlin' boy... Come to bed and forget about tomorrow...'

It was gone two when he returned. Peter had waited up, worried that he'd not come back. The fire in the grate had burned down to ashes.

'I'm sorry... I had some business.'

'Dad...' He could see the boy wanted to scold him, to tell him off. And not only for being late. For everything. For the whole damned mess.

'I'm sorry, lad. I shouldn't have stayed out. I...'

Coming back from Corfe he had hurried through the darkness, his thoughts in turmoil, not knowing what to feel or think.

He had not slept with a woman since Annie's death. Had not killed a man like that, up close, for what? Eight years and more. But today...

'Uncle Tom's not well,' Peter said, breaking into his thoughts. 'Cath came across an hour back...'

'An hour? Oh, shit... Has Mary sent for the doctor?'

'I said you'd come, as soon as you got back. Only you didn't...'

'I'm sorry... Look, I'll go there now... D'you want to come?'

Peter grabbed his coat and nodded, a surly look on his face. Boy at once jumped up out of his basket.

'Dad?'

'What?'

Peter looked down, embarrassed. 'Perhaps you ought to wash...'

'Wash?' Then he realized what Peter was saying.

'Oh...'

He went through to the old butler sink at the back of the house and washed.

Peter was right. It wouldn't have done to have turned up at the Hubbards' stinking of another woman. And not simply for the reasons Peter thought.

For that too had crossed his mind, even as he lay in Becky's arms – that in sleeping with her he was somehow betraying Mary.

Absurd, he knew, but true.

He went back through, joining Peter and Boy out front.

'Did Cath say what the problem was?'

'He's running a fever...'

'A fever?'

Jake stopped, then reached out and took his son's arm. There was so much anger in the boy right now.

'I'm sorry, right... It's been a hard day.'

And it isn't going to get any easier. But he didn't say that.

'Come on... let's see what we can do.'

Tom was in a bad way. You could see it as soon as you walked into the room.

'What is it? Jake asked quietly, not sure whether Tom, who had his eyes closed, was sleeping or not.

Mary turned, looking up at him. She had been crying.

'It's his shoulder. It's begun to swell up again.'

'And the doctor?'

'Cath went half an hour back. He said he'd come.'

Jake went across and, careful not to disturb Tom, had a look.

He winced. It looked bad. Looked like it was infected.

'But it was fine,' he said, looking to Mary again. 'The wound was clean.'

She took a shivering breath. 'I know...'

'Tell him, Mary,' Tom said wearily. 'Just tell him.'

'Tell me what?'

Mary's head went down. She was hunched forward, as if fending off some physical blow.

'What?'

He was conscious suddenly of Peter and the girls in the doorway behind him.

Tom opened his eyes. He turned his head slowly, looking up at Jake.

'I'm dying, Jake.'

Jake shook his head. 'You can't say that. The doctor'll be here any minute. He'll give you something...'

Mary turned, looking up at him. Her eyes were raw, her face pale. 'It's not the wound.'

'I don't get it…'

'I've got cancer,' Tom said. 'Liver cancer. At least, that's where it started. It's spread. And my immune system…' He smiled wearily, as if it were a cause for amusement. 'It's shot…'

Jake shook his head. It wasn't possible. It just wasn't. Only a few days ago, Tom had been striding along at his side, all ruddy-faced and healthy.

'You can't know that.'

'He went to see them. In Dorchester. They did all the tests.'

Jake looked to Mary, then back at Tom. 'That young doctor we saw…?'

'Had seen me before… three… no, four times…'

Tom had closed his eyes again, but he seemed much more relaxed now.

There was a sudden, sharp movement behind him. Jake turned, in time to see Meg turn away and rush off, bursting into tears as she went. Peter chased after her.

Cathy too was crying. Only she and Beth seemed calm. 'Is it true, Daddy?'

'It's true,' Mary said quietly.

'And the bullet?'

Tom smiled; a proper smile this time. 'One of life's little ironies, eh?'

But Jake couldn't smile. All he could see now was the damage in Tom's face. He hadn't seen it before now. Maybe he hadn't been looking properly. But now he could.

'How long has it been?'

'Best part of a year,' Mary answered, taking Tom's hand again and squeezing it. 'He thought it was simple tiredness to begin with. A sign 'e was growing old. But then the pains began.'

'Christ, Tom, why didn't you tell me?'

'You'd only have fussed…'

'Yeah, well, you should have let me fuss!'

Jake stood. His own anger surprised him. He felt like breaking something.

'Fuck it!'

'Jake...'

He looked at Tom, blinking through his tears. 'You *saved* me! You gave me my fucking life that time! I *owe* you. You can't just *die* on me!'

Tom's mouth trembled. 'Seems I can.'

There was a sudden knocking down below, then hurried footsteps on the stairs. The local doctor, Hart, appeared in the doorway.

'Jake... Mary...'

He went straight across, setting his bag down by the bed even as Jake stepped back.

'I've told them,' Tom said, looking up at him.

'Thank god for that. Now what's the trouble?'

While the doctor did his examination, Mary took Jake downstairs.

They spoke quietly but intensely.

'Why didn't you *tell* me?'

Mary shrugged. She was close to tears again. 'He asked me not to. He wanted things to be normal...'

'Normal? How could they be fucking normal?'

'Jake...'

'I'm sorry. It's just... No, I'm sorry... I really am. I love Tom.'

'I know.' But it sounded desolate.

Jake shook his head. Now that he'd been told, all manner of things came clear to him. Even Mary's behaviour the night of the gathering.

Mary turned away, busying herself, filling a kettle simply for something to do.

'We... talked about it... Tom and I... when we first knew... I... I wanted to tell you.'

'Did you?'

She glanced at him. 'Yes... only Tom didn't want that. Didn't want you looking at him in that way... you know...'

He did, and he understood. If he was dying the very last thing he'd want was for his friends to look at him that way – in that mawkish, over-sentimental fashion.

'So you just...'

Mary sighed. 'You know... it's been the 'ardest thing, watchin' him each day... seeing him diminish. You must have noticed something.'

'No. No, I... Small things, I guess, but you put them down to ageing. We're none of us getting any younger...'

'No...'

He frowned. 'You told the girls?'

Mary shook her head. 'No. Not till tonight... Not till...'

She turned to him, her face distraught. 'Oh, Jake... it was awful...'

'Oh, Mary...'

He took her in his arms and held her, letting her sob into his shoulder, the tears coursing down his own cheeks.

'We'll do our best for him, Mary, I promise you. Whatever you need... You only have to ask, you know that. Whatever you need.'

Jake barely slept. Long before dawn he was up and dressed, ready to go and do what needed to be done.

For once he was afraid. Afraid of seeing in the daylight what he'd glimpsed the night before. He had packed a bag with several old sheets and thick gloves and a shovel and was about to go – to get there at first light – when Peter came down and joined him.

'Peter... you didn't have to...'

'I couldn't sleep,' Peter said, coming across, taking his coat down from the peg.

'You don't have to come.'

The boy turned, looking back at Jake, clear-eyed. 'I know. But I want to. We share things from now on. Okay?'

Jake stared at his son, surprised. This was a new tone from him.

'Okay... How's Meg?'

'Not good. She never guessed. Cathy and Beth... well, they knew something was going on. But Meg... it's hit her hard.'

Jake nodded. Like it hit you, he thought, when your mother died.

'I meant to ask,' Peter said, 'did you...?'

'The ring? Yeah. I'll bring it back from Corfe later on. It's in my pack.' He smiled. 'It's really nice. Solid gold.'

Peter grinned back at him. 'Thanks...'

'Okay... then let's go.'

East Orchard was barely any distance across the fields. As they walked down the long slope in the early light, Boy gambolling along between them, both were silent, lost in their own thoughts. It was only when they came to the cottage that Jake turned to his son again.

'Look... if you find this disturbing...'

'Dad. I'm all right. Really I am. It's awful, yeah, I know that, but I have to deal with it.'

Jake wanted to argue, only maybe the boy was right. Maybe you did have to see the worst of it – the very worst – to understand the whole. Good and evil. They were delicately balanced in the world. And you needed to understand that, for without that you were fucked. Well and truly fucked.

He reached out and touched Peter's shoulder. 'Come on, then. But be warned. It's not a pleasant sight. Poor Margaret...'

Peter lowered his head, then nodded.

'We'll wrap her up in the sheets and bring her down. Bury her in her garden. That's where she'd want to be...'

'Dad?'

'What, boy?'

I know it might sound a bit ghoulish, but d'you think Meg and I could have the cottage?'

The question astonished Jake. 'I... I'll talk to Tom about it...'

'Only...'

'Go on...'

'Just that if it is all ending... if the Chinese are here... then I want to have some time alone with Meg. Just me and her...'

Jake wanted to say that he was only fourteen and that they had all the time in the world. Only fourteen was a different kind of fourteen these days – not like when he grew up and you were still a child. No, and they didn't have all the time in the world. No one knew how long they had. So why not?

'I'll talk to him, Peter, I promise... when I'm back from Wareham. Now let's do what we have to do.'

Becky was waiting for him when he got to the Bankes Arms Hotel, her wagon secured with thick straps, her packed bags on the pavement next to it.

Seeing him, she smiled and came across. She was dressed in her very best clothes and, most surprising of all, she was wearing her eye patch.

'Jake, my love... As you see, I'm ready.'

He put out his hand to her, but she ignored it, giving him a hug instead, and whispering in his ear.

'I wish you could 'ave stayed a little longer... I couldn't sleep...'

He moved back a little, feeling awkward. 'Tom wasn't well... We were up half the night... and then there was the burial...'

Her face changed, grew concerned. 'I'm really sorry...'

'That's all right,' he said gently, remembering how kind she'd been – how loving-generous – the previous evening. 'Let's get you to your husband, eh?'

There was something faintly wistful in her expression, and then she grinned. 'Come on, then... come up and sit next to me on the seat, Jake, and tell me what's been 'appenin'...'

It was an hour and more to Wareham in the wagon, and after the events of the past few days, Jake was wary. Letting Becky do most of the talking, he sat there, his eyes searching the horizon on all sides, looking out for any sign of bandits.

If Becky had had her way, of course, they would have stopped along the road, but Jake was strict about that.

'It was wonderful... really it was... you're a lovely woman, Becks... but this is your wedding day, and I'm not – you know – on your wedding day.'

Becky feigned disappointment. Or maybe she didn't. Maybe she really was disappointed. But that didn't matter to Jake. Sweet as it might have been, he was not succumbing to her again. And besides, his mind was full of other things. He only had to think...

It had been a lot worse than he'd thought. The look of Margaret's corpse in the dawn's light had caught him unprepared. It wasn't only that rigor mortis had set in, giving her a stiff, almost haunted look, but there was a marked discoloration of the skin. Already insects had found her and begun their hideous feast. But it was her hair – that lovely mane of silver hair of hers – that disturbed him most, for it was thickly matted now with clotted blood, like a black tar, fusing her to the pillow, such that when he came to try to lift her, the pillow came up with her, inseparable.

Awful it was, that moment when he'd lifted her. Simply awful. But Peter had helped him, had quickly brought the sheet and wrapped it about her. Between them they had carried her down-stairs – light as a child, she'd seemed – and out into the garden. Peter and he had already dug the grave, there between her roses and chrysanthemums.

It was such an end as she never would have dreamed. Such a lovely woman she had been in life. Such a power for goodness on the earth.

He had stood there, before they covered her, saying a few words, while Peter bowed his head. Boy edged forward curiously, tiny whimpers escaping him at the smell of the open grave.

Yes, but at least someone cared at the end.

He looked up. Becky had been saying something.

'What's that, Becks?'

'I was just sayin'... 'bout that craft we all saw.'

'Go on...'

'I was thinkin'... maybe they've come to 'elp us. You know... to set things up again. 'Elp rebuild... Everyone's thinkin' some'at else, of course... expectin' the worst... only... well, maybe we've all become too untrustin'.'

'It's only to be expected,' he said, made thoughtful by her comments. 'It's been twenty years and more since anything but trouble came down the east road.'

They were coming close now, the town and the river visible up ahead.

'Jake... before we get there... before I... you know... before I meet this man who's gonna be my 'usband... will you promise me some'at?'

He smiled, but he could see this once she was deadly serious.

'Depends what it is.'

'It's just that... Well... if it goes wrong... if for some reason things go bad between me and this Jack... then you'll come for me. That you'll bring me away from there.'

It was some request, and he was silent a moment, chewing it over.

'Well, Becks,' he said finally, shaking his head. 'I guess I could say yes... only that's not quite what you mean, is it? You mean you and your goods... your wagon and your pony and your bags and clothes and everything... have I got that right?'

She smiled, relieved that he'd understood. 'It's just that... a single woman is very alone in this 'ere world. Unless she's the most wicked o' bitches then she's vulnerable, and it 'elps to 'ave a good friend you can call on. 'Specially one that you've shared things with, if you know what I mean...'

'Becky... get it clear... it was a one-off...'

'Oh, I know,' she said, smiling broadly and laying a hand on his knee. 'But what a sweet one-off, eh? One of the best hours of my life, I'd say...'

'Becky...'

'Oh, I know. And I'm gonna try my 'ardest to make things right... to make things work between Jack Hamilton and me. Only sometimes one's best endeavours ain't quite good enough. Sometimes there's just no chemistry...'

He almost laughed at that but, again, she was in deadly earnest.

'Okay,' he said. 'I promise. But in return you've got to promise *me* something.'

She turned slightly, facing him squarely on the long bench seat, her good eye looking back at him kindly, her mouth set in a broad smile which showed her perfect teeth.

'Just ask me.'

'Okay... You've got to promise me that you won't fuck any of Jack Hamilton's sons...'

'Jake!'

She seemed almost offended by that, but he wasn't fooled.

'No... I won't have it... I know you, remember? You've told me what you're like, and I know it now for a fact. You're a girl with bad habits... very bad habits... but Jack's sons... they're off limits, you got me?'

'But why...?'

He spoke over her. 'Because they're your age, and strong and healthy and... do I have to spell it out?'

Becky pulled at the reins, bringing the wagon to a halt, then turned to him again.

'That's unfair... that makes me feel almost like I ought to turn straight round and go home.'

'What, that room you've got in that boarding house in Chikerell? You're going to give up the chance to be mistress of the best inn in Wareham for *that*?'

She looked down. For a time she was silent, then, in the tiniest voice, 'Okay... I promise.'

'Good... but if I hear any word... the slightest breath of tittle-tattle about a certain young woman's taste in young men... then the deal is off... and I'll come and tell Jack Hamilton myself, understand?'

'Oh, Jake... you wouldn't be so mean...'

'Try me.'

For a moment she stared at him almost angrily, and then, almost from nowhere, she began to laugh.

'What?' Jake asked, confused now.

'Just that I was thinkin'... what a good job it was I got a stock o' them old blue pills 'fore I set out...'

Jack Hamilton was sitting in his office at the back of the pub, in his leather apron, his lunchtime glass of whisky in front of him as Jake stepped in.

Jack stood, giving Jake a beam of a smile. 'Jake... good to see you... 'ave you?'

'I have.'

'An' is she?'

'She is. Only a word first, before you meet her.'

'She cost more than I gave you, is that it?'

'No, Jack. I didn't *buy* you a wife.'

'Oh?' Jack looked confused. 'You didn't?'

'No. But I did *find* you one. An independent woman of means.'

From the look on Jack's face, he wasn't sure whether that was a good thing or not. 'Go on...'

'All right... Well, first off, she's a good-looking woman. Strong and young. She'll bear you strong sons...'

Again Jack looked confused. 'Sons? I don't need sons... got plenny o' them from my first wife, may she rest in peace... What I need is a good woman in my bed every night and at my side throughout the day. Someone as'll take some of the burden from me. Someone who doesn't mind workin' her arse off.'

'Then I think I've found you the very woman, Jack Hamilton... There's just one little drawback...'

'Yeah? An' what's that?'

'Her eye.'

'Her *eye*?'

'Yeah... She's got a funny eye. It doesn't focus properly. It *wanders*... But if you can *overlook* that eye...'

'She could wear a patch...'

Jake smiled. 'Funny you should say that... Oh, and one other small thing... she gets to keep her stuff.'

'Her *stuff*?'

'She used to sell jewellery, in Dorchester market... She's got a wagon load of the stuff and some bags and clothes and other things. You've got to let her keep all of that. Draft an agreement before you wed, so that it's legal and binding.'

Jack was clearly still thinking about the eye, for he nodded almost absently.

'Good... You want to meet her, then?'

Jack nodded, then, realizing he was still wearing his apron, hastily took it off, then combed his fingers through the last few threads of his hair.

'Wheel 'er in, boy! Wheel 'er in!'

Becky stepped into the room.

Jake's heart was in his mouth. What if they didn't hit it off? What if they hated each other at first sight?

Only he could see at once that both were relieved, even perhaps happy that the other wasn't quite so awful as they had imagined. It wasn't perfect, but then what was?

'Jack...' Becky said, smiling as she crossed the room confidently and took his hand. 'I'm Becky... Rebecca Croft, that is, only daughter o' Leopold Croft, late of Weymouth, and I'm pleased to meet you.'

Becky's smile was one of intense satisfaction, like she'd seen the worst and it wasn't so bad at all. But it was no match for the smile on Jack's face. Jack was smiling like he'd just come into a fortune. Smiling because the woman standing before him was younger than his youngest daughter, and, more to the point, clearly was a fine figure of a woman.

'Becky... I'm *delighted* to meet you.' And, showing a daring that was quite uncharacteristic, he drew her close and gave her a kiss, full on the lips.

Becky laughed. 'Now, that's what I like, Jack Hamilton... a man of spirit!'

'Good!' the innkeeper answered, beaming now from ear to ear, looking over to Jake to include him in his delight. 'Then let's get things done and dusted...'

Jack sent two of his sons to accompany Jake as far as Three Barrows, to make sure he was safe. There had been reports of yet more strangers on the roads and a sighting of a war party of twenty or more heading west, but they saw nothing. The countryside was still and silent under the cloudless autumn sky.

As he walked the last section of the road, Jake found his mood darkening once again. For a brief time he had almost forgotten, but now, heading back, he found himself facing the fact. Tom was dying, and with him the world they had come to know over the last twenty years and more.

Slowly the castle came into view, a rough-edged sprawl of grey against the green of the mound in which it was embedded, its ruined towers set proudly against the blue of the sky. As he looked up, Jake glimpsed a brief flash of light from the topmost tower, and knew at once who it was.

As he came out beneath the East Hill, Peter ran out to greet him, Boy barking at his heels. He looked concerned, and puzzled.

'You all right, lad?'

Peter had Jake's field glasses about his neck. 'Dad... you've got to see...'

Maybe. But first he wanted to know how things were.

'Is Uncle Tom all right?'

'He was sleeping... the doctor gave him something...'

'And Aunt Mary...?'

'Dad... this is important... please... come and see... Aunt Mary's fine. The girls are looking after her...'

Jake let himself be led up through the gate and on, climbing the steep grassy slope to the Keep, then up again, until he stood at the top of the highest tower – the King's Tower. There Peter handed him the field glasses.

'Look to the north-east,' he said. 'Towards Bournemouth...'

Jake adjusted the settings, then looked in the direction Peter was indicating, resting the edge of the glasses on the brickwork to keep the image still. At first he didn't understand. Beyond the great urban sprawl of Poole and Bournemouth that lay just across the water from Purbeck was a patch of whiteness that hadn't been there a week ago. A pearled nothingness, like the world just ended there in a perfect geometric line.

'What is that? It's... like a wall of mist, or the edge of a glacier... only that's not possible... it's much too warm for anything like that...' He looked to his son. 'Who else has seen this?'

'No one...'

'Then keep it to yourself. Until we know for sure just what it is. No use scaring people, is it?'

But Jake could see that Peter was as disturbed by it as he.

'Look... I'm going to go and see Geoff anyway. I'll bring him up here... see what he thinks.'

'Dad...?'

'Yes?'

'I don't know. I...'

Jake could see that Peter wanted to be reassured; to be given some kind of explanation for what he'd seen. Only it made as little sense to him as it did to his son. It wasn't possible. It simply wasn't possible. It had to be some kind of natural phenomenon.

'Look... I've a couple of things to do. Go back home... make sure Mary and the girls are okay... See if you can help in any way. I'll be back as soon as I can.'

When Peter was gone, he went back to that high vantage point and looked again, fiddling with the magnification, searching the horizon and coming back to the fact, finally, that whatever it was, that block of whiteness, it really was there, in the far distance to the north-east.

He came back down, troubled by what he'd seen. The truth was, it had been as big a shock as seeing the craft the other evening. It had the same power to disturb the eye, and he had known at once that it was all part of the same picture. Whatever had produced that craft had produced this, whatever it was.

The Chinese... the Han...

Geoff would know. That is, if anyone knew. But first he'd go and see Josh and give him his presents.

Jake retrieved his pack from the old post office, then walked over to the hotel.

On the stairs, outside what had been Becky's room, he paused, recollecting what had happened there. It was only last night, but already it seemed a thousand years ago. Before he'd learned that Tom was dying. Before he'd seen that block of whiteness, there on the edge of things.

Josh was at the very top of the old building. You could hear the music coming from his room, a faint, muted sound that seemed to come from the depths of the building.

As he came to the top of the stairs and pushed the door wide, the sound grew suddenly louder, clearer.

Josh was bending over the old machine, looking at the jacket from some old piece of vinyl. Hearing the door, he turned and, seeing Jake, broke into a toothless grin.

'Ah, Jake... I wondered when you'd come...'

'I've brought you something,' Jake said, looking about him at the groaning shelves of records and CDs that lined every wall of that room and the next, which could be glimpsed through the opening on the far side.

'What's this?' he asked, not recognizing the song that was playing. Josh handed him the sleeve, which read Propaganda in what was a vaguely Chinese style of writing.

Jake studied it a moment, then looked to Josh again. He was grinning now.

'I love it... You know who that's meant to be...?'

'Chairman Mao, playing lead guitar, and those are his Red Guards...'

'I'm not sure about the music, though.'

Josh took the sleeve back. 'It's early Police... a live version of one of their B-sides... they used to put out records like this... samplers, they called them.'

Josh lifted the arm. The sound vanished.

In the corner, just behind him, was what looked like a truncated bicycle, from which a belt ran to the back of the makeshift hi-fi system. It was, as the old man said, 'very Heath Robinson', but it worked. It allowed him to play his music without burning up gallons of generator fuel.

'So?' Josh asked, excited now. 'What 'ave you got me, boy?'

Jack set his pack down then rummaged.

'There you go,' he said, producing the single. This was his 'teaser', his joke item. Only Josh was staring at it very strangely as he held it. A tear slowly formed in his eye and rolled down his cheek.

'Who told you?'

Jake was confused now. It was not the reaction he'd expected. 'Told me what?'

'This.'

Carefully, almost tenderly, Josh slipped the tiny seven-inch single from its red and black sleeve and placed it on the turntable. As he lifted the arm again, he looked to Jake.

'This song... no... I guess you couldn't have known, could you...? Only... the memories it brings back. One in particular. My wife, Gwen... she was havin' our first. Fifty years ago it was, maybe more... A boy, as it turned out, name of Andrew... I lost contact with him when things fell apart, but anyway... Gwen was havin' a hard time of it... a long labour it was... best part of a day... and part-way through I left her to it... had to get out of there for a while... so I went and 'ad a pint at a pub nearby and this was playin'... on one of those old juke-boxes they used to 'ave.'

'I didn't know...'

'No. I can see you didn't. But listen. It's a gem. Especially the bass line.'

Jake closed his eyes and listened as the sound from the speakers filled the room. But Josh was right. It was a gem.

As it ended Josh sighed. 'Beautiful, eh?'

'I've got something else,' Jake said, returning to the pack. 'Something special.'

Josh chuckled. 'Need to be something really special to top that.'

Jake handed him the album, watching as Josh's face lit up with a great beam of delight.

'Jesus! Where did you get this! It's priceless!'

Jake smiled. 'Rory had it... says it's a present... for being such a good customer all these years...'

'Good boy!' Josh laughed then hugged it to him, careful not to bend it. 'You got time to listen to a track or two, Jake, or you in a hurry?'

Jake really wanted to hear it. He loved what he'd already heard of Spirit, and the build-up Josh had given this album had been tremendous, but Geoff was waiting for him and, more to the point, Tom.

'Why don't I pop over tomorrow sometime? I could bring a few bits and pieces and we could listen to the whole album...'

Josh grinned. 'That sounds bloody wonderful! You don't mind if I listen to a track or two afore then, though?'

'Mind? Why should I mind? No, Josh... you enjoy it... only don't scratch the bugger...'

'Oh, don't you worry, boy... I'll treat it gently...'

'Then I'll see you on the morrow. You'll be here, I take it?'

But Josh was already removing the record carefully from its sleeve. 'Oh, I'll be here, Jake. Where else would I be?'

Peter watched from his elevated perch on the keep wall as his father stepped out from the front of the old coaching inn and looked about him.

Jake looked tired. His body language spoke of a man who had been pushed close to his limits. Lack of sleep was part of it, but it was much more than that. Peter had thought about it now and thought he understood. Killing the stranger had pained his father greatly. Had drained and damaged him. There'd been a moment when Jake had looked at him and he had seen it in his eyes. The shame of the act. Yet what was there to be ashamed of?

He had not understood at first. How could he? He hadn't seen her then. Hadn't seen what that scab of a man had done to that kind and gentle woman. No wonder his father had gone mad. But he knew his father prided himself on doing the right thing, and for once he felt he had transgressed. Down below, Jake hesitated, then adjusting his pack and his gun, set off down West Street. He was heading for Geoff Horsfield's house, at the end of that gently curving lane of grey, slate-roofed cottages, overlooking Corfe Common.

The 'school house', as they called it, though they only ever used the one room for lessons.

Jake was troubled. Peter could see it even from that distance,

even without seeing the expression on his face. His slightest movement conveyed it; the way his head was tilted slightly forward, the
hunching of his back and shoulders as he walked.

If anyone had answers, then it was Geoff. He'd been a historian,
after all, back in the old days. But even if he didn't, it would do his
father good to talk to someone. Someone who had a proper grasp
of things.

Peter sighed, then reached into his pocket and removed the ring.
He had taken it out and looked at it a dozen times now, trying to
imagine how Meg would react, rehearsing in his mind the words
he'd say in offering it to her; mouthing them silently, afraid in case
someone was nearby, listening.

If this was the end, if change *was* coming, then he had best do
this soon. Today, possibly. Only there was the small problem of
Tom and his illness.

Maybe it wasn't appropriate right now. Maybe...

Oh, he could maybe the day away. He would ask Aunt Mary. He
would do it now and get it over with. And then...

Then he would go and clean out the cottage. Burn all the old
sheets and blankets and get it all nice and cosy. Make it a little nest
for the two of them.

Or was that moving much too fast?

The whole business troubled him. It should have been so easy,
so natural, but now it felt a little like everything was having to be
rushed.

He looked through the field glasses one last time.

Down below, Jake had reached the last house. As Peter watched,
he unlatched the gate and walked up to the door, straightening up
as he did. Peter watched him knock, then, a moment later, duck
inside into the darkness.

He turned away, setting down the glasses. He would go right
away and speak to Mary.

And afterwards?

Afterwards he'd find Meg and give her the ring.

Boy barked. The wind had blown up and he was keen to get back.

'Okay, Boy,' Peter said, reaching down to ruffle his coat. 'Let's go find Aunt Mary. Let's go right now and get things settled, eh?'

Boy barked again, then leapt up and bounded off across the grass towards the gate. Peter watched him a moment, smiling, then followed slowly on behind, the glasses about his neck, his hand pushed deep into his coat pocket, cradling the ring.

Geoff came back through from the kitchen, carrying two cups of steaming hot coffee.

'There you are... white with two sugars, just as you like it.'

'Thanks...' Jake took the cup and set it down.

The room they were sitting in was Geoff's study. In one corner a huge desk was piled high with books, while the walls on every side were groaning, floor to ceiling, with shelf after shelf of yet more books. Books on every subject you could imagine.

They were text books mainly. A historian he might have been, but at heart Geoff Horsfield was an old-fashioned polymath, interested in and knowledgeable on everything under the sun.

'So...' Geoff said, settling behind his desk. 'You want to know why I was so quiet the other evening?'

'Well, it's not like you. You have an opinion on most things.'

'And I have on this... Only I wasn't sure people wanted to hear it.'

'I don't understand...'

'What you said... about the craft... about its markings...'

'The dragons?'

'Yes. I think you were right. I think... look, let me show you a couple of things. Articles... from old magazines, from before the Collapse. I think they clarify what's been going on.'

'It's been a long time...'

'I know. Twenty-two years. But they're still relevant. You want to look?'

'I'll take them away with me, if you want. But can't you summarize?'

Geoff smiled. 'All right. It's like this. Remember you told me once about those three days when it all happened. I mean... from the inside. In the... what did you call it?'

'The datscape.'

'Right. And do you remember what you said about how it seemed to you that it was the Chinese who kicked the props away, and not just from under us, but from under themselves, too.'

'How could I forget?'

'Okay... the first article I found, you see, was about the man who I think did that... Tsao Ch'un.'

'Tsao Ch'un?'

The name rang a bell, but after all these years Jake wasn't sure why.

'He was in charge, when it all happened. In charge of China, that is. And from what I can make out – the evidence is very sketchy – it was he who gave the order for it all to be trashed.'

'And destroy his own economy? Why would he do that? It's insane!'

'That's precisely what I've been asking myself for close on twenty years. There had to be a reason. Only I didn't understand it until very recently. Until I'd come across a few other bits and pieces. Essays in small, dissenting magazines. Pieces I had reprinted from the internet long ago. Podcasts and odd bits from here and there... from all over, actually. Jigsaw pieces, they were. Nothing startling on their own, but when you put them all together...'

Geoff was looking down broodingly.

'China...'

'Yes, China. It was they who initiated the great Collapse. And not only initiated it but, as you know, pushed and pushed until there was no way for the Market to go but down, on the biggest helter-skelter ride in history.'

Geoff sipped at his coffee, then set the cup down again.

'In fact, from what you said to me, and from what I've subsequently read, I can say with some confidence that it was no accident. I've looked at the state of the Market in the weeks before it happened, carefully examined and analysed the economic trends of those last few days before it all went off, and I can state with absolute certainty that there was no economic trigger, no failure of the system. It was deliberate – entirely deliberate. War. Not a shooting war, but war all the same. And now they're back. Now they've turned up, after all these years, to finish the job.'

Jake laughed. It seemed absurd. But at the same time he felt a deep foreboding. They *were* here. He had seen them with his own eyes.

'I don't want to sound like Ted Gifford, but why would they do that?'

'You said it yourself, Jake. To build a world state.'

'But...'

'I know what you're thinking. Why didn't they save themselves? Why did they subject themselves to all of that destruction, that chaos? And I can come up with only one answer. That Tsao Ch'un saw it as the only way of destroying the West without a nuclear war. A war he would most certainly have lost. By destroying the world's economic system, he destroyed the US as effectively as if he'd dropped ten thousand nuclear warheads. Russia and Europe too. And because he'd prepared for it – because he had instigated it – he was also prepared for the next stage of things.'

'Which was?'

'To prevent the West from rebuilding. To keep us down – broken, if you like – while they slowly took things over. That's why it's taken them so long. That's why it's only now that they've turned up on our doorstep.'

'That's an astonishing theory.'

'No, Jake. It's not a theory. It's what happened. That's what I'm telling you. All of those little articles and essays. They all add up. The signs were there, before it all happened. You only had to know where to look.'

Jake looked down. Since he'd first seen it, he had been wondering what on earth it had been, out there on the horizon. Now he knew.

'There's something out there, Geoff. On the edge of things...'

Geoff shifted slightly in his chair. 'Are we talking metaphorically now, or for real?'

'For real. It's something Peter noticed. I went up on the King's Tower with him earlier and he pointed it out to me. It's out past Poole and Bournemouth way. Right out on the very limits of what we could see with the glasses.'

'And?'

'It's a great mass of whiteness, out there on the horizon.'

'A block of whiteness?' Geoff laughed.

'Like a glacier. You want me to show you?'

Geoff seemed to blanch at that. He realized suddenly that Jake was serious.

'You mean...?'

'Like a huge glacier. Only you don't get glaciers this far south. And it's October. And I think I know now who's behind it...'

'China...'

'Yeah...'

'A glacier?' Geoff said. 'Or a wall, maybe?'

Jake nodded.

'But why would they build a wall?'

'Why do people ever build walls?'

'To keep their enemies out...'

'Or their people in.'

'Yes, but why build it there?'

'Unless it's not a wall...'

He took Geoff up onto the tower. There, using Geoff's glasses, which were considerably less powerful than his own, he had tried to point it out, only it was hard to get a clear view.

'I don't know,' Geoff said finally, lowering the glasses. 'It looks like *something* there, but what it is...'

'I'll bring my glasses... tomorrow... we'll look at it then... you'll get a clearer view.'

Geoff turned to him. 'It's like you said the other evening, Jake... The big question is what do they want with us? Do they want to rule us or exclude us? Help us or kill us?'

'You think those are the only choices?'

'Well... they sure as hell aren't going to leave us be. That's never the way of it. If history teaches anything, it's that an invading force makes certain it's secure, and by whatever means it can.'

'Then we're to fight? Resist them?'

Geoff shrugged. 'You saw their craft. Do you think we can?'

'No.'

'Well, then. Resistance isn't an option.'

Walking home, Jake thought about that. Was that it, then? Had Fate decided? When China came, was that their role in this – to acquiesce?

If so, it seemed ignoble. Not only that, but the dark historical parallels of it disturbed him. When the world changed, people died. That was the rule of it.

Yes, but maybe they could *choose* how they died... He was walking along the final stretch of the lane coming up to the church when he heard a noise, a strange animal whining, coming from just ahead of him, over to his left.

That's Boy, he thought. That has to be Boy!

Jake broke into a run. As he came out onto the main stretch of road, he paused, trying to get a fix on the noise.

There, he thought. The Hubbards' house...

His heart was pounding now. What if it was bandits... part of that huge army that Branagh's men had driven off? Jake hauled his gun from his shoulder and ran with it out before him, the safety off. Anxiety burned in him now.

Where's the whistle? Why haven't you blown the fucking whistle?

As he came to the gate, he leapt the low wall and ran on, down the passageway between the house and the garage and out into the garden space beyond.

There, crouched low, like he'd been told to sit, Boy was howling now, his head tilted skyward.

Jake turned, trying to make out what was happening.

Peter was standing in the doorway, looking in.

Thank god...

Only he didn't look right.

'Peter...?'

Peter turned his head, looking towards him. 'Dad...?'

He looked back inside, then quickly came across. 'Thank god you've come. I was going to come and get you...'

'Hey, hold on...'

He lifted Peter's face, saw it was wet with tears.

'He's dead, Dad. Tom's dead...'

'Dead...?'

The shock of it ran through him like a jolt of electricity.

He could hear it now, from upstairs. The sound of sobbing.

'Christ... when?'

Peter's face convulsed. 'He was sitting up talking to us. He...'

He shook his head, unable to continue. Jake gripped his shoulder briefly, then pushed past, hurrying across.

The sound was louder inside. For a moment he paused, looking about him at the kitchen. So many happy moments he'd shared with them, here about their table. So much joy. But now the room seemed desolate, untenanted.

He climbed the stairs, fighting gravity it seemed, his reluctance like some foul force draining his strength.

Dead. He couldn't be dead.

At the doorway he stopped, looking in, seeing how the four of them crowded the bed. Clinging to him, like they'd become one in their grief. Tom's girls.

The thought of it unmanned him. Tears rolled down his face. Tom's girls...

Sensing him there, Mary turned and, on seeing him, wiped her eyes on her apron and came across.

'What happened?' he asked, looking past her at Tom's face, where it lay, pale against the pure white pillow.

Tom looked like he was sleeping.

'I don't know,' Mary said quietly. 'His 'eart...'

She stopped, her face creased with pain.

Jake stepped close, holding her to him, letting her sob against his shoulder.

'I'm so sorry, Mary... So sorry...'

Her hands gripped his shoulders briefly. She took a long, shuddering breath, then moved back slightly. She was trying to smile, to reassure him somehow, only it came out like a grimace.

'It's good in a way, Jake. At least he won't suffer...'

But he could see she didn't believe that. She looked distraught. Besides, he knew how it had been between them. There was no faking that. Every second she had had with Tom had been precious. But now he was gone, and that vast gulf between the living and the dead had opened up between them; a vastness that made nothing of the distance between stars.

He had been dying, sure, but that was weeks off, months they'd hoped. To lose him now seemed cruel.

'I'll go back down,' he said. 'Make us all some tea...'

Mary was staring at him now. 'Thanks...' But as he made to turn away, she reached out, taking his arm.

'Jake... don't go home tonight. Stay here... please... Just tonight...'

'Sure…'

He went down, busying himself, trying not to think.

As if he had a choice…

It was the end of familiar life, he realized. Of normalcy. It was not just Tom's death. Not just the whiteness at the edge of things. Everything had changed.

And so it comes again…

Once before he had faced this. Once before it had all dissolved about him. Only this time he was scared, truly scared. This time it was sink or swim. This time it was for real.

CHUNG KUO

Chapter 9

ENDURING WILLOW

I t was a rest day and Jiang Lei was writing poetry.

At least, trying to.

Jiang Lei was a tall, elegant Han. A refined and dignified man, he had the self-contained air of one accustomed to command. Dressed in a pale blue silk, his dark hair, in which there were threads of grey, tied back severely in a bun at the back of his head, he might easily have been mistaken for a figure from an ancient painting. A study by Ku K'ai Chih, or Chou Fang, or the masterful Ku Hung Chung.

He was sitting on an ancient campaign chair his men had found for him some months back, when they had been in France; a relic of the Napoleonic Wars. Jiang liked the chair, even if it was somewhat uncomfortable. He liked its history. The thought that maybe it had belonged to a general like himself.

The view was a pleasant one. Of water meadows and a river, and, beyond a small outcrop of rocks, the sea. Another day he might have brought his paint box from the ship and spent the morning sketching. But not today. Today he was composing.

Or trying to.

The place he was in was quite beautiful. He had chosen it

himself having seen it from the air a day or two ago during their reconnaissance. Just behind him, to his right, was an ancient temple, what the locals called a 'parish church', and beside that a graveyard, curiously untended, the ancestor stones worn down and covered in moss, some of them hidden in the tangle of wild flowers and brambles. He had walked there earlier, enjoying the peacefulness of the place; the sense of timelessness.

Only its time had ended now. In a day or two it would all be gone.

Jiang turned his head, looking back at the encampment. His tent was on the near side of the field, in the shade of an old oak tree; a spacious thing of delicate rose-coloured silk with pale yellow panels. Beyond it, on the far side, were two rows of simple canvas tents, near to which his men – random specimens of 'Old Hundred Names', peasant soldiers with peasant faces – went about their business, washing and cooking and checking their weapons.

Beyond them, some way distant, was the city – or part of it, anyway – being built even as he sat there, a great slab of hexagonal whiteness that dominated the horizon. Closer to hand, not half a mile away, his men were busy putting up barbed wire fences, enclosing a large space in which stood six rows of dormitory huts made of the same opaque plastic as the city.

He turned back, looking down at the page, then tore the paper from the pad and, crumpling it, threw it down.

He was a good poet. A better poet, indeed, than he was a general. He was even famous, among his own people, the Han. But they did not know him as Jiang Lei, they knew him under his pen name, *Nai Liu*, 'Enduring Willow'. Indeed, for many he was the voice of his time, his verses reprinted in a thousand places. But life was far from easy for Jiang Lei, for he was also a general in the Eighteenth Banner of the great army of the illustrious and wise Tsao Ch'un, sole ruler of half the earth, and as such he was closely watched.

It was that watcher, a short and stocky man with a quite strikingly ugly face, who approached him now, walking towards Jiang Lei from the direction of the river. This was Wang Yu-Lai, the cadre appointed by the Ministry, 'The Thousand Eyes' as it was known. His task was to watch Jiang Lei, to ensure that things were done properly, and to report back to his Masters whether they were or not.

My dark shadow, Jiang Lei thought, seeing him approach.

Wang stopped two paces from Jiang Lei, his shadow falling over the older man's notebook. 'Might I have a word, my lord?'

Wang's head was bowed, his manner deferent, yet there was something in his voice that lacked respect. Wang thought that he had the power. That he had only to maintain the *semblance* of respect.

Not that that worried Jiang Lei too much. It was not that that rankled with him. Or not much, anyway. It was Wang's humourlessness, the absence of any charity in his nature. Wang was not a good Confucian. He did not understand that one had to lead by example; that benevolence was a virtue, not a weakness. No, the man was little more than a common bully. Jiang had seen with his own eyes how he treated the men.

It was disgusting. But Jiang Lei had no choice. Wang Yu-Lai had been appointed to him by the First Dragon himself, the Head of The Thousand Eyes. To watch him with his petty little black eyes, like a jackdaw watching a worm.

Jiang almost smiled. He would write that down later on. Make a couplet of it, maybe.

'Go ahead,' Jiang said, revealing nothing of his real self.

'It is just... I have had a word, my lord... with those at home and...'

'Go on,' Jiang said, noting Wang's hesitation. It was usually the prelude to some nastiness or other.

'Well, my lord, the feeling is that you have been too... *lenient*, shall we say. That you have allowed, perhaps, too many into the camps that should have been passed over.'

Killed, you mean.

But Jiang didn't say that.

'And is that how *you* feel, Wang Yu-Lai? Am I being too lenient?'

Wang bowed even lower. He seemed to be cringing, but Jiang knew that Wang's true self was smiling, even if his face showed something else.

'Oh, no, my lord... but my Masters...'

Wang's head lifted a little, his eyes taking a sneaky little look at Jiang Lei to see how he was reacting to the news, then went down again.

'Well... it would not harm to placate them, neh, my lord? To give them what they want.'

Only Jiang knew what they wanted. Annihilation. Genocide. Call it what you will. But this was better. This semblance of fairness.

'You may tell your Masters that I hear what they say... and will act.'

Wang bobbed as much as bowed. 'My lord...'

Jiang waited until the odious little bastard was gone, then, setting his book aside, stood up and walked over to the river's edge, looking out across the waterlogged fields.

He was a good Confucian and his service record was exemplary, but lately he had come to question his role in things, and some of that questioning had come out in his poetry. All of which disturbed him, for a good poem ought to possess '*Wen Ch'a Te*' – elegance – and of late his work had had a certain spikiness and lack of shape which he abhorred. Only what could he do? It was the path his creative instincts chose and they had always, until now, been right.

And yet it *felt* wrong. Not only that, but he knew that such poems could not be published, not in the current climate, anyway, and should the odious Wang get hold of them... well... there would be trouble.

Jiang closed his eyes, letting go of the turbulence within, letting his mind clear, his inner spirit grow calm, and in a moment all was well once more. When he opened his eyes what he saw was the simple beauty of the land. Its ancient mystery.

Ying Kuo... Inn-glaan.

Jiang formed the words in his mind the way his men would say them, in that crude peasant way of theirs. *Inn-glaan*. He, of course, could speak the language fluently, but sometimes it paid to feign ignorance when you were dealing with them.

Sometimes...

Jiang sighed, hearing the man's creeping footsteps approach from behind him once again. He waited and, after a while, Wang cleared his throat.

'My lord,' he said, speaking to Jiang's back. 'Forgive me for disturbing you but... another batch of processees has arrived. I thought...'

'I'll deal with it later,' Jiang said, making no move to turn and face the man; his voice brooking no argument. 'Just settle them in, neh?'

'Yes, my lord.'

Jiang Lei waited, listening to the rustle of the man's cheap silks as he retreated, then turned.

Wang was hurrying across the field towards the tents, lifting his skirts so as not to get mud on them. He was already some way off, but even from that distance Jiang Lei could see a kind of pent-up vindictiveness in the man. Wang was a busybody. He had an instinct for making others' lives miserable, and right now he was going to spread some of that misery among the men.

Jiang watched a moment longer, then turned away. The truth was he despised Wang Yu-Lai. Loathed Wang with a fierceness that was most unlike his normal self, not merely for his pettiness but for his cruelty.

Jiang shook his head slowly. He had given up on the poem.

There would be no composing today. Wang had seen to that. He was in much too sour a mood now to continue.

As for this matter of his leniency...

Jiang walked across, then stood in the doorway of his tent. He had told Wang he would do this later, but there was no real point in delaying. No. He would begin at once. Get it done and out of the way. Then maybe he could rest.

He went inside, into the right-hand chamber where his portable desk was. His papers were still there where he'd left them earlier, and his slate.

Jiang picked the slate up and took it through into his inner sanctum. There, sprawled out on his bed, he began, watching their faces come on-screen, quickly reading through their files, sorting through them one by one, deciding which would stay and which go.

Like Solomon, he thought, recalling the old story.

Only the wisdom of Solomon evaded him. At best he was a good servant to Tsao Ch'un. At worst... Well, some might have called him a murderer.

I have no choice, he told himself, not for the first time. *If it were not I, then another would do this, and cause much greater suffering than I. At least I am fair.*

Only it didn't convince him. It never did. And as he came to the end of it, he felt what he always felt – a kind of self-disgust. A self-loathing almost equal to that he had of Cadre Wang.

Only deeper and more profound.

'Curse my mood,' he mumbled, setting the slate aside. 'And curse the lack of poetry in me.'

But it wasn't the lack of poetry that really worried him. It was the lack of pity.

On that clear, beautiful autumn day, in the grassy space at the back of St. Peter's Church, they gathered to say goodbye. There were more than a hundred in all, friends of Tom, come in from the surrounding villages to pay their last respects.

Beside the grave itself stood Mary and her girls, the four of them dressed in black, distraught, clinging on to each other as that darling man, their father, was lowered into the earth.

For Jake, looking on, it was unbearable. His loss was vast, yet it was the sight of Tom's girls, weeping uncontrollably, that got to him. He felt bereft, his heart broken, yet his sorrow was but a shadow of theirs. Mary, particularly, seemed close to collapse. As Geoff Horsfield read the eulogy, she shook, like at any moment she would fall into that awful, gaping hole with the man she'd loved.

Afterwards, when all the guests had left, Jake went out into the kitchen.

Mary was standing with her back to him, at the window, looking out into the darkness of the garden.

'Are you all right?'

It was a stupid thing to say, but he had to say something, for they had barely spoken all day.

Mary's head dropped. For a moment she was silent. Then she turned, looking at him. Her voice was small, like it came from far away.

'Will you stay tonight?'

It was the last thing he'd expected her to say.

'Mary?'

She shuddered. 'Don't say no, Jake. I need you to.'

'But I can't. I...'

She came across and, putting her arms about him, kissed him. Her eyes, red-rimmed from crying, searched his own.

'Don't you see, Jake? You have to. Tom... Tom would understand. In fact, he said I must. For the sake of the girls. The end is coming, Jake. We all know that. And if that's true, then I want to face it beside you... you and Peter, that is.'

Jake stared back at her, stunned. 'But the girls...?'

'I've spoken to the girls. You can't be Tom... can't be their father. We all know that. But you're a good man and you've been alone too long.'

'But it's too soon...'

Mary looked down at that. 'Maybe. And maybe some would think it ill judged, but if we don't do it now... tonight... we never shall. Isn't that right? We'll let old ghosts come between us, and then...'

She looked down, her face breaking into a grimace of pain. 'Please, Jake... *Please*. For Tom's sake.'

But he knew, even as he told her yes, that this wasn't for Tom. This was for himself. He wanted her. But it was wrong.

That night, when all was quiet in the house, she came to him. She was wearing a plain white cotton nightdress. That pained him, for it was how Annie had dressed for bed, when she was yet alive.

'Mary,' he said gently. 'You don't have to. We can take our time.'

She stared at him, as if steeling herself, then peeled the white gown up over her shoulders and let it fall.

In the candle's light she was beautiful. She had the full figure of a mature woman. Her breasts and thighs were everything he'd imagined. And her eyes...

She slipped in beside him, putting her arms about him, shivering now.

'Don't speak,' she said, leaning over to blow out the candle. 'Just hold me, Jake. Just hold me.'

Jiang Lei woke in the night, thinking of his wife.

Chun Hua was far away, in Pei Ch'ing, together with his daughters. It was two years since he had seen them last, and sometimes, as now, their faces haunted him.

There had been a time when they had been inseparable. Chun Hua had been his secretary, his aide, truly his other self. In both day and night she had been there, at his side. Sweet Hua, the *yin yueh* – the music – of his life.

Now, however, it was different. Now it felt like he was a single goose making its lonely path across the sky.

As he stepped out from his tent, Steward Ho hurried across and, going down onto his knees, bowed low, touching his forehead to the ground.

'Master...'

Ho had been given a rare day off. But Ho was never happy when he was away, and he had hurried back, to serve Jiang Lei and make sure he had everything he needed.

Jiang Lei looked past the man towards the encampment. Fires were still burning. In their light he could see that the men were still up, sitting about the fires, talking and laughing softly.

He looked up. It was a clear night. The moon was high and almost full.

Jiang Lei shivered. It was much colder than it had been a week back.

'Master... shall I get your cloak?'

'If you would, Steward Ho...'

Ho nodded, then ran into the tent, emerging a moment later with Jiang's silken gown. Jiang slipped into it.

'Thank you, Ho. I think I shall go and see the men. See how they are.'

'Master...'

There was something in Steward Ho's manner that made Jiang Lei pause.

'What is it, Ho?'

Ho kept his head low, his manner utterly deferent. 'It is Cadre Wang, Master. I would have told you, but you were sleeping. He is gone...'

'Gone?' It surprised Jiang. 'When did he go?'

'An hour past, Master. He told me to notify you. He has gone to see his Masters.'

Ho would not even say the words. The Ministry. *The Thousand Eyes.*

'Was he summoned?'

'I do not know, Master. But he said he would return, as soon as he could.'

'I see... Thank you, Ho.'

Jiang walked across. As he came into the circle of the firelight, the men, seeing him, stood abruptly, bowing low, a dozen shaven heads reflecting the fire's golden light.

Jiang, seeing it, thought how fine an image it would be, if he could but find a poem in which to use it.

'Ch'un Tzu,' he said, making them all smile. 'Let us be informal... please... be seated.'

Ch'un Tzu... Gentlemen. They enjoyed his playful poke at their backgrounds. For not one of them was a gentleman, and never would be. And they were strangely proud of that. But they were good at what they did. Some of the finest soldiers he had ever served with.

Jiang turned, meaning to tell Ho to bring his chair, but Ho had anticipated him. He stood there, just a yard or two away, clutching the heavy chair.

Jiang smiled, then gestured to a space beside the fire, where he could see them all.

'Well... this is cosy, neh?'

Slowly the men sat once more, crouched down on their haunches, their eyes looking towards Jiang Lei, waiting for him to speak.

Jiang looked towards one of them. 'Chang Te... how are your parents? Is your father better now?'

Chang, a tall, quiet man, bowed his head.

'They are well, Master Jiang. Old Chang is much improved... and my sister has given birth to another boy.'

Jiang smiled. 'That is good news, Chang Te. How many is that now?'

330

'It is her fourth, Master Jiang.'

'Then both you and she are serving our country well, neh?'

There were grins at that, even some laughter. But none of them was at ease with him there, and Jiang Lei wondered why. Was it to do with Wang?

He looked towards another of them.

'Ma Feng... how are things with you? Your leg...?'

Ma Feng, a short, stocky little man in his thirties, nodded. 'I am well, Master Jiang. If it troubles me, then it is my own fault. I should have been more careful.'

Jiang was immediately concerned. 'Do you need treatment, Ma Feng?'

But the very idea had Ma Feng bowing low. He seemed embarrassed by Jiang Lei's concern. 'You are too kind, Master Jiang. It needs but a little exercise.'

Jiang Lei looked about him; saw how each one averted his eyes, afraid of being picked, of being the subject of his attention.

But why? It hadn't always been so. These men, after all, had been with him in Africa.

'Li Ying,' he said, picking the youngest of them, almost amused by the sudden panic in his eyes.

'Yes, Master Jiang?'

'Our friend, the watcher... our friend who isn't here... what do you think of him?'

Li Ying looked down, horrified. 'Master Jiang, I...'

Jiang had his answer. He waved his hand. 'No matter...'

He turned. 'Steward Ho... bring us two flagons of my best rice wine. It is some while since I had a drink with my men.'

Jiang looked back, his eyes going from face to face, seeing the relief there, the gratitude that he had not pursued his questioning.

'Liu... do you still play the pi-p'a?'

Liu lowered his head. 'You wish me to play for you now, Master Jiang?'

331

'It would be my delight. I have often said how fine your playing is.'

Liu almost blushed. 'You are too kind, Master Jiang. I am but a novice.'

It was a lie. Or, rather, a statement of extreme humility, for Liu Ke was an exceptionally fine musician, and his plucking of the four-stringed Chinese lute – the pi-p'a – matched anything Jiang Lei had ever heard. Indeed, it was one of the reasons he had hand-picked Liu Ke to be in his personal squad of bodyguards.

As Steward Ho poured the wine, and Liu Ke tuned his instrument, Jiang Lei looked about him.

Since he had made – and dropped – his query about Wang Yu-Lai, the men had relaxed. Without him having to have said a word, they understood. And now that that was so, something of their old relationship had returned.

Two months Wang had been with them. A mere two months, and yet his poisonous influence was strong. He had made these good men suspicious of their own commander, and how could that be a good thing? Only what could he, Jiang Lei, do about it? He was nominally in charge here, Wang Yu Lai's superior in every sense. But that barely mattered, not when the Ministry was concerned, for The Thousand Eyes was a law unto itself, and when one fell beneath its gaze...

He supped his wine. Liu Ke looked to him and, at his nod, began to play.

As the first notes rippled in the air, Jiang sighed, his pleasure unfeigned. It was the 'P'ing Sha Lo Yen' – 'Wild Geese Descend on the Smooth Sand'. He sat forward, watching Liu's fingers, astonished by his virtuosity. It was not an easy piece to play, and Liu was note perfect.

Jiang looked about the circle of faces, seeing how every one of them was trapped inside the music for that moment, their eyes attentive, each of them leaning towards the lute as if to breath it all in.

Jiang closed his eyes, feeling the hairs on the back of his neck stand on end.

As it finished, he looked at Liu Ke and grinned, standing up to clap him, the rest of the men joining him after a moment, whooping, filling the night air with their applause.

'Liu Ke... such fingers...'

Liu Ke looked down at his hand where it rested on the strings and blushed. 'I am pleased you liked it, Master Jiang.'

Jiang looked about him at the men. 'One more, neh, my friends? How about "The Moon On High"?'

He looked to Liu, who bowed.

'As my Master wishes,' Liu said quietly, even as the others settled.

They were enjoying this. Jiang could see it in their eyes. And that gave him an idea. Before Liu Ke could begin, Jiang stood again, raising his hand.

'Men... what do you say to a story? Maybe something from the *San Kuo Yen I*?'

He saw how they looked among each other, then nodded. Ma Feng, the eldest, spoke for them all.

'We would like that, Master Jiang. You do us a very great kindness...'

Jiang smiled. 'Not at all, Ma Feng. I love the *Romance*, and it is some while since I read it.' He turned. 'Steward Ho...'

But Steward Ho had already gone. You could see the back of him in the darkness, half running, as he went to get the book.

There was laughter; laughter that Jiang joined in with.

They had not felt like this for months. Not since Wang Yu-Lai came.

Jiang Lei sat once more, gesturing to Liu to begin, and as the first few familiar trills of the *'Yueh Erh Kao'* spilled out into the air, so Jiang sat back in the old campaign chair, his eyes closed, imagining he was back at home once more and not halfway around the world.

After all, what could be more Chinese than this? To listen to 'The

Moon On High' and read from the *Romance of the Three Kingdoms*?

Only what he felt at that moment was a profound, almost over-powering sadness that came from nowhere, descending on him like rain from a clear sky.

Exile. This felt suddenly like exile.

Jiang turned his head, looking down, away from the fire, even as the notes ran on and the hauntingly familiar melody filled his head.

So they must have felt a thousand years ago, patrolling at the very edge of the world.

It was the fate of soldiers, yes, and of poets too.

'Master...?'

Steward Ho knelt close by, his head lowered, the book held out before him.

'Thank you...'

But as Jiang stared at the cover, with its picture of the three great heroes of the ancient historical tale, he realized that his cheeks were wet.

He brushed his cheek with his fingers, then stared at them, surprised. He had been crying.

Across from him Liu Ke had closed his eyes, lost in the music, his fingers moving with a rapidity, a sensitivity, that seemed to belie his solid peasant face.

As he played the final note, Liu Ke gave a little shuddering sigh, then looked up, as if he had been travelling somewhere and was now returned.

The applause was deafening. Jiang was on his feet again, clapping Liu Ke.

'That was wonderful,' he said softly, wondering to himself if any from the camp nearby had heard it, and what they would have made of such a strange and alien sound.

For so it was. They were the aliens here, after all. Their stories, their poems, their music – these were all out of place, here in these ancient, rolling hills.

Chung Kuo... China... It seemed a million miles away right then. A million miles away and right up close.

As they settled again, he took the book and opened it at random. That was the thing about the *Romance*. One tale was as good as another in its pages. Not only that, but all of the stories were known to each and every one of them sitting about the fire.

'Tsao Tsao conquers Hang Chung,' he began, reading the chapter description. 'Chang Liao spreads terror at Chao Yao Ford...'

The words brought a great murmur of happiness from the men. Tsao Tsao was a particular favourite of theirs, and the chapter promised a battle...

Jiang Lei cleared his throat and began:

'The expedition against Hang Chung went out in three divisions...'

Jake woke with a start, alone, realizing where he was and what had happened.

He was in Tom's bed. And last night...

He rolled over and closed his eyes. If only he hadn't drunk so much at Tom's wake. If only he'd had the strength to say no to her.

Only he hadn't. Neither had he wanted to.

Hold me, she'd said, but how could he simply hold her? How could he not have made love to her, she had been so warm against him.

Six years he'd been without. How was *he* to blame? Yet he felt guilty now. What he had done was wrong. Tom was barely cold in the ground.

He could hear Mary, downstairs in the kitchen, pottering about, clearing up the last few things from yesterday's 'celebrations'.

Thinking of her, remembering her, naked beneath him in the moonlight, her nipples hard, her need clear in her face, made his cock grow erect again. If she had been there now, next to him beneath the sheets, he would have taken her again.

And yet... afterwards, after he had come inside her, she had lain in his arms, sobbing uncontrollably. For Tom.

He lay there a moment. Then, knowing he couldn't stay there all day, got up and dressed and went down to her.

Mary was at the sink. She turned and gave a tired smile.

Jake went over to her. Held her from behind, pressed in to her, his arms about her waist, his cheek against her neck, savouring the touch of her, the smell.

'Are you okay?'

He asked it gently, knowing how raw, how tender her emotions were. Knowing it could still go wrong between them.

Mary turned, snuggling in to him, letting her head rest against his chest.

'I'm fine... and thank you...'

She was trembling. The night, intimate as it had been, had brought them only a little closer. They were still strangers.

'Where's the girls?'

'Gone out.'

'And Peter?'

'He's with Meg. I thought...'

She looked up at him, reached up to smooth his face with her hand, then kissed him; a gentle, almost asexual kiss.

Jake smiled sadly. 'It'll get better.'

'Yeah?' But if there was any anger in that, it wasn't aimed at him. He knew that. It was aimed at circumstances. Tom was supposed to have been there, looking after her. Only he wasn't, so she had to make do.

Jake stroked her hair. Just being so close to her made him stiff. But if she noticed, she said nothing.

For a while they stood there, like that, then she pushed him away a little.

'We'd better finish off here, then get your stuff moved in.'

'Ah...' He was surprised by that. His stuff. He hadn't thought. If anything he'd thought they'd run two households. But they were a family now. As of last night.

'What about the neighbours?'

'They'll understand...'

'You think?'

'Jake.' Her voice was hard, uncompromising. 'They'll understand, okay?'

'Okay.'

She looked at him; a frank look, appraising him. And then she nodded. 'You'll do. And, Jake... you mustn't feel guilty... Tom loved you. He loved us both. He'd understand. And he was right...'

'Right?'

'Yes... you did need a woman in your bed.'

Jiang Lei climbed up on to the dais, then sat behind the table, facing the crowd.

His men were lined up either side of the detainees, masked up, their guns – big semi-automatics – resting against their chests.

If there was going to be trouble, this was when it happened.

Jiang Lei reached across, taking his slate from where it lay on top of the stack of official documents. Wang Yu-Lai stood just below, away from the dais, beside the nearest of the guards. He had that look on his face – the look he always had when they did this. Not so much a smirk as a sneer, like he was somehow superior to these poor creatures.

This – the 'processing' as it was called – was the part Wang liked the most and Jiang the least.

Jiang Lei sighed, then gestured for it to begin. The prisoners had all been given numbers, from one to one hundred and thirteen. It wasn't a big batch – Jiang had processed more than six hundred in a morning before now – but if he was to do it properly it would take him a while.

'Number one!' Wang yelled, moving towards the front of the

queue, his manner threatening now, his face suddenly ugly with rage. 'Present yourself!'

Unnecessary, Jiang thought, looking down at the image on the screen of his slate. *So totally unnecessary*.

He read the brief summary.

Miss Jennifer Oatley. Twenty-three. Unmarried. No children. No political affiliations and no criminal record.

So far, so good. He looked up, studying the young woman, seeing at a glance just how frightened she was. She hadn't a clue what was going on.

What if it had been the other way round? What if the West had taken over China and this was one of his daughters? Little Mei, perhaps. How would *he* have felt?

But he knew he was only tormenting himself. It had to be done, and if *he* hadn't done it then some other bastard – someone with far less tact or sensitivity – would have been doing it.

Or maybe not bothering at all. Maybe just rounding them up and 'dealing' with them, like they had in the Middle East.

Jiang sighed. It was going to be a long day.

'Miss Oatley? Miss Jennifer Oatley?'

He could see how surprised she was that he spoke such perfect English. Most of them were. But then most of them hadn't been to Cambridge, like he had. Most of them hadn't had the education.

Which was another reason why he was here. Because of a friendship he had made, years ago, in another part of this tiny island. In Cambridge.

He began the questioning. Have you a boyfriend? Have you ever taken drugs? Have you any debilitating diseases? What do you think of this and that and...?

Etcetera, etcetera...

Most of it, of course, was already on file. That is, if they were over twenty-two. This one was borderline. She'd been only one year

338

old when it all fell apart, and had known no other world. But some of them...

They didn't know just how much Tsao Ch'un knew about them. How, when it had all collapsed, he had hung on to their records, making copies of whatever he could get his hands on, storing it all, waiting for the day when it would be used to screen new citizens for his continent-spanning cities.

All of which ought to have made the job easier. But people weren't just good or bad, healthy or unhealthy, political or non-political. People were complex, and Jiang welcomed this part of it – the making sure – as much as he loathed its consequences.

It even made good sense to him not to let some in – to bar them and make life better for the rest. Murderers and rapists and the like – what right did they have to a new life?

Only it was rarely that straightforward, much as Wang Yu-Lai would have liked it to be.

They had taken this batch in a single raid, four days back. More than forty they had 'processed' there and then – away from the others, naturally. It didn't pay to panic them, after all.

There were certain categories that Tsao Ch'un didn't want. Criminals, the overtly religious, political agitators, so-called 'ethnics', Japanese, and the old.

All the rest were potential citizens. But not all of them were suitable.

Tsao Ch'un had set one simple and far-reaching criterion – would they make a good citizen? In that regard, any anti-social tendency was discouraged. They most certainly didn't want *difficult* people.

That was why they put them in the camps. To watch them. And to question their friends and neighbours, because who, after all, would know them better?

Jiang finished his questions and, nodding to the girl, indicated that she should go through to the cabin on the right, where two clerics sat at a table. He pressed his electronic seal against the face of the slate, then keyed the next entry.

She had got through. Providing the medical showed nothing serious, she would be a citizen within the year. After she had been 'inducted'.

'Number Two!' Wang bellowed. 'Move up! Quickly now! We haven't got all day!'

Jiang Lei looked to Wang Yu-Lai and groaned inwardly. Maybe not all day, but it was going to be a long session. He could sense it.

He touched the slate, changing the image.

'Mister Andrew James Stewart. Forty-seven,' it read. 'Widower. No children. No political affiliations. One conviction for Drunk & Disorderly.'

That's what it read, and the image matched the man standing in front of him, his identity confirmed by fingerprints, DNA and retinal scan. Only he claimed to be someone else. He said he was Arthur Hillman. Fifty-two and single.

So why was he lying?

Jiang had a good idea even before he asked. Knew because he'd seen this time and again. The man had taken on someone else's identity. Someone who had died in the troubles that had followed the Fall. There were countless reasons why, but most just wanted a fresh start, away from authority, and a new identity gave them that.

'Mister Stewart...' he began.

'That isn't me!' the man protested, taking a step beyond the black paint line that was drawn just in front of his feet. 'I'm Arthur Hillman. I...'

Wang rushed across and, slapping the man, pushed him back, shouting at him.

'Be quiet! Answer only when you are asked a question! Understand?'

Jiang waited, watched the man glare at Wang, then look back at him.

'Mister Stewart,' he began again, 'I would advise you to give up your pretence. My Master is all-seeing. He knows when you were born and when married. And he knows of your sorrows. He knows, for instance, how your wife died in giving birth, and how the child subsequently died. So please do not even think of continuing this deception. It would only be to your detriment. Now... speak clearly to me... you are Andrew James Stewart, is that right?'

As Stewart confessed, Jiang looked past him, seeing how the others were surprised and yet impressed by his detailed knowledge of their 'friend'. Such knowledge proved a powerful tool, and after over twenty years of being 'off the radar', most were frightened by it. They had got used to being free and unwatched. But now the eyes were back.

Literally so, Jiang thought, looking at Wang Yu-Lai and seeing how the odious little shit was rubbing his hands together, enjoying this. Enjoying their misery, their suffering and doubt.

Leniency? Jiang sniffed and, out of a sudden pique, changed his mind from the previous evening and passed Stewart as a potential citizen, ignoring Wang's angry pout, clearing the image and summoning up the next.

It was going to be a long day.

Jake turned and took Mary's hand, helping her up.

It was strange, standing there beside Tom's grave. He hadn't thought he would be here again so soon, but Mary had wanted to come, to make sure everything was neat and tidy, and to spend a moment alone with Tom.

Jake understood that perfectly. So it would be from here on. However well it went, they would always have these ghosts in their lives, these memories. Whatever lay ahead, it would always be second best, and they would need to live with that. To accommodate that fact.

Looking at her, at the grief in her face, Jake knew he would come to love her. It wasn't that hard. He already loved her as a friend. But they would have to find a way to live with the distance, that strange feeling of abandonment each of them would sometimes feel. Yes, and to deal with the fact that fate, not love, had brought them together.

A marriage of convenience. So it was. So it had to be. But he would try his best to make it work. Looking at her, at how fragile she was, he swore to himself that he would never let her down. Her or her girls. From now on they were his. Tom had handed them on to him, and he felt a sacred duty to look after them.

'Are you done?' he asked gently.

She nodded, her eyes questioning his momentarily, searching his to see if things were still all right between them.

Jake looked past her at the grave. The rich dark earth was piled high on top of the coffin. Above it, Mary had placed six sprays of winter jasmine, the tiny white flowers like exploding stars, their sweet, delicate scent filling the air.

Just then the crows in a nearby tree began to caw. They both turned, looking at the scattering of dark shapes among the leafless branches.

Jake took her hand, squeezing it softly. She looked at him and gave a small, sad smile.

'Come,' she said. 'I'll do dinner...'

They were at the gate, Jake standing back to let her go first, when they heard the sound in the air.

Mary looked to him. 'What's that?'

They turned, looking towards Corfe, towards the sound. Slowly it grew, the vague vibration becoming a droning pulse – the unmistakable sound of engines. And then they saw it, its huge, dark shape emerging from above the trees, not two hundred yards away.

The craft came on, growing larger moment by moment, moving slowly, a vast, almost spherical thing painted a perfect midnight black. It had no shine to it at all. If anything it seemed to absorb the light, such that its shape seemed more an absence than a presence.

Behind them the crows scattered, cawing loudly, raucously.

Mary let out a long, low moan. Somewhere, off to their backs, dogs were barking now.

The sound grew, shaking the earth, its roar now filling the air, making them hold their hands up to their ears, it was so loud.

On it came, moment by moment, until they fell beneath its shadow.

Mary sank to her knees.

Jake went to her quickly, kneeling beside her, wrapping his arms about her tightly, expecting, at any moment, some bolt of force, or a rocket to come hurtling down out of that darkness and destroy them.

He stared up at it, waiting for the killing blow, straining to make something – anything – out, even as Mary buried her head in his chest, terrified.

There... I was right.

Beneath the craft, on what looked like two long fins, was a circular design.

A dragon, its eyes fierce. Its talons sharp, its body coiled like a wheel, its mouth swallowing its tail.

It moved on, past them, following the curve of the road, slower than walking pace, as if some alien sentience controlled it.

As they came out of its shadow, Mary looked to him. She seemed in shock.

'What in god's name...?' she asked, her voice like a child's, trembling with fear.

Jake held her tighter. He wanted to let her know he was there for her, that she was safe in his arms, but he couldn't look at her, couldn't tear his eyes away from the massive alien ship.

It was directly over both their houses now, its huge bulk throwing them into deep shadow.

People were out in the street now, staring up at it. Some of them were standing, but most were on their knees, awed and appalled by the sight. Peter was there and the girls. They were in a little group in the front garden, staring up at it fearfully and hugging each other. Nearby, Boy was jumping up and barking, but you could hear nothing of it above those mighty engines.

On it went, slowly, so slowly now it seemed almost about to stop, following the line of the road, less than a hundred yards above the old slate rooftops.

Jake's mouth was dry, his whole body tensed against some sudden violence.

This was the future, this hideous juxtaposition of old and new. This was what it was like to have the aliens land. This awful feeling of helplessness. The intrusion of a brutal, overpowering force.

Like rape.

The sound changed, dropped down an octave. The very sound of it made him want to be sick. He felt his stomach fall away.

'Oh, Christ...'

For a second or two nothing, just this sudden stillness, and then the sound changed, like the old sound of jet engines powering up, and it began to accelerate, going from walking pace to fast velocity in seconds.

Jake watched it flash out of sight, his mouth agape.

Next to him, Mary was trembling.

Jake tried to stand, only his legs had gone. He waited a moment, then tried again, hauling himself up on to his feet this time.

He reached down, helping Mary up.

'Come on,' he said. 'Let's see to the kids. They looked terrified.'

Mary looked at him, his words getting through the numbness, making her forget her own fear. She nodded.

He tried to smile, only he couldn't. He felt right then that nothing could ever make him smile again. 'Let's calm them down... get them settled back indoors...'

344

He stopped. She was staring at him.

'That's what you saw, isn't it? At market...'

He nodded. 'It's China. They've finally come. They...'

He stopped, seeing how close to tears she was. Even so, she had to know. She had a right to know.

'Let's get the kids settled, eh? Then there's something I've got to show you.'

They climbed up onto the topmost wall. There, with the King's Tower at their back, he handed her the Bresser glasses.

For a long time she was silent, then she lowered the binoculars.

'Well?' he asked. 'Do you understand now?'

Mary sighed. 'You want to look?'

He took the glasses from her and raised them to his eyes, expecting to see what he had seen only a day or two before. But it had changed. In fact, it shocked him to see how far it had encroached in just a matter of days.

There were now five of the huge white shapes, like massive skyscrapers spread out across the landscape, four, maybe five miles distant at most. Now that it was closer, he could make out details, could see the tiny, ant-like figures of men and, dwarfing them, massive spider-like machines, clearly vast in themselves, like mobile cranes. It was these that appeared to be constructing it, weaving fine threads from vast tanks situated beneath their high platforms, and wrapping them, like a skein of silk, cat's-cradle fashion about the mile-high supports.

Everything on a giant scale. Everything – and he could see this clearly now – built over the top of what was already there. They weren't even bothering to knock things down, just confining the old world to the cellar.

Again, it awed him at the same time that it terrified.

'They're like glaciers,' Mary said, her voice quiet, clearly stunned by what she'd seen. 'Huge slabs of ice...'

'The whole country,' he said, taking in suddenly just what it was they were doing.

These outcrops were just the start of it. Outposts of a kind. Eventually they would fill the gaps between them, merging the whiteness until the whole country lay beneath.

A city! They were building a city the size of the United Kingdom!

He felt dismay at the thought.

Like a glacier, yes... everything under ice.

He jumped down, then turned back to help Mary down.

'Do they know?' she asked. 'I mean... the kids...'

He nodded.

'Ah...'

They walked down the hill in silence, both of them lost in their thoughts. It was only when they got to the gate that she turned to him again.

'I didn't think it would be so brief. I thought... well, I thought we'd have years together. I thought...'

She stopped. Tears were rolling down her cheeks.

'It's the end, isn't it, Jake? That craft... those things on the horizon...'

He wanted to say no. To tell her it'd all be fine. Only his gut said otherwise.

China had tried to kill him once before, years ago, before he had found this haven, this little heaven on earth. But now they were back, bigger and nastier than ever, and no one – no matter how hard they tried – was going to get away from them this time.

'Come,' he said, taking her hand. 'Let's make the most of what's left, eh?'

Mary looked down at where his hand held hers, then up at him again. There was the faintest of smiles now on her lips.

'Okay... but let's say nothing to the kids, eh? I don't want to spoil things for them. I don't...'

She stopped, as if she had come to the edge, her face puckering.

'Come here, my darling girl,' he said, pulling her to him, holding her tight, his eyes closed now, letting her sob against his shoulder.

So this is how it feels. This is how it is at the end.

Jake shivered, then looked across towards the encroaching whiteness, still just about visible above the fallen stonework.

'Mary?'

She sniffed in deeply. 'Yes, Jake?'

'Will you marry me?'

Chapter 10

EAST

Jiang Lei was woken by his Steward, Ho.

'It is six-thirty, Master. The men are already up...'

Jiang turned, then pulled the blanket up to his chin, looking across the tent.

Ho had cleared a space on Jiang's table and laid out his breakfast for him, a bowl of *ch'a* and a plate of various delicacies – things he knew his Master liked.

'Thank you, Ho.'

Jiang considered asking Ho to bring a heater. The tent might have been luxurious in summer, but in late autumn it was just cold. The thin silk did little to keep in any warmth. But to ask for a heater might be misconstrued as a weakness, especially in some quarters, so he did not ask.

'How *are* the men?'

Steward Ho bowed and smiled. 'They are in a very good mood, Master. Looking forward to the day ahead. Your visit to them the other evening...'

Ho fell silent, lowered his head a fraction. He realized he had let his enthusiasm run away with him.

Jiang Lei smiled and threw off the covers, risking the cold. 'It was a good evening, neh? We should do it again. It's good to raise the men's morale.'

Ho had hurried across, the moment he had emerged from the blankets, and now stood there, next to him, offering Jiang Lei his clothes for the day, his small, shaven head, as ever, bowed low.

'Steward Ho?'

'Yes, Master?'

'Do you like this land? Do you like *Ying Kuo*?' Again, he sensed he had asked too much in asking Ho for an opinion. But this once he genuinely wanted to know. Was it just he who found this country beautiful? Or was it all just 'orders' to the men?

Ho struggled to find the words, then shrugged. 'To be honest, Master, I had not thought about it. Should I?'

Jiang reached out for his leggings, shivering with the cold. 'No... I was just curious. Just that we have seen so many lands, neh?'

Steward Ho smiled and bobbed a bow. He was clearly much happier to be in a position to agree. 'We have, Master. Many lands.'

And many people, Jiang thought, recalling all those he had 'saved', all those he had cast into the pit.

And more today...

Jiang pulled on his padded jacket, feeling much warmer as he did, then went across and, letting Ho pull his chair out for him, sat at his desk.

The *ch'a* smelled heavenly. As it ought, for he paid a small fortune to have his special supplies sent from home.

He sipped at it then gave a nod.

It was the signal Ho was waiting for. 'Is there anything else, Master?'

'Only my boots.'

'Of course, Master.'

It was their ritual. Every morning they would say the same words, and every morning Ho would bring his boots and kneel before him to help him on with them.

Jiang Lei smiled. If he had been Wang Wei, he would have written a poem about it. Something on the lines of 'Steward Ho brings his boots'. Only between he and Wang Wei lay thirteen centuries. And besides, Wang Wei was a poet. A real poet. He would not have feared to set down what was in his head, however jagged and misshapen. He would have found a way to make it work – to give it *elegance*.

And now, with that thought, his mood had changed.

Jiang reached across and picked up the book he had been reading yesterday evening. It was something one of his men had found and thought he might be interested in. And so he was. Only knowing about these places didn't help. If anything, it only made things harder.

Jiang sipped his ch'a, picked at the delicacies, but his appetite was gone. He had that sour, irritable feeling he sometimes had on collection days. That awful sense that it was he and not Tsao Ch'un who ordered things thus. For why should they discriminate? Why, if all they saw of China was him, should they think it bore another's face?

He the murderer. He the arbiter, the life-giver.

Some days it was just too hard. Some days he felt like leaving it to Wang Yu-Lai; felt like crawling back between the covers and pulling the blankets up over his head, shutting it all out.

Only that was infantile. Unbefitting a man. He had been given this task and, awful as it seemed, he would carry it out to the letter.

After all, as the saying went, he was his Master's hands.

He turned. 'Ho... take it. I'm done here.'

'But, Master...'

Ho saw his look. He bowed low, then took the tray away.

Alone, Jiang stood. The book on Corfe had woken him to the age of this land. This culture, like his own, was rooted deeply in the landscape. Perhaps that was why the great *Kuoming* emperor, Mao Tse Tung, had striven so hard to emulate these people, exalting the Han to be like the *Ying Kuo*.

Only they were very different. He knew that now. And it wasn't just that they stank like babies from their habit of consuming milk products. No. It was something in their heads. Some belief they shared that life should somehow be fair. As if life was ever fair.

'The shadow of Magna Carta...'

'Sorry, Master?'

Jiang turned. Steward Ho stood there just inside the tent flap, his head bowed low.

'It's nothing, Ho. Nothing at all. Are the men ready?'

'Almost so, Master.'

'And Cadre Wang?'

'He awaits you, Master.'

Jiang looked past his servant, saw the figure pacing up and down outside, and sighed.

'Another day, neh, Ho? Another day.'

The pony was restless. As Jake tugged at the leather strap, trying to fasten it about the load on the cart, so the animal took a step forward then a step back.

'Peter! Keep it still!'

Boy barked. Peter bent down to ruffle his coat, then walked over and got hold of the pony's bridle, smoothing the side of its long face with the other hand to calm the animal.

Jake glanced at his son. Peter had a way with animals. He could, quite literally, make them eat out of his hands. But, then, his mother had been farm bred, not city-born like himself.

'You've not forgotten anything?' Jake asked.

'Not that I can think of...'

'Good. Because we need to get going.'

They had packed everything they'd need for the winter. Clothes, medicines and guns, and whatever jewellery and items they could barter. Everything else they'd left, giving it to friends or trading it for things they needed.

In an hour they would be gone. Off on the road again, heading west. There was no future here. They had realized that yesterday, when the craft had come, and when they'd talked of it last night, leaving had seemed the only option. Only now that it came to it, Jake wondered if it were. Wondered whether the few weeks they would have together were enough to compensate for the discomfort and anxiety that lay ahead.

Besides, who was to say what the Chinese had decided? Would they build their great city over every last piece of land? Or would they stop at some point, leaving the rest in peace?

Whatever, the future was not bright.

Right then his old friend, Geoff Horsfield, the history teacher, made an appearance. They had spoken earlier and come to an agreement. Jake had taken Geoff's pony. In return Geoff had 'inherited' all of Jake's books.

Geoff touched his forehead. 'Jake? All done with?'

Jake tightened the strap one last tiny bit then nodded, satisfied. 'Is now.'

'Where's Mary and the girls?'

'Inside, packing the last few things.'

'Are you sure about this?' Geoff hesitated. 'I mean...'

Jake knew what he meant, and he was conscious of Peter listening, but he had to forget any doubts he had. They couldn't stay here. Not with that thing coming over the horizon.

'I'm sure. We'll head for Dorchester. Stay there a few nights, then head on. We've friends in Bridport we can call in on. After that... well, nothing's guaranteed, is it?'

Geoff smiled sadly. 'It's the march of history, Jake. Though I must say, it isn't usually so fucking visible, excuse my French.'

'I guess that's the Chinese way...'

Geoff nodded. 'The Three Gorges and all that, eh?' He hesitated, then, 'I'll miss you, Jake. We'll all miss you. And hey... I've got something for you.'

He handed Jake the old-fashioned paperback, then watched as Jake's face lit up.

'Where the fuck did you get this?'

It was a copy of Ubik, the novel. A 'tie-in' version, with Drew Ludd on the cover, playing Joe Chip.

'I remember you talking about it, years back now. I meant to give it to you then, only...'

'This version... with Drew Ludd on the cover... I didn't think it existed.'

'I bought it, down in Exeter, the day things began to unfurl. I was there to see my sister, god bless her soul, and I was in a book-shop there, and... Well, there it is. A little bit of cultural history, eh, Jake?'

The two embraced warmly. As they stepped back, Mary and the girls emerged, carrying their heavily laden packs.

Jake slipped the book away in his jacket pocket, then looked to Mary. 'Shall we?'

Mary set her pack down next to the cart. 'I thought we'd all go. Say goodbye properly to them.'

Jake nodded, then looked to the girls. They could barely look at him right now. Not that they blamed him in any way for circumstances, only it was hard to say goodbye to their father. Hard to abandon him this way.

He looked to Geoff. 'Would you mind the cart for a while?'

'Sure... you go...'

The girls set down their packs, then came over to their mother. All except Meg. She went to Peter, putting his arm about her waist.

She was wearing his ring.

Together they went to the churchyard. There, side by side, lay Tom and Annie. Tom's grave was fresh, raw almost, like the pain they felt. But Jake wasn't just saying goodbye to his best friend, he was saying farewell to his wife. To the woman who had loved him. To Peter's mother.

It almost made him change his mind and stay. After all, how could he leave this place? This was home. The only real home he'd ever had. The place where he'd found himself again after all that loss.

He stood there, staring at the graves, realizing, perhaps for the first time, that it wasn't just rotting flesh and bones that were buried here, it was them, their essential selves. All that they'd been. All that they'd meant to those who'd loved them. Here was where they were, in an English country churchyard. Here for all eternity.

Or so he'd always thought. So he'd hoped. Only now, in a few days, it would all be gone. Cast into shadow.

As they came away, as each of them wiped the tears from their faces, so Jake felt as if they had been cast out, into exile, like the Israelites. He took Mary's hands and met her eyes.

'We'll not forget them.'

'Let's go,' she said bleakly. 'Now, before I change my mind.'

As the craft lifted, Jiang Lei leaned forward, looking out.

It was impressive. Had he been a native he would have been in awe. Sixteen craft they had, including his own, and a force of 1500 men.

On most days, like today, it was pure overkill. He did not need such a force. And yet he used it always, for that was what Tsao Ch'un had ordered.

'Gunboat diplomacy', Tsao Ch'un had called it, smiling nastily, when he had given Jiang Lei his commission three years back. 'Our revenge for the Treaty of Nanking.'

And so it was. Only the irony was lost upon the natives of this land. What had happened back in 1842 on the far side of the globe was barely relevant to their lives now. Or so it seemed, but history, for the Han, was very much alive, and the desire for revenge – to impose their new-found status on old enemies – was strong.

Not only that, but this was the part his men liked. The chance to play gods over these people's lives. To save them or destroy them, depending on their whim.

Not that Jiang allowed them total liberty. No. He was quite strict about what they could or couldn't do. Yet if one of his men was to make a mistake; to be too zealous let's say, then he would forgive them as likely as not. Or punish them lightly, just to make a point.

After the morning's chill, the day had brightened. Jiang Lei closed his eyes, humming an old folk tune.

Behind him, in the back of the massive craft, were his eight bodyguards, Ma Feng leading them. While in the cockpit...

'Master Jiang...'

Jiang opened his eyes again, his spirits sinking. It was Wang Yu-Lai. He had been up in the cockpit, talking to the two pilots.

'What is it, Wang?'

Jiang saw how that rankled with the man. Wang liked his full title, especially since he had come back from his Masters with the title of Senior Cadre.

'The pilot was asking, Master Jiang... Did you wish to make the same approach as before, over the castle, or...?'

Wang had clearly seen what he'd been reading. Even so, it was unusually thoughtful of the man.

What does the bastard want? He's never nice unless he wants something.

'We'll fly in as before, but slower this time. Oh, and, Wang... before you say anything... each captain knows his task. I have fully briefed them all.'

'Yes, General.'

Wang bowed, then returned up front.

Jiang let a long breath escape him. One of these days he would tell the man what he really thought of him.

But not today. Today was much too fine a day to ruin.

He hummed a little louder. Down below there was sunlight

on the water of the Bay, while to his right – four or five miles north-east of their current flight path – lay one of the city's outposts, a huge geometric chunk of whiteness consisting of a full eight stacks, each one mile high and two li in diameter.

Personally he found it an abomination. To his eyes it was little more than a massive plastic box. A giant storage unit for humanity.

Or, worse still, a giant hive.

Jiang had flown over parts of it while it was being constructed and seen the eight-sided, hive-like units. Had felt, momentarily, like he'd been shrunk and ingested into the stomach of a bee.

He had even written a poem about it. Not that it was any good. No. The last good poem he had written was a year and more ago. That poem for his eldest daughter. It was after that that his muse had soured. Had grown as dark and jagged as his moods.

They swung south, then, aligned with the castle, headed directly towards it.

Jiang came through; took Wang's seat between the two pilots, while Wang stood behind him, silent for once.

'Do you know how old that is, Cadre Wang?'

'A thousand years?'

Jiang laughed lightly. 'Precisely so. It was the king's castle. It was here he kept his treasury. Here that he kept his political prisoners. Impregnable, it was. Until a traitor let in the besieging rebel army. The rest is as you see. Even so, I feel, it is impressive, even in its ruination, neh?'

'How long has it lain like this?'

'Four hundred years. There was no need to rebuild, you understand. This part of the countryside... It is hardly London.'

Wang Yu-Lai nodded. For once he seemed engaged with Jiang Lei rather than watching him.

'See how it dominates the landscape,' Jiang continued. 'It must have been truly something when it was whole. A true statement of power, neh, Cadre Wang?'

'And soon it will be gone, neh, General? Will you let the men have their sport with it, perhaps?'

Jiang turned slightly, looking back at him. 'Their sport? You mean, let them *vandalize* it?'

Wang lowered his eyes, warned by the tone of Jiang's query. 'Surely, General, it could be little worse than it is now. I just thought... letting off a little steam could not hurt, surely?'

Wang was right. It wouldn't hurt. And the place had been vandalized for centuries. Even so, Jiang felt a sense of outrage at the thought of such desecration. Ruin it might be, yet his instinct was to harm those ancient stones no further. To leave it, buried beneath Tsao Ch'un's city, for later generations possibly to unearth.

'No, Cadre Wang,' he said decisively. 'We leave it be, neh? It would not be right...'

He saw that Wang was tempted to argue, only Wang let it drop. And that again was unlike him. The man usually pushed things until he, Jiang, was forced to bellow at him.

Slowly they drifted over it. Slowly it passed behind them. Ahead lay the village.

'Is everyone in position?' he asked, seeing the craft in the sky up ahead, forming a great circle about the place.

One by one they reported in. When the last had done so, Jiang gave the order.

'Okay. Set down. Everyone to containment positions.'

He cut the connection, then looked to Wang Yu-Lai again. 'Cadre Wang... you will stay in the craft this once.'

Wang looked stunned. 'But, General...'

'You will do as I say. You may watch things from the cockpit, but you will stay inside the ship. Do I make myself clear?'

Wang opened his mouth, then closed it again. And then he bowed.

All of this would go into his report tonight. Jiang knew that. And maybe he ought to have feared it, for the First Dragon had him in his sights. Only he knew Wang was up to something. Some manoeuvre or other. Something he had been asked to try by his Masters. But Jiang wasn't going to let him. Not here.

As the big craft juddered to a halt in the sky, Jiang pointed over to the left.

'Down there,' he said, speaking to the senior pilot. 'Behind the inn. Send a squad in... no, make it two... to make sure it's safe. Then we'll set down.'

He glanced back at Wang. The man was brooding now.

I'm right, he thought, seeing that. They had meant him to try something. To stir things up and cause trouble.

Not while he was still in charge. It was bad enough for these people that they had to suffer this... *humiliation*. Bad enough that they were to have their lives disrupted, everything they owned and treasured taken from them. At least, this way, they were given a second chance. To become good citizens. Yes, and to forge something good from this abomination.

Jiang Lei knew the damage he did. Knew it and hoped to mitigate it. To be his Master's hands, and yet... somehow to keep his soul unblemished. Like a polished piece of jade, buried inside his chest.

I am not a bad man, he told himself for what seemed the thousandth time. *And yet what I do...*

Jiang watched as, down below, his men ran here and there, securing the inn, bringing the first of the prisoners out and laying them face down on the lawn at the back of the building.

He blew out a breath, then, touching the pilot's shoulder, gave the order.

'Okay, Pilot Wu... set us down.'

Jake had watched the ships come down. Had counted them and knew their chance of escape was gone.

As he stood there, among friends and family, he wondered if this, then, was the end. Whether, within the hour, he would be dead.

It was not even that he was afraid. Not for himself. What he felt was a tiredness. A mental lethargy, one might call it. A sense that to struggle would be absurd.

So the Jews must have felt, during the Holocaust.

That part of history had always troubled him. Why hadn't they fought? What had they to lose, after all? But he realized now what it was. Now that it had come he understood.

He could see the soldiers coming into the village from all directions, some of them carrying loudhailers, shouting the same thing time and time again in broken English.

'Fro dow yo way-pon an' surreh-da. Re-sis an' we wi' kih yu or.'

He hadn't understood it the first few times, but now he did. If any of them fought, then all would die. That, too, was like the Holocaust.

So was that their fate? To be packed off in trains and slaughtered? Like animals.

Jake looked about him. All those he loved were here. Perhaps if they all died, now, together, it would not be quite so bad. Perhaps...

Only he couldn't bear any of those perhapses. To allow himself hope in the face of this seemed almost obscene.

Peter came across and put his arm about his waist. The boy was trembling. Beside him, Boy was growling. A low, hostile growl.

'Quiet, Boy!' Peter said softly, urgently.

Jake glanced round. Mary was clutching her girls, the four of them clinging together, fear in their faces.

He had seen that too in the old black and white documentaries of the camps. Seen how families clung together at the last, as if it could protect them, when all that awaited them was the ovens.

He closed his eyes and groaned.

This was why he'd packed the cart. To try to avoid this moment. To have a few last weeks with them. And yet he had known, this morning, even as he loaded up the cart, that it wasn't escape, only delay.

Now even that had been taken from him.

The soldiers were in among the buildings now. They were kicking down doors and searching every house, making sure that no one was overlooked. And then, suddenly, all of the villagers were being moved, four men in brutal-looking uniforms – their helmets and armour making them look utterly anonymous – driving them on before them like sheep.

Out into the space behind the New Inn.

There, like some monolithic alien spaceship, sat the Han craft, its huge bulk taking up almost the whole of the lower slope. It completely blocked the view, its blackness seeming to cancel out the daylight.

Jake felt his legs go weak. He had not thought such power still existed in the world. A cold, technological savagery seemed to emanate from within that blackness. It was not so much an object as a concept. Not so much a weapon as an instrument to implement their will.

Like the great city they were building, it was not a continuation but a breach. Seeing that awesome ship, Jake finally understood. What he had witnessed them begin, some twenty-odd years ago, had been but a prelude to this. A clearing away before they began anew.

Differently. With Chinese characteristics.

He looked to Mary and the girls, beckoning to them to come closer, only they seemed frozen where they were, terrified of what was to come.

Boy growled again. A long, low growl that ended in a bark.

They had not noticed Boy before, but now one of the soldiers – a captain by the look of him – hurried across, unbuttoning the holster of his handgun as he came.

Peter, reading his intention, screamed at him. 'No! Leave him be!'

Only the soldier didn't listen. Raising his gun, he fired at Boy, even as the dog jumped up and turned away, making to escape.

The man fired again, and then a third time, bringing Boy down. The poor dog was whimpering pitifully now, lying there in a pool of his own blood, the life pulsing out of him. Standing over him, the soldier delivered the *coup de grâce*.

As the shot rang out, Peter let out a cry. Seeing what was about to happen, Jake grabbed at him desperately. For a moment the boy tried to evade Jake's grip, fighting to break free, to throw himself at the soldier. Only Jake held on tight, wrestling with his son, knowing that if he let him go he was dead.

'Jesus,' someone said. 'It was just a dog...'

One of the soldiers came across at that, slapping the man, gabbling at him in his native tongue.

Peter was gripping Jake tightly now, his face pressed into Jake's chest, his whole body shaking as he sobbed.

The soldier stood there still, next to Boy, gun raised, as if hoping Jake would make something of it.

Jake glared at him. 'You cunt...'

The man's face twitched. Maybe he didn't know the word, for a moment later he backed away.

Jake looked about him; saw the shock in people's faces. But he just felt numb. He kept seeing how casual it had been, as if Boy were just an object, at most a piece of vermin to be disposed of, not a cherished pet.

He gripped Peter tighter, whispering to him so that the soldiers wouldn't hear.

'It's okay, son. We're going to be okay.'

Only he knew that wasn't the truth. Killing Boy was only the start of it. He could not see much of their faces beneath their helmets, but he could see their eyes, see how they enjoyed exercising their power.

A number of the soldiers, in black uniforms, not the more common green, had begun to go among the villagers, instructing some to stay where they were, others to move further down the slope, towards where a second, smaller craft was parked.

It seemed an ominous development. Only before Jake could work out what it meant, he was being separated from Peter, one of the soldiers dragging him by the arm, forcing him into one of the lines they were forming.

'In line,' one of them barked, pushing him roughly. 'Get in line!'

At the front of each of the queues, a helmet-less soldier now sat at a desk, a second soldier stood just behind, taking pictures with a polaroid camera. They were asking questions now: name, age, place of birth. Simple stuff. And they were conducting other tests, too: fingerprinting, swabs for DNA, retinal scans.

Jake looked around; saw Mary and the girls in one of the other lines.

The murmur of voices grew.

'Quiet!' one of the officers yelled, looking about him sternly, hands on hips. 'No talking in the lines! You hear me? No talking!'

It grew quiet again. The only voices that could be heard were those of the interviewing officials.

Peter was just in front of him, in the queue to his right. He was quiet now, his head down.

He's a sensible boy. He'll get through this. If only for Meg's sake.

As Jake looked away from his son, he noticed, to one side, away from the mêlée, another of them standing there and looking on. Only this one wasn't a soldier. This one wore flowing silks of lilac and yellow, like a mandarin of old; a long-sleeved, elegant gown that was in total contrast to the rest.

As he slowly drifted past the uniformed men, so each would bow respectfully, in the fashion of their kind.

Jake was surprised to see such traditional clothing. Then, beneath the silks, he glimpsed the teflon-plated jacket.

So just what was he?

Jake was curious now. All of this testing and questioning, what was it for? Or were they, like the Nazis before them, simply con-cerned with listing who they had 'processed'?

He hoped not.

Jake studied the stranger. He was older than himself, though probably not by much. There were strands of grey in his fine dark hair that was, Jake noted, as long as a woman's. Compared to the brutality of the soldiers surrounding him his appearance was almost effeminate, yet the man had an air of great refinement. He seemed to shine inwardly, like a crystal, clear and pure and clean.

Just then the Han seemed to notice Jake's particular attention. Calling a man over to him, he whispered something in his ear, then stood back, watching as the soldier ran directly to where Jake was standing and took him from the line.

Watched by all his neighbours, Jake let the man rough-handle him, half pushing, half dragging him across, until he stood there, not two yards from the Han in the silks.

The soldier forced his head down. Made him bow low. The other was watching him, as if awaiting his reaction. Only Jake knew almost instinctively not to speak. Not to say a word.

'I'm sorry,' the Han said, after a moment. 'About the dog, I mean... The guard... He was only acting as instructed.'

Jake was surprised by how good the man's English was. But then, why so? The Chinese had been learning English as a second language for fifty years now. Only this was polished. Was better English than any of the villagers possessed, himself included. If he'd not known better, he would have said it was Oxbridge.

The apology made him understand, however. Whatever rank this man possessed, however refined he might be, he was still only a supervisor, a carrier-out of orders. Someone else, Tsao Ch'un or his successor, called the shots. The rest of them danced like pup-pets to his command.

'I am Jiang Lei,' the man said, after a moment. 'And you are?'

'Jake Reed,' he said. Only even as he said it, he wondered whether it was wise to say it; whether, after all these years, someone still wanted him dead.

But why? How could he harm them? Look how powerful they were.

'Well, Mister Reed... who should I speak to were I to wish to find out more about these people?'

Jake looked away.

'Very well... Only it would have made things so much easier. Now, however...'

Jake moistened his lips. 'You could speak to me. Only...'

The Han looked at him, calmly, as one intelligent man to another. 'Go on...'

'Only what exactly do you want?'

'Exactly... Now that's hard to say. Nothing is exact, neh?'

The Han turned and snapped his fingers. At once, a small, servile-looking man with a shaven head came hurrying across.

'My slate, Ho... now!'

As the man brought Jiang Lei his 'slate', the Han studied Jake.

'I have been doing this two years now, Mister Reed, and I have witnessed many things...' He sighed, then, as if confiding, leaned closer, lowering his voice. 'This is always the trickiest time, you understand. If any of your people have concealed any guns and try to use them... well... it would be hard to restrain my men. Only that hasn't happened in some time. I pride myself on my restraint. Few generals of the Banners can say as much.'

Jake stared at him. A general? He almost laughed. Then he looked about him, saw how organized it all was, how efficient, and the laughter fled. He might wear silks, this one, yet he was still a powerful man.

The servant returned, bowing low as he handed Jiang Lei his slate.

Jiang took the slate and began to touch its surface. Jake, watching him, recognized the machine from before the crash. They had just been coming in. A lot of dealers had switched to them only weeks before it had all happened.

Another piece of the puzzle, maybe?

'Okay... R E E D, is that right? Jake as in Jacob. And what... forty-eight years old?'

'Forty-nine.'

'Born in?'

'Windsor... Berkshire.'

The general hesitated a moment, and then his face lit up. 'Well, I never... Jake Reed... so here you are!'

Jiang sat on his own inside the craft, musing over this latest, most interesting development.

He had sent Wang Yu-Lai back outside, telling Ma Feng to keep an eye on him. There was little Wang could do to mess things up, now that the initial processing was done; now that the villagers had accepted their fate. The very worst he could do was draw his gun and shoot one of them, but Jiang was pretty sure he wouldn't do that. Not without good reason.

As for Reed...

The procedure was straightforward. Though Reed had been removed from the official list more than fifteen years ago, his was still a file that interested the Ministry, and any news of him was to be notified to them immediately.

Only Jiang Lei hadn't.

Without Wang knowing, he had had Reed separated from the rest and kept under guard inside the inn.

Now, sitting there in the cool interior of the craft, Jiang worked his way through what was known of Reed, trying to gauge what kind of threat, if any, he was.

When the time had come, back in '43, there had been a 'list'. More than twenty-three thousand names had been on that list, Jake Reed's among them.

Tsao Ch'un claimed he had had the idea while watching an old

American movie, *Godfather II*, where a gangland boss dealt with all his rivals on the day of his godson's christening. Only Tsao Ch'un, as ever, conceived things on a different scale. With his scheme, he would take out not merely the heads, but the brains of the West's most powerful institutions. He would eradicate them totally, sending the system into shock. For without its keenest, sharpest minds, what was it? A megalith of mediocrity. A lumbering dinosaur of a system.

In the months leading up to the Collapse, Tsao Ch'un had carefully placed his men in position, like stones on a wei chi board – tens of thousands of them, sent to pose as trade delegates and businessmen, there in the West to serve the great cause of globalization; to feed the great furnace of consumerism. Only trade was the last thing on their minds. They were there to observe; to take in every detail of the behaviour of their chosen targets. To know where they went and who they saw, so that on the day, when the order came, they could act swiftly and decisively.

In the three days following the first assault on the Market, they had taken out more than five-sixths of the names on that list. The rest were in hiding, or were dead and untraced, victims of the bloody savagery that followed.

Over the subsequent years they had traced a number more. Yet in these past few years such 'sightings' had been rare.

It was a good enough reason to want to talk to one of them. Only there was another, more specific reason why Jiang Lei was interested. A *personal* reason.

Jiang Lei cleared the tiny screen, then sat back, considering what he was going to do.

It wasn't feasible to think he could hide the man from Wang for more than a day or two. He would have to hand him over at some point. Yet it would be nice to question the man alone – to *sound* him, without the odious Wang breathing down his neck and listening to every word.

He let out a long sigh. There was only one way. To put Wang Yu-Lai in charge of the *Kung Tso* squad.

Jiang Lei stood, then paced the cabin for a time. Which was the greater evil? To allow Wang Yu-Lai his sadistic sport, or to hand the man, Reed, over to Wang's Masters? Either course was an abomination. Yet there was nothing he could do about the fate of those Tsao Ch'un had excluded from his city, and it would, at the very least, buy him a day without Wang peering over his shoulder and looking into his every action.

He would do it. He would give Wang Yu-Lai charge of the *Kung Tso*, and turn a blind eye to whatever followed.

Even so, it troubled him.

And the dog, he thought. Why did they have to shoot the dog like that? Why couldn't they have taken it away somewhere and done the job? He had seen, from the faces of the villagers, just what an effect it had had on them, destroying whatever small trust they might have had.

Jiang Lei huffed. He would have to have a word. But first he'd speak to Wang. Give him the 'good news' and send him on his way.

'Steward Ho...'

Ho was there in an instant, head bowed, his back arched towards his Master. 'Yes, my lord?'

'Send for Wang Yu-Lai. Oh, and bring Ma Feng while you're at it. But tell him to wait until Cadre Wang has gone. I have a job for him.'

Jake sat there in that empty, familiar room, waiting for it to begin.

They had tied him to a chair, then left him to stew in his own fears. To imagine the very worst while still hoping for the best.

Was this how it felt, then? he asked himself. This sick uncertainty? This awful limbo of the soul?

Better dead than this, he thought. Only it wasn't true. For right then he knew he would do almost anything to live. Make any kind of deal to save Peter and himself.

And that was the worst of it. The not knowing how they were. Peter and Mary and the girls. Where *were* they now? What was happening to them?

What if they used them to get at him? What if they tortured *them*, not him? For he'd heard of such things.

He closed his eyes and gave the softest groan.

The door behind him opened, spilling sunlight into the darkened room.

'You are an interesting man, Mister Reed.'

It was the Han. The refined one. Jung-something.

They hadn't gagged him. He could speak if he wanted. Only he'd not been asked a question.

Jake waited, his heart beating twenty to the dozen.

The door closed. Soft footsteps came across the wooden floor.

'You don't understand yet, do you?'

The general had changed out of his silks. He was wearing a military costume now. A formal blue one-piece with a huge square of silk at the chest, some colourful, stylized animal – it was hard to say what it was – embroidered into the square.

Jake cleared his throat. 'Understand what?'

'What we're doing. Why we are doing it. I thought... well, I thought you would probably want to know, seeing as you were there, right in the very centre of things, when it began.'

Jake looked down. It was true. He *did* want to know. He had spent twenty-two years wanting to know.

The Han came closer. 'Can I trust you to behave?'

Jake looked up at him and frowned. What did he mean?

'Oh, I could threaten to kill your son, or... oh, many different things, but what I really mean is... can I trust *you*? If I were to unbind you...'

'Oh...'

Jake was surprised. He met the other's eyes, then nodded.

'Good.'

368

As the Han unfastened the cords, Jake found himself wondering what kind of man this was. Could he trust to appearances, or was this all some subtle game? Some devious scheme to make Jake reveal more than he otherwise would?

Only that made no sense. What could he possibly get Jake to say that simple, brutal torture couldn't dislodge?

As the Han came around to the front of him again, Jake looked up at him.

'Your name...? I didn't quite...'

'Jiang Lei,' he said pronouncedly. 'Zhi-ang Lay-ee.'

'And you're a general?'

'Of the Eighteenth Banner.'

'Ah... and how many Banners are there?'

Jiang Lei smiled but did not answer.

'Can I offer you a drink of some kind?'

'My wife, Mary... and my son, Peter...?'

Again Jiang did not answer.

Jake sighed, then nodded. 'Yes... Thank you.'

'Water? Or tea, perhaps? Or something stronger, maybe? You used to like whisky...'

'Water will do. I just thought...'

Jiang Lei raised a hand to silence him. He went to the door and, opening it a fraction, gave an order in his native tongue.

He returned.

'Your family will be all right. None of them will be hurt. But we are not here to speak of them. Not now, anyway.'

'Then why *am* I here?'

'Because you were there. You saw it, didn't you? On that last day, when Tsao Ch'un gave the order. I was there, you know, in the imperial palace. I had been giving a reading. And then suddenly it was all gone. The old world. And a new world had been born. Do you understand?'

Jake stared at him a moment, then looked down. He shook his

head. Only Jiang wasn't fooled.

'You do. As soon as you saw what was happening you got out. It's all on your record. Tsao Ch'un kept it all. Even after it was all gone. He needed it you see, to re-people his world. To fill the levels of his great city.'

Jake looked up. 'Is that what this is?'

Jiang Lei nodded. 'It's a new beginning, Mister Reed. A new chance. But first you must be re-educated. What you knew, all that you were, all of that must be shed. Only then can you enter the city. Once the past has been purged from you.'

'And my wife and family?'

Jiang Lei smiled. 'A man needs his family, neh?'

Jake looked away. There were tears now in his eyes. He couldn't believe it. Couldn't believe that he was going to live – that they were all going to live. It seemed too good to be true.

'However...' Jiang said, his voice darkening. 'There is a problem.'

Jake felt his stomach tighten again. 'A problem?'

'About your past.'

'Ah...'

Jiang was about to continue when there was a knock on the door. He went across, then came back a moment later.

'Here,' he said, offering Jake a glass tumbler of cold, clear water.

Jake took it, sipped, then looked back at the Han.

'They tried to kill me. Twice. They shot me out of the sky, then came after me at my girlfriend's house. They... they murdered her. I got away...'

'I know,' Jiang Lei said. 'Leaving three of our best assassins there behind you, neh?'

Jake let his breath out. 'And they won't forget that, I guess...'

Jiang Lei laughed. Then, more sombrely: 'The Thousand Eyes have a long memory. They forget nothing.'

'The Thousand Eyes?'

'The Ministry. There is a man here, Wang Yu-Lai is his name, who serves them. He reports back on all we do here. He does not know yet of your presence here, but he soon will. It cannot be kept from him for long.'

'But you said...'

Jake dropped his eyes. It wasn't Jiang Lei's fault.

'So what am I to do?'

'You must become another... temporarily... until I can think of something better. My man, Ma Feng, is finding a suitable name for you. Then, when you are out of Wang's sight...'

Jake didn't understand what he meant. Become someone else? Assume a false identity, is that what he meant?

'But if there's no file on record to match the name...'

'Do not worry,' Jiang said, looking away. 'There will be a file.'

Jake made to ask him what he meant, but even as he opened his mouth, he saw precisely what it meant. A dead man. Someone who had already been 'processed' and found wanting. Someone who hadn't made it through re-education and into their great city.

He sipped at the water, then let his head fall forward. 'Oh, god... what a mess... what a total bloody mess...'

Jiang was watching him, nodding now, his eyes filled with understanding and sympathy.

'I am sorry. There was probably a time, early on, when our two peoples could have come to some much more suitable arrangement... could have learned to live with each other and shared the world. Only that time passed, and afterwards... Well, let us be grateful for what we have. We must look forward now, not back. The past is dead. There is only the future now.'

'Jiang Lei...?'

'Yes, Mister Reed?'

'That accent. Where did you get it?'

Jiang Lei smiled. 'I was at Cambridge. I was a rower, you know. I had arms like pistons.' He laughed. 'Long ago now, neh? And in a far country. But tell me, now that I have you here... what was it like inside the datscape? What did it feel like, when it began?'

Old Josh had drunk the best part of a bottle of single malt. Now he lay there, sprawled out on the couch, his eyes closed, loud music filling that small room at the top of the inn, its golden sound spilling out into the darkness of the deserted town.

He was listening to Man. *Rhinos, Winos and Lunatics*. One of the best albums he had in his collection. Welshmen dreaming of being Californians.

Josh smiled, then belched. Ah, but it was such a glorious sound. That wonderful foot-tapping shuffle and the two lead guitars playing off each other. Mickey Jones, particularly. Oh, how he wished he'd seen the man in his prime. Only it was a long time – close on eighty years – since they'd made this and the man was long in his grave.

The thought stirred Josh to sit up. He rubbed at his left eye a moment, then looked about him blearily.

Where had he put the fucking bottle...

His hand found it, tucked beneath the faded pillow. He took a swig, then raised the bottle in a salute to the end of things.

'To the old world...'

That glorious world in which this kind of pure instrumental majesty could exist.

Josh hauled himself up unsteadily onto his feet, then went over to the open window, looking out across the moonlit landscape, that vision of grey slate and broken walls that was his home.

Or had been. Until today.

He'd been in the outside toilet when they'd come. Had sat there, his trousers round his ankles, afraid to move; listening to them as they bellowed harshly through their megaphones in the square beyond the inn, rounding people up.

He'd heard their voices in the back bar, only yards from where he sat. Heard his son's voice, protesting strongly as he'd been led away.

And still he'd sat there, afraid to come out.

They had come out into the garden where he sat, secluded, hidden from them, chattering away to each other in their hateful foreign gabble.

And then they'd gone. Overlooking him. Back into their craft and away. And when he had finally found the courage to emerge, an hour or so later, it was to find the place deserted, everyone gone. Taken.

After a lifetime of living in his own fashion, he knew this was it. The end. Roll the credits and play the theme tune, because the West was fucked. China had come, and those little fuckers didn't play games.

No, and they didn't like rock music, either.

Josh laughed, then looked about him at the cluttered shelves. Well, fuck the Chinese. This was his world. These remnants of the pre-computer age. All of that download stuff his generation had gotten into – all of that had vanished, along with the world wide web, with Google and Yahoo, MySpace and Facebook and all the other e-clutter. All of it gone without trace. But not this stuff. Not the vinyl and the plastic. That had survived.

'And thank God for it.'

He tottered back across to the turntable and changed the record. Something grand was called for. Something he hadn't heard in a long while...

Josh grinned, then looked about him. Where had he put it now? Or, rather, where had Jake left it?

Ah, there...

Josh took the album out of its sleeve, savouring the feel of it, the look of its old orange label with the black lettering – the CBS motif in a square little box about the spindle hole.

Yes, just the thing...

He crouched over the turntable, careful not to scratch the record as he lifted the arm and gently placed it on the gap between the fourth and fifth tracks.

He loved the look of vinyl, the black gleam of it as it revolved. CDs didn't have that, or any of the stuff that followed. It was fetishistic, maybe, but such things mattered. Without them, life wasn't worth the candle.

There was the faintest noise, an underlying hiss and hum, and then it began. The crystal clarity of those opening piano notes floating from the speakers sent a ripple down his spine. 'Aren't You Glad'. Spirit at their very best.

Josh turned, looking for the whisky bottle, grinning now, the music swelling up inside him.

'Beautiful... fucking beautiful...'

Wang Yu-Lai was sitting by the half-open door of the craft, looking down at the silent countryside, when he heard it, drifting up to him from over to his right, beyond the castle.

He leaned forward, speaking to the pilot. 'What's that?'

The man half turned. 'Sorry, Cadre Wang?'

'That music... where is it coming from?'

The man removed his headphones and listened for a second or two, then pointed. 'It seems to be over there...'

'Then find it!' Wang said, impatient now. 'Let's silence that awful din!'

The pilot nodded, then, adjusting the controls, banked the craft, heading back over Corfe.

Wang saw it almost at once, there, on the top floor of the old coaching inn, to the right of the moonlit castle. There was a light at one of the windows. In that light a small, hunched figure danced.

He was tempted to tell the pilot to launch a missile – to take out the whole inn – but he was curious. What did the fool think he was doing? And just how had he slipped the net?

It was slack. He'd have the men responsible whipped for this!

'Set us down in the square,' he began, then changed his mind. 'No... the other side of the inn. I'll go in with a couple of the men.' He looked round. 'Li... Cho... you'll come with me.'

He chose those two for a reason. Because, this afternoon, they had performed well, following his instructions to the letter.

And with enthusiasm, he thought, recalling it. He'd watch the tape later. Once he was back at base.

They set down. Wang waited while the craft's engines whined down, then, looking to the two guards, signalled for them to go ahead.

If anyone was going to get shot, it wasn't him. Not that he expected any trouble. The man he'd glimpsed looked drunk. Only it was best not to take a chance.

As he went inside, Wang grimaced. He hated the smell of these places almost as much as he hated the people who lived in them. Why they couldn't just eradicate them he didn't know. Tsao Ch'un, who was so exemplary in every other way, surely had a weakness in this. Had it been he who made the decisions, there would have been no one left but Han. And even then, only *pure* Han, none of these fucking ethnics.

As they climbed the stairs the sound grew louder. It was an awful, raucous noise. The kind of thing that only these barbarians could have come up with.

At least that much is well ordered, Wang thought, knowing that this, amongst much else, would be erased from cultural memory, once the Ministry had finished.

No. There would be none of this pop and rock in the new city. None of this retarded beat music. Nothing but traditional Han tunes, traditional Han instruments.

One flight from the top Cho and Li stopped, looking back at Wang Yu-Lai for instructions.

'Go in,' he said, mouthing the words exaggeratedly over the

pounding noise of the music. 'Secure the room, then I'll come in...
And shut that fucking row up, neh?'

Cho kicked the door in, Li at his shoulder as they charged inside.
There was the sound of a chair being knocked over, a brief scuffle,
and then the music stopped abruptly.

Wang let out a sigh of relief. 'Thank fuck...'

He climbed the last few steps then went inside, stopping dead
as he saw the shelves and shelves of books and records.

Kuan Yin! Look at all this stuff! The Thousand Eyes would have
a field day, going through all of this!

There was enough illicit material here to keep a team of clerks
busy for a month.

Wang Yu-Lai looked about him, then frowned. Cho and Li had
their heads bowed low. Of their captive there was no sign.

'Well? Where is he?'

Cho looked to Li, then, bowing lower, answered him.

'I am afraid he jumped, Cadre Wang. When we came into the
room he was beside the window. He took one look at us and...'

Wang walked across and, holding on to the frame, looked out
and down.

It was hard to tell, it was so dark, but it seemed like there was
something lying in the street just in front of the inn's front entrance.

Wang turned and looked to the two men. He could tear them off
a strip, maybe even punish them for not doing their duty properly.
Only no real harm had been done, and he could cultivate these two.
Use them to find out what the men really thought of their precious
leader, Jiang.

'It's a shame,' he said, nodding to himself, letting them stew a
moment longer; enjoying their discomfort. 'It would have helped
us to know how he evaded us. To know who among us was to
blame. But... never mind... We will leave this off the record, neh?
After all, I would not wish to see two such... useful men get into
trouble for some minor failing on their part.'

'Thank you, Cadre Wang,' the two men said, relieved, their heads bobbing.

'But Cho... Li... do not fuck up again, neh? Next time make sure we take our man. Next time make sure that I have a chance to talk to them. To have one of our special chats, neh?'

Cho and Li looked to each other again, then smiled, their understanding perfect.

'Yes, Cadre Wang...'

Josh groaned, then tried to move his hand. He could see it, lying there next to him on the cold stone floor, but when he tried to move it...

No. The pain was almost too much. Despite the numbing effect of the whisky, it felt like the whole of his back was on fire. And there was a tingling, from his toes through to the back of his neck. But when he tried to move...

Nothing. Not a damn fucking thing.

But what had he expected? He'd just jumped out of a fucking window. Stupidest fucking thing he'd ever done, even if those pair of goons had been a shock.

He closed his eyes, blacking out for a moment. As he faded back in again, one single thought assailed him.

I'm dying...

One moment he'd been in heaven, waving his arms about to that beautiful, powerful sound, and the next...

The silence was the worst of it. If he had to die, let some glorious piece of power rock be playing. 'Free Bird' maybe, or 'Whipping Post', or... yes, fuck it... Neil Young blasting out 'Cortez The Killer' full volume with a reggae beat. Something truly great in those final few moments. But this...

He hated it. Hated the silence, the cold, the numbness.

And that, surely, was wrong? To feel so much and yet so little.

His hand lay there, not an arm's length from his face, and yet it was a thousand miles away.

Dying... yeah, you're fucking dying, boy... This is how it feels...

How much blood he'd lost he didn't know. Probably a lot, because he felt faint now, nauseous. But it was the cold that was going to kill him. He knew it for a fact.

He heard their footsteps, then, coming across to him. Heard them talking among themselves. Not that Chinese gabble this time but proper English.

He heard them stop. Heard them register surprise.

'Cadre Wang... you want me to...?'

'No, Li... why waste a bullet?'

Why, indeed?

Right then he wanted to call out to them, to tell the arseholes to go fuck themselves, only he didn't have the strength. Even when one of them placed his booted foot on his back, Josh barely felt it. It felt like the memory of a memory of pain, sent through thick glass and vacuum across an infinite distance.

Like he was dying by degrees.

Which was probably the fucking truth.

If he could have laughed right then, he would have laughed. Just the one final time. For defiance's sake. Because that was how he'd lived his life. Defiant. With a finger up to authority.

Old Josh smiled, or thought he smiled... and was gone.

They turned the lifeless body over, looking for some form of documentation, only there was nothing.

The man looked old. Eighty if he was a day.

Wang stared at the corpse a while, then shook his head. It was no good trying to work out what motivated these people. They were not like his own.

Nei wai yu pi'e... the saying went. The Han and the *Hung Mao*, the Westerners, were different. They saw the world in different ways. So it was. So it would always be. To think that they could live together... it was a mistake.

'Come,' he said, gesturing to Cho and Li. 'Let's get out of here.'

But as he climbed back onto the craft, he found himself remembering the figure of the man, dancing in the light beside the open window.

Dancing...

Wang Yu-Lai shook his head. No good would come of this experiment; of this mixing of the pure and the impure. Time would prove him right. Only what was he to do? He had no voice in the matter. He was, after all, merely his Master's hands.

He sighed, then, reaching for his slate, began to write that day's report. And as he did, so other memories came back to him from earlier that afternoon.

Wang smiled; a cruel, lascivious smile, remembering, then cleared his mind, like the good servant he was. Loyal unto death.

But not his death. Not if he could help it.

Chapter 11

THE END OF HISTORY

Jiang Lei stood there atop the castle mound, staring out across the darkened countryside.

It was late, but you could still hear, faintly, in the distance, the sound of the machines as they worked into the night, building Tsao Ch'un's great city.

Those machines never stopped. Shift after shift the city kept on growing, encroaching on the land, populating it with its outposts, like a giant laying endless wei chi stones upon the board, filling it slowly, purposefully.

Jiang Lei could see it clearly from where he stood, its pearled, lambent forms scattered across the darkness.

Reed had left a while back, but their talk had made Jiang thoughtful; had brought him here to experience for himself what it was like to see the world from this vantage point. It was true what Reed had said. One seemed to shed the centuries standing there beneath its fallen towers.

He sighed. It would have to be destroyed, of course. Now that he'd seen it for himself he understood. The whole ridge would have to come down. Normally they would build around the more mountainous regions, encircling them, only this was too small a natural feature. No. They would flatten this, pushing the city on, over and above its pounded ruins.

Jiang Lei imagined it, holding the thought a moment, seeing how he could make a poem of it. A poem of ice and time and broken lives. Especially the last. A delicate, elegant poem. An observation from the edge of the world.

He turned, looking back down the hill. There, not fifty metres away, Ma Feng and the youngster, Li Ying, were waiting for him, sharing a cigarette, the glow of its stub the only sign of them in the darkness.

Jiang smiled. Today, for once, had been a good day. His talk with Reed... it was rare that he had such conversations. But then Reed seemed a rare kind of man. It was a pity he was *Hung Mao*. Much more a pity that he was on Wang's list.

Jiang sniffed in the cool night air. He was not sure what he would do about that yet. He had given Reed a new identity. One that would keep him from discovery for the next few days. But after that...

'Ma Feng...'

The man hurried up the slope, taking form from the darkness. 'Yes, General?'

'My talk this afternoon... with the prisoner... I want no word of it to get back to Cadre Wang, you understand?'

Ma Feng's head bent lower. 'Yes, General. I shall speak to the men.'

'Good. Then I am finished here.'

Ma Feng remained as he was, head lowered. He showed no sign of ever moving from that pose.

Jiang knew what it meant. Knew, of old, that Ma Feng would not ask directly, and so asked the question for him.

'You want to know why, neh? Why I, Tsao Ch'un's general, should be so interested in a simple villager? Well... I am... only the truth is, our friend Wang Yu-Lai would be even more interested.'

He paused, then, 'The man is on the list...'

381

Ma Feng looked up, shocked, then quickly down again.

'You understand, then? Why Cadre Wang must not know?'

'No, General, only... you must have a reason.'

'I do indeed. But what I said... no word, yes?'

Ma Feng hesitated, then, 'Yes, General.'

'Good. Then let's be gone from here.'

Jake stepped down from the craft and looked about him. It was a camp. A detention camp, complete with barbed wire fences and guard towers. As far as history was concerned, he might as well have been living a hundred years before. Only now that he'd met the man in charge, he found this strange. To be so cultured and yet so cruel. Or was it mere necessity?

He had not thought to live out the day. When he'd been sitting in that room, alone, his hands bound, he had thought himself a dead man. Only here he was, alive and, in a minute or so, to be reunited with his loved ones.

He looked back at the guard, but the Han wasn't interested in him any longer. He waved Jake on, gesturing vaguely towards the huts. There were people over there – prisoners, Jake thought, for what else were they? There was a single light on a pole in the centre of the camp, and the low hum of a generator.

He made his way across. A number of people were gathered beneath the lamp, next to a standing water tap. Jake looked about him, recognizing some of the faces from nearby villages. Some of them had even been there in Corfe the other night, when they'd had the barbecue.

The 'huts' were further on, twelve long low buildings laid out in three straight lines, their opaque material glowing faintly from within. Vague shadows moved within that glow.

Beyond them lay the fence, lit every twenty metres or so by spot-lights.

Light spilled from the doorway to each hut.

'You seen the Church Knowle crowd?'

'Middle row,' one of them answered, pointing. 'Down near the end. Can't miss 'em.'

'Thanks.'

He heard them long before he made out who it was. A few of them were standing by the door, just outside, talking like they were back home. Like this wasn't some bad dream they had stumbled into.

Will Cooper was there, and John Lovegrove from Corfe, and – to his surprise – Jack Hamilton from Wareham and his new wife, Becky.

Jake stepped out from the darkness, surprising them. Will Cooper said it for them all. 'Jake... fuck me, mate, where you been?'

'Thought you were for it,' John Lovegrove chipped in.

Becky stepped over to him and gave him a hug. 'Good to see you, Jake,' she said in his ear. 'Best go see Mary and the others... they've been worried sick...'

'They inside?'

'Down the end on the left... poor Petie... been crying 'is eyes out, poor boy.'

Jake gave her a gentle squeeze then went inside.

It all looked very spartan: a cross between a large dormitory and a massive tent made out of what looked like thick plastic. There were light sources actually embedded in the walls. Beneath those, pallet beds had been set up either side of the central aisle, army style.

He saw Mary at once, sitting on one of the beds at the far end. Cathy and Beth sat either side of her, holding her hands. Nearby, two beds down, Peter lay face down, Meg sat next to him, smoothing his hair.

The sight of them moved him deeply. For a while, earlier, he thought he'd lost them; thought he'd never see them again.

He walked across. They all had their backs to him. They didn't realize he was there, until Meg glanced up and saw him.

'Uncle Jake!' she squealed, jumping up. 'It's Uncle Jake!'

In the chaos that followed he was hugged and kissed, their happiness at seeing him again making his heart leap, the tears come flooding from his eyes.

Peter clung to him, as if he'd never let him go.

As it calmed, he sat between them all, Peter cuddled in beneath his arm, as he told them everything that had happened. Others had gathered about them, eager to hear Jake's news, fascinated by Jake's description of the man who seemed to hold all of their fates in his hands.

Only Jake didn't tell them everything. For once, instinct made him hold back; made him relate only the bare bones. He didn't know why, but he felt it a kind of betrayal. The man had clearly spared his life, and he ought to feel grateful for that, not repay him with idle chatter.

As for the false identity... Of that he said nothing. Not even to Mary. For who knew, in these changed circumstances, which of his erstwhile friends and neighbours would betray him?

Later, as he lay there, stretched out on his bed, Mary came across.

She sat down beside him, putting her hand on his brow, and smiled. 'Hi...'

He let his eyes take in how beautiful she was.

'Hi...'

He put his arm about her, pulled her down and kissed her.

'You know what? I never thought I'd ever do that again...'

'What, kiss me?'

'Yes... I sat there in that room and... oh, god... I dunno... I thought I was dead. And I kept thinking...'

Jake swallowed, choked up by the thought.

'I kept thinking of my promise, to Tom, and...'

She put her finger to his lips. 'I'm glad, you know... really glad you came back. I wasn't sure before... you know, about what I felt...

about us... but when I thought I'd lost you...'

Jake stared back at her, surprised by the tear that rolled down her cheek.

'I missed you, you know.'

'Did you?' She tried to smile, but she was crying now. 'Oh, Jake... what's going to happen to us? Why are we in this dreadful place?'

Wang Yu-Lai stood there on the podium, in the centre of the yard, looking out over the heads of the gathered prisoners. A handful of guards stood close by, their big automatics held casually, almost lazily. They knew nothing would happen. These people were as docile as sheep.

Wang himself had slept well. For once he was in the very best of moods. That little 'excursion' yesterday had whet his appetite for more. Which was why he was here, now, at this unearthly hour, welcoming the dawn.

He looked about him at the captives. They were a ragged bunch. Most of them had no more than the clothes they'd been wearing when they were taken. Few had coats. Most stood there, shivering in the cold morning air.

Wang smiled. He oughtn't to have been there. Not officially. This wasn't really his job. But what Jiang Lei didn't know about couldn't possibly hurt him. And besides, it would make the general's job much easier.

He summoned Cho, then spoke to him in a low whisper, so that none of the others could hear.

'Cho... I want you in the office. I don't want any of these fuckers trying to contact General Jiang, understand?'

Cho bowed low, then ran off to do as he was bid.

Wang straightened, pulling his cloak tighter about him against the chill. With Jiang absent, he was the senior ranking official here, and what he said went.

He jumped down, walking among them, seeing how they were cowed by his power, his eminence. Hate him they might, but they also feared him.

'This one,' he said, touching the arm of one of them. 'And this one, too,' he said, indicating another.

One of his men was filming this from the podium, while another, beside him, noted down those he selected. Others waded into the crowd to take those whom Wang had picked and dragged them off to one side of the main mass.

Wang shook his head, a sneer of disgust crossing his features. Jiang Lei was far too soft, far too undiscerning in those he let through. And that was bad for the city. For the city, if it was to have Hung Mao at all, must surely have the best of them, the strongest genetically.

No, his Master, the First Dragon, was right. General Jiang was far too lenient. *If he can't make the choice, I'll have to make it for him.*

He could see the old man in his mind, his Steward fussing about him, making him ch'a and bringing him a fresh sheet of paper, so he might compose another poem.

It made Wang want to spit. To have such a man as a general.

He did not like to criticize Tsao Ch'un, even in his thoughts, but in appointing Jiang Lei to such a rank, he had surely been mistaken. Jiang was not hard enough, not ruthless enough, for the task.

He chose another, then another, most of them older men, though there were one or two women among them. Women of advanced years.

Wang stopped. Now what was this? He gave a grunt, then shook his head. No, no... they couldn't have this. Look at the woman's eye!

He touched her arm. 'This one...'

'No!' someone nearby bellowed, trying to push through to grab at Wang. 'Leave her be!'

Wang backed off a step or two, almost bumping into one of them, even as two of his guards interceded, using the butts of their guns to club the man to the ground.

'Take her!' Wang ordered, his heart beating fast. 'And that one, too.'

They dragged the pair of them away.

Those surrounding him were watching Wang now, a shared look of hostility in their faces.

Wang sniffed. 'Enough for now...'

He backed away, letting his guards force a way back through the crowd.

It was a start, anyway. Another thirty or so they'd not have to bother processing.

'Load them up,' he said to the captain of the guard as he passed him. 'We'll do it now. Get it out of the way.'

The man bowed, his face a blank, then barked out orders to his men.

Yes, and maybe I'll have her, he thought, looking back at the one he'd selected at the end – the one with the lazy eye. Wang smiled. *Better than that... I'll tie her husband up and have him watch us at it.*

Like he'd done with the two crippled women last night. Kuan Yin! That had been good! He grew hard simply thinking about it.

And then, later on, he'd contact the Ministry and let them know what he had done – what he'd *achieved*.

Wang Yu-Lai turned, drawing up his silks so they would not be soiled, then hurried towards the craft.

Jiang Lei yawned, then stepped out from the tent.

It was a fine, clear day, the air crisp and chill.

'Can I clear the breakfast things, Master?' Steward Ho asked, hovering close by.

'Of course...' Jiang glanced at him, took a step away, then turned back. 'Ho... have you seen our friend this morning?'

'Our friend...? Ah, Cadre Wang, you mean?'

'Yes... the good Cadre... have you seen him?'

'Not for an hour, General. He left.'

'Left? But he's not due anywhere.'

Jiang frowned. What in the name of the gods was he up to now?

He was tempted to leave it. After all, it was quite pleasant without the Cadre here, following him about, making his nasty little comments. But if Wang Yu-Lai wasn't here making trouble, he was making it elsewhere.

He called out. 'Ma Feng... get the men together. I want to reconnoitre.'

Jiang didn't know where Wang had got to, but he could guess.

The camp. He had to be at the camp.

And if he was?

Jiang let out a sigh of exasperation. He looked to Ho again. 'An hour, Ho... you're sure?'

'He crept away at dawn, General. Why... should I have told you?'

'Yes, Ho... when it comes to Cadre Wang you tell me *everything*.'

Ho bowed low. 'Forgive me, Master...'

Jiang shook his head. What was that bastard up to now?

He turned, not quite sure what to do, then hurried across to the communications tent. 'Li Fa,' he called, addressing the young technician at the desk as he stepped inside. 'Connect me with the holding camp. And no delays or excuses. Anyone who attempts to stall me will be in severe trouble, make that clear. I need to know – *at once* – if Cadre Wang is there.'

Li Fa bowed, then turned and made the connection. He made his request. A moment later he turned back, looking up at Jiang.

'He was there, General, only he left five minutes back.'

'Put me in touch with the craft directly... Now!'

If this was what he thought it was, he'd have the man tried in the field, then stripped and flogged for his insubordination.

Only Wang had anticipated him. He was flying blind, with a full communications blackout, as if he was on a special mission.

That confirmed it for Jiang. The only question now was this –

was it done at Wang Yu-Lai's own discretion, or was he following the orders of his Masters at the Ministry? If the latter, then Jiang might find it difficult prosecuting a field trial against the man.

'Curse the little fucker!'

He left the tent. Ma Feng and his squad were waiting there just outside, their heads bowed.

'Come,' he said, heading across to the landing pad, the men falling in behind. 'Let's hope we're not too late.'

Jake slumped down onto the bed, all of the hope he'd carried away from that meeting with Jiang Lei crushed by what he had seen that morning.

That – that other odious little cunt – was the real face of China. That son of a prick, with his self-important sneer and his callous disregard for life.

He had no illusions as to what would happen now. The only hope he had was that it would be quick. That that dung-ball didn't toy with his friends. Didn't 'get off on' torturing them.

When he'd seen poor Jack clubbed to the ground by the guards he'd wanted to throw himself at them, to fight them to the death. Only what would it have achieved? He knew, from what Jiang had said, that that was what a lot of these guards wanted – the excuse to wipe them out. To *not* have to do their job properly.

And then there was his family. The promise to Tom. If he'd fought them, then they'd all have been killed. Peter and Meg and Cathy and Beth... and Mary.

He closed his eyes and groaned. Poor Becky. That poor darling girl, whose only earthly flaw was her lazy eye. How did she deserve that? Why should some bastard be allowed to come along and take her away just like that? If there was any justice...

Only there wasn't. Not one single fucking shred of it.

Jake looked up, saw Mary standing there, staring at him, her own eyes desolate.

'I thought you said it was going to be all right...'

He lowered his head. 'I know,' he said quietly, apologetically.

'So what was that?'

Jake shrugged. He didn't know. And maybe Jiang Lei didn't know. Maybe this was how they behaved behind his back.

Mary sat down beside him, took his hand. 'One thing, Jake. We're going to live through all of this, yes? We're going to do everything we can to survive. For the children's sake.'

He looked to her, then looked away again. He hadn't yet told her about the fake identity. About the trouble he was possibly still in.

'I'll try,' he said, squeezing her hand. 'You know I'll try, only...'

'Only what?'

He took a long deep breath, then shook his head. 'Nothing,' he said, hoping it would never become an issue. 'Only nothing.'

Jiang Lei pointed, almost jumping up out of his seat as he did.

'There he is... There's the bastard! Set us down, Pilot Wu, right bang on top of him!'

Ma Feng looked to his colleagues and made a face. They had never seen their general so angry. Where had the mild, considerate man they knew gone? And who was this demon who had taken him over?

Jiang turned to the men. 'You will take him and bind him, understand? And if he struggles, I give you permission to slap him, yes?'

The men seemed delighted by that order. 'Yes, General Jiang!' they said as one.

'Good... then let's hope...'

A fusillade of shots rang out. Jiang leaned forward, trying to see what had happened, then gave a sharp intake of breath.

Jiang slumped, he physically slumped, back into his chair.

Some men were just plain evil...

Yes, but he would have him now.

As the craft set down, not twenty metres from where Wang stood, on the ramp of his security cruiser, Jiang Lei barked an order.

'Arrest that man, Ma Feng... I want him roped!'

Ma Feng and two others jumped down and ran across. As they did, so Wang's men made to intercede.

'And if they try to stop you, shoot them!'

Li and Cho backed away at that, leaving Wang Yu-Lai exposed. Ma Feng grabbed him roughly, almost pulling him off his feet.

'My lord,' Wang protested, clearly angered by this treatment. 'What have I done to deserve this?'

But Jiang Lei was having none of it. He was furious. 'Get him inside!'

Jiang looked across, to where the bodies lay, grieved by the sight. This was not the way. This only made their job harder, not easier.

Inside, as Wang sat there, head bowed, his hands tied with rough cord, Jiang raged at him.

'What do you mean by this? Who gave you the order to do what you have done?'

Wang Yu-Lai looked up, glaring at Jiang Lei. 'I was merely doing what you ought to have done!'

Jiang stared at him, astonished by the man's impudence. 'You presume to tell me my business, Wang Yu-Lai? To tell me what I ought to be doing?' Jiang shook his head, knowing now that he had no course but to try him and deal with him as harshly as he could. 'I am Tsao Ch'un's general... his chosen man. And what are you?'

Wang laughed. It was the oddest sound, considering the trouble he was in. Jiang frowned, not understanding what might have caused such a reaction.

Had the man lost his senses?

Jiang calmed himself, then spoke again, clearly, like he was talking to a wilful child.

'What you have done, Wang Yu-Lai, is a most serious breach of discipline. I intend to try you, here and now. And if I find you guilty, which I will, I shall have you flogged and sent back to your Masters in a box. Do you understand?'

Wang looked up, meeting his eyes. He seemed strangely unconcerned, unmoved by Jiang's words.

'Oh, I understand, General Jiang... I know what you'd like to do... only if you try me it will come out...'

'*What?*' Jiang let his impatience shape his reaction. 'What in the gods' names are you talking about?'

'About Reed. About the list.'

Jiang stared at him, utterly deflated by his words. How had he found that out? Was there a spy among his men? Or had one of Wang's creatures overheard something?

Whichever, he would find out. Would rack them all, if he had to, until he had his answer. But for now he had a bigger problem, for if it came out that he had meddled, giving the man a false identity to keep him from investigation by the Ministry, it would be he, more likely, who'd be on the end of a severe punishment.

There was only one thing he could do now. Only one thing that might save him. But first he must deal with the odious Wang.

'Ma Feng!' he called, his eyes never leaving Wang Yu-Lai.

'Yes, General?' Ma Feng said, rushing in, head bowed.

'Take this one somewhere safe. Bind him and gag him and keep a guard on him day and night. And don't let anyone talk to him. I don't want him getting any messages out, have you got that?'

'Yes, General.'

'But you can't...' Wang began.

Jiang turned and slapped him. 'I know you, Wang. You think me a soft man. Well, you will find out now just how soft I am.'

He looked to Ma Feng. 'Take him. And if he tries to escape, shoot him.'

*

Jake was resting when they came.

Peter came and shook him awake, then stepped back, pointing towards the man who stood there in the doorway.

Jake sat up, then, seeing who it was, quickly stood, lowering his head.

'Jiang Lei...'

The Han came across, signalling to his guards to stay where they were, in the doorway.

'Shih Reed... I'm sorry, but you'll have to come with me. I am afraid that your existence is a known fact. The Ministry will want to talk with you. And I... well, I must follow the formalities now.'

It was what Jake had feared. To come so close. Now they would have him. Now they would finish what they'd begun all those years ago. He sighed and looked down.

'What you did... I appreciate that. It was a kindness on your part. But my family...'

'Will be well looked after, I promise. No harm will come to them.'

'And you?'

Jiang Lei smiled. 'I must fight now to save myself.'

The smile faded. Jiang looked down. 'Your friends... I am afraid I came too late to save them.'

Jake groaned.

It was what he'd feared. Even so, it was still hard to hear it confirmed.

Jiang Lei met his eyes, his own sorrowful. 'I am so sorry... But I promise you this... That man will pay for what he's done. It is not our way, I assure you. He is not typical of us. But there are many like him, and The Thousand Eyes uses them whenever it can. I might try to disguise it and call it necessity, only that isn't true. It is an evil, and I apologize, Shih Reed. This isn't how it was meant to be.'

Jake smiled and took the man's offered hand.

'Say your farewells,' Jiang said. 'You have half an hour.'

Jake bowed his head, Han fashion. 'Jiang Lei... Thank you...'

He watched the Han leave, then looked down thoughtfully. Was there still a chance? Probably not. Once he was in their hands that was it.

The Thousand Eyes... how apt it was. How very Chinese...

Later, by the light of a scented candle, Jiang Lei sat at his desk, writing the letter.

It was cold inside the tent. Much colder than it had been these past few nights. Winter was coming. You could feel it in the air. Even so, he did not summon Ho to bring a heater.

Earlier on, he had contacted an old friend, in Pei Ch'ing, who had agreed to be his intermediary; to hand deliver the message. For this had to be done discreetly or not at all. Were it to be sent through official channels, it would have no chance of reaching the one to whom it was addressed. It would be lost, or delayed, its purpose blunted.

Even as it was, it was a great risk. One did not write such letters every day. Then again, one did not often come to such a cusp, such a turning point, in one's life.

It was all his fault. He realized that now. It was he who had put Wang in charge. He who had given him the taste for it. Was it any wonder that such a sadistic little pervert should want more?

No. And so he shouldered the blame. Set it all down for Tsao Ch'un to read, humbling himself in words before him, even as he asked the great man a rare favour, begging him to remember the great services he had done him.

Done willingly, of course, with no expectation of reward, yet if he was in any small way valued, then...

Jiang stopped, the ink brush hovering in the air above the sheet, wondering just how to phrase it.

Whatever he said, he knew, was to some degree irrelevant, for Tsao Ch'un was a man of extreme moods, governed often by the

merest whim. It was what made him so unpredictable, so dangerous. What had kept him in charge all this while.

Even so, Jiang was a poet beyond all else, and, just as he took
care with his calligraphy, so he took equal care with the words he
chose to set down.

It was possible – maybe even likely – that what he was writing
here would be the last thing he wrote. That Tsao Ch'un would be
so annoyed by his request that, in a fit of pique, he would hand him
to the First Dragon, to do with as he wished.

But there was no other course. Even if he killed Wang, and all
those Wang had contaminated, the matter of Reed's identity would
come out sooner or later, and there would be an investigation. The
Ministry would insist. So why not face it now? Why not state his
objection to it loud and clear to the one man who had the power of
life or death over him? Why not say what a waste it was, to give one
such as Reed to those idle sadists in the cells of the Ministry building in Bremen?

Why break such a man when one could use him gainfully?

He wrote that down, ending with a small flourish of the brush.

There... All that remained was to place his seal upon the letter.

Jiang reached across and, taking two sheets of paper towel, lay
them beneath the sheet. Then, having carefully inked the seal, he
pressed it firmly at the bottom of the page.

The bright red ink of the seal seemed to glisten in the candlelight momentarily, the scent of the ink almost as strong as that of
the burning candle.

There was a poem in that, too. Only tonight he'd had enough of
poetry. Tonight he was just a general, begging his liege lord to
forgive him and spare his life. And the life of a man whom, until
two days ago, he did not know.

How strange that was. Or not, now that he thought about it. For
this had been brewing many months now. This disaffection.

Jiang Lei stood, taking a moment to yawn and stretch. Then,

seeing that the ink had almost dried, he picked up the sheet and, looking to the entrance flap, summoned his servant.

'Steward Ho...'

Ho appeared at once. 'Master?'

'Send for Ma Feng... Tell him I have a message I need delivered.'

'Yes, Master.'

Ho bowed and was gone.

Jiang took one of his official folders and placed the letter inside. There was no guarantee that it would ever get to his old friend, let alone to its intended destination. Even now, agents of The Thousand Eyes might be watching for such a missive, ready to intercept it, to assassinate Ma Feng then come for him. Who knew what the state of things was, and whether Wang Yu-Lai had had time to tell them what he knew? Only, fragile as this was, it was the only way. All other doors were barred to him. If this failed, he was a dead man.

Incongruously, Jiang Lei smiled at the thought.

Jake woke.

It was dark, and for an instant he could not remember where he was. There was a strong smell of wood polish and oil, so he knew he was not back in the camp.

He sat up.

'Hello?'

No answer.

Jake reached out, feeling blindly. The mattress he was on was resting on the floor. Nearby was a big tin of some kind. Paint or something. For some reason it felt like he was in a garage or an outhouse of some kind, only he couldn't remember how he'd got there.

What he did remember was the interrogation. That had been in the back bar of the Bankes Arms Hotel, only...

Only when he thought about it, he couldn't remember how it had ended.

Had they slipped him something? Given him some kind of drug?

Jake got to his feet, feeling unsteady. They'd filmed it all, that much he recalled. Everything he'd said. Everything he'd admitted to. Though what they'd do with it after all these years he couldn't guess.

He felt his way across the room, almost stumbling over a box filled with what felt like old wallpaper samples.

A garage. It had to be.

His head was pounding now, like he'd drunk too much.

He tried again, louder this time. 'Hello?'

There was silence for a moment, then, from outside, footsteps on the gravel. Jake turned towards the sound, then shielded his eyes as the big door swung up and back, spilling brilliant sunlight into that dark space.

He stumbled out. Through squinted eyes he saw that the guard held a big semi-automatic. It was aimed at him.

'You come now... See General Jiang...'

He hadn't seen Jiang Lei since he'd come to him at the camp. As he followed the soldier, he wondered what Jiang wanted with him now.

Jake looked about him, as his eyes grew accustomed to the daylight, not recognizing where he was. Wherever it was, it wasn't Purbeck. At least, not a part of it that he knew. So Jiang had had him moved for some reason. Maybe to keep him out of someone else's hands.

Jiang was waiting in his craft.

'Shih Reed,' he said, offering Jake a seat. 'Are you all right? I'm afraid the drug we had to give you—'

'It *was* a drug, then?'

'Yes, but its effects will wear off soon.' Jiang looked tired. He smiled apologetically. 'I did not wish to tie you up, so drugging you was the only real alternative.'

Jake looked down. 'Any news?'

Jiang shook his head. 'It is all in the hands of the gods. I have given it my best shot, as you say in the West, only...'

'Only what?'

'Only it's hard to gauge sometimes... how much power you have, how much influence you exert. Me...? Well, I consider myself a very small piece of the puzzle. And yet I have access to those at the very highest level. It is the world I was born into. A world of privilege. And, for once, I have used my connections in that world.'

'How do you mean?'

'I mean, I have written to Tsao Ch'un himself, asking for a pardon.'

Jake stared at him, astonished. 'A pardon...'

Jiang nodded. 'Yes... I have thrown myself on his mercy.'

Jake laughed. 'Jesus!'

Jiang too was smiling now. 'It is funny, neh? I mean... it isn't... and yet...'

'And until we hear from him?'

Jiang gestured towards a spot just across the cabin from him. There, beside the seat, were two fishing rods and a basket full of food.

Jiang stood and went across, picking up one of the rods and studying it with what looked like an expert eye. 'It is something I understand both our peoples are very fond of... You like fishing, Jake?'

Jake nodded.

'Then it is decided.' Jiang raised his voice, speaking to the cockpit. 'Pilot Wu... take us to that excellent stream we saw, three, no four days back. The one with the pretty stone bridge.'

He looked back at Jake.

'And Wang Yu-Lai?' Jake asked. 'What's happening to him?'

'Ah...' Jiang said, his face shadowed momentarily. 'Cadre Wang is with friends, let us say. Our friends, fortunately, not his.'

And Jiang laughed again, a warm and pleasant laugh that Jake decided he liked. Liked very much.

Wang Yu-Lai sat back, shocked, his cheek stinging from where the man had slapped him.

You'll die for that, he thought, glaring at him. I'll fucking have the skin stripped from your body, when I'm free again.

He knew they'd come for him. They always came. When he hadn't reported in last night, they would have put an enquiry in – to find out why he'd not been in touch, for that was their way – that was why they were so effective.

And for all Jiang Lei's stalling and subterfuge, they would find out where he was, and then...

Wang shuddered with indignation. He'd had the very worst of nights, sleeping on a damp, uncomfortable mattress that they'd grudgingly given him, on the floor of a cold cell, the stench of the drain nearby making him want to retch.

He would have his revenge, though. They might have their fun now, only he would have the last laugh, and oh how he'd enjoy that!

Wang had seen such 'work', in the special rooms in the cellars of the great fortress in Bremen. Had seen with his own eyes how a strong man could be reduced to a terrified child. How pain could be used to unstitch a man.

And that, he promised himself, was what he would do to these.

With his Masters' permission, of course. But then why would they not grant it? For he had, in his head, details of Jiang Lei's misdemeanour. Of his attempt to hide the man called Reed. That was his trump card. Was the kind of thing his Masters loved to hear. Not that they would expose Jiang Lei. Oh, no. They would use it, rather, to control him. To make him *theirs*.

For that was how they operated. How they cemented their control over Tsao Ch'un's great city.

For some time now it had grated on his nerves whenever Jiang had given him an order or contradicted him. The very falsity of their positions had irked him. But that would soon be ended. Just as soon as he was released from this.

He had begun to smile again, just thinking of it, when the soldier slapped him again, hard, making his eyes water.

Yes… but this one first. How he'd make the fucker sing out…

Seeing them down below, through the cockpit window, Jiang Lei knew the game was up.

They had brought a regular little army with them: six transporters and a massive cruiser. Their black, unmarked craft sat in the field beside his own men's tents. Some of them had remained there, guarding the ships, but the rest, a hundred or more in total, including four very important-looking figures, were waiting just outside Jiang Lei's tent.

'It looks like we have visitors,' Jiang said quietly.

'D'you think they've come for me?'

'Possibly… but it's more likely that it's because their man, Wang, is missing. They keep a sharp eye on their agents, especially one as prominent as Wang.'

Jiang took a long breath, then: 'Pilot Wu… Set us down.'

'Stay in the craft,' Jiang said to Jake, pulling on his dark blue jacket. 'If you need to come, I'll send for you.'

Jake nodded. He had enjoyed their afternoon together. Had found himself seduced by the simple charm of the man, his warmth and culture. He had seen for himself the brutality of China. But in Jiang Lei he saw another side to things. Saw in this one man the pure essence of the Confucian ethic.

Good luck, Jiang Lei, he thought, watching the man as the craft set down and Jiang walked down the ramp to approach the seated officials. *And don't take any shit from the bastards…*

*

Jiang Lei bowed low, even as the four men rose from their seats.

'Ch'un tzu... it is a great delight to have you here... to what do I owe this most pleasant and welcome visit?'

It was said plainly, without any obvious irony, yet they knew as well as he that they were as welcome as the plague.

The eldest – a minor Dragon of the Seventh Rank – returned his bow and answered him. He clearly felt he had no need to be polite, even to a general.

'Where is he? Where is Wang Yu-Lai?'

Jiang lowered his head respectfully. 'Cadre Wang is under arrest. He—'

The old man interrupted him. 'You will bring him here. Now!'

Jiang kept his eyes averted. 'Of course, my lord.'

He turned away, looking to his duty officer. 'Captain Shan... bring Cadre Wang here, at once...'

'Yes, General...'

Shan ran off.

Jiang turned, meeting the old man's eyes. 'As I said...'

But the old man was having none of it. 'Wang Yu-Lai will answer to us, and no one else, General Jiang. Just how long has he been detained?'

'Several hours...'

'And you did not think to contact us?'

Jiang lowered his head again. They were not going to let this go, it seemed. What Wang had done would be ignored or smoothed over.

It was evil. Purest evil.

But Jiang's priority now was to keep his family out of trouble, whatever happened to himself.

He met the man's eyes again; saw that he was still looking for an answer to his question.

'Oh... forgive me, my lord... it was just that I was busy...'

'Busy?' The old man stood. He had a long, sneering face, in

which the deep-set eyes were as cold as a lizard's. 'So busy as to neglect your duty?'

It was a leading question, and Jiang Lei realized suddenly just what was happening. They were filming this. Trying to incriminate him.

'I know my duty,' he said coldly, vowing not to say another word.

Jiang thought suddenly of Reed, sitting there back in the craft, waiting to see how things turned out. The old man had not mentioned him, so maybe he didn't know about him yet. Maybe Wang hadn't had the chance.

Had he been another man, Jiang might have considered using Reed as a bargaining chip. But he was as he was and had instantly dismissed the notion. For Reed was the whole point of this. To keep such as he inside the system. Good men. Sound, intelligent men. For if one did not carefully discriminate between who should be citizens and who excluded, then it might as well all be handed over to Wang and his kind. For their cynical amusement.

Jiang Lei met the old man's eyes once more, noting the contempt there.

Oh, this changed things. Definitely. But not his tactics. His only hope was still to hang on until word came from Tsao Ch'un.

And if it doesn't?

The Dragon's men stepped over to Jiang, surrounding him. They showed him enough respect not to manhandle him, yet they had drawn their guns against him, indicating that he should return to his tent.

The Thousand Eyes were in charge here now. As he turned towards his tent, he saw them, beginning to go about their business, getting every last piece of information they could find and piecing it all together.

He had misjudged them. He knew that now. To him, Wang had simply been a nuisance. An irritation. But to them...

This was how they worked. Stamping down on any challenge to

their power. Protecting their own. Making sure their eyes were kept open, their vigilance maintained. It was almost admirable.

Only it bred such men as Wang. Sneaks and bullies and sadists. Half-men parading as heroes. Little shits with vile, inbred imaginations.

How he hated them.

But they, it seemed, had won this time. Unless some small miracle occurred, they would find out everything. And then...?

Jiang Lei sighed heavily. It was no good fooling himself any longer. An hour he had at most, then it was over.

It was while he sat there at his desk, brooding, that Ma Feng came to him.

Ma Feng stopped, bowing low, not two metres from where Jiang Lei sat. Another of his men stood just behind him, out of Jiang's line of sight.

Jiang looked up. 'Yes, Ma Feng... what is it now?'

Ma Feng straightened. There was a half-smile on his face. 'Master... I thought, as things stood, you might wish to question our prisoner again.'

'Our prisoner?' Jiang frowned.

Ma Feng stepped back. There, in full guard's uniform, stood the *Hung Mao*, Reed.

'Ma Feng!'

'Forgive me, Master, if I have done wrong, only I thought, as there was so little time, you might wish to finish questioning *Shih* Reed.'

He ought to have been angry. Ought to have raged at his man for doing this, but all he really felt was a faint amusement.

Reed waited, head bowed, like a good Han. Jiang Lei smiled at the sight.

'*Shih* Reed... you can discard the costume now.'

'Thank you, Jiang Lei, I...'

He spoke over the man, not wanting Reed to get the wrong idea.

'Shih Reed... You must understand clearly how things are. I cannot protect you any longer. The Thousand Eyes are in charge here now, and they will shortly know of your existence, just as soon as they have debriefed Cadre Wang. And when they do they will come to me and I will have to hand you to them.' He sighed. 'It is not how I wished it, but there we are. Your fate was cast long ago, it seems.'

Reed gave a little shrug, then began to discard the uniform.

Jiang Lei stood. 'Ma Feng... you will stand guard outside. No one is to enter here without my express permission, neh?'

'Master...' Ma Feng bowed low, then went outside.

Jiang looked to Reed again and smiled. 'Please... pull up a chair.'

Reed hesitated.

'What is it?'

'My family...'

'You mean, my promise to you? Do not worry, Shih Reed. I will do everything in my power to protect them. Besides, they are not on the list. There is no reason why our friends should be interested in them.'

'But surely, my son...?'

'Does not have to be your son. We will give him another name, neh? Something that will keep him safe.'

Reed met Jiang Lei's eyes, his own filled with gratitude. 'Thank you.'

The two men sat.

'Well?' Jiang Lei said after a moment. 'Is there anything you wish to ask me?'

Reed hesitated, then. 'My friends... the ones I told you about earlier... is there any record of what happened to them?'

Jiang considered it a moment, then laughed. 'What the hell, eh? They will find out anyway...'

Reed sat forward. 'What do you mean?'

'I mean, the moment we access your file, alarm bells will sound. The only reason they didn't before now is because I kept my enquiries vague and general. But any *detailed* queries on your file are tagged to alert enquiring minds...'

'Our friends, you mean?'

Jiang nodded. 'Who else? But they will know about you anyway, just as soon as Cadre Wang has had his say, and then they'll be marching into this tent, demanding to know where you are and why I didn't hand you over...'

'And you will be in trouble...'

'Again.'

The two men laughed.

'Well?' Jiang asked, his expression suddenly more serious. 'You really want to know?'

Reed nodded. 'Yes. If we have time.'

Jiang was penning the last line of the poem when the silk flap whooshed open and a stranger – a tall Han in a simple black silk one-piece – stepped into the tent.

Jiang half rose, then sat again, knowing from the man's self-satisfied look that they had got what they wanted.

'So you know everything...'

'No thanks to you, General Jiang.'

'Does your Master wish to see me?'

'My Master?' The man almost smiled. 'You mean Huang Tzu Kung, I take it...'

'So the Seventh Dragon has a name.'

Only now that it came to it, Jiang did not feel like sparring verbally with this one.

'And Reed?'

The man walked across, picked up the sheet of paper Jiang had been writing on and studied it a moment. He put it down, then turned, facing Jiang again.

'You will forget the matter, Jiang Lei. He is ours now.'

Jiang sighed. So it had all been for nothing.

'What will happen now? Shall I be replaced?'

'It seems likely, neh?'

'And Wang Yu-Lai... I guess you'll reward the little shit. Give him another promotion, yes?'

'He has been a faithful servant...'

'He's been a...'

Jiang almost said it. That horrible c word. But why waste his breath on the man? His gamble had failed.

He was so distracted that at first he didn't hear it, didn't feel the faint vibration in the air that slowly grew and grew.

It was the stranger who noticed it first. 'What is that?' he asked, looking up through the thin blue silk of the tent's walls.

As they stepped outside, the noise grew slowly louder.

Jiang knew at once, from the craft's markings, who it was. His heart soared.

It was Tsao Ch'un's own cruiser!

As it set down, men spilled out, securing the perimeter.

Jiang looked to the man standing beside him. 'Just who *are* you, incidentally?'

The stranger sneered at him. 'It is not your business who I am.'

'But if I don't know who you are...'

The man thrust an ID card at him. It was purest black. Jiang did not have to activate it. He knew at once what it was. It meant that the man was *shou*. Was, quite literally, a 'hand'. One of the twelve personal aides to the Ministry's First Dragon. They were his 'hands', whenever he had to get them dirty.

A powerful man indeed. But right now he was outranked and outgunned.

Only as the ramp came down, it was not Tsao Ch'un who stepped out into the daylight, but one of his servants, a small, dark-haired man in lavender silks whom Jiang recognized immediately.

Wen P'ing... Tsao Ch'un has sent Wen P'ing.

Jiang groaned inwardly, then walked across to greet the new-comer, the *shou* beside him.

Ten metres from him they stopped, both of them bowing low. Wen P'ing looked from one to the other and smiled, making no attempt whatsoever to return their courtesy.

'General Jiang... Master Teng... I understand there has been a slight misunderstanding.'

Master Teng, the *shou*, looked up at that, a flash of irritation in his eyes. But he knew better than to argue with Wen P'ing, for of all Tsao Ch'un's men, Wen was the most slippery. And the most dangerous.

Jiang Lei sighed. Either Tsao Ch'un had not received his note, or this was his answer.

'No?' Wen P'ing continued, his smile fixed now. 'Or am I mis-taken, *ch'un tzu*? Has everything been settled in my absence?'

Jiang Lei wet his lips, then spoke. 'Forgive me, Lord Wen, but should we not wait for the Seventh Dragon?'

'Oh, heavens no!' Wen P'ing said, walking past them and look-ing about him as if admiring the view. 'I'm sure we can come to an agreement here and now, among the three of us, neh? After all... we are all our Masters' hands...' He looked to Teng. 'Some quite literally so.'

Teng bowed lower. His eyes, however, had narrowed almost to a slit, trying to work out just what Wen was getting at.

'You see,' Wen continued, 'my Master, the great lord of us all, Tsao Ch'un, gets most distressed when he hears of such rivalry between brothers. And surely we are all brothers, for we work towards the same fine ends, neh?'

Teng and Jiang looked to each other at that.

Seeing it, Wen P'ing smiled. 'Ah... I see you understand. Excel-lent... I feel we're getting somewhere. But let's make this absolutely clear, neh? Let's clarify things. General Jiang...'

'Yes, my lord...'

'You must learn to share what you know. In future there must be no secrets. No holding back of information. You must learn to be transparent. Is that clear?'

Jiang bowed. 'It is clear, my lord.'

'Good... and as for you, Master Teng... as representative of our most valued brother, the First Dragon, you must encourage your agents to know their place and practise restraint...'

'Restraint, my lord?'

'Yes, *restraint*.' Wen glared at him a moment, then let his face soften.

The smile returned. They were all friends again, that smile seemed to say.

'So, *ch'un tzu*... let us put this matter behind us. Let us agree to move on, in harmony. Hand in glove, so to speak.'

He paused, then looked to Jiang Lei.

'General Jiang, I understand there are future citizens to be processed.'

'There are, my lord.'

'Then you will resume your normal duties immediately.'

Jiang bowed low, surprised and relieved by Wen P'ing's words.

'Yes, my lord. Thank you, my lord.'

'As for you, Master Teng... your grievance has been noted. There will be no further obstruction of your agents. They do necessary work. Without them the empire would be endangered. Our Master knows that and greatly values your work. But in the matter of the listed one, Reed, he asks that you review the matter with a more... let us say... *sympathetic eye*.'

Teng's head came up at that, saw the hardness in Wen's face and quickly lowered his eyes again.

'It shall be so, my lord.'

'Good. Then we are almost finished here. There is but one final thing needs to be settled. General Jiang...'

'Yes, my lord...'

'Your comments on Cadre Wang are noted. That said, we cannot allow personal feelings to dictate our actions. Wang Yu-Lai will be reinstated, and all complaints against him erased, you understand? Like it or not, you will work with him. And he with you. That is how it will be. You understand me, General?'

'I understand.'

Wen P'ing smiled. 'Good. I am glad we have settled this. There is nothing my Master hates more than such... disagreements. And what my Master hates...'

Both Jiang and Teng bowed their heads again at the threat implicit in those words.

Jiang Lei could see that Wen was about to turn away; to return to his ship without another word, but he could not let him go. Not without asking.

'Lord Wen...'

'Yes, General Jiang?'

'Forgive me, but... have you seen Chun Hua recently? I just wondered...'

Wen's eyes narrowed. He knew *something*. Jiang could see that. Only he shook his head.

'I am afraid I have no news for you, Jiang Lei.'

Jiang bowed one final time, as if in gratitude for Wen's words, but inside he felt an anguish that only long separation could bring about.

We are our Masters' hands.

Jiang stood there, when Wen P'ing had gone, watching as representatives of The Thousand Eyes packed up and made ready to depart.

So Tsao Ch'un *had* received his note. Or so it seemed, even if Wen P'ing had not referred to it explicitly, for the matter of Reed had been dealt with, and to some satisfaction. Only...

Jiang closed his eyes. Could he bear to pay the price? Could he stand working with that odious little shit after all that had happened?

He didn't know. Only what choice did he have?

'Ma Feng!' he called, turning towards his newly promoted captain of the guard.

'Yes, General?'

'Bring the cruiser. There's work to be done.'

Old Sarum was a place, like Corfe, from another age. And like many of these last remaining sites, it would soon be lost to sight, buried beneath the footings of the great city which, even as Jiang Lei looked east, grew slowly before his eyes.

From high up on that great mound, he could see the machines – thousands of the things, some of them huge, some tiny – busy at their work, while small teams of armed guards looked on, there to make sure that, if one of the 'bots' malfunctioned, they'd deal with it before it ran amok.

The big machines, of course, never went wrong. They were simple mechanisms, brutal in their design, like massive spiders, six of their eight legs steadying them while the other two gripped the anchor pillars and hammered them deep into the earth. And while it did, another gargantuan mechanism rested nearby, ready to feed the big *chih chu*, as it was called, with whatever was required, the struts and spars that gave the city its strength, stacked on its back. Everything on a giant scale, not a single piece less than half a li in length, building the shell of the city, on which all else was hung.

Jiang knew very little about the engineering involved, but he did know that the great anchor pillars were earthquake proof – that they'd been designed to take shocks up to 8.8 on the old Richter scale, with little more than a severe buffeting.

What fascinated him, however, were the smaller mechanisms – the surveyor bots and the smaller *chih chu* – most of them less than a few *ch'i* in diameter. They scuttled about like living things, measuring, marking, then spinning out floors and walls from the big tanks of liquid ice they carried on their backs.

These, it had to be said, were both more complex and less reliable machines. From time to time they *would* go wrong, and then you'd see one of the teams of guards 'go hunting'. He'd seen one himself, two months back. The machine had suffered a knock when it fell from one of the struts, and had begun to act erratically. Before one of the supervisors could deal with it and shut it down, it had slipped away, firing off short bursts of ice into the air, the long gobbets of super-plastic hardening almost instantly, making strange, translucent shapes that sparkled in the sunlight.

At once the guards were off, chasing it. But it wasn't a simple matter of blasting the bot into pieces. Liquid ice was a dangerous substance, and if a tank of it went up, they were as like as not to get cut to pieces or covered in the stuff. The only proper way to deal with a malfunctioning *chih chu* was to shoot its legs away, then laser-roast its artificial cortex, and the men enjoyed showing off their skill at doing this. Only this once the damn thing tumbled over, just as one of the guards was roasting it, and the beam caught the tank.

The sound could be heard ten miles away. A great cloud of liquefied ice was thrown out by the explosion, which, on contact with the air, hardened instantly.

It was as if someone had fired off a whole shower of crystalline, knife-sharp shards. Anyone within thirty *ch'i* was cut to pieces, but the worst fate befell those who were closer, for they found themselves embedded in the ice.

It was like being buried alive in the very toughest kind of Perspex. There were special chemicals they could have used to 'melt' the stuff, but those in charge had decided that they'd rather lose a few soldiers now and then than let any of the chemical 'ice-eaters' fall into the wrong hands.

And wisely so, perhaps, only sometimes they would take hours to die, slowly suffocating and gasping for each breath, the hard plastic making it impossible to struggle.

On the occasion Jiang Lei witnessed, the guards were relatively lucky. They had lost two men and had three more badly injured, but most of them had got off relatively unharmed. It had all been a bit of a mess, but it wasn't a disaster. A disaster was when something happened that slowed down the construction work, like the earth subsiding beneath the big mechanisms.

The loss of a few men didn't matter. Not in the greater scheme of things.

Right now, however, Jiang could not help but think that in this his countrymen were wrong. The Han had always prided themselves on their ability not merely to plan but to deliver such great projects – the Great Wall, the Grand Canal, the First Emperor's Terracotta Army, all were fine examples – yet he had come to question that. To challenge what it cost in human lives, and in suffering. Why did they value the grandiose above the human? What was wrong in their make-up that they could not see how futile all of this was – this ridiculous, strutting pride of theirs that needed always to be expressed in some massive, costly endeavour.

Then again, wasn't this what they had always done? Wasn't it just a new phase in the age-old process of destruction and regeneration? A physical manifestation of Yin and Yang?

Jiang looked about him. Old Sarum was gone. Only the brick outlines of its ancient chambers remained, embedded in the earth.

All of those lives. All those long generations of people, with their hopes and desires, their fears and anxieties...

He looked up, sensing a faint vibration in the air.

In the distance, beyond the edge of the regularly serrated white line that marked the city's edge, one of the massive lifting craft made its slow way towards them. It was like some giant, hovering beetle, its huge load suspended on great straps of ice beneath.

Everything on a giant scale...

At another time there might have been a poem in it; something about the ghosts of Old Sarum and the coming of the Han. Of cultures so diverse, so distinct and separate in their ways, that they may as well have been different species. Only Jiang had other things on his mind, chief of which was how to cope with Wang Yu-Lai.

Wang. What he would like to do with Wang!

Mary stood in the queue, waiting to be seen. It was cold, and though most of them had been allowed to keep their blankets, two hours of standing outside had taken its toll. People were beginning to look frail, especially the old and the young.

In front of her, Peter stood with Meg, his arms wrapped about her as they waited there, keeping her warm. He had been so good these past few days. In spite of all that had happened, he had kept his chin up, worrying more about them than about himself. It was easy to forget that he was still only fourteen. Another of his age might have buckled under the weight. But not Peter. He was like his father in that. He had an inner strength.

She would have smiled, only she didn't think she would ever smile again. Not since they'd taken Jake that second time. It was hard enough getting through the day when he *was* there, but without him...

Mary turned, looking to Beth and Cath. There was a grim determination in their faces, only she knew they too were suffering. It wasn't just the physical conditions, it was the uncertainty; the not knowing whether they would get through all of this, or even what its purpose was. And in the back of their minds, at all times, was the dark shadow of the Holocaust. What if that was what this really was? What if all the hopeful talk of resettlement was just one big lie?

She couldn't even bring herself to speak of it. Only it never left her mind. Not for a single moment.

Mary went up on her toes briefly, looking past the heads towards the front. He was here again – the one in the silks who'd come to see Jake that time. He sat on the platform at the front, quizzing each of them in turn then referring to the machine he carried. Jake had seemed to think he was a good man, only how could any of this be good? How could anyone who did this kind of thing sleep at night, knowing the heartache and anxiety they caused?

Beth nudged her.

She turned, meaning to ask her what she wanted, and froze.

It was him. The one who'd come before. What had Jake called him? Wang... that was it. The one with the cold, sadistic eyes.

Her stomach turned at the sight of him. Only she realized now that he was looking directly at her and smiling, like he knew who she was.

The thought chilled her.

She turned back, hoping he'd go away. Only moments later, she had a sense of someone standing right behind her. She could feel his warm breath on her neck.

He spoke softly, quietly, as if to her alone.

'You're Reed's woman, yes?'

Mary closed her eyes. What did she answer? What was *safe*?

She shook her head.

The voice continued softly, insinuatingly. 'No? That surprises me. Because that was what you said, only the other day, when we questioned you. You said you were Reed's woman then... but now you're not.'

'He's gone,' she said, forcing the words out.

There was something awful, something almost satanic about him standing there, just behind her. Speaking in that soft, almost serpentine fashion. As for the other, who sat up front, did he condone this?

She wanted to turn and slap the creature's face. To scream at him to go away. But she was powerless, for if he knew who she

414

was, then doubtless he knew who her children were, and it was the way of such men to use such knowledge.

'What do you want?'

The man laughed at that. A hideous, corrupt laughter. 'Why should I want anything?'

Why, indeed? Only she knew he did. Knew that, for some reason, he had fixated on them. Was it something Jake had done? Or was it simply that – sociopath that he clearly was – he had *chosen* them?

It was too frightening a thought to entertain. Yet entertain it she must, if they were to survive.

She was about to say something more, when he stepped past her, his silks brushing against her arm.

Seeing him standing there, directly behind Meg and Peter, Mary felt an overwhelming aversion. The way he stood there, cold and threatening, so close that his breath mingled with theirs. She had never seen its like. Never experienced it. If she'd had a weapon she would have killed him, there and then, and damn the consequences. Only she had no weapon. And it mattered what she did. They had to come out of this alive. All of them. If they didn't she'd have failed.

Wang reached out, touching Peter's shoulder.

Peter jerked away, surprised, looking round as he did, his eyes growing wide as he saw who it was.

'You!' Wang barked, all the softness gone from him. 'What's your name?'

'P-p-peter,' he stammered, taken aback by the violence of the query.

'P-peter Reed.'

'And your father... is he here *with* you?'

'No... no, he's...'

The man was sneering now. Leaning over Peter threateningly and sneering.

'He's dead, that's what he is... fucking dead! And you would be too, if I had my way. Scum like you...'

Mary stared at Wang, both astonished and horrified. Where did that come from?

At the front, someone was shouting now. Soldiers were making their way towards them, pushing through the crowd now to get to them.

'Come on,' Wang was saying, pushing Peter back viciously. 'Just give me a reason...'

'Peter, no!' she screamed, seeing how Peter had stepped back, raising his fist.

Only right then someone else pushed through and, shoving Peter to one side, took a swing at Wang.

There was the crack of bone and Wang went down, holding his nose and howling.

Frank Goodman stood there, the big Swanage man towering over the fallen Han, gesturing for him to get up and fight him like a man.

Only Wang wasn't going to get up. As the guards arrived, a couple of them lifted him and carried him away, while others grabbed hold of Goodman and dragged him towards one of the huts on the far side of the camp.

Mary looked to Peter. He was looking down now, at the ground, his chest rising and falling.

'We don't know,' she began.

Peter shook his head. 'We do. He's dead. And I bet that bastard was the one who pulled the trigger.'

Someone else was pushing through towards them now, people moving out of his way. It was the tall Han in the silks.

'What's happening here?'

Mary looked to him, disappointment in her eyes. 'It's nothing...'

'Nothing?' The man's eyes seemed concerned, but who was to tell? It all felt like subterfuge to her. And if Jake *were* dead...

'Come,' the man said. 'Follow me. Let's get you processed now.'

Mary hesitated, not knowing whether he meant just her or all of them.

'Come on,' the man said, as if he read her mind. 'Yes, all of you... But quick now, before I change my mind and leave you in the cold.'

Sometimes it's best not to know.

Jake sat there in the belly of the cruiser, mulling over what he'd seen. When he'd asked Jiang Lei if he knew the fate of his friends, it was an altogether vague enquiry, the kind of question you ask because it's been in the back of your mind for years. The kind you think you'll never get an answer to.

Only there was an answer. In fact, there was a file on each of them, sub-files to the greater file headed up 'Jacob Reed'.

He had not read the full files, not seen more than a few minutes of the hours of taped material of their interrogations. He hadn't wanted to, not once he'd realized what it was.

They had been tortured – taken to what looked like an abattoir, stripped and strung up. There, while the cameras rolled, they had been asked all manner of things about their good friend Jake. Where he went, what he did, who he saw, where he was likely to go.

Endless questions, while between times they 'softened them up'.

He'd not watched those bits. He hadn't the stomach for it. Especially what they did to Jenny. Not in his wildest imagination would he have thought they could be so foul. And to what end? To get to him. To find out where he was.

If he'd known...

No, even that was a lie. If he'd known he'd have stayed where he was, in hiding and safe, for they would surely have done the same to him.

He had seen the final photos of them, laid out on the slab, their bloodless, lifeless bodies pocked with scars and burns, each mark the token of a separate agony. But it was their faces that haunted him; those pale, ravaged faces with their sightless eyes and damaged mouths. Lost, they were. Abandoned and despairing. Knowing that no one would come. Longing for death, long after hope had fled.

It had made him weep. How could one human being do that to another? And for what?

After all, what threat had he been outside of the datscape?

Or was it just some obsessive sense of tidiness on their part?

And how could that not sour him? How could he now go forward, trusting them, having seen what they were capable of? How could he believe in their brave new world, when it was built on such foundations?

The trouble was, he had no choice. It was conform or die. There was no third option. Jiang Lei had told him as much. One did not have a say in things.

His instinct to flee had been right. Only it had also been futile. There was no running from it. No hiding.

When China comes...

Jake sighed, then stood, pacing the cabin, restless now.

The writing had been on the wall for a long time. Only none of them had seen the danger. None of them had seen just how ruthless China could be when woken. They had thought that to share a world with them, to trade with them and buy each others' goods, would somehow change them, make them more democratic, more Western in their ways. Only China was China. And when it came, it came like a swooping dragon, fiery-breathed and vengeful.

Jiang Lei had told him much that he hadn't known. Tsao Ch'un, it seems, had overseen it all. Had played it like a game, never for a moment considering the suffering he caused, the death and desolation. For him only one thing was important: to destroy America without triggering a nuclear war. Geoff Horsfield had been right.

It was an immensely difficult and risky strategy, yet it had worked.

Huge fleets of submarines had shadowed their American counterparts, ready for the day, while teams of special agents, set in place and trained to hack into US defence systems, bided their time.

Coordination had been the key. An attack on the Market had been followed within hours by a lock-down of key computer systems throughout the West. Whole cities had lost their power and thus their working infrastructures, while the removal of key personnel by assassination made the decision-making process grind to a halt.

It was, as Tsao Ch'un had termed it, 'like cutting off both the head and balls and then tearing out the heart'.

At his order ten thousand sleepers suddenly woke, making their presence felt on the streets of Western cities – bombers and snipers and arsonists, spreading chaos and fear wherever they went. Feeding the flames.

Some missiles had got off, of course. Nine had landed on the Chinese mainland. The cities of Ningbo, Shenyang and Nanchong had been reduced to ashes. But the rest of them – some tens of thousands of nuclear missiles – had never been fired. They had either been shut down or their facilities destroyed by Tsao Ch'un's special units.

In China itself, there had been chaos in those first few weeks. Tsao Ch'un had expected as much, and let the storm blow itself out before sending in his troops. By which time people were glad to see order restored, a firm hand imposed. Tsao Ch'un was seen as a hero, a protector of the people.

It was the beginning of a new age. The old order – the *Western* order – had been destroyed. It had been shut down and switched off. To all intents and purposes it was dead. But Tsao Ch'un knew that if his new world were to be built, let alone last, he would have to make sure that the old world stayed dead.

What followed was the most critical part of Tsao Ch'un's scheme, known to all who took part in it as 'The Long Campaign'.

Whenever there was the slightest sign of 're-awakening' – the opening of a radio station, say, or the rebuilding of some key installation – Tsao Ch'un's men would be there at once to destroy it, wherever in the world it was. It was a campaign to prevent and suppress not only new growth but the repair and reconstruction of old technologies. The old world – the world of the Western powers – was not to be allowed to return.

It was not easy. Several times things seemed to have evolved beyond their control. But Tsao Ch'un's forces always triumphed. Until that urge to return things back to how they were, driven as it had been by the memory of the past, began to falter as a new generation grew up, a host of new people – innocents, one might call them – whose memory of that world was second hand at best. A new generation to whom the old machines meant nothing; to whom the idea of a world 'connected up', with instant news from every point on the globe, seemed more a fantasy than anything that had really happened.

And so a new Dark Ages fell. A time of warlords and marauding bands.

It was a simpler, more brutal world. A world ripe for the plucking, if you were capable. And one man was. Tsao Ch'un. For this he had prepared, and now the third and final phase began, as the great, spider-like machines were sent out from Pei Ch'ing, to build the great city that was to last ten thousand years. A city which, like some vast glacier, would stretch across the globe, from ocean to ocean, quite literally burying the past.

The very thought of it daunted Jake. It made his balls retract simply thinking of how small he was in the face of such mighty processes. To destroy a world to build a world. It was inhuman to think in such a fashion. Yet one man had dared and, having dared, had triumphed. Thus far, anyway.

Jake sat again, looking about him, wondering how much longer it would be.

It had been hours since Jiang Lei had left, but there was still no sign of Mary and the kids. No tangible proof that Jiang's promise would be kept.

Jiang Lei had told him what came next. Another camp. But this one different. A 're-education camp'.

'The past,' Jiang had said, 'is dead. There is only the future. You must embrace it, Shih Reed, for there is nothing else. You understand?'

He didn't. Not yet. But he was sure he would. In time.

Mary watched as Jiang Lei stood and, with the slightest bow, handed Beth her ID card.

Beth was the last of them to be processed. As she turned and looked across at her mother, she smiled.

Thank god, Mary thought. If any one of them had not got through...

Only they had. So now they must get on with things, without Jake.

They were about to follow the others over to the transport ship, when a couple of the guards came across and, barring their way, indicated another, smaller ship, just across from them.

'But we're through,' Mary said, pointing to the larger ship, afraid that this was one last horrible twist. 'Our people are all in there.'

'You must go,' one of them said, gesturing to the smaller craft. 'You not with the others now.'

Mary turned, looking back to the senior official, but he was already processing the next person.

The guard nudged her forward. 'Now... you must go. The general say you must go...'

Her head went down. So this was it. To get so far and then...

'Come on,' she said, looking to the others. 'Let's do as the man says.'

She could see, even from this distance, that it was a military craft, not a transport. Two soldiers guarded its ramp. As they got closer, the two stood back, gesturing with their rifles that they should get on board.

Mary looked about her. None of the others could meet her eyes now.

They all knew, just as she knew, that something had gone wrong.

At the foot of the ramp she stopped, looking back across the camp. It was probably the last time she would ever see her neighbours. All those friends. All those happy years she'd spent with them.

'Beth... Cath... come here... Peter, look after Meg...'

She took her two eldest under her arms, then began to climb the ramp. Only right then someone appeared in the darkness just above them.

'Mary...'

The girls squealed and rushed forward, hugging Jake, while Peter stood back, with Mary, looking on.

She looked to the boy. Tears were streaming down his face, but he was smiling. Grinning like an idiot.

Jake kissed all of the girls, then, stepping away from them, came down and hugged Peter, clasping the boy to him fiercely.

'Thank god... thank fucking god!'

Peter squeezed him back, then released him.

Jake turned, facing Mary.

'Well? You coming along?'

Mary still looked uncertain. 'That craft...?'

'Is Jiang Lei's own. His men are to fly us to the camp.'

'Another camp?'

'Yes, but a better one than this. That's where we're going to begin to become citizens.'

'Ah...' And she almost smiled.

But Jake *was* smiling now. 'You know, I thought I'd never see you again. I thought...' He shook his head. 'I can't tell you, Mary. Those people...'

'But it's okay now?'

'Yeah...' He sighed, then, 'Well? Do I get a kiss?'

She stepped across and put her arms about him, putting her lips to his. For a moment there was only that. Then, realizing that the children were watching, the two moved back, awkward again, like teenagers.

Beth looked to her sisters. 'Let's get inside. And, Jake...?'

'Yes, my darling girl?'

'We're glad you're back.'

Jiang Lei looked on as his men took down and packed his tent.

They were moving today, setting up a new encampment, ready for the push on Dorchester. Their job here was done, the villages emptied, the people processed. Across the way, near one of the big cruisers, he could see Wang Yu-Lai, talking with the men.

Wang had become more arrogant since the incident with Reed. What had been difficult before was now, Jiang felt, impossible, for Wang and his Masters had taken Wen P'ing's instruction to cooperate as an invitation to interfere.

That little skirmish the other day, at the processing, was, Jiang Lei knew, just the start. It had caused the death of yet another fine, upstanding man, a potential citizen, punished for something which, in essence, had been entirely Wang's fault.

A broken nose was the very least he himself would have given Wang.

And Wang would do yet more mischief. He would take every opportunity now to insinuate himself and make things hard for Jiang. Any pretence Wang had shown at showing him respect had vanished. He was there now to make Jiang's life hell, to wear him down until he quit and let one of their puppets take his place.

No doubt they already had a candidate in mind...

Only the business with Reed had hardened him. Had reminded him just why he had taken this appointment.

He was there to give some degree of reality to the semblance. To fulfil the ancient dream of wisdom in government – the Confucian ideal. If he let go his belief in that, then what was left? Only barbarism. Only the rule of naked force.

Even so, he found it hard some days, keeping that particular lamp alight.

Ma Feng, his new stripes showing on his arm, approached him.

'We are ready, General. Do you wish to come on board?'

Jiang hesitated. It was tempting to leave Wang where he was. To lift off, leaving him to travel in another of the craft, but that would only have resulted in yet another tiresome report, another petty complaint.

Besides which, Wen P'ing had ordered him to cooperate.

'Captain Ma... go and invite Wang Yu-Lai to travel with me. Tell him... I would welcome him as my guest.'

Ma Feng's eyes widened.

'Yes, General!'

As Jiang climbed aboard, lifting his silks up as he went, so he found himself frowning. Was this a punishment for some former incarnation? Had he, in some previous life, incurred this awful penalty?

To suffer at the hands of smaller men...

Jiang took his seat, strapping himself into the plush black leather, calming himself inwardly, knowing, even before Wang appeared a moment later, that he would need all of his patience in the coming weeks.

See it as a test, he told himself. Rise above such pettiness.

Only the very sound of Wang's voice grated on his ears, and as the man came into the cabin, Jiang found himself staring at him with contempt, unable not to.

He tried to smile. 'Wang Yu-Lai... please, make yourself comfortable.'

Wang's smile was equally fake. His eyes met Jiang's for the briefest moment, then looked away, like they had better things to look at.

'Pilot Wu...' Jiang called, leaning forward slightly, to look into the cockpit. 'Fly us over the old castle, neh? I'd like to see it one final time before we leave.'

He settled back, aware that Wang was watching him, no longer concealing it, like he was studying some specimen in a jar.

It made his flesh crawl. To be the subject of observation of such a man.

'What is it, Wang Yu-Lai?'

'I was just thinking... about Reed...'

'What about him?'

'Just that I would like to see him one last time. He seemed... special to you. It would be interesting to find out why.'

Jiang looked down at his hands, saw how they were gripping each other. Such little things no doubt gave him away, but he was damned if he would react in any other fashion.

Besides, Reed was safe. There was no way Wang could touch him now. He was in the programme. He and his family. As far from here as Jiang could send them.

He looked to Wang. 'Have you any family, Wang Yu-Lai? A wife? Brothers?'

Jiang knew the answer. Knew it because The Thousand Eyes did not use any other kind. Wang was an orphan. Neither was he allowed to marry. For the agents of the Ministry were to have no distractions. And no weaknesses to be exploited by others. A family made a man weak. Made him vulnerable. As Jiang knew to his cost.

Wang had turned away, scowling.

Good, Jiang thought, smiling to himself. Then there's still a chance I might stay sane. If I can get under his skin as he gets under mine.

Only would it be enough?

The craft lifted.

'Pilot Wu,' he called. 'Give me the front view.'

'Yes, General.'

At once the big screen in front of Jiang lit up, showing the view from the cockpit. As they climbed, so the view opened up before them, the countryside a tapestry of greens and browns to their left, the sea in the distance, while to their right were the city's new-built outposts, great hexagonal slabs of whiteness that rested like marbled mausoleums on the land.

'It's an impressive sight, neh, Wang Yu-Lai?'

Wang shrugged. It seemed his purpose not to agree with Jiang.

'Tell me, Cadre Wang... are you specially trained to be such an arse?'

Wang glared at him. 'I would be careful what you say, General Jiang...'

Jiang was watching the screen, seeing, as the craft turned, the mound of the ancient castle come into view to the far left of the picture.

'Oh, I know what Wen P'ing said, it's just...'

The words died in his mouth. They were gone! The great stone towers were gone! And the mound itself... it had been gouged in several places. Eaten away, it seemed. Massive diggers with caterpillar tracks were working away at it, chewing it up, whole teams of men shovelling the earth and rock into big tippers. Long lines of them that covered the once-green slopes.

Jiang felt a sadness at the sight. It was just as he'd said – they were not going to let such a small thing interrupt their path – only seeing it made him realize what a shame it was. Yes, and how much was being lost.

One whole world traded in for another. A world made of plastic, filled with reconstituted men.

That much he didn't envy Reed. Jiang looked down, remembering something. There was a film he'd seen, years ago, before the Collapse, when he was still a young man. Even then the film had been old. But it had been a classic. One of the West's finest critiques of itself. Jack Nicholson had starred, and a whole bunch of other eccentric characters. The one who'd caught his attention, however, was the nurse. The one in charge of the asylum. He couldn't remember now what the film had been called, but its ending had always haunted him. How the Nicholson character had finally been crushed, his brain lobotomized, his memories and his rebellious spirit taken from him.

That, it seemed to Jiang, was what they were doing here, only on a massive scale. Doing it not to an individual but to a whole population. Reducing it. Lobotomizing it. And, in so doing, turning it into a world where people weren't given a choice; where they were forced to conform, to toe the line. Or die.

And how, in supervising that, did he differ from the likes of Wang? Too far, he told himself. Much, much too far.

For wasn't that the ethos that had driven them, these past three millennia? To build a society based on conformity and acceptable behaviour? To reward virtue and punish errant behaviour?

Yes, only Jiang knew this was different. For the *Hung Mao* especially. For what they were in effect creating here was a breed of zombies, of amnesiacs, schooled to forget their collective past and embrace the lie.

Jiang swallowed, bitter suddenly, unsettled and angry at having had these thoughts awoken in him.

He looked across. Wang was watching him still, the vaguest suggestion of amusement in the corners of his mouth.

The castle was behind them now, ahead lay only countryside.

'Cadre Wang...?'

'Yes, General Jiang?'

'Do not try my patience. Not today.'

*

427

Jake woke, startled into wakefulness. Then he realized. It was Peter. Peter had been shaking him.

'Wha-ah?' he drawled lazily. He had been having a dream. About his childhood. About the time before the accident.

He closed his eyes again. ''S too early...'

Peter shook him again. 'Dad... you gotta get up. Didn't you hear? We've got to go to the main hall. We've got to assemble there...'

Assemble. Now there was a word he hadn't heard in years.

'In a minute...'

He tried to pull the sheets up over him, but Peter pulled them off.

'Come on... we'll get in trouble if we're late.'

Jake sat up, yawning. 'Trouble?'

Then he saw it all. The long rows of beds. The identical-looking people with their shaven heads and ochre-coloured one-pieces.

He reached up, felt the stubble on his scalp.

No dream then. This is it.

He turned sharply, looking to see where Mary and the girls were.

They had arrived late last night. He remembered that now. Remembered the showers, the electric shavers, how all dignity had been stripped from them. Oh, and especially the guards, who'd seemed to take a salacious delight in watching their public humiliation.

The four of them were there, only yards away.

'Yes,' Mary said, as if she read his mind. 'I know what it looks like. But it'll grow back.'

Cath, standing beside her mother, looked like she might cry at any moment, so too Meg, but Beth stood taller, looked stronger for it.

'Like Ripley,' he said, and saw her smile at that.

Peter too had been shaved. Only on him it looked almost natural.

'Come on,' he said. 'We've been called twice now!'

'Called...? What, for breakfast?'

'Here...' Peter said, shoving a sheet of paper into his hand. 'You're supposed to have read it.'

Jake yawned again. 'What's this? *Wan Chi Kong Ch'ian, Wo Chiang Lai...*'

'No, Dad... The other side...'

Jake turned the flimsy sheet of paper over. 'Forget Past, Grasp Future... A lecture...'

'And we're obliged to attend. So come on...'

He let Peter drag him by the arm, Mary and the girls following behind.

Jake looked round, blew Mary a kiss. 'You look stunning...'

'And you look like a wrinkled prune...' she said, and laughed.

The lecture hall was just ahead. Guards were hurrying people inside.

Jake slowed, then turned to them.

'Listen... whatever happens, we have each other, yeah? And we're going to get through this. We're survivors. We always have been. And this new city of theirs... we're going to make a new home there. That's the important thing, to make a new home. Somewhere safe. Somewhere we're not going to be moved on from.'

Mary stepped across, taking his arm.

'You heard your dad. Now come on... let's see what's in store for us.'

'Ma Feng...' Jiang said, talking into the radio connection. 'What's happening down there?'

They were hovering above the town. Below them they could see bitter hand-to-hand fighting as Jiang's men tried to take it from Branagh's men. Several buildings were on fire, and there was spo-radic gunfire.

There was a hiss and crackle, and then Ma Feng's voice came

through. 'It's no good, General Jiang... they're fighting to the last. We've lost a dozen men... maybe more...'

Jiang sat back. He had persevered for an hour now, and there'd been no sign of the locals giving an inch. There was only one thing for it.

'Okay, Captain Ma... pull our men out.'

'Sir!'

The hiss and crackle died.

Jiang took a long breath.

'Are you sure that's wise?'

Jiang turned, looking to Wang. 'Are you still here?'

'Where else would I be?'

Where else, indeed, but close enough to torment me.

Jiang sighed. It was no good. He would have to give it up.

There was a hiss and crackle. 'Okay, sir... we're out.'

Jiang could see his men down below, spilling out of the main gate, small groups of them giving covering fire.

All smart and efficient, Jiang thought. Only sometimes it wasn't enough. Especially against desperate men.

'Okay,' he said, 'withdraw as far as the landing craft.'

The craft were further down the Weymouth road, some half a kilometre distant.

Jiang returned his attention to the town. Now that they were not under fire, some of the townsfolk were taking pot shots at Jiang's ship. He could hear the bullets pinging off the outer hull.

Jiang took a long breath.

'Okay... Pilot Wu... return their fire.'

He felt the whole ship shudder as the rockets were released, four great salvoes of them, whooshing down into those ancient streets, the shock wave lifting them even as Pilot Wu edged the craft away from the roiling mushrooms of flame.

Jiang Lei screened his eyes. The city could not be stopped, or delayed, and if these people did not want to be part of the new world, then they would die.

Even so, as he watched the burning town, he felt a profound sense of failure. A sense that he was somehow tainted by the act. Brave men had died. And women and children too.

'Okay,' he said quietly, more to himself than anyone else. 'Let's be gone from here.' But as he sat back, he saw how Wang was watching the screen, a look of sheer delight lighting his face.

'Kuan Yin! Look at those bastards burn!'

Jiang had them set down by the landing craft, going out to speak with his men. Dorchester was gone, and Branagh's little army with it. It was now only a question of processing the surrounding countryside. But first there was one last thing to do.

'Captain Ma,' he said, beckoning him across.

Ma Feng bowed low. 'Yes, sir?'

'Bring two of your best men. There's something I want to look at.'

'Yes, sir!'

He was back in a minute, the trusty Shen and Chang in tow. Seeing them, Jiang Lei smiled.

'Okay... inside... we've work to do.'

As they spilled into the cabin, Wang looked disgruntled at having to share it with common soldiers.

'General Jiang... is this necessary?'

Jiang barely glanced at him. 'There's something I've got to go and see... If you want to be dropped off...?'

Wang looked intrigued. Jiang knew what was going through his head. He was wondering what they could possibly have to go and do so urgently.

'No, no... you can drop me afterwards.'

'Okay... then everyone strap in tightly. Pilot Wu...'

'Yes, General?'

'Set a course north.'

He saw how Wang narrowed his eyes at that.

The craft lifted, slowly turning in the air, then headed north.

'Captain Ma...?'

'Yes, General?'

'Remember what we were talking about, oh, a few weeks ago now...?'

Ma Feng began to shake his head, then stopped, surprise creeping onto his face. 'You mean...?'

'I mean precisely that.'

'But, General...' Only, seeing the certainty in Jiang Lei's face, he bowed his head.

Ma Feng unbuckled his belt, then, looking to Shen and Chang, nodded towards Wang Yu-Lai.

'Shen... Chang... give me a hand a moment. We need to show the good Cadre something...'

Wang looked about him, suspicion in his eyes. 'What is this? What...?'

Shen punched him in the face, silencing him, then lifted the semi-conscious Wang onto his shoulder with Chang's help.

'I want him conscious,' Jiang said coldly. 'I want him to know what's happening to him.'

The three men nodded. Shen and Chang went through, carrying Wang, but Ma Feng lingered.

'General...'

'Yes, Ma Feng?'

'Are you sure you want to do this?'

Jiang nodded.

'You know they will only send a replacement.'

'I know.'

Ma Feng hesitated again, then, 'You know he might be worse.'

'Worse than Wang Yu-Lai? He might. But until one of them learns how to fly...'

Jiang Lei chuckled to himself.

Ma Feng's eyes widened, then he too laughed, seeing the joke.

Wiping away a tear, Ma Feng straightened up then and made a deep bow to his general, his whole manner serious again. His eyes respectful.

'Then it is done, my lord...'

Just south of Cerne Abbas, out on the Black Hill, two men were walking, following the course of the river to their left. To their right and above them, dominating the view from the air, was the massive, one-hundred-and-eighty-feet-tall figure of the Cerne Abbas giant. The most ancient of fertility symbols, carved from the chalk, its whiteness contrasted with the green of the hillside, its massive phallus thrusting ahead of it, as it had these past three thousand years and more.

It was a clear, bright day. Hearing the craft speeding towards them from the south, they dropped down behind some bushes, afraid of being seen out in the open.

There had been a number of craft in the air that past week, but this one wasn't heading west. Neither was it a transporter. This was much smaller, much more elegant than the big troop ships. More than that, it was heading straight towards them.

As it flew overhead, something dropped from the back of the craft. It was a man in bright red silks, his arms and legs flailing as he fell, a long, shrill shriek escaping him, cut short as he impacted with the ground.

They hid, watching the craft slowly circle overhead, then turn and head south again. Only then, when it was gone, did they get up and, running across to where the man had fallen, stand beside the obscenely flattened body, spread-eagled on the exposed chalk.

When they spoke, it was in the rich Dorset dialect of the locality.

''Ow fast d'you think 'e were goin'?'

'Pretty fuckin' fast!'

The two men laughed.

'Well,' the first said. 'Best get packed, I guess. Get away from 'ere.'

'Who d'you think 'e were then?'

'Fuck knows. Don't really care, meself. Serve 'em right if they all topped 'emselves. The more as falls from the sky the better, I say. But those 'oo dropped 'im... damn fine shots, eh? At least one o' those buggers 'as a sense of humour.'

The other nodded. Thinking about it, it had the look of target practice. And they'd got a bullseye, no doubt about that... bang on the tip of the giant's cock!

'What a way to die, eh?'

The two turned away, chuckling now, slapping each other's backs and laughing.

CHARACTER LISTING

Adams, Eve	Popular diva and recording megastar
Adams, Jack	Farmer from Church Knowle
Alec	Young boy from Corfe
Alex	Close friend of Jake Reed and fiancée of Jenny Security Captain, Special Forces
Alison	Jake's girlfriend at New College for 3 years. Evaluation Executive at GenSyn
Boy	Peter Reed's dog – an eight-year-old border collie
Branagh, William Arthur	King of Wessex
Buckland, Eddie	Farmer from Corfe
Carl	Immersion director
Chang Te	Han soldier; member of Jiang Lei's bodyguard
Chao Ni Tsu	Grand Master of Wei Chi and computer genius. Servant of Tsao Ch'un
Cho	Han soldier; servant to Wang Yu-lai
Chris	Close friend of Jake Reed; gay partner of Hugo and multi-millionaire industrialist
Cooke, Dick	Farmer from Cerne Abbas
Cooper, Will	Farmer and resident of Corfe
Croft, Rebecca	'Becky', daughter of Leopold, with the lazy eye
Daas	DAAS4 – the Datscape Automated Analysis System, Version 4 – an enhanced intelligence Unit belonging to Hinton Industries

Ebert, Gustav	Genetics genius and co-founder of GenSyn, Genetic Synthetics
Ebert, Wolfgang	Financial genius and co-founder of GenSyn, Genetic Synthetics
Gifford, Dick	Farmer from Corfe and son of Ted
Gifford, Ted	Farmer from Corfe; father of Dick
Goodman, Frank	Farmer from Langton Maltavers
Grove, Dick	Resident of Corfe
Gurney, Tom	Watchman from Corfe
Haines, Billy	Landlord of The Wessex Arms in Wool
Hamilton, Jack	Landlord of The Quay Inn in Wareham
Hammond, Matthew	Butcher from Church Knowle
Harris, Ginny	Young girl from Corfe
Hart	Doctor from Church Knowle
Hewitt	Lieutenant to Branagh – leader of a horse patrol
Hinton, Charles	CEO of Hinton Industries
Hinton, George	Senior Executive at Hinton Industries
Hinton, Henry	'Harry'; Head of Strategic Planning, Hinton Industries
Ho	'Steward Ho', body servant of Jiang Lei when in the field
Horsfield, Geoff	Historian and resident of Corfe
Huang Tzu Kung	Seventh Dragon; servant of The Ministry, or 'The Thousand Eyes'
Hubbard, Beth	Second daughter of Tom and Mary Hubbard
Hubbard, Cathy	Eldest daughter of Tom and Mary Hubbard
Hubbard, Mary	Wife of Tom Hubbard and mother of Cathy, Beth and Meg
Hubbard, Meg	Youngest daughter of Tom and Mary Hubbard and girlfriend of Peter Reed
Hubbard, Tom	Farmer, resident in Church Knowle. Husband of Mary Hubbard and father of Beth, Meg and Cathy. Best friend to Jake Reed
Hugo	Close friend of Jake Reed; partner of Chris, and acclaimed classical composer

Jenny	Close friend of Jake Reed and fiancé of Alex
Jiang Chun Hua	Wife of Jiang Lei
Jiang Lei	General of Tsao Ch'un's Eighteenth Banner Army, also known as Nai Liu
Joel	Senior engineer in the datscape for Hinton Industries
Lampton, Sir Henry	Head of Security, Hinton Industries
Leggat, Brian	Farmer from Abbotsbury
Li	Han soldier; servant to Wang Yu-lai
Li Fa	Han soldier and technician, working for Jiang Lei
Liu Ke	Han Soldier; member of Jiang Lei's bodyguard; an adept at the *pi-p'a*, the Chinese lute
Lovegrove, John	Farmer from Purbeck
Ludd, Drew	Highest grossing actor in Hollywood and star of *Ubik*
McKenzie, Liam	Owner of the stables in Dorchester
Ma Feng	Han soldier; member of Jiang Lei's bodyguard
Mason, Harry	Landlord of The Thomas Hardy in Dorchester
Mel	Wife from Corfe
Mike	Self-appointed leader of barricade guards at Sonning Common enclave gates.
Miller, Harry	Local from Church Knowle
Nai Liu	'Enduring Willow'; pen-name of Jiang Lei and the most popular Han poet of his time
Oatley, Jennifer	Young Englishwoman 'processed' by Jiang Lei
Padgett	Retired doctor from Wool
Palmer, Joshua	'Old Josh' Palmer, father of Will and record collector
Palmer, Will	Landlord of the Banks Arms Hotel, Corfe and son of Josh
Randall, Jack	Farmer from Church Knowle and husband of Jenny
Randall, Jenny	Wife of Jack Randall
Reed, Jake	*Login*, or 'Web-dancer' for Hinton Industries. Father of Peter Reed
Reed, Peter	Son of Jake and Anne Reed

The Dead

Ascher, Walter	Account Overseer for Hinton Industries
Bates, Alan	English actor
Captain Sensible	English pop musician
Chang Hsuan	Han painter from the 8th Century
Christie, Julie	English actress
Coldplay	English pop group
Cooper, Charlie	Son of Jed and Judy Cooper
Cooper, Jed	Husband of Judy Copper and father of Charlie and John
Cooper, John	Son of Jed and Judy Cooper
Cooper, Judy	Wife of Jed Cooper and mother of Charlie and John
Croft, Leopold	Father of Becky Croft
Denny, Sandy	English folk singer
Depp, Johnny	American actor
Dick, Philip K.	American science fiction writer
Drake, Nick	English Folk Singer from the 1960s
Gaughan, Dick	Scottish folk singer
Griffin, James B.	Sixtieth President of the United States of America
Hendrix, Jimi	American rock guitarist/songwriter
Jones, Mickey	lead guitarist of Man
Man	Welsh rock band
Mao Tse Tung	First Ko Ming emperor (ruled AD 1948-1976)
Mattie	Young lover of Old Ma Brogan
Nicolson, Jack	American actor
Palmer, Andrew	Son of Old Josh Palmer
Palmer, Gwen	Wife of Old Josh Palmer
Presley, Elvis	American rock and roll singer
Reed, Anne	Wife of Jake Reed. Mother of Peter Reed and sister of Mary Hubbard
Spirit	American/Californian rock band
Stamp, Terence	English actor
The Verve	English pop group
Young, Neil	Canadian singer-songwriter

GLOSSARY OF
MANDARIN TERMS

Ch'un Tzu	an ancient Chinese term from the Warring States period, describing a certain class of noblemen, controlled by a code of chivalry and morality known as the *li*, or rites. Here the term is roughly, and sometimes ironically, translated as 'gentlemen'. The *ch'un tzu* is as much an ideal state of behaviour – as specified by Confucius in the *Analects* – as an actual class in Chung Kuo, though a degree of financial independence and a high standard of education are assumed prerequisites.
Hung Mao	literally 'redheads', the name the Chinese gave to the Dutch (and later English) seafarers who attempted to trade with China in the seventeenth century. Because of the piratical nature of their endeavours (which often meant plundering Chinese shipping and ports) the name has connotations of piracy.
Ko Ming	'revolutionary'. The *T'ien Ming* is the Mandate of Heaven, supposedly handed down from Shang Ti, the Supreme Ancestor, to his earthly counterpart, the Emperor (*HuangTi*). This Mandate could be enjoyed only so long as the Emperor was worthy of it, and rebellion against a tyrant – who broke the Mandate through his lack of justice, benevolence,

	and sincerity – was deemed not criminal but a rightful expression of Heaven's anger.
pi p'a	a four-stringed lute used in traditional Chinese music.
San Kuo Chih Yen I	*The Romance of The Three Kingdoms* is a long book of 120 chapters, covering a hundred years, from the downfall of the Han dynasty to China's reunification under the Tsin in AD 265. Based partly on fact, part on myth, it is still regularly read in public and is China's most engrossing heroic saga. Its opening words say much of the Han's attitudes towards history – 'The empire when united tends to disruption, and when partitioned, strives once more for unity.' Anyone studying Chinese history would see the truth in those words.
Wen ch'a te	'elegance' – this is much more the expression of a concept, that of a certain sense of perfection embodied within that elegance, than a simple descriptive term.
Yin yueh	'music'. Again, the word is used conceptually, almost poetically here.
Ying Kuo	England, or, more often these days, the United Kingdom.

AUTHOR'S NOTE & ACKNOWLEDGEMENTS

As the reader will have noted, SON OF HEAVEN introduces its major theme – the coming of China – rather late in the day, and for this reason I've not felt it necessary to provide more than the scantest note on Chinese words and phrases used – a mere handful are in the Glossary. Similarly, I do not intend to dwell too long on other matters, except to say that wei chi is the world's oldest and most challenging game, known more commonly in the West by its Japanese name, Go.

Thanks this time go out to Brian Griffin for reading the thing in its earliest stages, also to Mike Cobley for encouragement and insights, and to Nic Cheetham, my latest editor and newest champion, whose most radical suggestion – to remove 70,000 words and reconstruct the novel in two parts – has resulted in this current volume. To Caroline Oakley, who did such a superb hard edit on the creature, thanks immensely for that, and for telling me – clearly and with good reason – where to end it.

Finally, to Susan and my girls – Jessica, Amy, Georgia and Francesca, a big thank you for enriching my life. To think they were but babes when this began.

Here's to the journey ahead. *Kan Pei!*